THE SILENT ONES

Could you leave a child behind?

LINDA COLES

PROLOGUE

Matthew loaded groceries into the back of the small Fiesta as Blue watched on, chattering and pointing at other shoppers as they walked past with their own trolleys laden with bags. A cold breeze had him pulling his collar up against it, summer pretty much over now, the skinny fingers of autumn caressing his neck as he loaded the final bag. A fat raindrop hit the car roof, closely followed by another. He looked up at the gathering clouds with disapproval.

"Right, let's get you strapped in," he said to the child, who had no qualms about leaving his plastic trolley seat. In fact, he was glad to be out of the wind. Not that he could share his feelings at twelve months old. When Matthew was satisfied the boy was secure, he strapped himself in the driver's side and set off towards home as the rain began in earnest.

The roads were busy. Saturday morning shopping was the worst time in his opinion, but like many families, it was their best chance of getting provisions. There was always too much going on during the week and shopping on a Sunday was even worse. Plus, by the time he got back, she'd be at the gym, and that meant he and Blue could have the place to themselves. It was Matthew's favourite time of the week, when she was out, and he didn't to have to talk to her.

He could sit with a mug of hot coffee and the paper, while a jam sandwich and *Hey Duggee* entertained Blue for a while. The house would be calmer, more relaxed, at least for a couple of hours – the occasional outburst of a child's delight a welcome sound. He hadn't realised just how much he'd love the boy until he'd arrived. They weren't far from home as Matthew turned into Low Lea Road, the nearest to a quiet country lane you could find in the town of Marple, just outside Manchester. As he flipped his wipers from intermittent to constant, he sensed the car behind them before he saw it in his rear-view mirror. They were driving far too close for his liking, had come out of nowhere, and they didn't appear to want to pass even though there was opportunity to do so. He flicked several looks at the mirror, watching, but the silvery wet brightness cast an awkward glare on the windscreen behind so he couldn't see who was at the wheel, a man or a woman. Not that it mattered, he couldn't do anything about it except hope they passed him soon. He knew there was another open stretch around the next corner, the road coming out from the trees, perhaps they'd take the opportunity and pass then. As he drove into the bend, he resisted accelerating out of it and kept his speed deliberately low to give them more of a chance.

The vehicle stayed close behind.

Matthew wound his window down and waved them through with his hand, but still they ignored his request. The light faded a couple of notches as they drove under trees that would be bare in a matter of weeks. He kept an eye on the vehicle that had no intention of hanging back or overtaking him.

It didn't feel right.

There was a lay-by not far; he'd stop there, and they'd have no choice but to go on, leaving him to the rest of his peaceful morning. He thought about his coffee and *Hey Duggee*, his quiet time, without Tess. The last thing he needed was an idiot tailgating him for their own enjoyment. It was likely a couple of teenagers having a laugh at his expense.

A shiver hit his stomach and he wondered what might happen

next. Visibility was worsening by the second and he increased the speed on his wipers as rain poured down. He spotted the gravelly lay-by up ahead and indicated left to inform his follower he was stopping, but as he slowed and his tyres hit the loose stones, the car pulled off the road along with him.

"What the—"

It was then that he noticed a van had joined the convoy; it accelerated out in front before slamming its brakes on, cutting him off at an angle, and Matthew had no option but to do the same to avoid a collision. Blue groaned in alarm as he was pressed hard against the restraints of his seat, bags of groceries shot forward in the boot, and Matthew was yanked painfully against his own seat belt.

Then he knew.

They'd said they'd take him by surprise – it would be better all round. Was this it? He watched as the van door opened and two men got out and approached the car. Someone else from the other vehicle undid the rear passenger door and leaned in, unstrapping Blue from his confines. He repaid them with a fierce wail.

"Get out," a male voice instructed him.

He had no choice now. It was all happening so fast. He pulled his hood up against the rain which was falling in skinny rods all around them.

"Hand me your wallet and phone," the man said.

Matthew reluctantly handed them over and watched as they were slipped inside a jacket pocket. He wasn't sure if that had been part of the agreement or not, he couldn't remember. There had been little communication from them – less chance of error that way.

"Hurry up. Get in the van."

"Can I say goodbye to Blue?" Matthew asked.

The little boy was being carried away, back to the car that had driven so close to them only moments ago. A woman was securing him into another booster seat, and Matthew could hear his cries, the little boy clearly upset. He hadn't realised how hard this was going to be, on both of them, and he gulped down tears that threatened to fall from his eyes.

"There's little time. We have to leave – now," the man said as he ushered Matthew quickly towards the van. The others stood in the rain, watching and monitoring the road as the switch-over took place. Once seated, Matthew heard the other car drive off, heading back in the direction he'd just come from. As the engine revved and loose stones flew into the air, he was taken the opposite way.

It had started.

SATURDAY

Chrissy was more like an excited child bobbing up and down in her seat than an adult arriving in Doolin for an autumn break. As Adam turned the hire car into the driveway of their Airbnb accommodation for the next week, she couldn't have felt any happier. As soon as they stopped, she stepped out, gripping her hair with both hands to stop it whipping into her eyes as a brisk wind fought to strip it all from her head. Grey clouds overhead moved at full throttle without dropping any of the moisture contained within, and she watched them hurtle along, new ones replacing them and slotting into place just as quickly as their predecessors. Chrissy felt Adam at her side before he slid an arm around her shoulder and pulled her close.

"I'm ready for a break," he said, watching the clouds overhead with her.

"Me too. Long walks in the day and good food and company in the evening. What more could a girl wish for?"

Adam bent in closer to whisper in her ear: "How about just the two of us?"

Chrissy smiled her delight but was prevented from responding right at that moment. Julie's excited voice broke through the wind.

"Chrissy, it's divine!" her sister gushed as she bent to reach the handle of her trolley bag and make her way to the front door. Richard followed her dutifully, looking more like a butler than her husband. The wind caught the man's thinning wisps and every strand appeared to stand on its end, showing quite how balding he was underneath his normally carefully arranged hair. Chrissy smiled as he paused to try and flatten it, releasing one of the two bags he was pulling so it fell flat to the ground with a clatter. Julie instinctively turned and rolled her eyes but stayed quiet. Adam glanced at Chrissy knowingly and opted for silence as they both moved towards the boot and their own luggage. With their two large holdalls out, they were set. The two families were the polar opposites of each other but somehow it worked.

Chrissy had planned their autumn break not long after she'd returned from a case that had taken her and, unexpectedly, Julie to France and back. Mission accomplished, the two women had returned home safely and ready for a rest, and since Chrissy had always fancied the west coast of Ireland, she'd picked the holiday destination. There would be something for everyone. Julie had a couple of pubs and restaurants to choose from, Richard had his newspaper and Kindle, Adam had the cliffs to wander along and Chrissy? She had all the above and planned on doing it all with a few runs added in.

As long as the wind blew itself away.

She followed Adam inside and idly wondered which bedroom Julie had allocated for them since she'd have taken the largest for herself without a moment's hesitation.

"In here," Adam offered, turning right into a wide-open space.

"Hell's bells, look at that view!" she said, dropping her bag on the floor and heading closer to the large bay window that looked out over green fields and an ancient castle.

"Doonagore Castle, sixteenth century, now a private holiday home," Adam said matter-of-factly, as if he were a Chaser on *The Chase*.

Chrissy glanced his way enquiringly. "I'm impressed. Did you already know that snippet or did you just look it up without me noticing?"

"Two can plot and scheme, not just your good self. I was waiting for the opportunity to spread my hard-earned knowledge, though it came much sooner than I expected." He slipped his arm around her shoulder again as they both looked out at the rolling greenery and the old, single-tower castle. Cattle grazed nearby, their woolly brown bodies making them look like giant four-legged teddy bears. Other than that, there was nothing else in sight. Apart from the Atlantic Ocean that is.

"Oh, what a lovely room, and what a view," Julie exclaimed.

"Don't tell me you want it now?" Chrissy asked.

"No, we have a lovely suite at the back of the house with bags of room, so we're all set. I thought with Richard's snoring, we should be as far away from you two as possible. Don't want to keep you awake," she said, beaming.

"Thoughtful of you, thanks," Chrissy managed, trying not to roll her eyes yet again.

"Plus, there's an extra room equally nice next door, so there's choice if you want it?"

"Thanks, but I'm happy enough with this one."

"Well I'm going to unpack the food and get that bottle of bubbly into the fridge before I do anything else," Adam said as he left the two girls to do their thing. Since Chrissy was not a domestic goddess, Adam invariably took the lead and had shopped for a few bits to tide them over in the last town they'd driven through. At least until they decided on a dinner destination somewhere. Julie stepped closer to admire the old castle.

"Could you imagine living in that old thing years ago? It must have been cold and draughty. I bet it blows terribly on a foul wet winter's day. Not for me. No thank you." She shuddered for effect.

"Good job I didn't book it for our stay then."

"Goodness no, this is far nicer. You should see our room, it's better than what we have at home."

Chrissy doubted that very much. There wasn't anything Richard had not provided over the years to his sometimes-dramatic wife.

"Though we haven't quite got the view, I must admit."

"You'll have your eye mask on anyway, so you'll not be missing anything," Chrissy said as she humped one of her bags into the corner to unpack later. "Ready to go exploring?" Instinctively, she glanced at Julie's feet. "Perhaps not quite. Where are your boots?"

Julie looked down at her painted toes and pretty strappy sandals. "You think I'll need them now?"

"I would. It would be a shame to break those or scuff a toenail," she said, pointing.

Julie turned to leave the room and as an afterthought Chrissy shouted to her sister, "Grab your jacket too, it's cooling down."

A moment later, Julie was back, wearing the smallest and slimmest pair of walking boots Chrissy had ever seen. She'd always been the daintier of the two and continued to be so now as a grown woman. How they'd come from the same parents Chrissy had often wondered, but after a stay in hospital, blood tests had confirmed they had both been cut from the exact same cloth. Chrissy pulled her own jacket on and called out to Adam that they'd be back shortly as they left through the back door.

"Decide where we're eating tonight if you can," he called.

"Will do!"

Turning the corner, and facing straight into the wind, the two women headed out to explore the village of Doolin and report back.

"Let's take a closer look at the castle," urged Julie, almost tugging at Chrissy's jacket to steer her in the opposite direction.

"Somebody could be home; you can't just go wandering over."

"I'm not going to peer in through the windows, just get a better view of it."

"It's not like you to be interested in old relics," she said as they approached the building slowly.

"I live with Richard, don't I?" Julie added with a laugh. At that Chrissy had to join her.

About ten minutes later, they were about as close to the castle as they dared go when a door opened, and a flash of long deep-auburn hair could be seen briefly before it vanished back inside.

"Told you there would be someone home," said Chrissy. "We'd better not go any closer. Come on, let's find where we're going for dinner later," she said, turning to leave. Julie caught her up and the two wandered off back towards the village.

"Who was that, I wonder?" Julie asked.

"I don't know. Holidaymaker, I expect. Great hair though."

CHAPTER 2

The two women walked towards the small village centre in relaxed silence, each enjoying the fresh air and scenery, their holiday cottage behind them. Not that it was a cottage really, far from it, but the name felt apt for their break away.

Fisher Street was where most of the eateries and small shops were situated, some of which were painted in bright pastel shades that made them look like liquorice-allsort buildings stuck on a picture postcard. The sweater shop was the most visual of the first few, painted in a deep bright pink, and Julie immediately wanted to slip inside. It was right next door to an equally bright orange crafts shop.

"For a quick look. I might need a sweater while I'm here," she said, as if she needed an excuse to browse.

Chrissy followed her sister inside, slightly annoyed that she was shopping already and not taking in the sights as she herself was doing. Still, Julie had at least wanted to see the castle first, so she'd show willing and pretend to look at the garments on offer, feigning interest.

The small cramped space was filled with heavy knitted sweaters and cardigans in all shapes and sizes. Throws and scarves, hats and gloves all fought to be seen, some draped from already full drawers or hung loosely, dangling over the backs of chairs or from hooks on any available wall space. The room had a distinctive but pleasant oily wool smell and Chrissy breathed it deep into her lungs – the essence of a warm woolly sheep. As Julie picked out a creamy cable-knit sweater and held it to herself for size, Chrissy couldn't help but admit how good she'd look in it, the colour perfect to complement her hair and complexion.

"You should get Richard one too. You could matchy, matchy," she said, mocking and smiling at the same time.

"I know when you're taking the mickey, you know," Julie said.

"I wasn't."

"Yes you were, so don't bother denying it. Anyway, if the weather turns cooler, I might just come back and yes, get us both one. If that's okay with you?" Julie was being petulant, and the question didn't require an answer so Chrissy smiled her understanding as they headed back outside.

"Which way?"

"From memory of my research, there's a pub up this way," Chrissy said, pointing. "Let's take a look at the menu for dinner. I'm thinking informal tonight since we've been travelling all day. I really can't be much bothered for dressing up."

"Sounds good."

The two made their way further along Fisher Street and a moment or two later, Gus O'Connor's pub came into view, its smart black facia set back in local stone. It looked inviting. Two planters filled with late pansies added a splash of colour to the entrance and the two women headed inside. The dark-walled interior gave the place a warm and welcoming feel which was added to by the huge open stone fireplace where logs burnt brightly, crackling from new wood recently added. Various prints and documents hung in frames along the walls adding to the feeling the place had been around a good deal longer than its owners. Wooden tables and chairs stood on a tiled floor, or was it stone flags? Pointing to the various musical instruments adorning one wall, Chrissy said, "I bet they have live music in here regularly."

"I wonder if they will tonight then."

"I expect so on a Saturday evening, that could be fun. And I bet it's traditional Irish."

They approached the bar where a tall man with tight blond curls meandered over and asked, "What can I get you?" He wasn't a local, he sounded more Oxford than Doolin.

"I fancy a whiskey of all things," announced Chrissy. "Want one?" she asked, turning to Julie. Somewhat unsure, Julie took her time to decide and the barman made a suggestion.

"If I may?" he said, reaching for a bottle of Dingle single malt and offering it to Julie. "I suspect you enjoy the finer things in life, and if you're not really a whiskey drinker, I can almost guarantee you'll enjoy this." He had an easy way about him that was in no way pretentious or cloying and Julie nodded her approval as two glasses were poured. Chrissy watched for her reaction before taking a sip of her own. A perfectly sculptured mouth took the tiniest of sips followed by a deeper, much longer drink as she gained confidence that it was in fact delicious and wasn't going to bite her. Chrissy smiled inwardly and followed suit, enjoying the warmth and fruitiness as it slipped down her throat. She outwardly groaned.

"Now, that is nice," Chrissy said, watching Julie take another large mouthful that drained most of the glass. "Steady on, sis. You might not weigh much but I don't fancy carrying you all the way home." The barman caught her eye and smiled. While he was cute, he wasn't a patch on Adam. She was reminded of the woolly-sheep-smelling shop; his curls weren't too dissimilar. Licking her lips, Julie placed her empty tumbler on the bar. "I'll have another one when we come for dinner later," she said matter-of-factly. "Do we need to book?"

"Best to, yes. It gets busy in here, particularly on a Saturday when the band is on. Be here by 7 pm, just the two of you?"

"Four actually," offered Chrissy. Did she imagine it, or did he look a little disappointed at that piece of news? They were two women in their early forties. Still, they were both in good shape, though with rather different physiques and outlooks on life. Julie in particular turned heads wherever she went, both men and women, and Chrissy observed their reaction almost as a hobby. She knew her sister enjoyed the attention and acted purposely dumb as though she never noticed it. She gave her details for the booking.

Chrissy was glad of her jacket as they stepped outside since the temperature had dropped a handful of degrees. She pulled her collar up around her ears, Julie did the same, and they linked arms.

"He was nice. As was that whiskey," said Julie.

Chrissy raised an eyebrow at her. She wasn't normally one to comment on the male form.

"What? I'm not allowed to look?"

"I've not said a word. You just tickle me sometimes," Chrissy said, smiling and pulling her close for a moment. "I'm sure we'll be seeing more of him, and his whiskey choosing talent."

"Starting with dinner later."

"Indeed." Chrissy turned to face her sister. It felt great to be getting on so well, getting closer again as they had once been as children. Their father dying and their mother not speaking to either of them had somehow drawn them together again. A trip to France on a case had also helped renew their friendship. "Let's have the best time while we're here, eh?"

"If I can have another of those whiskeys, you can bet on it," Julie giggled.

They arrived back to the house just as a fine misty drizzle began to fall. Julie almost stumbled through the door and a waiting Adam raised his brows at his sister-in-law and the comical smile on her face.

"Don't ask," said Chrissy, thieving a cracker as she passed by a tray of nibbles he'd organised.

"In that case, I won't."

CHAPTER 3

By the time everyone – read Julie Stokes – was ready to head out for dinner, it was almost 7 pm, and they still had a good walk ahead of them.

"I'll drive, else we'll miss our table," a concerned Richard suggested as he checked his watch yet again. Even though he was used to his wife being behind schedule, it still frustrated the hell out of him. He knew, though, exactly why she did it, but in this instance it was totally unnecessary. They were going to a pub for an informal dinner; there would be no grand entrance to be had, no one would be watching or waiting for Julie Stokes to appear. He figured in a spot such as Doolin, they'd be more focused on their beer or the plate of food in front of them than a woman on holiday. When she finally breezed in wearing a glorious pair of leather trousers and a cashmere sweater, she achieved her grand entrance anyhow, even if it was to her own small group. Chrissy had to admit her sister had impeccable taste in clothes, though usually a good deal more formal than her own style. Lately, she'd noticed the relaxed change in what Julie wore, and it suited her.

"Finally!" Chrissy quipped as Richard grabbed the car keys anyway.

"Let's get moving then," he said and everyone filed out to the hire car. Julie got in first as usual; it meant she'd be last to get back out.

A few minutes later, they pulled up just along the road a little from Gus O'Connor's pub. It sounded like it was busy already. As the front door opened and others went inside, snippets of loud conversation drowned out the music as both fought for ear time. Chrissy thought back to what the barman had said earlier. If it got busy later on, the place must physically heave. She waited for Julie to get out and the two women led the way, Adam and Richard bringing up the rear quietly. As they approached, Chrissy caught a fast-paced fiddle on the airwaves and wondered if it was coming from a jukebox or if the band had struck up already. She held the door open for Julie, who went inside, followed by Richard and Adam. Another couple, a young woman and a man, waited to enter and Chrissy played doorman for the two of them.

"Thanks," they chimed. The woman had long, wavy red hair and Chrissy couldn't help but wonder if it was the woman she'd seen at the castle earlier.

"You're welcome."

When everyone was safely inside, she joined her family at the bar, which already was a bit of a crush. Conversation and spirits were high, and the tourists among the locals stood out like heavy rockers at a folk festival. She hoped their spot booked for dinner was in a quieter back room someplace or else conversation would be pointless.

She was amused to see the barman from earlier was still on duty. As she watched Adam get the drinks in, she considered his tight blond curls again. It was unusual for a man to have such coiled hair, though it suited him and would be low maintenance for sure. Adam turned her way to enquire about her drink choice using a mixture of rough sign language and facial expression. She was normally a white wine drinker, but it seemed appropriate to have a Guinness and she pointed to the beer tap. Adam nodded his understanding with a downturned smile, and she wondered if Julie would opt for another whiskey. No sooner had she thought it, a tumbler of deep, honey-coloured liquid was handed across and she watched Julie take a sip. She could see her sister was enjoying it and wondered quite how many more she'd have before the night was up. Still, if you couldn't relax on holiday, when could you? Adam must have told the barman they had a table booked because the moment everyone had a drink in their hands, a waitress was at Chrissy's side, ready to escort them through.

She'd been right. The dining room was a good deal less raucous though filled to capacity, suggesting the only empty table left must be theirs. The four arranged themselves around the large table, Julie and Richard with their backs against the wall, looking out into the room, and Chrissy and Adam facing them. At least they had plenty of room to spread out; the table meant for six. The pretty young waitress handed out menus and explained the night's specials, before leaving them alone to decide.

"Beef and Guinness stew for me," Chrissy announced, laying her menu down and taking a sip of her drink. Adam dittoed her choice, as did Richard, leaving Julie to ponder between the seafood and the chicken. The waitress returned with a basket of bread to nibble on in the meantime and took their orders. Julie opted for the supreme of chicken, which was a good choice in Chrissy's book since she couldn't see her sister picking out crab claws or dealing with mussels. When the waitress had everyone's order down, she hovered for a moment looking a little sheepish. Then, in a broad local accent, she asked:

"Would you mind awfully if two people joined the end of your table, so? Only we've had a booking mix-up and there's nowhere for them to sit and eat." Chrissy could see the young woman's cringe in anticipation they would say yes and unburden her of a problem. And possible trouble from her boss most likely. The waitress added, "Of course it's our mistake and it's perfectly fine if you decide not to, we don't want to spoil your evening." She smiled in hope. Chrissy glanced around at the table. Surely no one would object? She made the decision for them.

"Of course they can, that's fine. As long as they don't mind us!" she said, laughing, allowing the waitress to relax her shoulders and smile.

"A round of drinks on the house, as a thank you," she said, before leaving them to give the table-less couple the good news. A moment or two later she was back, a young duo right behind her.

The woman had long, wavy deep-red hair. Her name was Ciara.

CHAPTER 4

It turned out that Ciara *was* the same woman Chrissy and Julie had noticed at the castle, or rather it had been her distinctive hair on view. After initial introductions, which were only mildly awkward, the couple had eaten their meal alongside the rest of the group and kept themselves to themselves. Until coffee and more drinks that is. Chrissy had complimented her new acquaintance on her hair, and Adam being Adam, and always easy to get along with, had talked in great detail with the man whom they now knew as Lorcan. The two, it turned out, were staying in the castle for a while. They were on an extended break, though neither of them alluded to the reason behind the extended part. Chrissy being the more curious of the group would find out, of that she was sure. Being a private investigator, her antennae were naturally tuned into anything even slightly out of the ordinary, even when she was away on an autumn break with her family. Richard hardly said a word to the couple though, in his defence, he was sat at the far end of the table and likely couldn't hear much of the conversation with the music and loud chatter that had risen a notch or two. Julie sipped on her drink quietly and people-watched from her spot next to him.

"So, you are all staying nearby?" Ciara asked. Her Irish accent was as warming as the fire in the hearth nearby, as soothing as a mother's kiss.

"I guess you'd call us almost neighbours," Chrissy replied. "We're just over the way from you – the big house with the lovely front-deck area? I imagine you've probably seen it. An Airbnb actually, though I wish it was ours. It's a real find, beautiful inside and loads of room. Perhaps you might pop over for a coffee at some time. We're here all week."

"Thanks, I might do that. The castle is lovely and all, but it's tiny inside. Great view from the top though. And the stairs keep me fit, though a bit awkward with Flynn."

"Flynn?" enquired Adam, joining in the conversation.

"Sorry, yes, Flynn. He's the little one, coming up to twelve months old now," she said. Chrissy could tell the woman doted on the little boy, her wistful smile giving her feelings away.

"Such a lovely age," Chrissy said. "Our two are almost grown now, boys, fifteen and sixteen, and right at that age where they don't want to be anywhere near their parents. So enjoy the early years while they let you," she said, laughing. Chrissy wanted to ask where Flynn was now since both his parents were at their table. It would seem rude though and she assumed the young boy would be with a relative or being babysat, perhaps by a local. Since neither Ciara nor Lorcan volunteered where he was, Chrissy didn't push it. Her antennae buzzed a little.

"So, Lorcan," Chrissy said, turning her attention to him. While he didn't have Ciara's fiery red hair, he was as equally natural blond as the barman. She imagined little Flynn would have beautiful hair colour himself with such parents. "What do you do when you're not on an extended break?"

"The fancy title is logistics and distribution, but between you and me, it's a glorified lorry-driving role," he said. The smile told her he'd used that particular line before, though he sounded almost embarrassed about his occupation.

"I bet you see the country doing that then."

"And the continent. I go all over Europe throughout the year, though most of my journeys are across to the main northern England ports."

"And your accent, I can't quite detect where you might be from, but I'm guessing you've spent some time away from Ireland?"

"You're very perceptive," he said, smiling somewhat slyly. "I'm from Galway originally, a good many years ago, but I've been living in Manchester for the best part of my life."

"That is a change. And here you are now, in a Doolin pub sharing a dinner table with us four from Surrey."

"So it seems."

Chrissy was about to carry on her interrogation of him when a man with a microphone announced the live music was about to start and no sooner were the words out of his mouth, a fiddle made its spirited entrance. Even from the dining room, there was no way to have anything resembling a conversation, all words drowned out by either the button accordion, the tin whistle, or folks joining in clapping their encouragement to the beat. A man at a table nearby asked his companion for her hand in dance and the two performed a pretty good jig, spurring on the hand clapping and foot tapping. Chrissy glanced across at Richard and Julie who seemed a little uncomfortable in their seats, unsure what to do. Not one to be shy, Chrissy stood and took Richard's hand and she almost dragged him up to join in the fun. Lorcan, almost a local, took the hint and made a beeline for Julie, who looked as startled as a rabbit at the prospect of dancing like the others now enjoying themselves. He wasn't taking no for an answer and after whispering something in Julie's ear, Chrissy watched her smile broaden as she escorted him and let him lead her in what to do. Looking over Richard's shoulder, Chrissy vowed to find out exactly what he'd said that had persuaded her to dance with him. Since there was only Adam and Ciara left at the table, the two joined in the fun effortlessly, Adam as confident in Irish dance as he was in everything else he did, even though he'd no clue what he was doing. With a redheaded stranger on his arm, he allowed her to take the lead and instruct him, making it look like it was all his own doing.

It was the call of last orders when everyone finally stopped for a nightcap before eventually heading home – Chrissy and her family to one house, Ciara and Lorcan back to their castle. As she watched the two casually stroll away, she wondered once again about their extended holiday.

And where their son was.

SUNDAY

CHAPTER 5

The following morning, Chrissy sat in the sun-drenched kitchen on her own, with a pot of tea to herself sat on the wooden table in front of her. It was almost 8 am and she was the only one in the house that had stirred, the others sleeping heavily after an exhausting and late night dancing at the pub. She smiled to herself at the memory of Julie and her version of a jig, something far away from her normal more sedate style of dancing, but it was good to see her laughing so voraciously. Even Richard had had to admit on the way home that he'd had fun, though Chrissy wasn't sure if he'd be up for another rendition on another night later in the week. Maybe the redheaded Ciara had cast a spell on him; Julie certainly hadn't complained, but then Lorcan was a good-looking bloke to enjoy the company or attention of. What exactly had he whispered in Julie's ear? She sipped on her tea and stared out the huge glass window towards the castle, the Atlantic Ocean visible to her right, falling away from the cliff edge. Ciara had said it was a cracking view from up the top of their castle, and Chrissy wondered if she might get an invitation to take a better look. Footsteps padding about made her turn, someone was up and moving.

"Any tea in the pot for another?" Adam asked, grabbing a mug from the cupboard and adding a splash of fresh milk.

"There is, though you might want to make a fresh one," she suggested, receiving a quick peck on the cheek as he bent down to greet her. He had bedhead like she'd never seen on him before and pointed to it as he picked the pot up.

"Rough night's sleep by chance? Only you look like you slept on the beach."

He ran his fingers through sticking-up hair as if to inspect what she was referring to. "I guess I must have been more active than usual in my sleep," he said, grinning, "though I don't remember tossing and turning. I was out like a light."

"Clearly you weren't totally extinguished," she added, winking.

"Did we?"

"No, we didn't, you were too out of it." She watched him tip the old pot of tea away and make fresh.

"You didn't what?" Julie asked as she joined them, looking like she'd been up for hours though still in her pink robe. Perfectly made-up, hair a stark contrast to Chrissy's and, even more so, Adam's. She too grabbed a mug and added milk. Chrissy glanced at her husband and smiled. Julie caught it.

"Oh, too early, please!" she said, screwing her face up in disgust.

"You asked 'what'," said Adam in a sing-song voice, rubbing it in a little. He put the fresh pot on the table in front of Julie and sat with the two women in his life that he adored the most. Julie rubbed her temples.

"I'm not surprised it hurts," Chrissy said. "Have you had a painkiller?"

"I meditated for a few minutes, but no, not yet. I was hoping it would be gone by now."

"That amount of single malt might need more fuel to remove it than a bit of kumbaya, sis."

"Don't dismiss it as woo-woo, it does actually work," she said, sounding peeved. "It might just need a little extra help is all." She carried on rubbing both sides of her head, staring into her empty mug. Adam exchanged a glance with Chrissy; his turn to wink.

"Well, fresh air will shift it and I know just the thing," he said.

"Shift what?" Richard asked as he entered the room, sitting straight down and looking around at the gathered individuals. It felt like *Groundhog Day* to Chrissy who turned a smile on and answered her brother-in-law, refraining from rolling her eyes at him. Normally she'd stick her tongue out when she knew he wasn't looking, but the opportunity hadn't presented itself so far. Plus, Julie had told her to stop being so childish on many previous occasions, and that he knew she did it. Still, it felt good to act stupid even if she was in her forties. She never meant it maliciously.

"Your wife's hangover, primarily."

"It's a headache, not a hangover," Julie said indignantly. "It'll be gone in a while."

Adam set a packet of paracetamol down, which he'd found in a kitchen drawer after she'd said her kumbaya hadn't helped.

Changing the subject, Chrissy asked, "What do you have in mind, Adam?"

"Well, you've a veritable plethora of activities on offer since it's such a nice day," he said theatrically. He was still standing, leaning against the kitchen cupboard alongside the cooker. Counting out on his fingers, he reeled off the list he'd made in his head: "We've got the Cliffs of Moher, a spot of mountain biking, there's horse riding, and then Doolin Cave, though we should leave that one for a rainy day." He looked around for takers and interest, but apart from Chrissy there was a complete lack of enthusiasm. Adam carried on with suggestions of a different nature: "And then there's Father Ted's place for afternoon tea, though we have to book and it's only just gone 8 am."

Julie perked up a little. "I could fancy that, though I couldn't face a boat ride," she added dramatically, resting her head in her hands.

"There isn't a boat ride, so you're safe there," Adam continued.

"Craggy Island is fictious. The old farmhouse is about a forty-minute drive from here, at Lackareagh."

Julie visibly perked up. "Then I vote we try and go this afternoon then, and maybe a light walk this morning?" she said, looking round for interest in her idea.

It was Richard that surprised them all by saying, "Well, I think since it's such a lovely day, we should do something longer outdoors while the sun stays out. Let's add afternoon tea to the rainy-day list." His beaming smile was so totally out of character that Chrissy sat open-mouthed and speechless. He couldn't have surprised her more if he'd dropped his trousers down to his underpants right there and then. She glanced at Adam who looked as aghast as her.

"I'm with you, Richard. Great idea," he said finally, sealing the deal. "You choose the cliff walk, and straight after breakfast, we'll head out. Is that all right with you, Julie?"

She continued to rub her temples dramatically. "You three go, I might stay here and read."

"The fresh air will do you good," Richard said. "Plus, I'll miss you if you don't come."

She lifted her eyes to meet his as both Chrissy and Adam watched on dismayed. Had someone brought a different Richard along with them by mistake?

"Oh, that's so sweet," she cooed. After a moment, she added, "Of course I'll come, there'll be coffee somewhere along the way I expect. Perhaps we can stop then."

Chrissy and Adam hadn't the heart to tell her otherwise. Craggy cliff walks were not renowned for having frothy coffee establishments dotted along the way for the Julies of the world. Adam bent down to retrieve a frying pan from a cupboard nearby. He twirled it like a baton in front of his audience.

"That's settled then. Who's for scrambled eggs?"

Feigning nausea, Julie took that as her cue to leave.

CHAPTER 6

Chrissy, Adam, and Richard ambled back up Fisher Street, towards the pub where they'd drunk and danced the night away only a few hours before. The start of the 10 am guided Doolin cliff walk was from outside the pub, Gus O'Connor's, which was now no stranger to the trio. Julie had changed her mind at the last minute and had gone back to bed for a lie-down, even Richard's promise of finding a coffee somewhere hadn't been enough to persuade her. That was probably a good job, a conjurer he was not. The rest of them had left her snoozing her hangover off, eye mask firmly in place, and wished her a speedy recovery. They'd grab lunch out at the end of the walk since it would take them until around 1 pm to complete it. There was a visitor centre at the other end, and a bus back to Doolin. They were wrapped up in their coats and Adam carried a backpack containing woolly hats and gloves along with bottled water and a bag of local toffee to suck on as they walked. With winds of around twenty-five miles per hour expected, it could well be draughty along the clifftops and a hat would be a welcome addition if it turned cold. Chrissy watched as a few stragglers approached the pub and joined the small group that had gathered in the morning sun. There were people of all ages, and since the walk itself was on man-made tracks, it promised to be easy enough to complete for most. She wondered about the climb though. The highest point they would reach was seven hundred feet above sea level, and the views of the Atlantic Ocean promised to be spectacular. She hoped the elderly couple standing nearby were up to it. A male voice called them all to attention. Chrissy had no doubt he was a local, she could barely understand a word of his strong Irish accent. She glanced at Adam, who appeared not to have any trouble in that department, and cocked an eyebrow enquiringly at him. He replied in a whisper, "Tell you in a minute." He needn't have bothered since they set off the moment the man's words had finished leaving his mouth. Still, Adam filled her in.

"He's Pat, a local farmer and the one responsible for organising and creating the trail," he said easily, slipping his arm around her shoulders as they all set off, back, as it happened, towards their own holiday home.

Richard said, "Maybe I should call in and see if Julie has changed her mind?"

"Knowing Julie," Chrissy said, "she'll be soaking in a bath with lavender oil or some such, eye mask on, hair tied in a towel, her idea of tranquillity."

Richard nodded his acceptance though Chrissy thought she saw a little disappointment in his eyes. She hoped it was a one-off and that her sister was going to join in with the holiday plans from this point on, and not leave Richard like a third wheel to herself and Adam. While she didn't mind, Richard just might. She thought about his unusual behaviour the previous night, his enthusiasm for dancing as the night had worn on, of Ciara and of Lorcan, and of course their baby, Flynn.

As the small group approached Doonagore Castle on the left, she could see their own holiday home away in the near distance, but the trail wasn't taking them towards it. They were heading up onto the cliffs, the steeper rise visible for all to see. While it promised not to be a difficult walk, it wasn't for those scared of heights. The local farmer and guide was out ahead up front, seemingly in a world of his own as the group appeared to be struggling to keep up his pace.

Chrissy turned to Adam and said, "Shall I run on ahead and ask him to slow down, do you think? Only if you look behind us, the old couple look like they're about to collapse."

Adam pointed; the guide had stopped a while, maybe to let people catch up. "No need, I don't think," he said as they came to a stop and waited for the last of the group to gather round. A stiff wind whipped hair around faces. People wobbled slightly as stronger gusts caught them from behind and nudged them forward. The guide had his back to the ocean as waves crashed on rugged slate-grey rocks many feet below. White caps of water bounced over the surface and broke randomly, generating another and then another. Even with the sun shining, it didn't look the sort of day for a pleasant boat trip and Chrissy was glad she was on foot. She struggled to hear what the guide was saying and caught every other word or so, putting together the main points, slowly getting used to his accent.

"By the time we get home, I'll just about be able to understand the man," she whispered to Adam. "I don't know why I'm struggling; accents aren't usually an issue for me." Adam pushed her ahead of himself slightly in the hope it would make it easier for her to hear, but the wind was the stronger force and won out. Finding her own enjoyment, she marvelled at the lush green grass on one side and the ferocious swell on the other as she slipped her hand inside Adam's to feel his closeness. Once the walk resumed, they fell back slightly, allowing the others, including Richard, to go on ahead a little. There'd be time to catch up when they reached the end.

After nearly three hours of walking, they reached the rest of the group that were milling around the visitor centre. Even the senior couple had overtaken them after they'd chosen to saunter along and enjoy not only the rugged views but each other's warm company. Overhead, the lunchtime sun warmed them as they each slipped their jacket zippers down and Adam reached for the bottled water in his pack.

"That was breathtaking," Chrissy said. "Utterly breathtaking. I can see why they've filmed movies along there. Stunning."

"We should do the other half tomorrow. Hopefully Julie will join us," Adam said, taking a long drink from the bottle. He passed Chrissy a piece of toffee and took one for himself. Scanning the small car park, he asked, "Can you see Richard anywhere?"

"Perhaps he's inside."

"Well, I need to take a pee so I'll go and check."

"Okay. I'll stay here until you come back."

Chrissy made herself comfortable on the grass and waited for both Adam and Richard to return before they headed back on the shuttle bus. Adam returned, alone.

"Where could he be? Have you tried his phone?"

"Yes, I got Julie," Adam said disappointedly. "He left it plugged in beside their bed apparently."

"Now she'll be worried."

"I said I must have pocket dialled. I think she believed me."

"Then all we can do is sit here and wait a while and hope he turns up soon. Maybe we missed him somehow?" It was the only explanation Chrissy could come up with.

An hour later, Richard still hadn't returned.

"Let's head home," Chrissy said. "If he got on a bus, he's likely back by now."

CHAPTER 7

"Maybe he got chatting with someone and just forgot about us," Chrissy said. "I must admit it's unlike him to do something like this, totally out of character, don't you think?"

"I agree," said Adam, turning towards Chrissy. The shuttle bus was packed heading back to Doolin, and Chrissy and Adam were sitting at the back, squashed in with backpacks and anorak-clad strangers as they bumped along the road towards 'home'.

"I'm ready for something to eat. Is there any more toffee left?"

"Sorry, no. We've eaten the whole packet. We'll be back soon enough and I'll make some sandwiches. Maybe Richard or Julie will have something ready?" he offered.

"Don't be so sure," she said as the shuttle bus pulled up in the village centre. They waited until almost everyone had got off then slid out from their cramped seat. Adam stretched his long legs which had been pushed up against the seat in front of them. At a smidge over six feet tall, it was a regular problem for him when travelling. The average seat was for the average-sized person and he most certainly was not one of them.

"We could have got off back there," Chrissy said, pointing backwards with her thumb. The bus had gone almost right past their house.

"Come on," he said, taking her hand. "It's not far. And can I suggest you go easy on Richard? I know you when you get a bee in your bonnet about something, so just let it go, eh? We don't want an atmosphere all holiday."

As it turned out, creating an atmosphere was the least of their worries. Richard wasn't home when they arrived back.

As they opened the door and went inside, Julie slipped out from behind her magazine. She was sitting curled up on a comfy chair in the window, with the grey-blue of the Atlantic filling the frame around her blonde head.

"Great timing! I'm famished!" she said enthusiastically. "I thought I'd wait until you all got back, though I had thought you'd be a little earlier than this," she said, glancing at the huge old clock on the wall. "What's Richard doing? Where is he? Don't tell me he's stopped off at the pub?" She stood up and put her hands on her hips.

"We were kind of hoping he was here with you," Chrissy said, slowing her words as if she was talking to someone who struggled to understand English.

"With me? No, he went out with you. Don't tell me you've lost him?"

Adam stepped in. "Not lost him per se, more... more misplaced him."

"Will someone explain? I'm clearly having a blonde moment." She didn't sound like she was.

"Adam and I dropped back from the group a little to go at a slower pace. Richard was up front taking photos and whatnot, and when we got to the other end, to the visitor centre, he wasn't there. We waited an hour just in case, but figured he must have got on a shuttle bus and come back without us."

Julie waved her arms around her dramatically. "Well, as you can see, he's not here."

"Then where can he have got to?" Chrissy asked, turning to Adam.

"So, you have lost him!"

"Don't go getting all hysterical yet, sis, he's a grown man, not a toddler. I'm sure there's a perfectly obvious explanation to all this. He's likely found a nest or something and is still lying in the grass with his camera, looking at a gull, and we all walked by without noticing."

"Well I hope you're right," she said, walking from the room and leaving Chrissy and Adam to wonder what she was up to. A moment later, Julie returned, smart new hiking boots in one hand, top of the range jacket in the other. "So, I'm guessing you didn't 'pocket dial' earlier, you were phoning him to see where he was, am I right, Adam?"

"Yes."

"Well, I'm going out to find him. Anyone coming?" There was a fierceness to her words, a heat somewhere between warm coals and a hot oven.

"We'll all go, Julie," Adam said. "But first we need something to eat and drink before we set out. Let's be sensible and have a sandwich then go. Yes?"

"I agree," Chrissy added, moving to get the required bread from the cupboard and pull plastic tubs from the fridge. "We will be out of here in less than thirty if we get our skates on. I'll make sandwiches, you make the tea," she ordered. "Adam, why don't you see if you can get hold of the tour guide? He might know a likely spot that Richard could be holed up in."

"Good idea, on it." He picked up his phone and searched the internet for the number. As the girls busied themselves in the kitchen, Chrissy did her best to keep the negative thoughts from her head. Richard wouldn't be injured, would he? Of course not, she told herself, why would he be? He was likely wandering back on his own right now, famished, and hoping for a sandwich too. By the time they were ready to go, he'd have come around the corner and through the back door with a grin on his face because he'd photographed a spotted something or other in the grass. She felt Adam at her shoulder. He spoke quietly so only Chrissy could hear.

"It's a bit late in the year for the nesting season apparently. I just looked it up and it's only until late July, so long gone." The frown over his eyes told her he was concerned about Richard's absence too.

"Did you get hold of the tour guide?" she whispered.

"Answerphone, so I left a message."

"God, I feel awful about all this now, don't you?"

Adam nodded then took plates from the cupboard, and along with the sandwiches, the three hunched over at the table. A pot of tea sat in the centre and Chrissy poured three mugs before tucking into a chicken sandwich herself.

"I don't suppose we have a first aid kit between us?" asked Julie. Two sets of amused eyes turned towards her and she stopped chewing. "What?"

"There'll be one in a cupboard I expect," offered Adam. "Good idea, Julie," he said soundly. If Richard had in fact had an accident of some kind up on those cliffs, a plaster wasn't going to cut it. Still, her heart was in the right place, even if her thinking was a little off. Chrissy rose, grabbed an empty plastic tub and placed a sandwich inside it. She took a bottle of water from the fridge, found a small first aid kit in a kitchen cupboard and loaded everything into Adam's backpack. "He may be hungry," she said matter-of-factly before stuffing the remains of her own sandwich in her mouth and refastening her boots. If this wasn't nesting season, perhaps they should get moving right away.

"Let's get going," she encouraged. "Bring your sandwich with you. Adam, should we drive back to the visitor centre in case we pass him on the road coming back this way?"

"Good idea." He grabbed his own jacket, sandwich held firmly in his mouth as he slipped it on. Julie left hers on her plate.

"I'm worried," she said. Her bottom lip began to quiver.

"We'll find him," Adam said, smiling, trying to keep her spirits up. He hoped he sounded more positive than he felt.

Richard wasn't likely lying in the grass photographing a gull after all.

CHAPTER 8

By the time they'd travelled in virtual silence back to the visitor centre, they knew Richard wasn't out on the road. Since no shuttle buses had passed going in the opposite direction, there seemed only one place left to look. The cliffs. Adam parked up in the car park and the three climbed out. The wind had cranked up a notch and Julie fought to pull her hat on without it being snatched from her hands. Having already braced the cliffs once that day, both Chrissy and Adam knew how fierce the wind would be gusting further on up the trail and glanced a little nervously at each other, hoping Julie didn't cotton on to their thoughts. Adam readjusted his backpack and together the trio set off up the path back towards Doolin.

"Do you think he carried on and walked the rest of the cliff walk to Hags Head? We might be going in the wrong direction," Chrissy suggested as they set out.

"I'd doubt it, but anything's possible," said Adam. "We'll look if we don't find him this way," he said, pointing. Even though the 10 am tour was well and truly finished, there were still plenty of people milling about doing their own thing. Not everyone was interested in the history of the place and therefore didn't need a guide. Many travelled for the stunning ocean views and the remote and blustery feel of the place as they imagined fantastical scenes from days gone by in their heads, or scenes from the great movies that had been filmed in the spectacular surroundings. And not everyone wanted to be on a timetable on their holiday.

By the end of the first mile in, other walkers had thinned out somewhat as the early afternoon marched on into late. Chrissy was thankful the sun was still shining, and they weren't having to deal with horizontal rain on top of the fierce wind as they ploughed on. The three alternated who called out for Richard, and Adam and Chrissy walked as close to the cliff edge as they dared, peering over the top. If there had been an accident, neither of them wanted Julie to be the person to spot his body lying on the rugged rocks below, bashed and smashed by the roiling surf. It hadn't been lost on either of them that, with the tide going out, Richard could have drowned and been swept out to sea. It wasn't a pleasant thought. Adam's phone buzzed in his pocket and as he retrieved it to look at the screen, he noted it was a local number. He ducked down to shield the phone from the wind as he answered the call.

"Adam speaking."

A heavy Irish accent boomed back at him;. It was the tour guide from earlier.

"Have you found your friend?" he asked.

"We're on the track again now, and not as yet. Any ideas where he might be, places of photographic interest? I believe it's a bit late for birds nesting."

"No birds nesting at this time of year, no. There are so many places he could be, even out of nesting season, sorry."

"Thanks anyway. I did wonder."

"Did he go on to Hags Head, do you think?"

"I doubt it, but it's a possibility. We'll search this side first then check back at the house. I guess we'll have to get help if we don't find him."

"Right. You will, so. Keep me up to date, will you? I know those cliffs like the back of my hand, every crevice."

"I will. And thanks."

Adam slipped the phone back into his pocket as Chrissy and Julie stood nervously by.

"What's he say?" Julie asked urgently.

"There's several places, not far up here." It was the right time for a white lie, to give Julie hope. He just hoped Richard was only a little way ahead.

"And if he's not there?"

Panic was starting to set in with Julie. While Richard could be a bit of a bore at times, he was her Richard and she wouldn't be without him.

"If he's not there, we'll carry on to Doolin and you go back to the house. He may be there. I'll run back to the car this way then drive home. If he's not at the house reading his newspaper, we need to alert the authorities before much longer and it starts to go dark."

Tears started to trickle down Julie's cheeks and she hurriedly wiped them away, not wanting the others to see. Chrissy slipped her arm around her sister's shoulder and comforted her.

"We'll find him."

"Why didn't he take his phone with him!" she demanded, her lower lip quivering again. "He could be lying in a ditch with a broken leg, cold and frightened."

"Then let's get a move on, shall we?" Chrissy said in encouragement. "Let's get him home in time for dinner."

Julie nodded furiously. As the two women set off, Adam hung back behind them. He felt mean at the fib, but it was for Julie's sake, in an attempt to keep her spirits high. The two girls called out as Adam continued to scan over the edge of the cliff.

Another five hundred metres or so further on something caught Adam's eye. What looked like the sleeve of a red jacket was flapping in the wind, and it was on a ledge a good few feet down.

Richard's jacket? He had been wearing red.

Peering over for a closer look, Adam called his name and waited. "Richard!" Wind whistled by his ears and he turned his head and cupped his ear to find a spot with less noise as he listened for a reply.

A sound came back to him, but could he be sure of what it was? He called out again and stood stock still. "Richard!" The red fabric arm seemed to move again, and this time Adam was certain of a voice on the wind. It was Richard!

"Help! Down here!" It was faint but there.

"Hold on!" he yelled back, still not sure what the situation was that Richard had found himself in. Was he hurt? If so, how badly? What the hell had happened? Adam called ahead to the girls who came running back, Julie more awkwardly than her sister, not used to rough terrain under her boots.

"Chrissy," Adam said urgently. "Fancy a run back to the visitor centre, see if they have a rope to lower me down?" She was the best bet, the fastest of either of them, even with Adam's long, lean legs.

"On it. But call for help in the meantime. If he's hurt, we can't move him."

"My very next job. Now, you go. Be quick!" he called as Chrissy set off at pace back towards the car park and assistance, leaving Julie and Adam to mark the spot.

"Help is on its way, my love," Julie called down. "Hang on!"

As Chrissy raced back towards help, all the times she'd poked her tongue out behind Richard's back flooded her mind. It was a childish habit, and one she vowed never to do again. "You'd better be all right Richard Stokes," she panted. Emotion taking over, she suddenly felt extremely concerned for him. "I'll not take the mickey ever again!"

She concentrated on her stride, as it wasn't the easiest run in walking boots. The last thing she wanted was a sprained ankle, but she pressed on quickly regardless.

CHAPTER 9

Back at the holiday house, Richard teased, "Please, Julie. I'm fine, stop fussing," as she tucked the blanket around his shoulders for the umpteenth time.

"The doctor said to keep you warm and that's what I'm doing."

"Warm, not sweating," he said, pushing the blanket back off gently. While he didn't want to offend his wife, he wasn't going to stifle for her either. His badly sprained ankle was elevated on the couch in front, but it had been his dislocated collarbone that had prevented him from climbing back up from the ledge he'd found himself on after his tumble. Back in place now, it had a pulse all its own and throbbed like an idling engine. The effort of pushing the blanket back made him wince.

"See, now stay still."

Chrissy and Adam watched on with amusement as Julie played matron and Richard rolled his eyes good-naturedly, though it was plain to see he was hurting. Miraculously, nothing was broken, but he was going to be sore for some time, and with a swollen foot, there'd be no more cliff walks on Richard's autumn break. By the time they'd arrived home from the small local hospital, and settled him on the sofa, it was gone 7 pm.

Adam clapped his hands together as a diversion in their conversation. "I'm hungry, and since we won't be going out tonight, I'll see what I can create with what we have in the fridge," he announced, standing, ready to go.

Chrissy stood beside him, "I'll help," she offered and the two left the room, leaving Richard and Julie to carry on playing doctors and patients.

Once out of earshot, Chrissy said, "He's lucky, isn't he, that he didn't go all the way down. It doesn't bear thinking about." She refilled her wine glass from the bottle of red on the worktop.

"I know, but he's home now, and to all intents and purposes he's fine. I bet he won't sleep much tonight though, so he'll be tired tomorrow." Chrissy watched as Adam all but emptied the fridge and placed ham, eggs, cheese, salad, and cream on the side. He looked over the selection thoughtfully. "Is there any pasta?"

"Pretty sure I saw some," she said, opening cupboard doors and on finding an unopened packet of pasta bows, tossed it across to him.

"Creamy ham carbonara it is then," he announced and got to work with his ingredients, putting a pan of water on to boil.

A knock on the rear door surprised them both. Glancing at Adam, Chrissy said, "I'll get it," and went to open the door.

Ciara's voice filled the room as both she and Lorcan moved into the kitchen, all smiles as if they owned the place. Chrissy glanced sideways at Adam as the pair plonked two bottles of wine down along with what looked like a tray of tiny stuffed potatoes. Steam rose from their cheesy tops and they smelled delicious. What was going on? At the same moment, Julie walked in and shot her hand to her mouth.

"Oh heavens!" she cried. From her wide eyes, it was obvious she was startled by something, or had she forgotten something? "Damn! I'd clean forgotten all about it," she said, finally removing her hand from her mouth.

"Forgotten what?" asked Chrissy, though she almost figured it out at the same time. People didn't usually walk in holding hot snacks and red wine uninvited.

"While you were out, I went for a walk and bumped into Ciara and suggested they both come over for drinks and something to eat this evening. But then we lost Richard and it went clean out of my head," she said, moving her hand to her temple, rubbing, as if it was going to help her feel better for forgetting.

Lorcan stepped in, smiling, "You lost Richard? Have you found him?" he said, trying to lighten the moment and make it less embarrassing for them all.

"We have, but not before a dramatic cliff rescue and a visit to the hospital, mind," Adam filled in, laughing the events off. "Anyway, it's not a problem, so why don't you all go through to the living room where Richard is, and take the wine with you," he said, passing the bottles back. "Julie, grab some glasses and the tray of nibbles, and I'll be through in a moment. Then we'll fill you in properly before I rustle dinner up," he said.

"No, please, we can reschedule if it's inconvenient," Ciara said. "Don't worry about dinner, it sounds like you've had a hectic day. It's absolutely not a problem at all." She turned to Lorcan for backup, but Adam beat him to the punch.

"And it's not a problem here either," he said, encouraging everyone to move inside to the living room. "It won't be gourmet, but it'll be tasty. Chrissy, might I utilise your chopping skills?" She understood, it wasn't her knife skills he needed, but it was another set of hands to make use of and cook for an unscheduled party of six. She hoped he had a plan to feed everyone, because she certainly didn't. "Absolutely, go through everyone. I dare say Julie will recite the story a tad more dramatically than either of us anyway."

Julie took a mock bow.

"Adam and I will sort dinner and join you shortly. Just don't eat all those nibbles before we get back, okay?" Smiling, she left them in the capable hands of Julie the storyteller. No doubt Richard would get a word in at some point. When they were alone once more, Chrissy asked, "What's the plan, Stan?"

"A big bowl of cheesy pasta, side salad, and garlic bread if the bread rolls are still in the bread bin," he said, searching a pantry cupboard for inspiration. It was a good job the house came with a reasonable stock of pantry staples. Past guests had likely added to the range, leaving behind what they hadn't consumed for someone else to enjoy. Plus, the rule was if you used something, you replaced it with another item. Adam pulled out two tins of apricots and set them down along with a bag of pasta shells. "Shells and bows mixed will have to do. Can you remember how to make crumble?" he asked as he searched for a bottle of vanilla.

"I've got Google if all else fails," she quipped. "Apricot crumble and vanilla sauce, I'm guessing?"

"Custard to you and me, babe," he said, chopping ham. Sometimes the best meals were made when ingredients were scarce. In any case, they wouldn't go hungry.

"It will be lovely. Now tell me what you want me to do."

It was while she was fingers-deep in flour and butter that she realised something – and not for the first time since they'd met their new friends.

Where was baby Flynn, again?

CHAPTER 10

As it turned out, there was plenty of food to go around. Adam had worked a small miracle and turned humble pantry items into a delicious meal any TV chef would have been proud of. Chrissy would have liked to have said it had been her doing, but there was little point in embellishing the truth. She'd mixed flour and butter together and opened the apricots, but it had all been Adam's doing. Domestic goddess she was not. It was just before midnight when Ciara and Lorcan drunkenly left the house and headed across the way towards their own place, the tiny castle off in the distance. And presumably back to their son Flynn, Chrissy thought as she watched their torchlight as they walked back. There was only a tiny white pinprick to see when Chrissy finally closed the door. Julie was washing glasses in the kitchen behind her.

"That turned out to be a nice evening after all," Julie said, rinsing soap suds from a wine glass. "Poor Richard though, he's totally wiped out. He'll never live down going to sleep on dinner guests," she said, laughing.

"Hmm?"

"Did you hear any of what I just said, Chrissy?" Julie asked.

"Sorry, sis. No, I was miles away. Thinking about young Flynn again actually."

"What about him?"

"Well, he wasn't with them when we met them at the pub, and he didn't come tonight, and he could have done. I just wonder who looks after him when they go out, that's all." She picked up a tea towel and started to dry a wine glass. "Do you think they leave the little boy alone?"

"I don't know, I doubt it. Why didn't you ask earlier? There's likely a perfectly reasonable explanation, that he's with a sitter in the village, perhaps."

"Mmm. Something tells me otherwise, though I can't place what it is. I wanted to ask them tonight, but it seems a little rude to enquire. And if they did leave him all alone, what would I do with that knowledge anyway? Am I likely to report them?"

"I doubt you would, but it's not ideal, is it?" Julie passed her another glass to dry as they both stood at the sink chatting. Chrissy spotted the plate that Ciara had brought her nibbles on earlier. It gave her an idea.

"Well, first thing I'll take their plate back and invite myself in for coffee. Maybe the child doesn't actually exist?"

"What? That's a bit out there, isn't it?" Julie said, turning to face Chrissy properly. "Why would someone make up having a child for goodness sake?"

"Part of their cover story?"

"What cover story? And why would they need one?"

"They're on an extended holiday, Lorcan works all over the country, and we've never seen the child. They could be up to anything.

"Clearly, you've been playing private investigator for too long already," she said, turning back to the sink and more glasses. "You're fantastical."

"Inquisitive mind is all." They carried on in silence a while, Chrissy thinking about what she'd just said. Was there something adrift or was she looking for a story where there wasn't one?

Nobody else would think their friends' situation was odd for any reason, and maybe it wasn't. Still, Chrissy's nature let her thoughts idle away as she dried and returned glasses to their cabinet. A yawn behind told her Adam was ready for bed; it had been a long and eventful day.

"That was an unexpectedly fun evening."

"Chrissy thinks there's something suspicious about them, about their set-up," Julie spouted, like a ten-year-old child telling tales. Chrissy groaned at her sister. Some things never changed.

"Oh? And what's that?"

Chrissy was about to speak when Julie jumped in again.

"Because there doesn't appear to be any sign of their baby, Flynn. Chrissy thinks he might not exist since they are always without him. What do you think?"

"I don't think anything actually. He's probably with a sitter where he should be."

"Well, Chrissy is going over tomorrow for a snoop, so I guess we might find out then," she added somewhat tersely. She dried her hands on the towel and untied her apron. "I'm done. I thought I'd take a sleeping tablet tonight. It's been a hectic day so don't try and wake me too early in the morning."

"What about Richard?" Chrissy asked. "If he wakes in the night, you'll be knocked out in the other room and won't hear him. He might need you."

"He'll be fine. I dropped half a tablet in a glass of water for him, he'll sleep like a baby all night."

Chrissy kept her shock under control. With the painkillers the poor man was on, she doubted the doctor would have prescribed a sleeping tablet on top, but it was done now and not officially her business or concern. Maybe a good night's sleep was for the best.

"I'll see you late morning," Julie said. "Goodnight."

Chrissy and Adam watched her go before turning the light off and heading to their own room via the living room where Richard lay asleep. In the lamplight, he looked peaceful as he snored lightly. Chrissy flicked the lamp off, plunging them into moonlight, and turned once again towards the tiny castle in the distance. A small creamy light still glowed at the top of the structure and she wondered whose room it was. Perhaps it was the nursery, little Flynn awake, maybe having a late feed. Perhaps it was Ciara and Lorcan getting ready for bed. A moment later, the light was gone before Adam led her to their own bed, and sleep.

She dreamed of a baby floating towards a full moon on a navy-blue sky.

MONDAY

CHAPTER 11

Maybe it was the change of air or that they'd all had a stressful day previously, or maybe they'd all been late to bed having entertained unexpected dinner guests, but whatever the reason, all four had slept like tired children and it was gone 8 am when the first of them rose. Richard had woken around 4 am and, realising where he was, had taken himself to the kitchen, rather gingerly, for more painkillers before heading to his bedroom and slipping in alongside Julie. There he'd lain until the pain had finally eased and he'd dropped off back to sleep again. Four hours later, he was ready for more relief and so settled himself on the comfy old sofa by the window, foot elevated and sipping tea. The house was silent, not a sound from any room. Richard folded his paper over and tossed it to the seat beside him, having read the whole thing the previous day anyway. He attempted to rest his hands behind his head but the fierce shot of pain in his shoulder quickly persuaded him otherwise. While the dislocation had been put back in place, shoulders weren't meant to move in and out the way his had and whatever had been disturbed internally took its opportunity to growl at him. He rubbed at it as his good arm allowed him to.

Sitting in the tranquillity of the morning sun was relaxing. It was a shame his holiday had been curtailed so early on and not more conveniently on the last day. Still, he was sure he could manage afternoon tea at Father Ted's place when they went. Doolin Cave, on the other hand, might have to wait, though he couldn't see himself returning just for that particular damp, dark, and wet experience. A floorboard creaked somewhere further back in the house and caught his attention. A moment later, Chrissy padded barefoot into the room. On catching sight of Richard lying by the window in his pyjamas and robe, she stopped short, slightly shocked.

"Morning, Richard. I wasn't expecting anyone to be in here, I thought I was first up." Instinctively, she pulled her own robe a little tighter around her middle in an attempt to make herself more presentable in front of her brother-in-law and ran her fingers through her hair to tidy her bedhead. If she'd known he would be sitting there, she'd have dragged a brush through it first. Too late now. "Can I get you some more tea?" she asked. Richard struggled to stand, and Chrissy went to his aid. "No need to move, stay where you are and I'll get the pot."

"Thanks."

"Did you sleep okay?" she asked, busying herself with the kettle.

"Until about 4 am when I needed some more tablets. I hadn't realised I wasn't in my own bed." He rubbed his temples with the palms of his hands. "I don't remember much about last night actually, and I certainly don't remember falling asleep on the sofa."

Chrissy smiled at him. "Do you remember our dinner guests?"

"I do, yes. God, how rude of me. Did I fall asleep while they were still here?"

"Out like a light." She poured boiling water onto fresh teabags and added milk to two mugs.

Richard groaned at the awkwardness of it all. "I'd better apologise when I see them again."

"I wouldn't worry too much. They could see you were unwell last night; you'd been through quite an ordeal on that ledge. You were lucky the doctor didn't insist you stay in hospital overnight."

She spotted the plate that had held warm nibbles a few hours ago. She'd take it back later. And hopefully meet the little boy.

If he existed.

"Anyway, I'm popping over there shortly so I'll pass on your apology, if it'd make you feel better?"

Richard leaned forward to pick his fresh mug up and winced again. "Thanks, please do. I don't suppose I'll be moving a great deal myself today."

Chrissy could see the pain reflecting in his eyes and immediately felt sorry for the man. While they weren't the closest two members of the family, them both being so different in many ways, he was her sister's husband and she cared about him. She took a long drink of tea, tipped the rest down the sink, and placed her dirty mug in the dishwasher.

"Right, I'm off to get changed and I'll run on over, take the plate, then carry on for a while, I think. Do you want me to wake Julie before I go? Or get you anything?"

"No and no, thank you. I'm fine here. You go and enjoy yourself, and I'll see you when you get back." Chrissy left him to his tea then rinsed the sleep from her eyes, pulled a brush through her hair, and changed into her running gear. Adam lay sprawled out on the bed watching her. He smiled.

"Can't I tempt you back under the covers?" he asked slyly.

"No, you jolly well can't. I know your moves, Mr Livingstone," she said, chastising him a little. "It takes time and effort to stay in shape so unless you want me to turn soft and mushy to the touch..."

"I wouldn't mind."

"Well, I do. Plus, I'll drop Ciara's plate back at the castle. I'm hoping to see for myself if there really is a child."

"Trust you," he said, groaning. "Miss Scarlett of the modern age." His underpants, which had been tossed to the floor late the previous night, suddenly found themselves airborne before settling on his head. Chrissy was a good shot.

"And if there isn't really a child? Wouldn't you think it odd to make one up?"

"Here we go..."

"Mark my words, there's something not sitting right, and I intend to find out what that is."

Adam groaned loudly then pulled a pillow over his own head in an attempt to tune her out as Chrissy fastened her laces and left the room. She passed through the kitchen, grabbed the plate, and set off towards the castle on the hill.

If there actually was a child, surely she'd see it during her own unannounced visit?

CHAPTER 12

Once outside, the weak morning sunshine did its best to warm her shoulders, but it was the ever-present wind blowing off the ocean that did its damnedest to chill her, which won out. With the absence of a jacket to keep the nip at bay, she'd have to wait a couple of miles at least to warm up. She'd reach the castle before then. Still, with gulls calling overhead and woolly brown cattle off in the distance, the green grass and uneven surface was far more enjoyable than the grey tarmac of roads and pavements back home in Englefield Green.

It was only a handful of minutes before she was at the perimeter wall of the castle where Ciara and Lorcan were staying. Seeing her new friend ahead of her, she called out, waving with her empty hand. Ciara waved back and waited for Chrissy to approach so they could hear each other over the sounds of birds calling.

"Good morning!"

"It is, isn't it? And good morning to you too," said Chrissy, appearing through the entryway in the stone wall. She gave her new friend a brief hug as a flash of movement caught her eye. A beige bundle of fur and wet tongue hurled itself out to join in the greeting.

"Rupert!" Ciara scolded as the Irish terrier pranced excitedly about, weaving at pace between Chrissy's legs and finally settling beside her. She bent down to pat his shoulders and the dog dutifully rolled over for a belly rub.

"Please, don't mind him. He's not the best-trained hound in the world. My bad."

"Pleased to make your acquaintance, Rupert," Chrissy cooed obliging with a tickle. "He's delightful. And such a cool name, it really suits him."

"He is a good lad actually. Quiet and gentle, hardly hear a peep from him. Useless as a guard dog, mind."

"Well, if there's no need for a doggy alarm, I'm sure his warm personality is worth more."

"Definitely, a real softy." Changing the subject, she asked, "Have you time for coffee or are you just starting out on your run?" Ciara pointed to Chrissy's attire. "Coming or going?"

"Well, I was going, but coffee does sound good, thanks."

"Come on in, make yourself at home then," Ciara said, taking the plate as the two women walked towards the old wooden door. Rupert followed, relaxed once more and behaving for the visitor. Before they entered, Chrissy turned to admire the view. Fierce grey waves crashed against the cliffs, white caps of water as far as the eye could see.

"Stunning," she said, turning back to Ciara.

"Come on in, I'll show you the view from the top."

Entering the tiny space, it was everything Chrissy had imagined something so old would be. There'd be little point making the interior of a sixteenth-century castle all sleek lines and minimalistic. While it had been brought into the twenty-first century, it still held fantastical charm.

"It's beautiful!" she exclaimed, taking her cap off. It never felt right to wear a hat indoors. "And so tastefully done."

"Come, I'll show you around."

The two women moved from room to room on their way up to the top. They passed tiny rooms off tiny landings until finally, at the third floor, they could climb no further. Before windows that faced directly out at the Atlantic Ocean, Chrissy stood mesmerised for a moment, taking in a view that could only be described as out of this world. The ocean went on forever. Finally pulling herself away, she took in the rest of the space. It looked like it had been set up purely as a place to sit and relax, read a book maybe, or just ponder. No matter which way you looked, the view was spectacular.

"Four floors in total, plus a cellar, so even though they are not big rooms, there's enough space for what we need."

"I'm speechless," Chrissy said as they started their descent.

Ciara paused by a door and leaned her ear close.

"Flynn is down for his nap," she said by way of explanation.

"That's a shame, I was hoping to meet the little one. Maybe another time."

"You might still be lucky, he's due up any minute," she said, smiling. "Anyway, coffee, and I bet you he's howling before the kettle does."

They made their way back to the kitchen, which, like every other room she'd seen, was small. Sandstone walls kept the castle's character alive with modern additions for comfort and convenience. An AGA range wouldn't have looked out of place, but since the property was a holiday home to its owners, there was little need. Nor was there space. Ciara busied herself doing the necessary while Chrissy gazed out of the ground-level windows and generally looked around as far as she could without being rude. There were no children's things anywhere. Not even the smallest teddy bear or toy train.

"Do you know the owners?"

"Heavens, no. Not us. I'm not sure where Lorcan found it, but I'm glad he did. But no, we don't move in those circles. Could you imagine how much a castle with views like would this cost? We'd have to be drug barons or something," she said, laughing. "Though, out here, that's probably not a bad job to be in. You should see the cellar, perfect hiding place."

Chrissy assumed, like anyone would, that Ciara was joking. She certainly hoped so but her antennae were once again nudged. Two steaming mugs of coffee appeared along with a biscuit tin.

"Help yourself," Ciara said.

"Thanks." The two settled down at the table. Chrissy took a biscuit since she'd still not had any breakfast and instinctively dunked it then realised she was in someone else's home.

"Oh, sorry, I wasn't thinking," she said through a mouthful of soggy digestive. "I'm being rude."

"Relax, you're fine," Ciara said, waving the suggestion away with her hand. "I dunk too. Go ahead." Permission or not, Chrissy kept herself in check and refrained from doing it again.

"You keep it very tidy, and with a dog and a small child too. How on earth do you manage to keep all the clutter that comes with a little one at bay?" She hoped she didn't sound like she was snooping since that's exactly what she was doing.

"The cellar."

"You keep him in the cellar?" asked Chrissy, feigning shock.

"No, of course not, though there are days, I can tell you," Ciara quipped. As if on cue and to shut Chrissy up with any more questions about his existence, the small cries of a baby waking up could be heard coming from a baby monitor that was hidden somewhere in the kitchen. "And as if by clockwork... I'll be back shortly."

Chrissy watched her go and sipped her coffee, amused at Adam's words from underneath the quilt earlier on: modern-day Miss Scarlett indeed. Rupert appeared by her side, and she leaned down to give him another scratch and listened as footsteps descended the stairs. A moment later, Ciara was back, a sleepy bundle in her arms, rubbing at his eyes with his knuckles.

It was Flynn.

CHAPTER 13

By the time Chrissy reached their holiday home after a slower than usual start to her run, it was almost 11 am. Ravenous from having not eaten breakfast beforehand and run solely on a coffee and two digestive biscuits, she filled a bowl with muesli and fresh milk, and took it out onto the deck where the others were all gathered. Richard had been given an extra chair and was sitting with his leg elevated, an ice pack in place and a blanket draped across his shoulders. He looked a little brighter than when she'd seen him earlier on, the painkillers were obviously doing their job. He was reading a book, something she couldn't recall ever seeing him do — it was generally the *Financial Times* or some other broadsheet. Julie was sitting next to him, huge sunglasses almost covering half her face, a large floppy hat keeping the sun from her skin. As always, she looked stunning, and she was only relaxing with a magazine. With everyone in a world of their own and reading, Chrissy felt like a spare part, and not wanting to interrupt anyone, worked on emptying her bowl. After almost five minutes, it was Adam that surfaced from behind his local paper and spoke first.

"Miss Scarlett returns," he said, teasing her. "What clues did you find, does the child exist?"

"Ha ha," she said. "And yes, a child does indeed exist, and he's gorgeous. As does the most adorable Irish terrier, Rupert."

"And which one was your favourite?"

"Rupert of course, as you'd expect me to say."

"Anything else to report, any other suspicious sightings?"

"Only one really."

"Oh?"

"Well, it sounds like nothing on the surface, I'll admit, but I asked if they knew the owners of the castle and they don't."

"What's wrong with that? We don't know the owners of this place," he said, flicking his head back towards the building behind them.

"This isn't a sixteenth-century building and we found *this* on the internet. I googled the castle and it said it was owned privately by a family who use it as a holiday home. There aren't any photos of the interior online, not that I could find. So, that means one of them must be connected to the owners in some form, maybe through a family member."

"You don't think they are just on an extended holiday, as they say they are?"

"No, I don't, though I can't be sure why. Call it a gut feeling. I don't know, there's something piquing my interest. Maybe it was Ciara's mentioning of it being a great place to smuggle and store drugs."

"Really? I doubt she'd be telling you if they really were drug-running."

"Oh, I don't know. You hear of things going on in plain sight. Maybe they are up to no good." Chrissy mulled it over for a moment before carrying on. "Plus, the little boy Flynn? He's not got blond or red hair."

"Would you expect him to have?"

"Lorgan is blond, so the allele for blond hair is dominant. Ciara, is red-haired, which is neither dominant nor recessive, so it's an incomplete dominant, meaning I'd expect, with their colours mixed, little Flynn would be perhaps strawberry blond."

Adam looked impressed, his mouth falling open at the revelation. Chrissy was an intelligent woman, but he often wondered where she picked such seemingly useless information up from and, furthermore, how she managed to retain it. From somewhere in the back of her brain, she'd just pulled out something she'd likely learned at school years ago.

"And what colour is his hair?"

Chrissy glanced across to her left and noticed both Richard and Julie were waiting for the answer too.

"Dark brown."

"And you don't think that's likely?"

"No, I don't."

"He could be adopted," suggested Julie. "They're not going to simply drop that into the conversation, now, are they?"

"True."

"Well, I say you've solved the puzzle of the fictitious child, so don't be looking for another where there isn't one. You are supposed to be on holiday, relaxing, remember?"

"I know. You're right, of course." She clapped her hands together loudly just once then stood. "Right. I'm off to have a shower. What's the plan for today?"

Three faces stared back at her as if they were expecting her to decide on the activities. "Don't look at me for the answer, but do chat amongst yourselves and let me know what you decide on when I get back," she said. With that, she headed back indoors to get ready. By the looks of them all, she figured they wouldn't be going far after yesterday's over-excitement, and as she shampooed her hair, she wondered if that was even a bad thing. It was turning out to be a glorious day and spending a little time on one of the sun loungers which were stacked neatly in the corner might not be a bad idea. Certainly until lunchtime anyway. The deck was nice and sheltered out of the wind – unless it changed direction of course. After that, she'd need to be up and doing something.

"I'd rather break than rust," she said to the shower cubicle, rinsing soapy suds away and wrapping herself in a fluffy towel. With

Richard laid up, perhaps she and Adam could slip out and do something after lunch, maybe finish the rest of the cliff walk to Hags Head.

Either way, she'd join them and be quiet for a while.

After lunch? Who knows?

CHAPTER 14

Lazing around is good for the body as well as the soul. For some it's a blissful activity, and for others, like Chrissy, it gets monotonous extremely quickly, and an acute dose of the fidgets sets in. She was lying on a sun lounger, staring ahead at nothing in particular, fingers drumming on the navy canvas beside her. She glanced at the rest of the group, each and every one of them content and concentrating on their own book, or in Adam's case, listening to one. Black headphones covered his ears, and with his eyes firmly closed, he could have been asleep, the story washing over him, not realising its audience had long since tuned out. Would the book detect no movement from his skull or his brain and stop courteously so he didn't miss the story? She'd ask him when he came out from wherever he currently was. Turning to Julie, she could see no more than the top of her huge hat and was reminded about their trip to Albi, in France, where she'd last seen her in it. Julie had played her part in finding a lost friend and had eavesdropped on an important conversation to help bring a criminal to justice. And then there was Richard, leg up, blanket on top, his thinning comb-over the only protection from the sun should he find himself in it.

Her fingers drummed, and drummed again. No one seemed to

notice. Not big on anything that was longer than a fifteen-minute read at a push, Chrissy found her mind drifting back to her castle visit earlier, the wonderful view from the top and finally meeting the little boy. His hair so dark, his parents so fair. Would Ciara have volunteered the information if he was indeed adopted? Letting a long sigh out and changing her thoughts to her own boys, she wondered what they were doing right at that moment. There'd been no interest from them in following their parents on holiday to Ireland, and when their friend Gary had suggested they all hung out at his place for the week, she knew there'd be no point dragging them along. She and Adam couldn't compete with friends their own age, and could only hope they hadn't planned on using their own house for an out-of-control party at some point. Gary's parents were fine with the idea and so everyone was happy. She retrieved her phone from the table beside her and sent a text to the two of them. Thomas would be the one to respond, as he was the more sensitive of the two young men, and while they were growing up so fast, she'd take the small amount of love and affection they tossed her way, for now. In another handful of years, they'd be into nothing else other than parties and girls, and she hoped they'd still make a little time for her and Adam, the aged parents. Until then, she'd keep them as safe and as happy as their young worlds would allow.

Hi boys. What are you up to? Is everything ok?

She hit send and waited. No little bubble popped up to say someone was replying immediately so she placed her phone back on the table to wait for a response. It could be a while. They were most likely kicking a rugby ball around the local park, their sweatshirts as goal posts, their phones in the pockets. Or the party had in fact happened and they were busy cleaning red wine out of the carpet. Chrissy cringed. It would happen one day, of that she was sure. She smiled to herself at the image, but it was the sound of an incoming text that made her sit up. With the generic tone as it landed, Chrissy instantly knew it wasn't either of the boys, they each had their own. She grabbed her phone to see who it was and didn't recognise the number, it wasn't a saved contact. The message, however, gave the sender away in an instant.

You left your cap earlier. I'll drop it over, heading out for a walk.

She'd noticed it missing not long into her run, as sweat had started to run down her temples, which she always found irritating.

She tapped back, *Great, thanks. Lounging out the back. Come on round.* Hitting send, she headed to the kitchen and made sure there were a couple of extra beers in the fridge, and added more diet coke before going back to her sun lounger. Julie looked out from behind her giant shades enquiringly.

"Ciara is popping over. I left my cap there earlier so since she's out for a walk, she'll drop by."

"Oh, I might get to meet the little one," she cooed, standing and stretching her back out a little. Since both of Julie's daughters were constantly at boarding school, Chrissy knew she missed them. It was Richard that had insisted they focus on their education, and to do that they wouldn't live at home. Chrissy couldn't say she agreed with the notion, but respected their decision anyway. While Julie spent a huge chunk of her time looking after her two boutique shoe stores, Jooles, Jooles, the rest she spent looking after herself. There was little time for anything else in her life so the girls were probably in the best place. That didn't mean she didn't miss them though.

Since their trip to Albi, Chrissy had noticed a change in her sister and a good one at that. While Julie had always been the more formal of the two, in every way possible, their trip away together had taught Julie to relax a little. Gone was the severely lacquered blonde hair, and in its place was a chic blonde bob that now caught the breeze naturally. She still looked stunning, and younger with it.

"I assume she'll be bringing him, but who knows. I didn't see Lorcan this morning, maybe he'd gone to the shops?"

"Well, it doesn't matter," she said, pointing with her chin. "Because they're here now, all three of them actually. And the dog."

Chrissy turned to see the trio walking down the side of the

house towards them. Young Flynn, sat comfortably in his buggy out front, was carrying her cap, while Rupert strained on his leash.

"Maybe you should ask about his hair," suggested Julie and received a warning look for her trouble.

"Hello again!" called Chrissy, stepping forward to meet their guests. "You were quick."

After pleasantries and refreshments had been offered, the six adults chatted over beers and cokes while young Flynn wriggled around on the deck by Ciara's feet, placing anything in reach into his mouth for a chew test. It seemed rude now their visitors were relaxing to ask about a child's heritage, particularly when it was out of sheer nosiness and nothing else, it served no purpose. Neither Chrissy nor Julie raised the subject.

About an hour into their visit, Lorcan's phone rang and he excused himself for a moment, taking the call at the end of the garden to talk in private. Through dark sunglasses, Chrissy watched the man's body language and tried not to appear as though she was spying on his conversation. But by the man's movements, his shoulders, his bent head, she could see something was troubling him as the conversation progressed. It also appeared to be fairly one-sided – the caller's side. When he finished the call, he stood for a moment, looking out to sea, before placing his phone back in his pocket. From behind her shades, Chrissy attempted to read his face, which was now devoid of the rosy cheeks he'd had on arrival. Something was clearly bothering him. Had Ciara noticed, she wondered.

When she glanced to her side, the answer was plainly visible. She had.

CHAPTER 15

Within five minutes of the call, Lorcan, Ciara, Flynn, and Rupert were all gathered up and had set off back towards their holiday castle, leaving Chrissy wondering what had just happened. And it wasn't just her that thought it odd, Julie had picked up on the vibe and it wasn't a good one. Gathering bottles and cans up, the two women headed for the kitchen, leaving Adam and Richard to their reading.

"I didn't imagine that hasty retreat, did I?" Chrissy asked, filling the recycle bin.

"No, you didn't. Quite odd. I wonder what that call was all about?"

"Whatever it was, it was obviously a worry to Lorcan, his colour changed in an instant, and when I glanced at Ciara, she didn't look much better either. I've never seen visitors leave so fast. People stay longer when I've cooked a meal, and that's saying something."

"Do you think something's up?"

"I do, yes. I've no clue what though," she said, loading odds and ends into the dishwasher. "I hope everything's all right, that they don't have to rush off back from their break."

"Wherever 'back to' actually is. We know nothing about them save for he travels to the English ports on a regular basis."

Chrissy wiped the side down while she processed her thoughts, such as they were.

As if reading her mind, Julie asked, "And how did she get your telephone number, to text you?"

"I was wondering the same thing. I didn't give it to her, I've no reason to do so." She screwed her face up as she concentrated on her thoughts, trying to come up with a perfectly reasonable explanation as to how a relative stranger would get her number. Perhaps Adam or Richard had given it to her, back at the pub on their first night? "Well, you obviously didn't give it to her since you're wondering the same thing. Either of the men, do you think?"

"I doubt it," Julie said, "but I'll go and ask."

Even though it was October, it was still warm on the deck, ideal for relaxing. Chrissy pondered as she watched Julie check first with Richard, and then with Adam. Shakes of their heads added more curiosity to the conundrum. While she could call Ciara's mobile and ask, was she really going to enquire how she got her number? It seemed rude.

"No." Julie entered, shaking her head slightly in answer. She looked as perplexed as Chrissy felt.

"Well, I guess it doesn't matter, not really. Though I am still curious."

"You'll have to drop it into a future conversation somehow. No doubt we'll see them again during our stay. They are here for a while, an extended break, they said," said Julie.

Folding the tea towel up and looking at the kettle that had boiled, Chrissy said, "I don't much fancy tea now. Let's go and get a frothy coffee instead. Richard can't move on foot and I dare say Adam will be asleep in five minutes, he's been drowsy all day. They'll not miss us."

Julie wasn't convinced, she only allowed herself one caffeinated drink per day.

Chrissy tried another tack to tempt her for a walk. "We could take another look in that sweater shop, if you like?"

"Deal. I'll grab some shoes," she said in a flash and set off to find suitable footwear. There had been a time, not so long ago, when heels were the only thing that ever adorned her dainty feet, but spending time in France had introduced her to flats – as long as they were gorgeous. A moment later, Julie was ready, with red-beaded loafers to match her bag.

Chrissy looked at them and raised her eyebrows. "I like those. New range?"

"Just a sample, but yes. I think they'll do well. Got them from the shoe fair on my buying trip last time."

"Lucky you," she said, grinning.

Chrissy checked for her purse and the two set off, arm hooked through sisterly arm. They chatted about their evening dinner options, poor old Richard and his lack of mobility, the fortuitous weather they were having, and eventually they circled back to their new acquaintances.

"I'd like to be a fly on their kitchen wall right now," said Chrissy. "I wonder what's got them both in a tizzy?"

"I guess you won't know unless you ask and I'm betting you're not going to."

Chrissy replied with a simple 'hmm' as she thought about it. By the time they got to the sweater shop, she'd managed to banish her earlier thoughts and settle on the task of getting Adam a gift. Unlike Julie and Richard, there was no way she and him were going to have matching knitted jumpers and she amused herself looking at a woollen waistcoat that she knew he'd look handsome in with his jeans and casual shirt. She chose a not-too-pretty printed scarf for herself, not that she'd ever wear it. Still, it might remind her of her time in Ireland at some point in the future. She headed across to the cashier to pay. A burly older woman admired her purchase and took payment as Julie approached the counter, the requisite two matching jumpers in her hand. Chrissy wanted to groan but refrained, catching the cashier's eye instead.

"You'll be needing them by the end of the week," the woman offered. "There's a real cold spell forecast. Shame, after such lovely weather, most unseasonal for October. Still, it's better than rain."

"It could be cold in the little castle then, I don't expect there's much heating in there," Julie offered by way of conversation.

"Owners only come in summer; it'll be empty now."

Chrissy glanced at Julie. She was concentrating on paying for her items, but Chrissy instinctively knew the news had landed in her sister's head, together with its implications. She certainly wasn't deaf. Or daft.

"I thought someone was staying there," Chrissy offered. "I'm sure I've seen a light on at night."

"There's a light on a timer apparently, though I don't know why. But no, there won't be anyone visiting in the off season. Of that I'm certain."

CHAPTER 16

Chrissy still yearned for a coffee; there was a small café a little way further up the road and since it was still pleasant and warm, the two women ambled along in no rush, chatting to one another.

"What do you make of that?" Julie asked.

"She's obviously wrong. I've been inside myself, I've seen all around it, met Ciara there, so she's mistaken on that."

"She sounded pretty certain about it to me, and even mentioned the light at night."

"She's out of the loop then. Not as up to date on the local grapevine as she might think."

"Unless..."

"Unless what?" Chrissy said, coming to a standstill. Julie turned back towards her and shielded her eyes from the sun, which was low in the sky; her giant sunglasses were not enough to do the job on their own.

"Unless Ciara and co are there when they shouldn't be. Maybe that phone call was someone telling them they'd been spotted, and they should leave?"

"You think so? It's a bit far-fetched, isn't it? Moving into someone's holiday home without permission?"

"I'm simply putting it out there that they could have moved in in plain sight. Who would question them? Only the owner, or perhaps a caretaker."

Julie had a point. Sometimes the best place to plant your marijuana was by your front door. Nobody would think it could possibly be what it actually was and so dismiss it out of hand. Marigolds looked suspiciously similar but weed didn't bloom bright orange. Was that what was happening here, at the castle?

"Squatters then really, I suppose."

"Glorified ones though." Julie grinned at Chrissy as they carried on slowly up the lane towards the little café. "Have you ever noticed the light on at night, like the woman in the shop mentioned?"

"I've never *not* noticed it, if that makes sense. We've only been here two nights and both of them were late ones to bed, so when my head hits the pillow, that's me done. But I'll be checking tonight."

"Me too, out of curiosity, though it won't prove anything, and by that I mean anything untoward or even normal. By the sounds of it, a light off should be out of place, not a light on."

Chrissy stayed quiet as she mulled things over. The whole Ciara and Lorcan matter was getting more and more peculiar with every contact they had with the couple. And receiving a text from Ciara was perhaps the oddest thing of all. They were about to pass Gus O'Connor's, the pub they'd eaten in on Saturday night, when they'd first met them. Something was triggered in her brain's hippocampus and a memory hit her as sharp as a dagger. She groaned outwardly.

"I know where she got my number from. It's obvious now I think about it."

"Where?"

"In the pub! I had to give my number when we booked, remember? In case we were late or something." She slapped her palm to her forehead. "I knew there'd be a simple explanation somewhere."

As they passed by, Julie reflected on what she'd just said: it still didn't explain it fully, not to her. "I'm not so sure it's that simple actually."

"What do you mean?"

"You gave your number to the *barman*. How did Ciara end up with it?"

That stumped her. She'd no reason to have seen it; it wasn't like she worked there. Plus, it would have been a breach of privacy for someone to hand it over, or for Ciara to have taken it without permission. The table booking only half-answered the question.

"I'm sure the full explanation will come to me at some point. Anyway, let's get a move on before the café closes, I still haven't had my frothy coffee yet," she said, increasing her pace somewhat and leaving Julie trailing behind.

By the time they arrived back at the house, the men were asleep in the living room, Adam on one sofa and Richard on the other. A book lay oddly on the floor, having landed as if it'd slipped off Richard's chest as he drifted off, its pages bent back, uncorrected.

"You'd think they worked in a coal mine or something, wouldn't you?" Chrissy said, amused at the sight in front of them. "How tired are these guys of ours?" It was like a nursery for grown men. Richard's mouth was open, a low gurgle coming from somewhere deep at the back of his throat. Neither was aware they were being observed by their loved ones. Chrissy dropped her bag on the coffee table and flopped down in a chair.

"It's a good job we're not burglars, the family silver would be long gone."

Julie made herself comfortable in another chair and leaned her head back, closing her eyes. "The trouble with holidays is they can be tiring," she said quietly, almost to herself. "I think I'll have forty winks too, before we go for dinner later. Wake me up in an hour if I haven't woken myself, would you?"

Chrissy looked round the room at the three and, fuelled by her recent caffeine fix, decided to let the sleeping dogs lie and make herself comfortable on the lounger outside. She grabbed one of the fleecy blankets that were stored in a basket by the door and headed to the sunniest spot, out of the breeze. She pulled the fleece around her shoulders and stared out towards the Atlantic Ocean. The peacefulness of the property, the view, and some time away with Adam and her sister was just what she needed after such a hectic year. Her father would have liked the spot, and so would her mother, though since Chrissy was no longer on speaking terms with her, she hadn't even considered inviting the woman along. Her father's death had stirred up a rat's nest of deceit and lies that both she and Julie were finally coming to terms with. She missed her father, no matter his sins, and as she gazed at the lowering sun, hoped he'd died a happy man.

CHAPTER 17

Bronagh Bowen had been running the sweater shop in Doolin for the last twenty years, give or take, and had been part of the friendly holiday community virtually all of her sixty-two years. Her own mother and father, both long gone now, raised her in the small coastal town along with her brother Brocc, who owned the garage in the village. The two, like many siblings, had had their fallings out from time to time but, on the whole, cherished a close relationship with each other and were in contact almost on a daily basis. Both now single, they kept each other company, though still led their separate lives and worked their own businesses.

When Brocc received a call-out for his pickup truck to remove the mangled wreckage of a car off the road some twenty kilometres out of town, he put his jacket on as usual and headed out to the location he'd been given. It was a night like any other. That was until he arrived at the scene and spotted the registration plate that lay broken in two nearby in the grass. It was then he knew what the police would find when they checked the identification of the driver: it was his sister, Bronagh. Frozen to the spot and staring at the plate that lay before him, he wasn't aware of an officer speaking, didn't hear a word the young guard said until there were two officers stood alongside him. The arrival of the sergeant did the trick, and he did his best to focus on the man's face, looking for a clue as to his sister's fate: dead or alive. Glancing at the wreckage again, he wanted to ask if the woman driver had perished, but his tongue felt like it had doubled in size, unable to form words. He turned, still unhearing, towards the first guard that had arrived, before finally managing to get his words out.

"Is she alive?"

Brocc recognised the younger officer, Garda Drew Harris, from previous call-outs. His thinning hair moved gently in the stiff breeze and his bird-like nose glowed pink in the manufactured light of the emergency vehicles as he looked to his colleague.

"She is, miraculously," the older of the two said. "How do you know the driver is a female, though?" This was Sergeant Michael Staines, a man Brocc had worked with on numerous occasions, though none as close to home as this one was going to be.

He breathed a deep sigh of relief. "That's my sister's car," he said, pointing. "Bronagh Bowen. She has the shop, back in Doolin."

Again the two officers glanced at each other, the younger waiting for his sergeant to perhaps offer more information, keeping quiet himself by default.

"You obviously didn't recognise her, did you? How badly injured is she?" asked Brocc.

"No, I'm sorry, I didn't," Staines said. "She's pretty banged up, and we haven't found a handbag, so no identification, so we didn't know. She had to be cut from the wreckage and she's on her way to hospital, but she's conscious, just."

Brocc had always been a man of few words, no matter the occasion, and with the news Bronagh was alive, knew there was nothing more he could do but hope she pulled through. He nodded his understanding before adding, "Right, she's in the best hands, so... I may as well get her car back. My yard then, I'm assuming?" He would keep himself busy. He kept his head bowed as he spoke, not wishing to make eye contact for fear of someone seeing the worry there. Brocc Bowen was a proud man.

"Yes, nothing suspicious here, no other vehicle involved," the sergeant added.

Brocc nodded his understanding and set to work. The two officers watched on as the older man made a start on the removal of what was left of his sister's vehicle, as he busied himself with gloves and chains and various levers to get it hoisted on board his truck. But Brocc was intrigued as to what had caused the accident, likely because it involved his kin. Normally he didn't give it much thought, just cleared the aftermath away. It was always someone else's family member.

When he'd loaded up and preserved the wreckage as best he could, he presented himself to Sergeant Staines once more. Brocc had a question.

"Michael, do you have any clue at all what happened here? Only there's no power pole or tree to hit, and no other vehicle involved, no other debris that I can see."

"So far, no, not a great deal. There could have been a medical event, perhaps. Was Bronagh unwell at all? On medication?"

"Not that I know of, no."

"On her phone, maybe, distracted with something. We see it all the time. A quick text can be deadly."

Brocc felt himself pale. "I doubt it. She was a good driver, conscientious."

"Well, it's a good straight stretch of road, dark or not, and there's nothing obvious right now. If there was another vehicle involved, and it left the scene, there's likely evidence on her car. My gut is telling me it was solo though."

"Well, I'll get this lot back and head off to the hospital I expect. Taken her to Ennis, have they?"

"I believe so. Will you be all right?" Michael asked. He'd known Brocc for most of his life. A placid, unassuming man, a community member that blended into his surroundings but was often there quietly paying attention. There wasn't much that escaped Brocc Bowen. He nodded silently and headed for the cab of his truck.

Brocc pulled back onto the road with his sister's mangled car on the back of his flatbed, and Michael Staines watched his tail lights disappear into the night. Finding out a family member had been involved in a serious accident was bad enough, but to find out by attending the scene unknowingly must be even more distressing. Drew Harris arrived beside him and said, "Poor sod, I hope she makes it."

Staines glanced down at something that had caught his attention, something his officer had in his hand. He pointed to it. "What's that?"

Drew lifted it so his colleague could see. "It's a baby's bottle. I found it just down the road slightly. I doubt it's anything to do with this lot though," he said, motioning with his hand. "There's a pack of nappies too. I don't think she has any children, so she's unlikely to have grandchildren. I can't see why she'd be carrying baby stuff."

Sergeant Staines nodded in agreement. "Curious" was all he said.

TUESDAY

CHAPTER 18

Chrissy and Julie were finishing a relaxing breakfast out on the deck in the morning sunshine. As usual a stiff breeze blew, though it seemed to have changed direction; normally coming straight off the sea, today it came more from the south-west.

"That's odd," Chrissy said, gazing off into the distance, towards the castle.

"Hmm?" Julie asked, not really paying much attention, intent on the gossip pages of her magazine.

"Rupert. He's been barking most of the time we've been sitting here, and now I think about it, I heard him last night too, which is unlike him. He's been so quiet the whole time we've been staying here."

"Probably a rabbit that's caught his eye."

"I'm not so sure," Chrissy said slowly. "It's been too constant. Plus, it sounds like he's indoors and not in the garden." Perhaps it was the direction the breeze was blowing that made it seem so much clearer. Noise carried on the wind. She stood to take a closer look, to see if the dog was bounding about outside, but it was a little too far to observe properly. All she could see was the single-tower castle and it looked quiet in the distance, save for the barking sound. There was no one to be seen, no movement to note. Just the dog yapping.

"Pass me Richard's binoculars, they're by your elbow."

Julie did as she was asked, and Chrissy looked again. There was nothing to see, no dog, and all seemed quiet. Yet it wasn't.

"I might pop over," she said, standing.

"Maybe Ciara has accidentally locked him in and gone shopping?"

"Doubtful."

"Well, go over there then if you're concerned."

Julie hadn't taken her nose out of the magazine all through their brief conversation. Chrissy slipped her feet into her trainers, which were sat nearby. "I think I will," she said, leaving Julie to soak up the contents of her magazine in peace. Without another word, she left her sister to it and stepped off the secluded back deck area where they'd both been sipping coffee.

Doonagore Castle wasn't far from their holiday home as the crow flies, but it meant a straight line across fields that held cattle. While Chrissy wasn't frightened of the bunch of furry brown animals, she didn't want to chance a bull being among them and it becoming upset at her intrusion. On the other hand, it seemed silly to get the car out for the short drive around to check on a barking dog. She looked down at her feet; her shoes would do the job if she ran – carefully. A bull would likely be more interested in a female cow nearby than her.

It was another glorious morning and while it wasn't a cold one, it wasn't a warm one either. As she took off at a gentle jog, the only sound she could hear was the wind forcing its way past her ears, filling them with a constant loud whooshing that tuned everything else out, including the dog's barks. Only when she turned her head to the side slightly did she get relief from the briskness of it, but she couldn't jog and face a different direction at the same time. Not without falling over. A handful of woolly brown heads glanced her way, obviously undecided about whether to run or not, and if so, in which direction they should go.

It wasn't far to the boundary. Chrissy slowed her pace as she reached the perimeter stone wall of the tiny castle. Once she had reduced it to a walk, she could hear Rupert barking furiously, but now there was something else in the wind as she approached the door. Something even more concerning.

It sounded like a baby crying. And not a whimpering cry either.

Urged on by the realisation baby Flynn might also be in distress, she quickly passed under the stone archway and knocked on the front door.

There was no answer.

She called out, "Ciara! Lorcan! Are you home?"

Still Rupert barked, much louder now she was only outside, and she could hear Flynn screaming at the top of his lungs. The boy was certainly distraught at something. Chrissy made her decision – she had to go in. She tried the handle; the door was unlocked. As she opened it further, a manic Irish terrier hurtled out and ran past her, but she took no notice. It was Flynn she was concerned about now.

"Ciara! Lorcan!" she called again, but there was no reply. It appeared nobody was home. Following the sound of Flynn, she mounted the stairs two at a time and headed up to where the noise was coming from, his nursery, she assumed. She'd only been in the tiny castle once before and felt like she was intruding, but Flynn's cries were not abating. It was easy to find his room, and she slipped inside. His crying stopped almost immediately as he realised someone was now in attendance. His face was the colour of a ripe strawberry and soaking wet from his tears. Two little rivers of thick goo ran from his nose and he hiccupped as he settled down a little. His dark hair was damp and stuck to his forehead. He must have got himself in a terrible state and appeared to be all alone.

"Hey little man," Chrissy said, cooing and reaching down into the cot for him. "What's all the noise, are you okay?" She picked him up and held him close in comfort, his little body overly hot to the touch.

"Where's your mum and dad, eh?"

Flynn could only blow a sticky wet bubble in response. Chrissy looked around the room, though for what she wasn't sure.

"Let's see if anyone's home upstairs, shall we?"

Carefully, she carried little Flynn on up the stairs and checked the bedroom. There was no one else there, the place was empty. She glanced out of the window: no car; nothing but grass in one direction, the Atlantic Ocean in the other. Flynn gurgled and started to whimper, and Chrissy turned her attention back to the little boy.

"It's strange all right, little man," she said. Patting his bottom gently, she noticed for the first time how wet he was. And how smelly he was. "Let's get you changed into a dry nappy, that'll make you feel a bit better, eh?" Heading back down to the nursery, Chrissy tried to come up with a reason why Flynn was all alone in the house, but couldn't find anything that immediately fitted. She took Flynn back into his room and placed him in his cot for a moment. The sound of a dog bounding up the stairs broke into her thoughts as she pulled dry clothing and a fresh nappy from a drawer then lay Flynn on the changing mat nearby and took off his wet clothes. Rupert entered the room and sat quietly, watching.

"Gracious," she said in her soothing baby voice. "You have been busy." It had been some years since she'd last changed a nappy, but she knew instinctively what a full one looked like and what an over-full one looked like. It was obvious the child hadn't been changed for a while.

"I think a quick bath is needed," she cooed, slipping next door to put the plug in and turn taps on. A moment later, she was back. Tears filled the little one's eyes again and he began to wail, and she did her best to soothe him. If he hadn't been changed in a while, perhaps he hadn't been fed either. Nothing added up. Where were his parents? Why such a full nappy?

"You're hungry, aren't you? Let's see what we can do about that." Picking him up and laying him in his cot for safety, she paced downstairs to the kitchen. On the work surface, empty feeding bottles lay waiting to be filled, a tub of formula nearby. Creamy powder stared at her as if someone hadn't wiped around after making his last bottle. When had that been? She was flummoxed. Quickly, she put the kettle on to heat up, made a bottle then took it back upstairs with her just as Flynn's wailing cranked up again. She turned the bath taps off on her way and went into the nursery.

"Shhhush, little man," she said wrapping a semi-naked baby in a blanket from his bed and sitting with him in the nursing chair. "This will help," she said, offering him the bottle. He drank greedily from the teat, so much so she had to gently pull it away from time to time to pace him, not wanting it all to come back up as vomit. It was acutely obvious he hadn't been fed in some time. She wondered about his nappy again. And the strength of his hunger.

Someone had abandoned him.

Surely not?

Right there and then, she couldn't come up with any other explanation.

CHAPTER 19

When Flynn had devoured half of his bottle, Chrissy gave him a short break to wind him. She'd almost forgotten the water running earlier and since there was way too much for an infant, pulled the plug out and let most of it go. It gurgled noisily through the pipes of the ancient building and when there was just enough left for the little boy, she replaced the plug and returned to her charge.

Her charge? There was no one else on the horizon for the boy, not at this point.

"Ready for a little more?" she asked as she reached in to pick him up. She pulled the blanket closer around him and repositioned him in her arms. Two small hands reached up, instinctively knowing what a bottle meant for him and he resumed his feed at a slightly slower rate than a few moments ago. Chrissy focused on him while he fed, and when the bottle was finally empty, wondered if she should make another smaller one up. She was a little rusty on infant formula knowledge and had had to check the tin for the amount to give him and hope she hadn't overdone it. Flynn gurgled his approval at his own full tummy and Chrissy was promptly rewarded with a wet belch that deposited milky goo over one wrist.

"Thanks, buddy," she cooed. "You needed that, didn't you?" She spent the next five or six minutes comforting him and getting his remaining wind up before her mind returned to the bizarre situation she now found herself in. How long had he been all alone, sitting in an overfull nappy and, by the look of it, having missed meals too? And there was no sign of either Ciara of Lorcan. The more she contemplated the situation, the more concerned she grew. Flynn whimpered in her arms and she remembered the bath. He needed a wash before she could put a fresh nappy and clothes on him. But should she call the police, the Gardai, before doing so? Had a crime been committed, and was she now trampling over evidence with each action she took? She felt sure Flynn's welfare was more important right at that moment.

"Come on, let's get you cleaned up and dressed, then we can decide what to do. How does that sound?" she asked, stroking his forehead lightly. At least he'd calmed down, his tears stopped, his face returning to a more normal colour.

A few minutes later, Flynn had his clean clothes on, and Chrissy placed him back in his cot while she quickly made her way down the stairs for another look around. Rupert greeted her again and woofed a little.

Maybe he was hungry too. She spotted an empty bowl on the floor by the fridge then found his biscuits in the nearby cupboard and filled it up. She topped his water up and watched for a moment as he tucked in hungrily. He'd had an accident, a deposit sat on the floor in the corner of the kitchen. She stroked his shoulders as he ate.

"What's gone on here, eh? How long have you two been alone? Are they coming back, or has something happened to them?" She wasn't expecting him to give her the answers, but asking the questions out loud helped to sort through the situation in her mind.

"If I call the authorities, I might be making trouble for your mum and dad if there's a simple explanation," she explained. "On the other hand, you can't just abandon a child and dog like this; it's not fair, not to mention dangerous." She topped his bowl with a few more biscuits before returning the packet to the cupboard. "I don't want you being sick too," she explained and scratched his shoulder before leaving him to it.

She had to do something, but what? She stood looking out of the window. There was no vehicle parked outside. She looked around the room: everything was neat and tidy. She made her way back up to Flynn, but first checked each level to peer again into the rooms. All was tidy, as if nobody was staying there. In the main bedroom, she checked inside a small wardrobe to find it empty. Bending down to look under the bed for a suitcase or holdall, she only saw a couple of dust bunnies. She made her way back to Flynn's room. It seemed his was the only place where there was any sign of habitation. The words from the woman at the sweater shop filled her mind, *Nobody in there at this time of year. Owners only come in summer; it'll be empty now.*

But what about Flynn? And what about Rupert? And where had Ciara and Lorcan disappeared to? Because on taking stock of the situation, Chrissy could only conclude they'd left the pair to it. Chrissy was torn about what to do next. Should she call Julie, tell her to come over? Damn, her phone was back at the house. She glanced around looking for a landline, but there wasn't one. It was a holiday home after all, visitors would have their own mobiles.

"Damn!" she spat. What next? She couldn't leave the two alone, and with no phone, that left one course of action.

"There's only one thing for it, Flynn. I'll have to take you both back with me," she said, gathering him up. "Let's get you wrapped up and go and find your buggy, okay?" Having found a jacket for him, the two headed downstairs to the kitchen. "Where does your mum keep the buggy?" she said before spotting it collapsed and wedged behind a kitchen chair across the room. "Gotcha." Reassembling it quickly, she placed Flynn in the seat and strapped him in. They were almost ready to go.

Drug baron sprang to mind, they'd only been laughing about it recently. Ciara had mentioned a cellar – she could take a look quickly, no one would be any the wiser. "I'll just be a minute," she explained to Flynn, who was watching her every move.

But first she had to find the cellar entrance and since the kitchen area was all in full view as she stood there, unless it was through a cupboard like in an *Indiana Jones* movie or a *Mr Benn* episode, there was no visible door. That left through the floor.

The rug!

She threw it back in the hope that some sort of entrance would materialise. She wasn't disappointed.

"Got you," she said, before bending down to open it. Cold air greeted her and she shivered as her eyes adjusted to the darkness below. Stone steps went down into the blackness, but how far? She couldn't see further than two down. There had to be a light. Taking the first couple of steps, she let her hands search either side of the rough entrance wall until one of them found the switch. She flicked it on. An explosion of bright white fluorescent light filled the space as she carried on down into the room. When her head was finally below the bulkhead, and she could see all the way into the space, Chrissy pulled up short at what lay in front of her.

CHAPTER 20

Chrissy was aghast as she took in the contents of the cellar. Yes, it was odd that so many wicker storage boxes, of all shapes and sizes, almost filled the room, but it was what was propped up against the wall straight in front that made her gasp out loud. There, standing proudly, were two coffins, both made from wicker, like a laundry basket might be. There were no fancy brass handles, no fine, polished surfaces, and if she looked inside, she knew there would be no silky lining. But they were definitely coffins.

"What the—"

Who were they for? Were they empty? Oh heavens! Were they full? Chrissy approached one then reached out with her forefinger knuckle and rapped on the surface. It sounded hollow. She did the same with the other one, and surmised they were both empty. A saving grace. Had she really expected them to contain bodies?

"At least nobody knocked back," she said out loud, relaxing a little as she studied the room a bit more closely.

A gurgle from above caught her attention, and she remembered young Flynn, sitting up there all alone. It was time to head off. She'd seen and experienced quite enough for one morning and was acutely aware of how long she'd been gone. Julie would be wondering where she'd got to.

"What to do, Flynn?" she asked him back in the kitchen. "There's too much weird stuff going on for my liking." She glanced at the hole in the floor, the bright light looming up from it like an apparition.

"Whose are those coffins? Surely they don't belong to your parents, do they?" As an afterthought, she added, "Though I suppose they could do." Chrissy sat, thinking out loud, looking for a reasonable explanation for the events so far that morning. There wasn't much coming to mind.

"As cute as you are, young man, I need to talk this one over with an adult."

Flynn wore an uncertain look, and Chrissy hoped he wasn't going to start crying again.

"Time to go for a ride, so I'll go and find a spare blanket then we'll get off," she told him, before heading back to the nursery to get what she needed. A moment later, she tucked the blue blanket across his body, and they were ready to go. They couldn't go over the fields back to the house, not with a buggy, and the road meant a longer journey for the two of them.

She was drawn to take another look in the cellar. "I'll be two seconds, promise," she said and slipped down through the cellar opening. The two coffins stared back at her like something from a Stephen King film. She certainly hadn't been expecting to stumble on such a disquieting discovery. Other than the coffins, the space looked like any other cellar and smelled just as fusty and damp. A type of whitewash peeled off the stone walls, the flagged floor clear of any other debris but for the wicker bins. There was nothing else to see or do, so Chrissy made her way back up to a waiting Flynn, turned the light off and dropped the trapdoor back in place. The rug followed and all was back exactly how she'd found it only a few minutes ago. Could such a lot have happened since she'd left her coffee to investigate a barking dog? Apparently, it had.

"Time to go, little one," she said, reaching for the buggy and steering it out of the door. Rupert spotted them from his place in the grass and strolled over, not in any particular rush. "I guess you'd better come along too," she said, grabbing his leash off a hook on the wall and attaching it to his collar. She closed the door and paused for a moment, deep in thought.

What an odd morning.

When Chrissy was satisfied she had everyone secure, they set off on the journey back to her own holiday home, and no doubt a great deal of questions from the others.

The trouble was, Chrissy didn't have any answers.

CHAPTER 21

As Bronagh came to, she was aware of someone flitting about nearby, of strange voices she couldn't fathom and a bright overhead light. One thing she did know was that she wasn't at home. And one leg felt like it was encased in cement. It was.

A broken wrist and a broken leg meant she wasn't going to be leaving her hospital bed today. Add the cuts and bruises to her head and chest area, and she looked like she'd taken on a cage fighter and let them pummel her half to death. The airbag had saved her neck but added to her facial bruises when it had punched its way out from inside the dashboard. With her good hand, she tried to wipe her eyes, which had run slightly. The inside of her head throbbed, and her mouth felt like the bottom of a canary's cage.

"There you are," a voice said brightly. "I'm nurse O'Brien. Can you tell me how much pain you're in, on a scale of one to ten?"

Bronagh tried to sort through the cotton wool in her head and make sense of what the woman was asking, but nothing seemed to function correctly, and the question dissolved from her mind. She stared vacantly up at the nurse.

"You've had a nasty accident, and you're in the hospital. The

Guards are here, waiting to ask you some questions, but I don't think you're up to it yet, are you?"

Bronagh tried to shake her head 'no', but the slightest movement sent pain spiralling through it. She winced involuntarily.

"I'll get you some pain relief," she said, smiling. "Oh, and your brother is here too," she said, pointing with her own head.

Deciding not to move again, Bronagh forced a whisper from her lips, "Thanks." The word barely made a sound, but it was enough and the nurse vanished for a moment. Or so it seemed. When Bronagh came to again an hour or so later, it was a different kind of light around her as she struggled to open her swollen eyes fully. Gingerly, she turned her head to one side and realised the light was in fact a weak sunshine climbing the sky, fluorescent replaced by natural light. A chair in the corner contained a crumpled body and judging from its clothes and the faint odour of oil and diesel, it was her brother, Brocc. How long had he been there? she wondered. More to the point, how long had *she* been there? She tried to raise herself up a little and as pain shot through her head again, she remembered the same thing happening not that long ago. But how long ago was it?

And then something far more important hit her. She had to leave! She had to get back home and quickly! Bronagh struggled, but looking down at the bed in front of her, it wasn't hard to see the white plaster cast of a broken leg. Another cast covered her wrist. She'd never broken a bone in her life and she was annoyed that she now had two limbs in plaster. Someone had obviously seen her movement and another nurse put her head around the curtain and smiled.

"Good morning. How are you feeling?" she enquired as she approached Bronagh's pillows and straightened them.

Gathering a deep breath, she replied urgently, "I've got to get back, I have to go," and struggled with her good arm to sit herself up. It was no use, she simply hadn't the strength and the pain sent torrential waves of nausea through her stomach, making her gasp and swallow deeply.

"You're not going anywhere for a while," the nurse said firmly as she gently leaned in to stop Bronagh getting up any further. The figure in the chair stirred at the sound of conversation and immediately went to the nurse's aide. Groggy from his own lack of sleep, he was still able to take charge of his stubborn sister. Her feistiness, however, was a good sign she was feeling better and was on the mend.

"Come on Bron, lie back down and stay still, will you? You've had an accident and you're not going anywhere, not for a while at least." He gently lay an oil-ingrained hand on her shoulder, ready to stop her moving if he had to, and watched as she closed her eyes for a long moment. When Bronagh opened her eyes again, tears were on the edge of spilling free and she blinked them away as best she could.

"Hey, don't go getting all upset, you're safe now. A few bits broken, but you'll live." His pink-tinged, weather-beaten skin crinkled around his eyes and mouth as he smiled down at her, willing her to stay still and rest.

"You don't understand!" she said more urgently. "I can't be here. You've got to get me back!"

"What's so important? The shop? I'll put a sign up, folks will understand."

"No, not the shop..." Bronagh knew it was no use saying any more. He wouldn't understand. The nurse relaxed a little, safe in the knowledge that her patient wasn't going to try and get out of bed again, and busied herself writing notes on her chart and checking her blood pressure. Eventually she slipped away, leaving Brocc and Bronagh to talk in private.

"The Guards still want to talk to you. About the accident. What happened, Bron? On your phone, were you?"

"What? No, of course not."

"Then what happened?"

Bronagh ran through the events in her head as they came to her. She hadn't been on her phone. It had been dark but clear, and then suddenly she'd noticed something in her rear-view mirror, a glint of light. And then her car had lunged forward and spun out of control, slamming into the banking and rolling over and over. She couldn't remember anything other than that. Had another vehicle come at her, run her off the road, caused her to have the accident? On such a quiet back road? It was not beyond the realms of possibility. Not with what she had volunteered for.

CHAPTER 22

He couldn't imagine why. "Are you serious?" Brocc asked his sister. "What on earth makes you think you were run off the road, woman?"

"Because it came up behind me, and didn't want me to see it – there were no lights on the vehicle, that's why."

"It'll have been ne'er-do-wells, too much drink in them, I'd say. They'll have been local lads trying to stay away from the Guards."

"I wish I could be as sure as you." She tried to moisten her lips and Brocc passed her a glass of water with a straw sticking out.

"Here," he said as he offered it to her. Bronagh took a couple of long slurps. "Does that feel better now?"

She managed a nod.

"Now, tell me what's so important that you have to get out of bed for."

Bronagh sighed deeply and turned her head away from him so he couldn't see her eyes filling with tears again. She needed to think, there was too much at stake and telling Brocc what she was up to was quite simply out of the question. He wouldn't understand. Men like him never did. What on earth was she going to do? A blue-uniformed guard entered the room and made his way over.

Bronagh recognised him immediately, his thinning hair was legendary on a young man: Garda Drew Harris.

"Hello Ms Bowen," he said. He'd been calling her Bronagh for most of his adult life, but in his official capacity he stuck with formal. It sounded odd to her ears, but she let it go. He was here to do his job. Brocc nodded his greeting and the officer nodded back. "I have some questions about your accident – if you're up to it?"

"Better to get it over with I suppose, then you can get on."

Brocc offered the single chair to the officer but he declined it, leaving it for the older man who gave a suit-yourself shrug and sat back down. Harris took his notebook out and revisited what he'd learned so far before asking his first question.

"Let's start at the beginning then. Can you tell me what happened, what you remember?"

Bronagh hadn't had time enough to think about quite what she'd say but it was too late now. She had to think on the hoof and hope she didn't say too much.

"I didn't see a thing," she started. "One minute I was minding my own business, and the next I was being hurled through the air like I was in a tumble dryer. The whole thing lasted a few seconds."

"Did you see any other vehicles before your accident?"

Had it been a vehicle she'd seen in her rear-view mirror? If not, what could it have been?

"I couldn't be sure now," she said slowly. "I don't remember seeing any headlights if that helps." Vague would have to do.

"Were you distracted in some way. Perhaps changing the radio station, or your phone rang?"

"Definitely neither of those," she said with as much force as she could muster. "I drive in silence usually, and my phone was in my bag. Like I say, I can't really remember anything."

"We found your phone on the road. Maybe it had been thrown from the car?"

"No, that can't be mine. I keep it zipped away, inside my bag. It must be someone else's." She glanced around the room for her belongings and Brocc took the hint. Standing, he said, "I'll get it for you," and retrieved her handbag from the bedside cabinet. The zip, she noticed, was undone. "That's odd," she said thoughtfully. "Brocc, check and see if my phone's in there, please." He did as he was asked and came up empty. He shook his head 'no'. Realising her phone had been taken somehow, Bronagh tried to think about what to do or say next.

"Do you have it, officer?"

"I do," he said, taking it from a jacket pocket and handing it to her. It was in a small plastic bag. "That's yours, I'm assuming? Only the home image is of the shop."

Bronagh held her good hand out for it. "Yes, that'll be mine." The glass had been cracked badly, hence the bag to save any cut fingers. It certainly looked like her iPhone. The battery was almost dead. She was glad of the locked screen, that no one could get inside it, not easily anyway. As if he read her mind, he added, "'It's locked, so many aren't," and smiled.

"There's too much on them these days to not lock them."

"Hate the damn things," Brocc added from his seat. "Always interrupting my thoughts when they go off."

Bronagh smiled at her brother's logic. He still carried an old fashioned one that was actually a phone and offered nothing else save for texting. He certainly didn't carry his life in his back pocket.

"I'm not sure I can tell you much more, officer," she added, trying to end the meeting. There was thinking to do, and she needed to get on with it in private. Plus, she was suddenly incredibly tired.

Taking the hint, he said, "Well, I'll be on my way then. If you think of anything at all, let me know. Something was responsible for an accident such as you've had and since you say you didn't come across another vehicle on the road, then..." He shrugged his shoulders.

"I will. Thanks for coming. Maybe I'll remember something when I've had more sleep," she said, smiling. Drew Harris gave a quick nod of his head and left Bronagh and her brother alone.

When he was well out of earshot, Brocc said, "You don't fool me. So why don't you let me in on whatever it is you're keeping from me?"

She looked up into his concerned eyes and wondered for a moment if she could. There was so much at stake if she got it wrong, if Brocc didn't understand. Could she risk it?

"I'll think about it. But first I need you to do something for me."

CHAPTER 23

Brocc left the hospital with so many questions whizzing around the inside of his head. He knew his sister was up to something – even if she wouldn't tell him what – but having known her for sixty years, he knew when to push and when to wait. She'd come around eventually. In the meantime, she'd asked for his help, and with no further questions asked, he had said yes. He could tell by her demeanour that it was important, though he'd no clue what he was supposed to do with the child in the meantime. All she'd instructed was for him to keep the child safe and that she'd fill him in later. He couldn't wait for the story she'd concoct, because from experience he knew she'd not tell him the truth first off. It was a big favour to ask, but he'd do it. At least she'd looked a lot better this morning, and her spirit was gathering energy; she'd given him enough worry for the both of them the previous night.

It wasn't far from the hospital back to his small home, but he had a detour to make before he could have the luxury of a shower and toast. Calling first at Bronagh's cottage, he let himself in with his own key and headed straight for the cutlery drawer, the teaspoon section in particular, and retrieved another key, one attached to a small pebble with a hole drilled through it. Once it was in his hand, he smiled to himself as his fingers became familiar with the smooth surface once again. He'd made the key ring as a Christmas present for Bronagh when they were young teenagers. The fact that she'd kept it all these years surprised and delighted him all at the same time. But there was no time to dawdle and think of the past. Slipping the key into his pocket, he locked the door again and headed on to his next port of call – the castle. She'd instructed him to be as quick as he could, so he wasted little time in driving across to the old building. Once at the front door, he slipped the key in the lock and turned it.

"Hmm," he grunted. The door was already unlocked. He stepped inside. All was quiet, not a sound could be heard as he made his way up to the room on the second floor as directed. When he put his head around the door, he was shocked and almost grateful to see the cot was empty.

Baby Flynn wasn't where he should have been.

Brocc hadn't been too keen on the idea of transporting the little one to the address she'd eventually given him; it had been a long time since he'd had anything to do with a small child. He stared at the empty cot as if the child would suddenly appear before grunting his consternation and heading upstairs to check the other room. The boy wasn't there either. Confused, he made his way back down the stairs, and returned to his van where he sat for a moment wondering what to do next. Bronagh had been precise in what he had to do, where to take the child to, and he'd agreed to help if she told him the full story once he'd done as she'd requested. When Harris had left, she'd become extremely anxious and upset, so he'd had no choice but to get involved, if only to calm her down. Now he was puzzled and unsure about what to do next. He checked his watch; it was coming up to 11 am. He was about to pull away when he noticed a Garda car approaching in the distance and, not wishing to be seen anywhere near the castle, he quickly set off in the opposite direction. With a child missing, he rightly assumed the Guards would be heading to the castle themselves. What the hell had Bronagh got herself involved in? And where was the child?

And, more to the point, where was the child's family? It hadn't escaped his notice that the place was empty save for the boy's room. Watching the Guards in his rear-view mirror, he wasn't surprised to see the vehicle pull up on the grass outside, where he'd been parked only moments ago, and two officers get out. Were they looking for the boy too? If he'd been confused before, he was doubly so now, and with no way to inform Bronagh of the situation, he had no choice but to drive back to the hospital and press her more to find out quite what she was involved in.

He pulled up at his own place, washed and changed, made himself a late breakfast of eggs on toast, and sat for a while deep in thought. Obviously Bronagh had meant to tend to the child herself the previous evening and had been unable to do so, what with the accident and all. Had she been run off the road like she'd suggested? She'd also been adamant her phone was safely zipped away in her bag, as it usually was, yet it had been found out on the road. Did it all mean Bronagh was in danger? Leaving his breakfast crockery where it was, he grabbed his keys and headed back to the hospital to see his sister. A smashed screen would have made it impossible for anyone to swipe the phone open, that much he did know. When Jake, his young apprentice, had smashed his own, he'd cut his finger badly trying to do the same thing. Yet it sounded like someone was interested in it, – how else did it get out from a zipped-up bag? He thought back to Jake's broken screen.

"How did he get back in then?" he asked himself. Finding his own phone, he called the garage and waited for him to answer.

"Brocc's Garage, Jake speaking." He sounded monotone and uninterested like many male youths that lacked a little confidence. The lad was all pimples and hormones encased in black denim that hung off his skinny backside. One day he'd grow into his jeans.

"I'll be late in," Brocc said. "Could be after lunch."

"No problem," Jake informed him.

"Need a favour. Need to know how you get into one of them fancy phones everyone has, when the glass is smashed. Must be a way."

"There is. You just install your backup onto your new phone directly from the cloud."

Brocc made a mental note of the gibberish. He was much more conversant with the inside of a diesel engine than a phone or computer. Perhaps Bronagh would know what the lad meant. Give him a piston or crankshaft any day.

CHAPTER 24

The wind was much cooler off the water than it had been yesterday, and Chrissy shivered, remembering the words from the lady in the sweater shop. The colder spell was well on its way, sunshine or not. She was glad Flynn had a blanket over his knees. As she approached the holiday home, Chrissy could see Julie watching for her from the front door of the house. After all, she'd been gone ages, far longer than she could have imagined, and with no way of calling back to the others, to the house, she'd been stuck. She waved, steering the buggy and Rupert with the other hand. Julie started walking towards her and, as she got closer, Chrissy could see the look of confusion on her face.

"It's a rather long story," she called. When the two women finally reached each other, Chrissy stopped for a moment and wrapped her arms around her sister, pulling her close. Julie must have sensed all was not entirely well and stayed quiet for a moment or two, squeezing her back. When she was ready, Chrissy let go and started to speak.

"Let's get inside first and I'll tell you all what's happened. And I need a coffee too, and something to eat." To her own ears, she sounded weary, the adrenaline had long since surged and evaporated, leaving her system, her being, feeling drained and empty. She handed the leash to Julie, who took Rupert the rest of the short distance as they turned the corner towards the deck and the back door.

Adam and Richard met them as they entered, and Adam's eyes searched Chrissy's before she flopped down onto a nearby chair and closed hers for a moment. Richard opted to stay silent for the time being, obviously confused. Julie took charge.

"Give her some space, will you? She'll tell us when she's caught her breath." Julie busied herself putting coffee on and bread in the toaster. She grabbed butter and jam and placed them on the table. "The sugar will get you going again," she said. "No rush." Chrissy nodded. When the toaster popped, Julie slid a plate of hot toast over for Chrissy to fix her own. Everyone waited as she sipped her coffee. Flynn was sitting quietly in his buggy. Rupert lay sprawled out on the warm floor tiles. Her hands busied themselves spreading butter and jam, though she didn't pick the toast up and eat. She took a deep, cleansing breath and then started at the beginning.

As she spoke, the others gathered around the table together and listened. Chrissy recalled everything that had happened, finding Flynn and Rupert, her lack of phone to call them with, and attending to the youngster. "It was obvious Flynn had not been fed or changed for some time, maybe even since yesterday."

"Poor mite," added Julie, then allowed Chrissy to carry on.

"So I thought I'd bring him back here since I couldn't leave him and with no phone..."

"Of course," said Adam.

"But it gets worse."

Three sets of eyes glanced at each other before she carried on. As Chrissy explained about the contents of the cellar, Julie gasped out loud, while Richard and Adam opted for curses. There was no way she could have left everything as it had been and run back for help, which was why she'd arrived home with her hands full.

"You did the right thing," said Adam, placing his arm around her shoulders. "What does everyone think we should do next?" he asked the group. Chrissy tucked into her toast, feeling better the story was out and the problem could now be shared. And sorted.

"I feel the authorities must be informed," said Richard. "A young child that has been abandoned in some way is a serious offence. We can't simply keep him, even temporarily. He's not a kitten."

"I agree," added Adam. "We don't know Ciara and Lorcan from a bar of soap so, to be on the safe side, we *have* to notify the authorities. As for the coffins, that's just strange, really strange," he said, shaking his head in disbelief. That left Julie's opinion. Chrissy looked at her sister and waited for her advice.

"Agreed. Though the poor child entering the system doesn't fill me with hope either. I wish there was another way."

Nobody spoke. A possible lifetime of being fostered and passed around rarely ended well for a child.

"Plus, I'm confused about the coffins and where they fit in," Julie added, trying to change the subject away from his Flynn's abandonment.

"You think they do fit in, do you?" asked Richard. "I mean, it's a holiday let, and they could be the owners' own. You hear of people planning their own funerals, maybe they're theirs?"

"He's got a point," said Adam.

"Well, whatever the issue with the coffins, young Flynn needs looking after and if Ciara and Lorcan have gone missing, we should call the police now," Julie said firmly.

"Gardai."

"Pardon?"

"The Irish police, they're called the Gardai."

"Then let's call the Gardai," Julie said, a little exasperated.

"I don't see we have a choice," Adam added. As Chrissy looked around the group, each face wore reluctance. While nobody wanted young Flynn to go into the system, each of them knew they couldn't take him in, not even temporarily. There were strict processes to be followed, for the child's own good. It wasn't like they were even remotely family members.

Standing, Chrissy said, "I'll make the call."

As she reached for her phone, the woman's words from the sweater shop came back to her: *Nobody in there at this time of year. Owners only come in summer; it'll be empty now.*

Why hadn't she mentioned that part of the story to the others, she wondered. Perhaps deep down she was chewing over the intrigue of it. After all, she was a private investigator.

Chrissy dialled the number anyway.

CHAPTER 25

Brocc drove the same route Bronagh would have driven the night of her accident. As he approached the crash scene, he slowed down slightly and pulled in. There was no one else on the road, no one behind him, no one off in the distance. Broken glass still lay at the edges of the tarmac, but there was little else to tell anybody that there'd been a bad accident there recently. He stepped out of the car and walked over to the banking that Bronagh had hit and put his hand on the soil that had been ripped loose into clumps. There was no real need to do so, and it helped in no way at all. It just felt like it was something he should do, feel the impact with her as she hurtled through the air. Had someone run her off the road? Or was she being conspiratorial? There were plenty of conspiracy theorists around with views on a variety of subjects, whether it was mobile masts, vaccinations, mobile phone tracking, or Princess Diana's death. He didn't believe in all that. He led a simple life with simple things and kept himself to himself. He stood there for a moment and let the sun shine on his head. It was barely warm but still it felt good that something so far above could touch him. At least she'd survived the mangled wreckage, that was the main thing. He didn't know what he'd do without her in his life, they were good friends as well as siblings.

So why wouldn't she trust him with her secret?

With nothing else to see or do, he returned to his waiting car and headed across to the hospital. She wouldn't be expecting to see him so soon; he should have been travelling elsewhere, taking the child to the address she'd given him, but all that had changed now since there was no child to take. Somebody had got there before him. The more he thought about the whole situation, the more intrigued and confused he became, and he wondered once again just what Bronagh had got herself mixed up in.

By the time he'd parked up in the hospital car park, morning visiting hours were well and truly over. But he hoped the ward sister would let him in, just for a few minutes, so he could explain, because she'd be worried. He crossed his fingers for compassion. As he arrived on the ward, a senior nurse scurried over, a stern crease on her mouth and he knew what was coming. He put his hands out in front of him by way of surrender and said, "I'll be five minutes, I promise. Just need to tell Bronagh something since her phone is broken and then I'll leave. Ah, go on."

He put his hands down and waited for her response. Her eyes softened a little, her shoulders slumped down to the normal position, and a small smile crept across her cheeks.

"Five minutes. I'm counting."

Brocc headed straight for his sister and hoped she was still awake. He wasn't disappointed. As soon as she saw him, she tried to sit up in bed, her face covered in confusion. He shouldn't be back so early, what had gone wrong? He didn't waste any time making himself comfortable and simply said, "He's not there. I don't know where he is."

She was about to say 'what do you mean?' he could see it written on her face, the questioning look, the doubt.

"How can he not be there?"

He repeated himself: "The place was empty."

"That can't be," said Bronagh. "Nobody knows."

"Come on, Bronagh. Why don't you tell me what it is you're involved in because I can see it's troubling you, and if there's a child involved...?" He let the question linger, waiting for an answer. She had to say something soon; there could be a life at stake if someone had kidnapped this child he knew nothing about. He had to tell someone, alert the authorities perhaps. But he didn't want to drop Bronagh into any trouble. He needed to find out what was going on before making his own mind up.

"Come on, Bronagh," he said. "We're family. Whatever you're mixed up in, I'm already helping now, I could help you more."

"I can't involve you any further," she said. "It's not safe. And anyway, you wouldn't understand."

"You obviously trusted me enough to go to the child in the first place. And I might understand, if you let me. Come on, Bron, I can keep a secret."

She knew from experience that part, at least, wasn't true, that there had been many times during their lives together he'd taken pleasure in dumping her in it, but he'd been a different man back then. Could she trust him now?

"I need to think what to do next. But I need a telephone. Can I borrow yours?"

"We'll swap. You give me your broken one and I'll get it fixed while you're in here. You take mine, at least then I can ring you on it from the home line. You have the number you need?"

"No. It's in the broken one," she said resignedly.

He remembered what Jake had said, he'd need to install the backup to a new phone from some sort of cloud. He knew what a new phone was, but what he didn't know was what a backup was. Maybe Bronagh did.

"Have you got a backup?" he enquired, not sounding confident he'd got the terminology correct.

She raised her eyebrows slightly. "I do, it's in the cloud."

He'd heard of that before and only hoped Jake knew which cloud he needed.

"Then you'll need my password," she said. He passed her bag

from the bedside cabinet and watched as she wrote the details down and handed them over.

"Right," Brocc said, wondering what to do next.

"It'll take too long to repair, so just get me a new one and I'll settle up with you when I get out. Have you got your credit card with you?"

"I'll do it tomorrow. How much are they?"

"About 800 euros now." She knew he'd got enough money to make the purchase since he rarely spent any of what he earned. As his face blanched, she said, "It's important to me," by way of justification. "I can claim it back on my insurance, what with the crash." Brocc grunted and, catching the eye of the nurse, said his goodbyes and headed out to get his sister a new iPhone.

Watching her brother leave the room, she concerned herself with the problem at hand. Who had taken baby Flynn, and why? Nobody knew he was there on his own. She glanced at the old Nokia phone her brother still used. It felt sticky from oily fingers and it was a wonder it still worked. Now all she needed was the telephone number.

CHAPTER 26

Two guards entered the kitchen, their blue uniforms adding a touch of authority to the situation. In the background, Julie flitted around and made fresh coffee for everyone while Chrissy gave her account of what had happened so far during the morning. Adam and Richard stood nearby and listened to events over again. The taller of the two guards, a sergeant called Michael Staines, busied himself taking notes and allowed Chrissy to carry on until the end without interruption. Another guard took notes of his own. He'd introduced himself earlier as Drew Harris and while he was the younger of the two men, he had the least hair on top. His thin lips and pointed nose reminded her of a bird, a crow, perhaps, which on the surface didn't feel like much of a compliment. Best she didn't say anything. When she reached what she'd found in the cellar, both guards stopped writing as they digested the sinister tale. When she was finished, she had a question for them.

"What will happen to Flynn?" It seemed the most important aspect of the whole sorry tale, and a question each of the holiday party wanted to know the answer to. Sergeant Staines took it.

"We'll organise for him to be picked up by Tusla and taken into emergency care first off, while we figure out where his parents are. He'll be safe then."

"Tusla?"

"Our child and family agency," he said before carrying on. "From there, it depends on how the investigation goes. Hopefully, we'll find his parents quickly and the whole thing can be sorted out, but if they have abandoned him, then the agency will decide on his future." The guard had kind eyes, and Chrissy could see the compassion they held as he spoke. It couldn't be an easy job dealing with children in need.

"I'll go back and get some of his things, shall I?" she offered.

"It's best of you stay away. Let us take a look first. If there has been a crime, and we don't know that yet, apart from the little boy left alone, we may need forensics in there."

"But he'll need things..." started Chrissy.

"Tusla will have that covered, he'll be well cared for."

Chrissy wondered about what the sweater shop woman had said: *Nobody in there at this time of year. Owners only come in summer; it'll be empty now.*

"The castle," she started. "It's privately owned, isn't it?"

"I believe so, yes," Sergeant Staines said.

"Only, the woman in the sweater shop said it was empty at this time of the year. And yet Ciara and Lorcan were staying there? With Flynn?"

"My guess is maybe she was wrong. We'll track the owners down of course, and see who their missing guests were, since we know nothing of them as yet, not even a surname. If they've cleaned out their possessions as you say they have, I doubt we'll find much either, but that's for us to deal with," he said, slipping his notebook away. Flynn reminded everyone he was still in the room with a loud gurgle followed by frantic hand waving. There wasn't a person in the group that didn't smile back at him, likely each wondering where he'd find himself spending the night. And who with. Sergeant Staines checked his watch.

"Someone will be here to pick him up shortly, I've made the call.

Garda Harris here will wait with you before handing young Flynn over. In the meantime, I'm going over to the castle myself then I'll start making enquiries." He turned to his colleague and added, "Let me know when they've been."

Chrissy wasn't sure if she was supposed to shake his hand and thank him or not. It seemed rude not to do anything, so she stood and offered her hand anyway. From Sergeant Staines's facial reaction, she shook a little too firmly, again. An old habit.

"I'll let myself out," he said before turning to leave. The remaining officer, Harris, attempted small talk while he waited but nobody was really that interested, or in the mood. What would happen to young Flynn next filled the room like a heavy weight, and even though nobody said anything, they each knew the others were feeling equally low about the whole thing. Richard was right though, Flynn wasn't a kitten looking for an old blanket and a tin of food at the end of the day, he needed much more than that. A vehicle pulled up outside and the officer stood to look.

"That's them now," he said, heading for the door. Voices could be heard outside as they conferred about what would happen next, and just where Chrissy and her family fitted into the puzzle. A moment later, a busty middle-aged woman with a welcoming smile introduced herself.

"Tilly Murphy. I'll be taking charge of Flynn today."

Chrissy stepped forward and almost threw herself in front of her, her own eyes searching the woman's in a fidgety way that Chrissy wasn't used to. The whole process of handing Flynn over, she knew, was going to be excruciating.

"Chrissy Livingstone. I found young Flynn earlier."

Walking towards the buggy, she said, "And this must be Flynn?"

"Yes." Nobody else said a word, as if they were afraid of saying the wrong thing. Even though they hardly knew the child, it was a distressing moment. Everyone watched as she removed the brakes on the buggy and rested her hands on the handle before moving towards the door. Her colleague was waiting in the doorway. Chrissy rushed forward and bent down in front of the buggy so Ms

Murphy had to stop abruptly. She reached out to Flynn and stroked his arm before placing a light kiss on his forehead. "Take care, little one," she said, trying hard to hold back the raw emotion that threatened. Adam went to her side and rubbed her back a little in comfort before they both stepped to one side to let the woman through.

"He'll be taken good care of," Tilly said, smiling as she pushed the buggy from the room, leaving four adults staring after them. No one said a word. Garda Harris followed close behind, informing Chrissy he'd be in touch soon. As soon as the door was closed, Chrissy did something she hadn't done in more years than she could remember.

She burst into tears.

CHAPTER 27

Chrissy surprised herself at her own reaction to seeing the boy go. Normally the emotional side of life didn't faze her, she pushed through and didn't let sentiment worry her, but this was different somehow. Why? She'd no clue. Maybe it was more the shock of finding Flynn than handing him over to be cared for by the professionals. Judging by the fact that Ciara and Lorcan's belongings had all gone, they obviously hadn't planned to go back for him. How could someone abandon a child, of any age, particularly when they had no way to fend for themselves? It was barbaric, unthinkable, and if she ever caught up with the two of them again, she'd tell them so. But not before she'd strangled them both. Still, the chances of catching up with them were almost zero.

Or were they? A renewed energy forced her eyes to flash open and they locked with Adam's who was sitting on the sofa opposite, watching.

"I'm going to find out what's happened to them," she announced, flitting her eyes from Adam to Julie to Richard and back to Adam. A slight smirk clung to Adam's mouth and he let it develop a while longer until it was almost a full grin. Chrissy looked to Julie, who was peering over her magazine, for moral support. "Do you fancy helping, Julie?" she asked. Two perfectly shaped eyebrows rose another inch before slipping back down behind the glossy pages. Richard unsurprisingly said, "Well, I can't move from here so don't look at me," sounding disappointed. "Otherwise I'd lend a hand, somehow." He rubbed his still sore shoulder as if for effect before burying himself behind his newspaper. Chrissy didn't believe a word he'd said, he'd only added the last sentence because he knew he'd be of no use.

"Adam?"

He raised both hands out in front of him, palms facing her as he added, "You're the PI in the room. I'll keep Richard company." Julie had to be listening and Chrissy picked up on the fact she hadn't turned a page in a while. The articles weren't that long.

"Julie? You know you want to say yes. Come on, help find that little boy's parents." Julie shoved her magazine down roughly and glared at her sister. "Don't try and make me feel guilty about enjoying my break away. If you want to go looking, that's for you to decide, but count me out, please." The magazine was forced back into place as Julie pretended to carry on reading. Chrissy let out a long sigh.

"Right then. I'll do it on my own," she said, standing. Glancing at the clock on the wall, she frowned. It was almost 4 pm, a bit late to go over to the castle, and since it would be taped up as a possible crime scene there would be no way to snoop around. The property was the only clue she had to anything concerning the couple's disappearance; she couldn't think of another starting point available. The local Gardai seemed pleasant enough, but they were highly unlikely to let her in on developments, either now or later on in the investigation. Why would they? She was a civilian, an English civilian at that, with absolutely no jurisdiction whatsoever. Her investigator's licence would be as much use to her as an inflatable policeman on crowd control.

She headed to the fridge, popped the top off a lite beer, grabbed a notepad, pen, and a blanket from the basket by the door, and went out to the deck. She dragged a lounger to a sheltered corner, wrapped herself up warm and settled down to work, making notes of everything she knew. There'd be a thread of an idea to pick at when she was done. After fifteen minutes of searching every tiny space of her brain, the list was a short one. She tried a different tack. Turning her pad horizontal, she drew a bubble in the middle at the top and filled in Ciara's and Lorcan's names. A smaller bubble off that held Flynn. Another for Rupert.

"Rupert!" With all the concern over baby Flynn, she and everyone else had completely forgotten about the poor dog. Where had he got to? Looking around her immediate vicinity, she found he was nowhere to be seen, so she threw off her blanket and headed back inside. The living room resembled the quiet room in the local library.

"Has anyone seen Rupert?"

Three hushed 'no's. She headed to each of the bedrooms in turn, half expecting the dog to be lying sprawled out on one of their beds, but each room was empty. Where had he gone? Chrissy sighed heavily; it had been a stressful enough day so far without the added angst of losing the dog too. *He'd be wanting a feed soon. In fact, not only would he be hungry, he'd surely be feeling frightened because of all the upheaval too.* All she remembered was handing him over to Julie when they'd first arrived back. Surely, she'd tied him up and not left him to wander? Back to the living room she went.

"Julie, did you tie Rupert up when we first arrived back?"

Julie stayed behind her pages. "Of course not, there was no need, he wasn't going to run off."

"Well it looks like he has..."

"I'd expect then he's gone back home."

"Helpful, sis."

"You are welcome, hun," she said without conviction. Clearly they weren't concerned.

Chrissy left them to their quiet state and grabbed her boots and jacket before heading out back towards the castle in the distance. This time she didn't forget to take her phone. There was no way she was going to let the dog fend for itself, that was one life she could look after – if only for a while at least.

CHAPTER 28

It was a pity she couldn't draw and walk at the same time and so had to be content filling in the bubble map in her head. By the time she returned back to the house, hopefully she'd have retained most of it and not forgotten anything majorly important. Plus, she had her phone's recorder if she needed to make notes of her thoughts and could easily transfer the information to her physical map on her return. As she walked across the fields, she ran through the short list she'd prepared while sitting on the deck and slotted various names and notes in bubbles with lines to link them to something else. So far, it was looking rather simple, but there wasn't much she knew.

Who else had she come in contact with since their arrival? There was the barman. He had her mobile number. Had he been the one to hand it to Ciara? Then there was the woman in the sweater shop. She'd said the castle was empty when it clearly wasn't. Did she know for sure? Then there was Lorcan himself. He'd said he was in logistics and distribution, a lorry driver that travelled all over Europe but spent time toing and froing between northern England ports. And Ciara? Nothing came to mind, since she hadn't had a chance to ask her anything while they were in the pub and conversation never arose the night of Richard's accident. All they'd talked about that particular evening was the local sights and poor old Richard before he nodded off to sleep on the sofa. If she thought she didn't know much of the pair, she knew absolutely nothing of the woman herself. Nothing. Flynn was the only other human being in the equation, and not a great deal of use on the conversation front – save to say Chrissy had suspected he might have been adopted, but she was only basing that on his hair colour. Since he couldn't speak and had now been taken into care, that was one dead end. Rupert fell into the same group as the youngster.

By the time she reached the castle, she could see the dog lying on the front doorstep, collar with leash still attached. He must have got bored and headed back to his own place. Sadly, there was no one to take him inside. Crime-scene tape across the door billowed in the stiff breeze and Chrissy wondered what, if anything, the Gardai might have found that would be of use. She bent down to pat him and took hold of his leash. She'd have to take him back with her, she couldn't leave him on his own, but not until she'd had a quick snoop around herself. Gardai or not, another set of eyes on the scene wouldn't be a waste of time and she was happy to volunteer her own.

"I suspect it's locked up," she said, trying the door. She pushed the handle down, but the door stayed firmly shut. They must have got keys from somewhere. "Thought so," she added as she looked around for another possible way in. A tiny castle wasn't exactly constructed like a Barratt house with UPVC double-glazed windows for easy access. No. Tall and skinny was what faced Chrissy as she strode around the perimeter of the building. There was no way she could get inside via one of those. Rupert barked, distracting her thoughts of how to gain entry.

"Any ideas?" she asked the dog. Whether it was the sound of her voice or something else, Rupert ambled over and sat down in front of her. He barked again, watching her intently. That was when she saw his collar. Not only did it have his details etched on a disc, but there was also a small silver cylinder dangling there. Smiling, she hoped it contained what she thought it might. She reached out, unscrewed the top off, and tipped it up. There in the palm of her hand lay a Yale key.

"Ha. Would you look at that." she said in a mock Irish accent. Standing up, she moved to the door and placed the key in the lock before turning it. It caught and the door swung open to reveal the kitchen she'd been in earlier that day. Had it only been that long ago? But Chrissy knew if she stepped inside, she'd not only be trespassing, she'd also be tampering with a crime scene. She was standing in the doorway, wondering what to do, when Rupert barked again. In her mind, she recalled Flynn's cries from earlier as she'd approached. The door had been unlocked then, which had been a good job under the circumstances, so who had locked up since? It couldn't have been a locksmith, since the key she'd used still fitted, meaning the lock hadn't been changed. If it had been the Gardai, and that was the most likely choice, where had the key they'd used come from? No matter how much she thought about it, she remained none the wiser, and didn't want to hang around much longer. Pulling her jacket a little closer around herself, she shivered, realising the temperature had dropped a couple of degrees more. The sweater shop woman had been spot on about the weather getting a lot colder and she shoved her hands into her pockets to keep them warm. It also deterred her from touching anything further. As her eyes adjusted to the light, grey fingerprint powder stared back at her in messy blobs, clinging to various surfaces by the grease and moisture from someone's hands. She wondered who those prints belonged to – anyone other than Ciara and Lorcan?

Well, yours are there...

The Gardai would likely know by now who she was, or who she had been at least. While they'd asked her to drop in at the station and give her prints for elimination purposes, there really was little point. Chrissy hadn't wanted to explain that particular insight in front of Julie and Richard. No doubt an officer would be back to talk to her at some point soon.

Chrissy headed upstairs to the top of the building, intending to look at each floor more closely on her way back down.

CHAPTER 29

The view from the top floor was as spectacular as ever and she stood for a moment watching the Atlantic Ocean out in front of her. It was deep grey as far as the eye could see. Where the sky met the horizon, it was difficult to distinguish which element was which. It would be dark soon, she'd left it a bit late to start inspecting what the professionals had already gone over, but she had to at least satisfy her own curiosity. Even the best technicians could miss something and if they had, she intended to find it. Time was of the essence.

There was virtually nothing left in the upper room, only the furniture and bedding. Any personal belongings had been removed and the space felt cold and unloved almost, a body with no warmth to it. She moved down to the next level, to where she'd found Flynn in his cot, the tiny bathroom to one side. As with the other floors of the property, dark powder decorated various surfaces, though this room still felt lived in, most likely because it still contained everything a small child needed. Drawers had been opened and searched, clothes left untidily, and Chrissy wondered why they hadn't been collected up to pass along to Flynn's caregivers. Surely, he'd be better with his own things nearby and gain comfort in his strange surroundings from fragrances he recognised. With his parents since disappeared, the little boy would be feeling confused and upset. She pulled open a drawer and reached inside, searching with both hands through baby-soft fabrics, hoping to find something that wasn't there. She repeated the exercise with the other drawers but it was fruitless. Had the Gardai found anything? Had there even been anything to find? Apart from the cot and changing mat, there was nothing else in the space to examine. Her deep sigh bounced off the walls and she stood, hands on her hips, frustrated. Taking a step forward, she pulled on the chest of drawers itself and moved it away from the wall, peering behind. Cobwebs and a spider were all she could see, and they didn't look like they'd been disturbed anytime recently. She pushed them back into place and headed down a level to the living room. A flash of light way out to sea caught her attention as she entered the space. Perhaps a passing ship; it couldn't be anything else.

As with the upper level, the room was absent of belongings and since the light was fading fast, she wasted no time. She lay down on the floor to peer under the sofa. Had anything been missed? She was desperate for something, some clue as to what had happened for a young couple to suddenly run off, leaving their child and dog behind. But she struggled to see, the gap between the base of the sofa and the floor was far too shallow. She stood and heaved the sofa forward into the room a little, allowing the space underneath it to become visible. She scanned what was now on full display, but as with the rear of the set of drawers in Flynn's room, only cobwebs and general debris lay in front of her. Rupert strolled in and reminded her of his presence.

"There's nothing here to find," she told him despondently and pushed the sofa back into place. "Come on, let's take a look in the kitchen and then we'll head back." Down the steps they went until they were once again in the kitchen. Each cupboard she opened was still filled with crockery or packets and tins of food. Not many would pack this lot up before they disappeared. Packets of rice and pasta and other staples stared back at her. The fridge held cheese and milk and little else, the can of baby formula still visible on the work surface. All was as it had been earlier in the day. Satisfied she wasn't going to find anything earth shattering that could help her investigation, she turned back to the door where Rupert was now sitting waiting, patiently. Then she spotted the rug on the floor and thought of the cellar below. Had the Gardai been down there? Surely they would have, yet the rug looked untouched, as if the area had perhaps been overlooked.

"Strange," she said to the empty room. Not wanting to turn a light on and attract attention to her presence, she yanked the rug back once again and opened the trapdoor. The same freezing-cold air from earlier seemed to grab her around the ankles, pulling her in as she peered down into the darkness. She found the torch on her phone and shone it down in front of her as she descended into the cold, wishing the mains overhead light could have been more contained, and not glow into the kitchen like a beacon. There was no way she could turn it on. The passing ship on the ocean outside sprang to mind. Once she'd ducked under the bulkhead again, her eyes refocused in the light available and for the second time in one day, she gasped out loud.

And it wasn't from the temperature.

The two coffins, which had been propped up against one wall, were both gone. As were most of the other wicker items.

"Now why would someone remove them?" she asked the empty room. "And when?"

CHAPTER 30

"We were just about to send out a search party for you," Julie said sarcastically as Chrissy entered the toasty kitchen. The temperature outside had plummeted even further and though she had a thick jacket on, her hands and face felt like they'd never be warm again. Her nose glowed like a radish. Rupert strolled in right beside her and flopped on the floor.

"No need, I'm back," she said, unzipping her coat. She tossed it onto a nearby dining chair and flicked the kettle on to boil. "Damn, it's cold out there now. And as you can see, I found Rupert. Poor lad was sitting on the step at the castle, looking ever so forlorn." She bent down to stroke him and he rolled over onto his back for a tummy rub. Chrissy obliged.

"What are we going to do with him?" Julie asked.

"I don't know. He can stay here tonight, and we'll have to decide from then on." Chrissy approached the kitchen door and closed it quietly so that anyone in the living room wouldn't notice she'd done so. Julie looked at her sister quizzically, tilting her head slightly in question. Chrissy was just about to speak when the door opened, and Adam walked through so she stayed shtum.

"Ah, the wanderer returns," he said, pecking her cheek lightly as he pulled a bottle of red from the nearby wine rack. He studied the label then returned the bottle, pulling another out instead. Satisfied with his choice, he unscrewed the top and sniffed. He nodded to himself. "Who wants a glass?" The two women nodded in unison, 'please'. They both watched as he poured then filled another two glasses and took them through to the living room. Chrissy again closed the door before turning the kettle off. The red wine would warm her through just the same. Julie moved closer to her sister, conspiratorially.

"So? What is it? Do tell."

"I went back inside the castle."

"How on earth—"

Chrissy raised her palm to stop her going any further. "That's not important at the moment, but this is."

"Well come on then, what?"

Chrissy checked the door was still firmly closed and leaned in a little further, her head nearly touching Julie's. "The coffins in the cellar? Both gone."

"Really? How? When?"

"I've no idea but they have. Now, is it me or do you think that's strange, and so quickly too?"

"No, you're right there. That is strange. Of all the things the Gardai would do, that wouldn't be on their priority list to remove. None of the contents would be removed by them, it's not their property to do so."

"My thoughts exactly. And I wouldn't expect the owners to have 'popped over' and taken them either."

"So you're thinking someone else, obviously. Though who?" They sat pondering for a moment then Julie asked, "The door was unlocked, I take it, since it was unlocked when you went inside this morning?"

"And that's another strange occurrence. No, the door was locked but not with a new set-up. I found a key and it still worked."

"You'll get in trouble, entering without permission," Julie admonished.

"Only if I get caught." Chrissy said and brushed the comment off. It was all part of the job. She'd done far worse.

"Then someone else does have a set of keys to the place, and that someone must know all about the cellar contents."

"And be able to move them quickly, so in a van maybe. They wouldn't fit in a SUV."

"Or a hearse? A funeral director?"

"The likely answer, yes, but two wicker coffins are a far cry from two ornate and highly polished vessels you'd expect them to use. And why store them at the castle? It makes no sense."

"Are you going to tell the Gardai."

"I can't, can I? Not without them knowing I've since been inside."

"True. No, you can't. Forgot about that bit." Julie said quietly, once again contemplating the situation. "You really think there's something sinister going on, don't you? That they fled in the night out of desperation, desperate enough to leave their child behind, and that the coffins are somehow linked?"

"The more I find out, yes, I do."

Julie stood to refill their glasses. "What do you want to do about it?"

"Find out what's happened, obviously."

"Then we'll have to be discreet about it. And not upset the men, we are supposed to be on holiday after all."

Chrissy couldn't help but smile at her sister's change of mind. Maybe it had been for Richard's sake, a show of 'count me out'. They'd been a good team chasing around France for a missing woman and now here they were about to get involved all over again, but in rural Ireland. Julie had her uses. It turned out Julie's pretty little nose was as sensitive as her own when it came to be digging something up. A truffle pig came to mind, though the image wasn't nearly as endearing as the sentiment she intended.

"Right then. I've got to submit my fingerprints tomorrow, so I'll have a chance, I hope, to glean what the Gardai know up to now. Let's hope I get to see Sergeant Staines or the other one, Harris. It can't be that big a station. I bet they still use a kettle rather than a vending machine."

"What time are you going?"

Chrissy didn't want Julie to tag along on that particular journey. She may have some explaining to do, in private.

"Early, so I can get back. You'll still be drinking your tea by the time I return. I won't be long." Thankfully Julie didn't read too much into it and accepted it would be a waste of time to accompany her. A knock on the kitchen door was followed by it opening a little. Richard's head peered around.

"Sorry to interrupt, and not wanting to sound like whiny children, but Adam and I are hungry. Have you decided where we're going for dinner?"

They must have thought that was the topic of conversation – far from it. Since sustenance hadn't been mentioned during their chat, Chrissy made the decision for them all. And she wasn't in the mood for a tablecloth dining experience. Not tonight.

"We have," she announced, standing. She caught Julie's eye who was also quite clearly waiting for the news.

"Back to the pub for another round of Guinness pie and song," she said, waving her arms around theatrically. She glanced down at Richard's leg. "We'll drive up though, this time."

"Right you are," he said before turning to hobble back. If nothing else, it would give Chrissy a chance to talk to the barman about Ciara getting her mobile number from the booking register. Plus she was ravenous herself.

CHAPTER 31

Even though it was a Tuesday evening, Gus O'Connor's pub was almost fit to burst by the time Chrissy parked up outside. Having decided to drop Richard and the others at the door, she'd driven on to park further down the lane and walked back. Once she made it inside and to the bar, through already rather merry customers, Adam had her glass of wine ready and a table secured, though they wouldn't be seated for another twenty minutes. Not bad given they didn't have a reservation. Chrissy took a large mouthful of a full-bodied red and winced slightly as it forced its way through the narrow entrance at the top of her throat. It felt like she was being stretched for a moment, before it returned to its normal width and the warmth cascaded downwards. Adam caught the wince and noted the half empty glass in her hand.

"Steady on. You downed that like a seasoned drinker in desperate need. Everything all right?" he asked. "Do I need to get you a refill already?"

"Perfectly fine," she said, beaming up at him, taking a deep breath and releasing it. "And no, not just yet, I'm driving back, remember?" The two moved further along so customers behind them could get to the bar. Adam struck up a conversation with

Richard on his other side. Chrissy, spotting the same barman that had served Julie and herself late on Saturday afternoon, watched him work for a moment or two. There were three staff attending behind the bar, and it looked like the territory of the one she wanted was at the opposite end to where she was currently standing. Had he been the one to give her mobile number out to Ciara, or had the woman helped herself somehow? Thinking as she watched, she came up with two possible ways to find out: by asking him directly or indirectly. The problem was, if she went the direct route, he could well be angry at her accusation. Go the indirect route and either she could land herself with some explaining to do, or he might not take the hint if she was too subtle. A hand appeared waving in front of her eyes like a fan, and it had beautiful nails attached to it.

"Chrissy, you're staring," Julie said, trying to break her sister's gaze.

Refocusing on her immediate vicinity, she replied, "Sorry, I was deep in thought."

"I can see that." Julie leaned in closer. "So, what are you going to do now? How are you going to find out? I gather that's why you suggested we come back here for dinner?"

Chrissy glanced at Adam and Richard, who were now deep in conversation nearby, before deciding on which approach to go for. Without answering the question, she handed Julie the remains of her wine and said, "I'll be back in a moment."

Chrissy made her way over to the curly haired man and struck up a conversation while he poured her a sparkling water. A slice of lemon floated on top like a tiny yellow raft on a bubbling sea.

"It's busy again tonight," Chrissy said. "Is every night like this?"

"It is, mostly. The live music brings the tourists in, they seem to enjoy joining in."

"I didn't think we'd get a table when we walked in."

"We can usually squeeze you in somewhere, even if you end up sharing."

"That's exactly what happened to us on Saturday night actually."

Chrissy couldn't believe the direction the conversation was moving in, right along to their table guests. "We shared ours with a lovely couple, and thoroughly enjoyed ourselves." Chrissy waited a beat before carrying on, searching his face for any kind of recognition, a twitch of a facial muscle perhaps, anything that could guide her in how to put what she about to ask. "In fact, Ciara left something behind, and I wondered if perhaps you may have taken her number that night. Perhaps she booked for dinner? Maybe someone could get hold of her, let her know?" A slight tilt of his head then his eyes locked with hers for a moment longer than necessary. She ploughed on: "I don't suppose you could pass it along to me, could you?" she said, grinning. He looked sceptical. Chrissy filled the gap: "It's just that I'm sure she'd like her bracelet back. I found it out on the lane the following day and I noticed she'd been wearing one just like it." She hoped her best innocent smile would do the trick and kept her mouth shut while he weighed her request up. Chrissy could almost see the wheels turning in his head. Had she said enough?

Finally, he said, "I'll check the bookings and see if we have it. Do you know her surname?"

"Sorry, no, but it was around 7.30 pm and he was called Lorcan, I think." She made a big deal of looking unsure as she lied through her teeth. In her PI role, exaggerating the truth or full-on lying didn't faze her. In her non-working role, she just didn't do it. He looked up and down the bar area, and Chrissy followed suit. There were only a couple of customers actually waiting, and there were two others serving. He could get away. In anticipation of his thoughts, she said, "Thanks, it might be sentimental to her," and watched him move to a separate screen a few feet further down. Fingers tapped as he presumably looked for Saturday's bookings and searched through the list. He scribbled something down on a nearby piece of paper and returned to her. Was he going to hand it over?

"I have a number that could be it, so I'll drop her a text and let her know. Hopefully she'll reply. Will that work for you?"

Chrissy wanted to say no, that she'd be the best one to contact her. It seemed there was no way he was going to hand it over anytime soon. Maybe he hadn't given Ciara her own number that night after all. "Great, thanks. I'll give you my number so she can let me know and I can get it to her." By the man's eyes flicking up and down the bar, he was conscious of gathering customers waiting to be served. He needed to move on. He nodded quickly and Chrissy recited her own number. When both were on the piece of paper, she watched as he placed it back on the counter near the booking terminal and resumed his work further up the bar serving thirsty customers. She had to get the contents of that note. Thinking quickly, she took her phone out of her back pocket, found the camera app and was ready to click as she deftly took the piece of paper. Watching him as he served, she snapped the photo then slipped the note back in place before heading straight to the ladies to see what he'd written. Once behind the closed door, she took a look. Her own telephone number was written on the bottom half, but the other number, above her own, made no sense. There surely was no such mobile telephone number as 07123 45678.

He'd obviously made it up, a charade for her sake, and was not intending to contact Ciara at all.

Why?

CHAPTER 32

By the time Chrissy had returned to her small party, they were ready and waiting to sit down for dinner.

"There you are," Adam exclaimed. He slipped his arm around her waist, and Julie handed back her half glass of wine. The sparkling water with its lemon raft still sat on the bar.

Chrissy was somewhat relieved to find their designated table sat only four, as she wasn't in a sociable mood, not tonight. Catching Julie's eye, she willed her sister to wait for the phone number results with a slight shake of her head. Richard, who had not witnessed the subtle exchange, dropped his menu on the table dramatically and announced he was sticking with the steak pie again. Adam concurred. Chrissy went along with them; it was easier than thinking. Julie perused a while longer before choosing the poached salmon. With their food order placed, it was Adam that kicked off the topic of conversation: the following day's events.

"Since the weather is now decidedly colder than the last couple of beautiful days have been, perhaps we should do two different activities rather than a whole day affair?" He looked around for approval.

"And don't worry about me," Richard said, "I'm not going to

hold your holiday up, I can't get far, so please, choose around my attendance." He smiled before taking a sip of his Guinness.

"Then how's this for an idea," Julie started, "how about we go to Father Ted's for afternoon tea tomorrow, then at least Richard can come. Then afterwards, you two can wander off and I'll stay and keep him company. So, somebody else choose an activity for the morning."

Chrissy felt as if she'd missed a whole day of her holiday already, even her run hadn't happened, and so she was anxious to get out and do some exercise. "I have to drop into the Gardai tomorrow and give my prints, but I'm heading over early so I can get back early enough. Today vanished on me."

Adam gave her a mock pitiful look and pulled her close.

"Then why don't those that wish to, take a picnic and finish the rest of the coastal walk, do the other side?" he suggested. "Hags Head back to the information centre, then home in time for a trip over to Father Ted's. It's an eight-mile round trip so if we get over there early enough, we should manage everything. Or is that cutting it a bit fine?" The idea of another refreshing cliff walk, with a gusty wind whipping her hair around, sounded ideal to Chrissy's ears. If she didn't get out and do some form of exercise during the day, she began to feel restless, like a child with too much sugar inside them.

"I'm game. Julie?"

Tilting her head to one side, thinking, she said, "On reflection, I'll leave you two lovebirds to your walk and stay back with Richard. We'll be out later for tea, so it's not as if I won't have been somewhere." Julie took Richard's hand in hers in a rare public display of affection. It wasn't the first time on the holiday Chrissy had noticed the sentiment; the pair were usually far more restrained. She wondered what had been going on behind their closed doors since Julie was doing a good deal more than simply tolerating her husband as she usually did. "And I might walk into the village again, if I feel like it."

"Well that's settled then," Chrissy said. "Picnic for two, then afternoon tea for four." Changing the subject, she asked, "Who wants another drink?" Three empty glasses were offered, and Julie took the opportunity to help. "I'll give you a hand," she said, and the two women rose. Chrissy smiled inwardly. For someone who wasn't particularly interested in using up much of her holiday time, she sure was interested in how things were going with the missing couple. Chrissy felt her sister's hand on her arm, steering her towards the bar. When they were out of earshot of the table, Julie couldn't contain herself any longer.

"What did he say, the barman? I'm going slightly nuts wanting to know."

Chrissy quickly filled her in about the nonsensical number.

"But that makes no sense."

"Quite."

Julie managed to attract the attention of one of the bar staff, something she was exceptionally good at. As she placed their order, Chrissy scanned the rest of the bar.

"He's nowhere to be seen now."

"He'll be on his break, I expect. Or changing a barrel?"

"Maybe," said Chrissy absentmindedly. She didn't sound convinced. The pair returned to their table just in time to see their food arrive. Of course, the man could be in the loo for all they knew and just because he wasn't behind the bar right there and then didn't mean there was anything suspicious to think about.

The small group ate their meal with relish then settled back to listen to the live music. Several deep male voices accompanied a woman on a button accordion and another on a fiddle, which increased the volume as well as the energy in the room. Adam, Richard, Chrissy, and Julie all sat with their feet tapping away to the fast and vibrant Irish tune, a rather different version of 'Galway Girl' to Ed's. When the song eventually came to an end, glasses were raised in celebration and a new song played out in front of them.

Chrissy glanced across at the bar just in time to spot the blond barman from earlier as he slipped through the rear door, which no doubt led out back. Had he a thick jacket on though? She'd only caught his distinctive hair and part of a shoulder before he'd vanished from sight, but she'd put a glass of wine on it he had. She looked around the pub. The place was heaving still and would be for another couple of hours more to come. Brushing it off as unimportant, she tried to focus on enjoying herself. She was on holiday after all.

It wasn't until they were driving back towards their holiday home that Chrissy spotted the man again. This time, however, he was leaving the woollen sweater shop. At gone 11 pm? What on earth was he doing in there at that hour? As she drove the group home, no suitable explanation surfaced, but she added the snippet of information to the rest on the bubble map in the back of her mind. No doubt she'd recall it again later – when the jigsaw piece fitted another.

CHAPTER 33

Even though she'd only drunk two glasses of wine, Chrissy awoke during the night feeling totally dehydrated. Maybe there'd been a good deal more Guinness in the pie than she'd realised, though more likely, with all the excitement, she hadn't drunk enough water during the day. Her mouth felt like it had a woolly lining. Trying to find moisture and realising she had little spittle to lick her lips with, she slipped out from under the covers, grabbed her robe and quietly headed down the hall to the kitchen. One of the stark differences they'd each discovered between here and Surrey was that when the lights went out in Doolin, it was pitch black – their nearest street lamp a good way away. Feeling with bare feet and her right hand down the hall wall, she managed to steer herself to the right room and fill a glass of water without banging into anything along the way. By the time her eyes had adjusted in the weak moonlight filtering in through the windows, she'd downed half of it. The liquid felt good as is made its way, refreshing her from the inside; like a parched camel might feel at a cool watering hole. Rupert fell in beside her, and she reached down to tickle him behind his ears. He seemed to sense he should stay quiet. She turned towards the ocean and gazed out for a moment while she sipped the rest of her drink. The sky above was almost ink black, the moon only glimpsing through the thinner edges of the clouds as they passed in front of it. Gazing up as it made a brief appearance, Chrissy saw it was almost full. In another couple of nights, it would be whole again. She tipped the remaining water into the sink and placed the glass on the drainer before passing the large patio window on her way back to bed. Something caught her attention, and she stopped, almost mid-step. Had she imagined it? Did something just flicker, off in the distance? She waited, her eyes searching the horizon, for whatever it was to return. A white speck broke through the ink. There was a light, off in the distance somewhere – another ship, perhaps? She'd seen a light out to sea when she'd been in the castle, it was likely that. It flashed again, and Chrissy realised the light wasn't coming from directly in front of her, it had come more from her left. Was it on the ocean? She couldn't be sure. Not wanting to wake the whole house up, she quietly moved to close the door and flicked a wall light on. Richard's binoculars might be still knocking around. Spotting them on a side table by a chair, she picked them up then turned the light back out. And waited. Before long the light materialised once again and she was ready with the binoculars, searching to lock on to her target and understand what it was. But she wasn't quick enough and she waited once more. This time she would get it. When it finally came, Chrissy gasped out loud as realisation struck her. It wasn't a ship in the distance out on the ocean, it was in fact much closer than that. With the power of the strong lenses in her hands, Chrissy could see she was looking at the castle. There was someone inside. Somebody was passing the windows carrying a light of some kind. Who was it and what the hell were they doing there in the middle of the night? Right at that moment, the overhead light flooded the kitchen as Julie walked in.

"I thought someone was up. Can't you sleep?" she whispered, tying the belt of her robe at the same time.

"Turn the light off!" Chrissy hissed urgently and Julie did as she was asked.

Fumbling in the dark a little, she made her way over to her sister and said, "What are you doing in the dark?"

Chrissy still had the binoculars up to her eyes as she replied. "There's someone in the castle, with a torch or something."

"But it's nearly 3 am," Julie said, as if that was reason enough.

"All the more reason for it to be suspicious, don't you think?"

"Can I take a look, please?"

Chrissy passed the binoculars over and waited.

"There's not a great deal to see, is there? I wonder who it is."

"Well, there's only one way to find out."

"What? You surely can't be serious?" Julie asked. It was a dumb question to have asked her sister.

"Coming?" said Chrissy as she pulled on someone's jacket that was hanging by the door. It smelled like it could be Richard's, it wore his fragrance. She rummaged around on the floor nearby for her trainers.

"You're mad."

"That's a no then?"

It didn't take Julie long to reconsider. "My walking boots should still be there, can you pass them, please?"

Chrissy smiled in the semi-darkness. The woman who used to be so stiff and starched was now beginning to bend with the breeze a little more. It hadn't gone unnoticed with Adam either. Finding what felt like Julie's boots, she handed them across. "You'll need a jacket," she said, taking hers off. "I think this is Richard's, so you have it." Fumbling for another, she found her own and put it on. "I need my phone, or yours, just in case and for a torch."

"I left mine plugged in to charge by the kettle," Julie said help-fully, moving to grab it. She slipped it into her pocket. "We must be mad. Walking boots, dressing gown, and a coat over the top. I hope we don't get stopped by the Gardai," she added.

"We won't be long. Plus we need to get back before the menfolk awaken. If Richard finds you gone, he'll start to panic."

"And Adam, surely."

Chrissy didn't bother replying. He knew about Chrissy's old

occupation, as well as her curiosity, not to mention her bravado in weird PI situations. It was what she'd done for many years. Julie didn't know the half of what she'd got up to. Her life in HR had all been a ruse for friends and family and she was never likely to correct any of them.

Rupert stood expectantly. "Sorry, Rupert. You're not invited on this visit." He slunk over to a mat and lay back down. She turned to Julie: "Ready? Let's go." Opening the back door, the two headed out towards the fields and the castle beyond.

"The road would have been easier," Julie grumbled as they half stumbled in the semi-darkness. Their eyes had got used to the lack of light, but it wasn't easy going.

"It's much shorter going this route. I've done both, remember?"

"Well, I hope I don't get a twisted ankle to match Richard's," she grumbled. "Why don't you shine the torch?" Chrissy was about to tell her to stay home but bit her tongue and answered her question.

"I don't want to attract attention to us."

"Who's going to see us? They're all in bed."

"All except the person in the castle that is," she said, pointing.

CHAPTER 34

The two women carried on their way in silence. When they were almost at the perimeter wall of the castle, Chrissy ushered Julie behind her slightly, for protection. Force of habit. The light inside still flickered, as if someone had a light and was moving from room to room with it. A generic-looking dark transit van sat silently nearby. Chrissy pointed to it and, in the half light, Julie nodded.

"Now what?" she whispered to the back of Chrissy's head.

"I'll take a look through the window, you stay put."

"I don't think so," she said. "I may as well have stayed in bed as do that. Why don't I watch your back, like they always do in the movies?"

Chrissy turned towards her sister and even though Julie likely couldn't see her facial expression, she gave her best incredulous look. It was Hollywood quality.

"Right," she said, conceding eventually. "You watch my back, but do it from here." And she left Julie squatting down behind the wall as she deftly ran across the grass towards a ground-floor window. A stiff and cold breeze wrapped itself around her lower legs and she was glad she was wearing pyjamas and not her usual nightie. Finally, she arrived at the side of a lower window and took a moment. She rolled herself away from the wall at one shoulder and took a quick look inside. A small handheld lantern was on the kitchen table and Chrissy could see the rug, which usually covered the trapdoor, had been flung to one side. Someone was down in the cellar. She flipped herself back against the stone as she processed her thoughts then peeled herself forward for another look. As quick as a flash she slammed herself back flat against the wall as the front door opened only a handful of feet along. Surely, she'd be seen standing here? Luckily, the intruder was looking the other way as they headed around the corner to where the van was parked. But how long would they be gone? Was there time to slip inside and hide? Then do what? Chrissy strained to listen for any sounds she could hear, but whatever the person was doing, they were doing it quietly. No, there was no point getting locked in, or confronting them quite yet. After all, they may have a legitimate reason for being there. Perhaps the owners had flown in from overseas? A moment later, the figure returned and from the shadows of her hiding place, she was able to see it was a man. And he was wearing the same jacket she'd seen the barman in earlier. His blond hair confirmed his identification.

Not the owners of the castle then. That posed the even bigger question of what did he want both in the sweater shop and the castle, all on the same night? And skulking to boot? As he went back inside, oblivious to Chrissy standing nearby, she sprinted past the open door towards the van, hoping to see what was inside it. It appeared even darker round the other side of the building and with no interior light on to help her, all she could make out were what looked like large cartons, like what a removal firm might use when moving someone to a new house. Since the barman, as she now knew it was, didn't appear to be adding or removing from what she'd seen so far, the boxes weren't much help to her. Perhaps the contents would. Had she time? She was just about to climb in and squat behind one of them, ready, when Julie appeared by her side from nowhere. She must have been watching and decided to join in. All Chrissy could do was deliver a surprised and outraged look and hope her sister could see it. There was no chance of even an agitated whisper with the barman so close by. If Julie saw the facial message, she ignored it and at the sound of returning footsteps, both women dashed further back around the castle and away from the van. From the shadows, all Chrissy could do was watch as the rear of the van was closed and the man got in the driver's seat and made a telephone call. It was the light that glowed in doing so that allowed Julie to see his face.

"That's the barman!" said Julie, incredulous.

"I know. But what's he doing?"

As the van drove off, the two women slipped out from their hiding place and ventured back around to the front door, which was now closed. Chrissy tried the handle. It was locked.

"So, he has a key. I wonder if he'll be coming back, or if he's done whatever he was doing?"

"How can we find out?"

"We'll have to keep watch."

Julie shivered. In the small amount of light available, Chrissy noticed that Julie was only wearing a nightie under her coat; her legs would have been frozen without the draught. "Come on, that's enough for one night, let's get back," she offered. Julie had no complaints to the idea and the two walked back deep in thought, wondering about what they'd just witnessed. When they reached the house, which thankfully was still in darkness, they crept in through the back door and took their coats off. They'd been gone an hour according to the clock on the cooker. Julie slipped into her robe and sat down, rubbing her arms and legs, trying to warm herself.

"I'll make you a hot drink to warm you up. If Richard reaches out and you're ice cold, he'll think you've died in the night. A heart attack, on top of his other injuries, we don't need." She busied herself with chocolate and a pan of warm milk, which was a good deal quieter than the kettle. With two mugs ready, Chrissy joined her sister and sat down. At least if Richard or Adam came in, they could legitimately say they were awake and fancied a warm drink. It wasn't a lie.

"What are we going to do?" Julie asked.

"Find out what's in those boxes that is so important they can only be moved in the middle of the night."

WEDNESDAY

CHAPTER 35

Julie had eventually gone back to bed and, with her eye mask firmly in place, hadn't stirred as Richard slipped into his robe. He glanced down at her. Experience had taught him that sleeping dogs should be left to lie and so he crept out and headed for the kitchen, silently. Adam was sitting with his own mug, flicking through Julie's discarded gossip magazine as Chrissy fastened her boots in the doorway. She hadn't gone back to bed after the night's activities but had chosen instead to have another mug of hot chocolate and to watch the sun rise on the horizon, wrapped in a woollen throw. At 7 am, she'd headed for the shower and was now ready to go and give her prints to the Gardai. A job she wanted to do alone.

"Why would anyone want to read this utter rubbish?" Adam asked as he tossed the magazine to one side. "Who cares who's dating who, or who's looking paunchy around their middle? Really?"

Chrissy smiled at the sudden outburst and caught his eye.

"I've been saying that for years," Richard piped up as he entered the room fully. He'd obviously heard Adam's words and agreed with them. "Maybe it's a woman thing?" he asked Chrissy, raising a greying eyebrow at her.

"Don't look at me. A waste of good money, not to mention my time."

The men had obviously slept through peacefully since neither raised the subject of a midnight adventure.

"Where are you off so early?" Richard asked. "You're not dressed for a run."

"Giving my prints in then I'll be back," she said cheerily, blowing a quick kiss over her shoulder and heading out. "See you later." Richard, Adam, and Rupert were left staring after her.

It was only a fifteen-minute drive to the local Garda station at Ennistymon and she parked her hire car easily in the small car park. The building would have looked like a small hotel were it not for the Victorian-style blue Garda lamp stood proudly out front. She wondered again about if they had a vending machine or still used the kettle. Heading inside, she made herself known to the officer on the desk and asked if Officer Harris or Sergeant Staines were in yet. She'd come down early to give her prints.

"Garda Harris is in, yes," he said. "I'll let him know you're here." The inside of the station looked like any other, clean and functional. They were never meant to be welcoming, not like a hotel reception, though if you were staying overnight in a cell, you wouldn't be using the main entrance anyway. She sat down to wait and glanced around the walls for something to occupy her mind in the meantime. Various posters and information leaflets begged her to read them up close, but she stayed where she was and scanned the headlines she could from her spot. Driving drunk or drugged was to be avoided. Another urged people to call the confidential crime line and help put the bad guys away. She thought back to her early morning adventures at the castle and the suspicious movements of one barman, in two locations. A male voice broke into her thoughts. It was Drew Harris. His thinning hair wafted about in exactly the same manner as when she'd spoken to him yesterday morning. It needed some gel to tame it. Was it only that long ago she'd seen him? The kindness in his eyes was ever-present.

"Thanks for coming in. This won't take long," he said, smiling, and Chrissy stood to follow him.

"How's the investigation going?" she asked nonchalantly. "Have you managed to locate the little one's parents yet?"

"I'm afraid not."

He wasn't for giving much away. She tried a different tack. "Don't you have number-plate recognition cameras in Ireland?"

"We do, indeed. Plenty in fact."

It was like pulling teeth. Obviously, the cameras hadn't shown anything. "Were they in their own car? Or since they were on holiday, maybe a hire car?" Harris let the question linger without answering. Chrissy carried on. "Poor Flynn, I bet he's missing his mum and dad. I hope he's all right. Do you know where he is?"

"He'll be well looked after in a foster home by now," he said, holding a door open for her. Once they were inside another nondescript room, he explained the procedure to her. There was no ink, it was all done by scanner these days. She placed her hand palm down on the glass and it did its thing. It would take both finger and palm prints; both were collected as a matter of course. Realising he wasn't going to tell her anything about the case, she changed the subject. "What happens when it's done its scan?"

"It does a number of things. If I was printing you under arrest, it would bring results back in just a few minutes. So now might be a good time to mention if you've committed any crimes," he said, laughing at his own joke. He'd used the line before. Chrissy wanted to wince but stayed straight-faced while the other hand was scanned. "We only need your prints for elimination, so I'm not expecting anything to pop up," he added. When both were completed, she gave her contact details once again and was about ready to leave. Maybe her prints weren't in the system after all. Harris paused for a moment then turned and looked her square in the eye.

"Let me guess: I can see your prints and a file I can't access, so I'm assuming by the questions you've been asking that you have an interest?"

"Ah, yes. Though I'm a Private Investigator now." She tried not to look sheepish.

"And on holiday, I gather?"

"What can I say? If there's a case needs my help…" She shrugged as if that explained everything.

"Then don't go getting in the way or do something stupid with this one. Are we clear?"

"I may be able to help, if you'll let me."

"Let me suggest you leave this one to the Guards. We'll find the boy's parents, I'm sure." His kind eyes had taken on a different persona, there was a warning tone in them.

"I get the message. But can I ask you don't mention this, my print results, to anyone in my family."

"You can be assured of my discretion," he said, almost bowing.

With nothing left to say and nothing left to find out, Chrissy kept her newly found barman knowledge to herself. Young Flynn was being looked after safely, his parents on the run. If the local Guards didn't want her help, that wasn't going to stop her finding the truth.

CHAPTER 36

Sergeant Staines pursed his thin lips as he watched from the staffroom as Chrissy got back into her car. Part of being an officer of the law was working with your gut as well as facts and data, and one thing he'd picked up while they'd interviewed the woman and her husband at the holiday home was a certain vibe. He couldn't put his finger on it, but he'd gone back to the station and done a little digging of his own. It seemed Chrissy Livingstone wasn't all that she pretended to be. She had a past, a closed file, and that meant one of a couple of things.

It was a shame what had happened to the child, to be left abandoned. That wasn't what was meant to have happened. They had people in place to prevent that type of error, and now the boy was in the system and it would be almost impossible for them to get him out. There were often casualties, somebody invariably got hurt; it was often dangerous, but never the children. They often ended up being a pawn in a game and it sickened him. At least the boy would be looked after and they'd figure out how to get him back sometime in the future. Staines joined his colleague, Drew Harris, and made polite conversation, all the time wheedling his way around to what he really wanted to know.

"Was that the Livingstone woman I saw leaving?" he said nonchalantly.

"Yes, Chrissy Livingstone. Seems she has a past."

"Oh?"

"Her prints are on file, a closed file," he said.

"Did she have much to say?"

"She had plenty of questions, but I told her to keep her nose out. The last thing we need is someone sticking their beak in like Miss Marple. I've told her to be on holiday and keep out of the investigation. Best to leave it to the Guards; we'll see if she does."

Staines grunted his approval and carried on his way, satisfied that his colleague hadn't said anything to the woman. He didn't need anything else going wrong. He placed coins in the vending machine and waited for his Twix to drop into the tray below.

CHAPTER 37

By the time Chrissy arrived back at the house, Julie had surfaced and was making fresh coffee in the kitchen, looking as composed and well put together as ever. Since their impromptu trip to France a couple of months back, Chrissy now appreciated that her sister was a naturally beautiful woman and a genius when it came to speedily applying make-up and doing her hair just so. There wasn't the sign of a bag under either of her eyes. Chrissy, on the other hand, was content with a daily flick of mascara, a pencil through her brows, and lip gloss, unless the occasion required more. This morning, though, she could have used some concealer. Her bags resembled the holdall she'd brought with her.

"Perfect timing," Julie said, turning as Chrissy entered through the back door. She busied herself pouring a mug and added warm milk to the top before handing it over. She noted Chrissy's clean fingers. "Where's the ink?"

"All done by scanning now." She took off her jacket and hung it up on a corner of the table as she flopped down. Julie frowned and hung it properly by the door.

"Where are the men?"

"In the living room, reading. I swear it's like having our own library; I've never known either of them to be so absorbed in the written word." Chrissy smiled at her description – couldn't she just say book or paper? Julie joined her at the table and huddled in close. "So, did you glean anything from your visit?"

"Not a sausage, actually. Officer Harris gave nothing away and all but warned me off looking into it. Like I'm really going to do that!"

"Hmm. That doesn't help then, does it. That's like putting a word down on the Scrabble board that doesn't allow for any further expansion." Chrissy inwardly smiled at her sister's metaphor, though she was correct. "And just as annoying actually." The two sat silently sipping before Julie said, "Oh, I almost forgot. I went up to the shop to get Richard a paper, and guess what?"

"Go on."

"Remember the woman from the sweater shop? She had a nasty car accident the night Ciara and Lorcan vanished and is in hospital. Broken leg and wrist, so she'll not be at the shop for a while I don't expect."

"Poor thing. I don't suppose she will be. That might explain why we saw Mr Curly Blond Barman coming out of the shop last night then. Perhaps he's helping out somehow. They might even be related. A small village like Doolin? I'd bet everyone knows everyone else. And their business."

"Maybe, but I can't see how that would explain his early hours castle visit, with boxes. Can you?"

"Permission to store stock now it's empty? Maybe temporarily?" Chrissy was clutching for a reason. "I guess it's possible, though unlikely, I'd say. That cellar was cold and damp, not the place for storing clothing."

"Have we still got the key?"

"Rupert has, yes. Where is he by the way?"

"In the library."

Chrissy knew exactly what her sister was referring to. "What are you thinking, going back inside for another look?"

"It's the only way we'll find out, assuming of course those boxes are in the cellar since there were a stack of them in the van. We'd have to expect the same contents in both?" Chrissy glanced at the cooker clock; she was supposed to be going on a picnic walk to Hags Head with Adam. Had she time to slip out and back beforehand? Julie read her mind.

"If you go now, no one would be any the wiser you've even come home from the Gardai yet."

"I'll need the key."

"I'll go and get it."

While Julie nipped to the other room, Chrissy noticed the folded newspaper and speed read the article on the accident. It appeared to be perfect driving conditions and no other vehicle was involved. The Guards were scratching their heads as to what had happened, and the reporter suggested perhaps the driver had been distracted. At 7 pm, it was unlikely she'd fallen asleep at the wheel. An accompanying photograph showed quite how crumpled the car had finished up. She'd been lucky to survive and end up with only moderate injuries. The Guards were appealing for any witnesses to come forward. On that stretch of road, they'd be lucky. Julie returned with the key.

"I don't think they even noticed I was in the room," she said.

Chrissy took the key. "I'll be back soon."

At that moment, Adam walked in. "I thought I could hear voices. Are you ready to go? I've made us a picnic," he said, bending to retrieve a couple of plastic boxes from the fridge. Before she could answer, Julie filled the space. Standing up, she said, "You lovebirds have a lovely morning and I'll slip out for a gentle walk myself," slipping the key from Chrissy's hand as she spoke. "Then we can all go and enjoy Father Ted's for afternoon tea. I've booked a table for 3.30 pm so there's plenty of time."

It made perfect sense, though Chrissy would have preferred to be the one snooping. What if someone came back? All she could do was show her concern by contorting her face while Adam was standing behind her.

"I'll get my boots on," she said resignedly as Adam placed their picnic in his backpack.

"I'll see if we can borrow Richard's binoculars to take with us," he said, leaving the room, unaware of the silent discussion the two women were having behind him.

When he was out of earshot, Chrissy said, "Just be careful. Text me what you find out."

"I'll be fine. If I can run boutique shoe shops, I'm sure I can check the contents of a box or two. I'm a grown woman, as are you."

She had a point, but still Chrissy would have preferred it to be herself going in. At any sign of trouble, Julie would likely fall over and faint. Adam returned with the binoculars dangling from his neck.

"All set?"

"All set."

CHAPTER 38

Once the pair had left for their cliff walk, Julie sat for a moment or two until they'd driven well away. It would have been just like Chrissy to have changed her mind and found some excuse to stay behind, but after a good ten minutes, Julie was content that they were staying away. Now all she had to do was explain to Richard why she wanted to do something so out of the ordinary for her: go for a walk by herself – for no apparent reason. Unless there was something at the end of it like a morning paper, she could count on one hand how many times in their marriage she'd done so. She popped her head around the living room door and watched for a moment or two as he sat, head bent, glasses on, totally engrossed in what he was reading. The hardback in his hands must have already been in the house since it wasn't something she recognised from home. The books on their shelves were purely for show. He turned the page slowly, unaware of her presence until she spoke.

"Would you mind if I went out for a walk myself? Only I'd hate to leave you on your own if you're going to be bored, hence my question."

Richard looked up and refocused his eyes as he removed his glasses and smiled. If he was surprised, he didn't show it.

"You go, I'm happy here reading," he said, showing her the front cover. There was a tear in the jacket; it was an ageing Agatha Christie book. How apt, she thought, given what she was about to do. Equally surprised at him not being surprised, she replied, "I won't be too long," and headed back to get her jacket and boots. Rupert trotted towards her, expectant.

"Come on then," she said as she clipped his leash on and opened the back door. She felt like Anne, one of Enid Blyton's Famous Five, along with Timmy the dog, as she set out on an adventure all her own. Chrissy could have been the other female of the crew, Georgina, or George, as she'd preferred to be called, a bit of a tomboy. A rush of cold sea air hit her square in the face, and she pulled her hood up to keep the wind out of her ears.

The journey across the fields was somewhat easier than it had been only a few hours ago in the pitch-black night, and with jeans covering her legs, she was a good deal warmer than she'd been when she was wearing her nightdress. It had taken her ages to defrost once they'd got back to the house and she'd lain in bed trying not to shiver and wake Richard. Thank goodness for the couple of pints of Guinness he'd drunk in the pub, and the same for Adam. They'd not heard a sound as the two women had returned and made hot chocolate while chatting in the kitchen.

Gulls and other equally noisy seabirds gathered overhead and they squawked and squabbled as they flew, some heading to the sheer, slate cliff face, others in search of food and whatever else birds did with their time each day. Rupert strolled easily alongside her and she chatted to the dog as if he were a human. No answers to her questions were required.

All was quiet as she approached the stone perimeter wall again, the bright blue sky all around making the property look all the more like a picture postcard. She wondered whether many couples had been married out by the castle, the photos with the backdrop of the ocean would be dramatic to say the least. There were no vehicles present. She checked over her shoulder as she neared the door and slipped the key in the lock. If anyone was inside, they'd have gone on foot as she had, though she wasn't expecting to see anyone sitting at the kitchen table or asleep on the sofa. Entering, she was relieved to see the kitchen was empty, naturally, and she breathed a sigh of relief and closed the door. Rupert had opted to stay outdoors and inspect the grass instead. The room felt eerily quiet and unlived in, and even with the sun shining outside, it was cold. Having never been inside the castle before, she was tempted to climb the stairs and look at the view she knew she'd find at the top, but that would have to wait. What she'd set out to do came first. The rug lay neatly across the floor and she pushed it to one side. Last night's visitor must have put everything back in place before he took off. She lifted the trapdoor and peered into the darkness, letting her eyes adjust. Chrissy had mentioned the overhead light and she felt around blindly until she found the smooth plastic plate with the switch. Bright light illuminated the space and she was glad she'd remembered to close the front door in case anyone noticed it. She picked her way slowly down the steps towards a pile of boxes stacked neatly two-high in the centre of the room. There was nothing written on them, they were just plain brown cardboard. She reached up at one randomly and nudged it lightly to see if it moved. While it wasn't particularly heavy, there was definitely something inside. She picked it up and rested it on the floor beside her before picking carefully at the tape to open it. She hadn't thought about that aspect, that whoever they belonged to would realise someone had looked inside, but it was too late now. Why hadn't they simply tucked the flaps in to secure the top? That would have been more convenient for her and her nails. As carefully as she could she pulled the brown tape back and tentatively opened the lid.

"Well, I wasn't expecting that," she said to the empty room. She reached inside and pulled the first blanket to one side, reaching down into the box only to be greeted by even more blankets. It was a box of bedclothes. She did her best to seal it back up, and then rearranged the boxes so it became a bottom one rather than a top one. Perhaps that would hide the fact it had been tampered with, if only a little more. She selected another box at random and repeated the process. Sheets and towels peered back at her, looking particularly harmless. Since there were no plastic wrappers on anything, she figured everything was either second-hand or someone's possessions. She sealed the box back up as best she could and hid it under an unopened one.

"What an anti-climax," she mumbled as she made her way back up the stone steps, turning the light out as she went. Back up in the small kitchen, she closed the trapdoor and pulled the rug into place and stood for a moment contemplating a quick look at the view from the top floor.

She should have left there and then.

CHAPTER 39

He'd seen her enter the castle, as he'd approached in his van along one of the narrow lanes. The dog, Rupert, was with her. He was glad someone was taking care of him, hadn't dropped him at the nearest pound, or worse. Perhaps he could retrieve him somehow? He pulled over and watched rather than let her hear his engine or see him again because he knew exactly who she was. Her nosey sister had been asking questions, not that he'd given her any answers but still, the woman was snooping, putting her nose where trouble most certainly lay. Who were this pair and why were they involving themselves? He waited a while longer before finally deciding to walk the rest of the short journey. If she was simply out for a walk, then he was too – what a coincidence. That would be the ideal scenario but, as he got closer, he instinctively knew it wasn't likely. As he approached the door, only the dog was outside, a dog that knew him well and greeted him with a lick to his cheeks, demanding a belly rub for afters. He declined, held his finger to his lip in a sign to keep quiet and peered in through the lower-floor window. The rug was tossed to one side. That meant one thing: she was in the cellar. He clenched both fists into tight balls and punched the air by his side in an attempt to keep control of his annoyance. And stay silent himself. He thought about the contents of the boxes in the cellar below, undoubtedly her target since there was nothing else in the property worth her nosey attention. Household items, nothing of value. Not to her anyway. Opening the door quietly, he watched the cellar entrance for movement before stepping into the room, his own key in his pocket and not needed to gain entry, this time. He had to know where she and her sister fitted into all this; he couldn't afford another project to be picked undone like the last one had been. Too much planning, organisation, man- and woman-power, not to mention the funds required to make them a success. It all added up, and when something toppled from its position, it threatened the rest of the structure. He waited in a dark corner at the base of the stairs that led to the upper floors, hoping to hear her make a phone call or at least enable him to discover something he could use to understand how much she knew.

Footsteps returning from below, the light switched off, the rug pulled back into place. He needed to get into that cellar before any more time passed and that left only one thing for it. He couldn't risk any more setbacks, not now. Glancing to his left, he saw the lamp just out of arm's reach and so quickly moved closer, and bent to remove the plug from the socket, quietly. A slight click hung on the air for a moment too long and he prayed she hadn't heard the sound. But Julie had.

As she came around the corner, to investigate, he assumed, he raised the lamp high before bringing it down on the base of her skull.

She fell to the floor with a thump. He bent down and checked for a pulse. Murder had not been a part of the plan. He breathed a sigh of relief; it was still there. He lifted her up and laid her on the sofa before racing back outside to his van and driving right up to the building. There wasn't much time, she could stir at any minute, and he contemplated tying her up. With what though?

"Forget it," he scolded himself and, as quickly as he could, loaded the boxes into his van before closing the cellar door and replacing the rug once more. Daring himself, he checked her pulse again, it was there but she was still out cold. She'd have a headache to match any hangover when she came to, likely accompanied by a lump the size of an egg. Needs must.

"Sorry, beautiful woman."

He left the main door unlocked and raced back around to his van where he hoped the sound of the engine starting wouldn't bring her to, not just yet. Give him ten minutes at least. As he drove back down the lane, he glanced a couple of times in his rear-view mirror, half expecting to see her watching his van disappear into the distance, but she never did. Once out onto the main road, he switched the radio on, more to relieve the tension, for something else to fill his head with, than to listen to music as he made his way to his destination. Someone else needed him.

Back inside, Julie lay on the sofa looking to all the world as if she was taking a nap. It was the sound of her own phone ringing that finally raised her from her slumber, and she struggled to orientate herself before crying out at the pain that shot up her neck. By the time she'd realised where she was and what was happening, Chrissy had rung off. She leaned forward, trying to head the nausea off as her stomach rolled. She felt the back of her head where the pain was coming from. A smudge of blood clung to her fingers, just enough to tell her that her skin had been broken. But how? She hadn't seen anyone. Had someone else been inside? What other explanation could there be? She spotted the unplugged lamp lying nearby. Had someone used that on her skull? She remembered the strange click sound, just before it had all gone dark. Her phone rang again and this time she was able to answer it.

"Hi Chrissy," was all she could force out before the pain took over.

"I thought you were going to text me? Are you okay?"

Julie glanced at the time on the phone. It was almost 11 am. She should have been back long ago.

"Sorry, I'm fine. Nothing but blankets and towels in the boxes," she explained, rubbing her temple with her free hand. She had to get out of there. "Listen, I've got to go, we'll talk when you get back." Then she hung up, something she couldn't ever recall doing to her sister. As she stood, the room began to sway, but eventually she gained her balance and made her way outside into fresh air. The blinding bright light stung her eyes and she felt for her sunglasses which were no longer there. They must have been dislodged when she went down. There was no way she was going to leave her Victoria Beckham aviators behind; they were hard enough to come by to be disposed of so easily. Plus, she didn't want to leave any evidence she'd been there, though it appeared somebody else knew she had. She spotted the sunglasses lying on the floor and gingerly knelt to retrieve them before returning them to her head.

That's when she heard it.

CHAPTER 40

Brocc knew well enough that his sister was in trouble and that worried him. She was too old to be getting involved in risky stuff and even though he had no clue what it was, the fact that he'd seen tears in her eyes, and that she'd mentioned perhaps being run off the road, gave him cause for concern. While he wasn't particularly bright in the technology department, he knew that, like many, her life was on her phone and he intended to find out what he could while he had it. He'd no idea what the cloud was apart from those above him in the sky, so he didn't have to put much of an act on when he went to the shop. If he could convince the salesperson he was just an old technophobe with no clue, they might just help him out. He opened the door and went inside. After a few moments of browsing the variety of phones on display, a young man approached him and asked if he could help. Sundip likely knew the answers to everything Brocc wanted to ask. Phone-related at least.

"Broke my phone," was all he said as he pulled it from his pocket still in its plastic bag. "Time for a new one."

Sundip took the phone from him and agreed. While he could probably get the screen replaced, Bronagh didn't want to wait and likely the young man was looking at full commission on a replacement.

"Do you want the same again?" he asked.

"I do," said Brocc as he watched him move to the counter and retrieve a small box with a replacement phone from the shelves behind him. As Brocc approached the desk, he said, "Can you update it for me? I've got the password. It's in the cloud, like."

Sundip smiled, though looked at him a little sceptically. Brocc needed to push a little.

"Only I'm not very good at this technology stuff, would you mind?" He tried a smile, something Brocc didn't offer very often.

"I'll see what I can do," he said and turned the replacement phone on. Brocc watched as he tapped the screen at various prompts. He answered the simple set up questions but when it came time to do the upload, he left the password with the young man and browsed the rest of the shop to keep away from questions he didn't have the answers to.

Looking at the display, he wondered if it was time for a replacement phone of his own. For the amount of money, it seemed a lot for such a small item. His trusty old phone was on its last legs, but he'd seen Jake's back at the garage and knew he could take photographs with it. He'd quite like to be able to do that himself. There were so many birds along the coastline, yet he'd never indulged himself with a camera. He walked back to the counter to see how things were progressing. "I won't set the passcode, so you can do that yourself, but I'll show you how to do it." Brocc watched, even though he knew Bronagh would be able to do it herself.

"And all your calls and texts have transferred across too," he said, tapping each green button in turn to show him. When he'd finished, Brocc handed over his credit card to pay for it then said, "Actually, can I have another one?" Bronagh was right, he rarely spent money on himself, he'd treat himself and have the same one. Sundip looked at him as if he'd just grown an extra head and said, "Sure." Brocc watched as he retrieved another one from the cabinet and placed it on the desk. "Do you want me to set this one up too?"

"Go on so," said Brocc. "But don't do the update."

"Whatever. Do you need a SIM card for this one?"

Brocc had no clue and it showed.

"A telephone number."

Brocc was beginning to catch up a little. "Can I use one I already have, in my old work phone?"

"Yes. Do you have it with you also?"

"No. But I can get the lad to do it for me." That seemed to be enough. Likely pleased at double the commission, Sundip busied himself doing the basic set-up. When everything was complete, Brocc paid for the second phone and left the building feeling quite pleased with himself. He hadn't done too bad. Perhaps Jake could show him how to get his few contacts from his old phone transferred across. He headed to a bench further on down the high street and pulled out Bronagh's new phone. He stared at it, not entirely sure what to do to get into it, then remembered the young man had used his finger to swipe. He had a go.

"Would you look at that," he said and tapped the green telephone icon. The screen filled with the last calls all listed by their names. He didn't recognise any of them as he scrolled through the last few and then went back to the beginning to check the time of the last call. Bronagh hadn't been using her phone at the time of the crash because her last call had been a couple of hours beforehand. He clicked on the text icon and read some of the texts. It didn't feel right snooping, but with Bronagh lying in hospital he wanted to make sure she wasn't in any danger. And he had questions of his own. The texts didn't really say a lot and he didn't recognise the names of those that had sent them. Bronagh appeared to know a good few people. He searched through a dozen or so more and realising there wasn't much of interest, put the phone back in his pocket and carried on back to the car.

As he drove, his brain ticked through what he'd read and the common denominator that each text seemed to have. They talked of delivery and pickup. Was it to do with the shop? He couldn't think she would have so many texts from suppliers about the same thing. He certainly didn't get a text at the garage when a delivery was due. The courier just dropped it off. So, what else could they refer to?

He knew very well it was nothing to do with woollen sweaters.

CHAPTER 41

It was late morning by the time Brocc got back to the hospital and he wondered whether the nurse with a stern face would allow him access to drop the phone off. He'd already asked a favour of her and he suspected he'd have to leave it at her desk, something he didn't want to do. As he approached the ward and opened the door, he peered round before inserting his whole being into the room. He couldn't see her. Maybe she was on her tea break. He did his best to walk across to Bronagh's bed without being seen. At the last minute a young voice called him back. He stopped dead in his tracks, wondering what to say and went with simple.

"I'm just dropping her new phone in. I won't even need to speak to her," he said. The whole exercise would take less than a couple of seconds. What was it with these nurses? She had a frown to match her older colleague's. Brocc again raised his palms in surrender and she tutted and left him to it. Thankful for small mercies, he quickly approached Bronagh's bed and could see she was sleeping. It took no time to retrieve his own old phone and slip her new one into the top drawer of the bedside cabinet. She'd find it later when it rang. At least now she'd have everything she needed to put her mind at ease and stop whatever it was that was troubling her. He'd told the young nurse he wouldn't stay for a moment longer and waved a little, so she knew he'd left the room.

Brocc drove back towards the garage in silence, mulling over what he'd learnt in the last twenty-four hours: a lot, yet not much at all, and what he did know made little sense. He went straight back to the garage and slipped into his overalls. Jake was busy underneath an old Audi and grunted 'hello'. Brocc called him over.

"Need your help, Jake."

The young lad ambled over, sleeves rolled up, black grease up to his elbows, a smudge on his chin, likely from having a cigarette earlier on.

"What do you need?"

Brocc took his new phone out of his pocket. Jake whistled.

"Fancyyyy," he said.

"The shop set it up, but I don't know how to use it, get my numbers in it. Can you show me?"

He wiped his hands down his overalls before taking the brand-new phone in still grubby fingers. Brocc was about to say something, but since it was going to get covered in oil anyway it didn't really matter whether it was his oil or Jake's. The two moved to the small office area that was equally as grimy as the rest of the garage. Brocc sat down on his old swivel chair, Jake on another nearby. "What made you buy such a nice phone?"

"Time for an upgrade. And you can take photos and all with this one."

"You can do a whole lot more than take photos with a smart-phone," said Jake. "Here, I'll give you the whistle-stop tour. He wheeled himself across to meet Brocc's chair and show him more closely. After ten minutes, Brocc knew the basics of taking a photograph, a video, sending a text, and making a call, as well as a couple of other things that he'd no doubt forget and never use in the lifetime of the phone. One thing he was pleased about was that he could use his phone as a torch, so when the light bulb outside his house went again, at least he'd be able see where to put the key in the lock. It was the small things that pleased him, that's just how Brocc Bowen was.

When the lesson was complete, and his few contacts were added, he checked the time, and hoped Bronagh would be awake. He dialled the number and waited. After three or four rings her voice filled his ears and the first thing she said was 'thank you'. He smiled. The simple things.

"Do you need me to bring anything later?" he said.

"No, thank you. I'm hopefully leaving here tomorrow, so I'll be back home fairly soon. There's no need to come back today, but perhaps call in the morning? I should know more then."

"Will you manage at home?"

"I'm sure I will. It's only a broken leg. Plenty of people have them and manage so why can't I? My wrist won't be a problem."

Brocc grunted. He'd be the same, not one for hanging around lying in bed. He liked to get on with the day and Bronagh was no different. Plus, she had a business to run. He thought for a moment about the deliveries.

"Are you expecting any deliveries at the shop?" he asked.

Did he imagine the pause before she answered?

"No deliveries expected," she said and left it at that.

Satisfied, he said goodbye and slipped his own phone in his pocket and felt for his keys. He had one on his keychain for the shop as well as for Bronagh's house. The pebble was still there also, and he thought about the child that should have been in his cot. Where was the boy now?

"Be back shortly," he called to Jake, who was now busy back under the Audi.

CHAPTER 42

No sooner had Julie collected her sunglasses than she heard the sound of a vehicle approaching. Had he come back? If she tried to leave now, whoever it was would undoubtedly see her, but she didn't fancy staying put either. Could it be that whoever had whacked her on the head had returned, perhaps to cart her away, never to be seen again? The more she thought of various scenarios, the more frightened she got. No, there was no way they were going to take her trussed up like an oven-ready chicken.

"Steady on, Julie," she said quietly to herself, needing convincing.

She staggered off the couch and went straight to one of the narrow windows to peer out. There was a van, but it wasn't the same size or model as the one from during the night. Was it the same driver though? She waited the extra moment and noticed it was a much older man, not the tall blond from the bar, the one that had almost locked Chrissy in the van with the boxes. This one looked like someone's father, or even grandfather if you were young enough. Dressed in casual manual-work clothes, he walked hunched over, his face rough from the elements. His stomach told her he liked a pint or two. He made his way over to the front door and Julie tried her best to blend into the wall, her plan being to dart outside when he'd gone either way, the kitchen or the living room. She could only hope he didn't catch her in his peripheral vision as she ran back towards the holiday home. That aspect could prove tricky but, sizing the man up, she figured even her small feet could move faster than his old ones. She stayed pressed back against the cool stone and closed her eyes like a ten-year-old. If she couldn't see him, he couldn't see her either. At the last minute, she remembered the lamp still lay nearby and reached to grab it. She held it tight in her right hand and resumed her position as the door creaked open. Through closed eyelids, she could just make out the change in light as more sunshine filled the room. She held her breath and prayed that whoever it was left the door open so she could flee.

It wasn't going to be her day. What felt like a lifetime was only a few seconds as the figure made his way into the living room where she was hiding in plain sight, and Julie did the only thing she could think of under the circumstances. She raised the lamp base high above her head and prepared to let it crash down against the intruder's head. Whether the sun caught it she'd never know, but the bright reflection caught Brocc's eye and he turned just in time to avoid getting a cracked skull. Quick as a flash, he raised a strong meaty arm and caught the lamp base before it could make contact. Julie screamed as she realised he held a firm grip on it and wasn't for letting go, her hand clamped next to his. She prepared for the worst and with scrunched-up eyes, waited for yet another blow to her head. A moment later and she tentatively opened them, coming face-to-face with the older man with wizened skin. He looked like a farmhand, but her nose picked up grease. A closer look at his fingernails as he grasped the lamp base in front of her gave more of a clue to his occupation. Mechanic of some kind. She dared herself to speak since neither had yet said a word.

"Are you going to hurt me again?" She knew she sounded feeble.

"Again?" Confused.

"You hit me earlier, with that lamp base," she said, pointing a pale pink fingernail.

"Not me. Who are you? What's your business here?" He lowered the lamp base onto the nearby table, out of arm's reach for either of them. Since she'd still no idea who the man was and what he wanted, Julie wondered how much to tell him.

"Julie Stokes. And you?" She may as well try and get some details. Chrissy would be proud.

"Brocc. Where do you fit into all this?"

That explained the grease, she'd seen the sign for Brocc's garage in the village. "I'm not sure I fit in at all actually."

"Makes two of us," he mumbled.

"So, who was here earlier then, the one that hit me?"

"No idea. Nothing to do with me." Trying again, he asked, "So what's your business here then?"

Julie let out a long sigh. There was something about the older man that she felt she could trust, maybe it was his worldly wise eyes. Plus, he hadn't used the lamp base on her, even though he could have.

"Before I tell you, do you know anything about the child or his parents?"

Brocc frowned, pulled up a hard-backed chair and sat down. Julie followed, resumed her place on the sofa.

"All I know is he's gone. I've no idea what 'this' is, but I was asked to check on him. Boy was gone when I got here." That must have been yesterday, Julie correctly surmised, after Chrissy had brought him and Rupert home. Where was that dog anyway?

"And the parents?" she asked.

"Don't know anything else. So, where do you fit in?"

Julie watched the man carefully as she spoke, looking for any sign of recognition or otherwise. "My sister found him alone yesterday. He's with the authorities now. The Gardai took him away, to a foster home, I expect."

Brocc nodded at the news. At least the boy was safe.

"The parents? Know anything about them?"

"Nothing. One minute they were here on holiday, then they'd

vanished. We met them on Saturday night at the pub and they seemed decent enough."

Since Brocc still wore a look of confusion, she was confident he couldn't possibly be involved. "How about you, where do you fit in?"

He stayed silent for a moment and Julie was about to repeat the question when he spoke.

"There's something going on. No idea what. But I know someone that does."

"Have you asked them?" Julie asked excitedly. "A little boy was abandoned for heaven's sake."

"I have. She won't say anything. Believe me, I wish she would."

"Then talk to the police, I mean Gardai?"

"Can't do that."

"Why not?"

Brocc paused before adding, "Because she's my sister."

Julie couldn't imagine giving Chrissy up to the police no matter what, so there was no point asking this man to either. But the child?

"So, what did you come for just now then?" Julie asked.

"Don't know really. Another look."

"Me too. Morbid curiosity, I suppose. And to look in the cellar." She could have kicked herself for adding the last part. While he seemed non-threatening enough, she had no clue who he was really. Or what he was capable of.

"What's in the cellar?" he asked.

Should she say? He could just look for himself, and since she wasn't going to knock him out with the lamp base, there was no point in not telling him.

"Boxes of belongings – sheets, towels, and the like. In removal-type boxes."

That confused him even more as he chewed on his upper lip. Could those be the deliveries Bronagh's texts had talked about? Boxes of belongings? If so, what were they for and why the secrets? It still didn't explain the child. He needed to press harder with his sister if he was going to sleep at night. A child now in care and its parents gone: it wasn't the usual run-of-the-mill situation he found himself involved in. It didn't sit right with him. Julie, realising there was nothing else to be gleaned from the man, stood to go; she'd been gone way too long.

"I'll leave you to it."

Brocc nodded silently and let her pass before standing in the doorway to watch her go.

Back outside, Rupert padded across and she grabbed his leash and led him home, back towards the house, sifting through her conversation with the older man. She eventually turned her attention to what she might say if Richard asked where she'd been for so long. Hopefully Agatha had kept him entertained and a lamp hadn't been used in that particular story. It had been used twice today already.

She needed to talk to Chrissy.

CHAPTER 43

Adam and Chrissy were sitting upon a grassy knoll on the cliff. The Atlantic Ocean crashed below against weather-beaten grey rocks, the noise almost therapeutic in its rhythm but not noisy enough to drown out their conversation. Between the wind, the gulls, and the water, it was a scene off any movie, likely a love story but Chrissy's mind was on anything but romance. As she gazed out to the silvery water on the horizon, the wind flicked her hair back and forth and she scraped it out of her eyes before taking another bite from an egg mayonnaise sandwich. Adam could see her faraway look and said, "Penny for them?"

"Sorry?" she enquired.

"You're miles away."

"That obvious, eh?" she said.

"I've known you long enough. So yes, that obvious. I'm guessing it's the child?"

"What else *could* it be?" she said, "I feel so sorry for him. I just hope that he's not in the system for too long and his parents are found sooner than later, whatever the consequences."

"Well, since they abandoned him, he's likely to be taken into care anyway."

"I know. I just hope that he finds somewhere decent. You hear of such terrible stories."

Adam shuffled along closer and tucked into his own sandwich, chewed thoughtfully for a moment before adding, "The majority are well cared for, I'm sure. The system isn't totally broken, and yes, you hear stories, but they are the minority, only a small amount, thankfully. The few that fall through the cracks as it were. Maybe in the past things were really bad, but not these days. We've had too many reforms in recent years and I'm sure Ireland will be just the same in that regard."

"I hope you're right," she said. The pair sat in silence for a moment or two, gazing way out to sea, enjoying each other's company and the solitude. Chrissy's mind was still wandering.

"Did you ever see a car at the castle? Lorcan and Ciara's?"

Adam thought for a moment and said, "I don't think so now you come to mention it. Why do you ask?"

"Because they're on an extended holiday, so they must've come from somewhere. We know he's a lorry driver, yet I don't remember seeing a car or any other vehicle."

"Well, they left somehow," said Adam.

"Did someone pick them up, perhaps?"

"Possibly, yes, I suppose. But the question remains, why didn't they take Flynn with them?"

"I've been wondering about that too," she said. "The only thing I can think of is maybe he's not theirs?"

Adam turned to Chrissy, gobsmacked. "Oh come on, Chrissy. How can he not be? What, you think he was borrowed in some way? For what, exactly?" Adam, visibly astonished at her notion, stopped chewing as he stared back at her.

"I know it sounds a bit of a stretch, but what parent leaves a child behind anyway?"

"A desperate one," said Adam.

"Desperate about what though? And then there's the small matter of the wicker coffins," she added, wagging a finger in his face, "in their cellar."

Adam put the remains of his sandwich back in the tub. "Are you going to spend all holiday thinking about this? I thought we were away having a break."

"Yes, I know, though it's hard not to think about it. Plus, it kind of fell in our lap, didn't it?"

"No, it didn't actually, Chrissy. The police are looking into it and the boy is in care, so the whole thing has nothing to do with any of us, it's none of our concern. No laps needed." He sounded final in his words and Chrissy knew when to keep quiet, a disagreement they didn't need. She reached for the flask and poured each of them a cup of warm coffee and they sipped in silence, once again looking out over the ocean. It was an idyllic spot just off the path where a few stragglers walked by braving the cold and the wind. The ocean view made up for it. She was thankful for their warm jackets and sheltered spot. It was the perfect place to stop and enjoy for a while.

She wondered about Julie and her visit to the castle. There was something about the way she'd spoken, distracted almost. Why? Or was she imagining it? There was no way she was going to share with Adam that they'd been snooping in the cellar, not the night-time visit and not Julie's daytime visit either. Boxes of second-hand bedding and the like, it got weirder and weirder. It made no sense. Letting out a deep sigh, she changed her thoughts to something else. Adam was right. They were supposed to be away on a relaxing break and with Richard hurting his shoulder and ankle, the holiday had already taken a turn of its own. Never mind. They were going out for afternoon tea to Father Ted's place later on. Maybe she should forget all about the castle, the boy, and the cellar, let the Guards do their job and concentrate on enjoying the last few days away. Work would be back on the agenda soon enough. Question was, could she do it?

With their picnic lunch finished, Chrissy collected up their few things and put them in the rucksack.

"I guess we should head back," she said, standing. The wind had picked up another couple of notches and the temperature had dropped while they'd been enjoying their picnic and both felt the urge to get back to their warm car as quickly as possible. They set off back towards the visitor centre at a brisk pace.

"I bet Richard's been bored silly," said Adam. "Not much of a holiday for him."

"Oh, I don't know. He seems quite content, I think. Richard isn't really one for much activity anyway, group or otherwise. It's probably been a godsend for him, sitting reading in peace."

"Yeah, but there's Julie to think of. She didn't want to come out with us today, play gooseberry, three's a crowd, and there's only so much gossip even she can read in a magazine."

Chrissy, of course, knew exactly what Julie had been doing, though nipping back to the castle wouldn't take long. She couldn't wait to catch up with her, maybe there was something that she hadn't mentioned on the call. Her voice had certainly told her she was distracted, and Chrissy had got the impression she'd wanted to get her off the phone. The question loomed again: why? Feeling the need to know sooner than later, Chrissy suddenly said, "Race you back to the car," and set off at a fast jog, leaving Adam to struggle with an awkward backpack and catch her up. So much for thinking about something else.

CHAPTER 44

Chrissy eventually slowed down to wait and the pair walked back at a fair pace instead. In a little under two hours they reached the visitor centre and their hire car. Adam touched it first and declared he was the winner, and Chrissy let him have his moment. She tossed his backpack onto the back seat and got into the driver's side. She wanted to be in control – no detours. Right now there was an urgency to get back to the house and speak to Julie. If Adam was driving, he'd be tempted to digress somewhere and she couldn't have that, not today. She struggled out of her jacket, the car toasty from the sun. She checked her appearance in the rear-view mirror, her cheeks glowed pink from being wind-whipped in the fresh air, her hair loose tangles. At least it hadn't rained though. She looked up through the windscreen at the threatening clouds that were tightly squashed together in the sky. They'd likely burst sometime later on in the day, it was October after all. Once they were tucked up inside at Father Ted's for afternoon tea, it could do what it wanted.

"We made good pace," said Chrissy. "By the time we get back and changed we'll be about ready to set off for the second activity of the day," she said, smiling.

"I hope you are enjoying your holiday," Adam said, looking at her somewhat sideways. He didn't sound too convinced.

"Of course I am. Why wouldn't I be?"

"Well, like I said earlier about you getting wrapped up in something, I want you to have a nice break too, both mentally and physically."

"I'm relaxed," she said. "Don't worry about me. I promise you I'll be going home happy as Larry." She hoped she believed it.

With them both safely seat-belted in, Chrissy pulled out of the car park and headed back towards home. Since it was only a short drive, by the time they arrived back, they'd had a change of subject and were planning the evening's entertainment. Adam was keen to eat somewhere different, having been to the pub a couple of times now. "Maybe we should let Richard and Julie choose for a change. I think we've chosen the pub twice, haven't we?" he asked.

"I fear if Julie gets her say we'll be fine dining with white linen tablecloths and dressed in our fancy clothes and quite honestly, I'm just enjoying casual, aren't you?"

"I am, but if we do white tablecloths one night then at least it's done."

As they neared their holiday rental, they could see the vivid pink of Julie's jacket. She was sitting outside on the deck. In the cold.

"I wonder why she's not indoors. It's bit chilly now," said Chrissy.

"I'll never understand your sister," said Adam light-heartedly. Chrissy parked up and they grabbed their belongings and headed inside. Richard met them at the back door. "Great timing," he said. "I was just about to make some tea. Anyone want some?"

"Me please," chimed Adam and Chrissy in unison. She glanced at the clock on the cooker. They'd got about half an hour before they needed to leave. It was a forty-minute drive to the farmhouse, the scene of Father Ted's.

"Where's Julie?" asked Richard.

"She's out on the deck," said Chrissy, and at that moment Julie entered the doorway, wrapped up in a coat and woolly scarf.

"There you are," said Richard. "I wondered where you'd got to, you've been gone ages."

The sentence wasn't lost on Chrissy and she glanced at her sister who caught her eye.

"I've got a headache and I thought sitting outside in the fresh air might help it disappear." She looked pale around her eyes, and Chrissy could see she was in pain.

"Have you had a painkiller?" asked Chrissy. "Or more kumbaya?"

"Painkiller actually, though it's not shifting it."

"If you're not feeling well, do we need to cancel this afternoon?" Richard enquired.

"No," she said faintly. "I'll be fine."

Chrissy didn't look persuaded, but Julie was an adult and could decide for herself. She'd been the one that had suggested afternoon tea in the first place. "We can easily do it tomorrow," Chrissy tried again.

"I'm fine really. Just a headache," she said with a little more snap than usual.

It wasn't like her to grumble and it hadn't gone unnoticed by the others as she strode from the room and headed through to the living room and beyond. No one in the kitchen said anything, but everyone felt it. Richard, ever the diplomat asked, "Did you have a nice picnic?" as he opened the fridge and pulled out bread and cheese.

"Have you not eaten?" Chrissy asked without answering his question first.

"I was waiting for Julie then I got engrossed in my book and didn't realise what time it was."

"She's been gone all this time?" said Chrissy. "That really isn't like her."

He shrugged his shoulders, "I don't how long she's been sitting outside with a headache. Like I say, I was engrossed in my book."

"Well, I'll go and get changed ready and then we should go. I'll check on Julie," she offered, glancing across to Adam that he should stay away from the conversation. He took the message. Richard, oblivious, buttered his bread and laid cheese on one slice. Chrissy took the opportunity and disappeared to find her sister and gently knocked on the bedroom door. She peered her head round to look inside. Julie was sitting on the bed nursing the back of her head.

"Are you really all right?" Chrissy asked.

Julie swung round. "I said I'm fine." Chrissy made her way over, sat down next to her and put her arm around her shoulders.

"I know when you're not fine. So why don't you tell me what happened?" Chrissy said gently.

She stayed silent for a moment or two and then said simply, "I feel a bit of a fool."

"Oh?"

"Somebody came to the castle."

"What!"

"I know. As I was coming out of the cellar, walking into the living room, someone whacked me from behind with a lamp base." She pointed to the back of her head as if Chrissy could see the exact spot.

"Heavens, somebody hit you?" Poor Julie. She wasn't built for dealing with aggro.

"Knocked me out cold. I woke up on the sofa. That's why I've been gone ages. I don't how long I was out for."

"Did you see anyone?"

"No, and it gets worse, or better, depending on your view."

"How so?"

"Because then I spoke to you and as the call ended, I heard a vehicle, so I hid in case it was somebody coming back to finish me off. I ended up almost attacking someone else."

"Someone else?"

"Yes, but it wasn't the man that attacked me the first time. I say man, I'm assuming it was a man, but this was another man, the man from the garage. He's called Brocc. I almost knocked him out." Chrissy was having trouble following which man was which.

"How do you know he's not involved in whatever is going on?"

"Because he told me he wasn't, and I believe him. But he did say his sister is involved and even though he's pressed her, she won't say what."

"I'd like to know what it all means."

"He's not going to the Gardai because it's his sister, says he can't do that to her."

"So, let me get this straight, somebody knocked you out and you tried to knock someone else out?"

"Yes."

Chrissy thought for a moment, but it didn't make sense. "You looked in the cellar before you were knocked out?"

"Yes."

"Did you check again after you'd been knocked out?"

"No, why would I?"

"Just curious. And then this other chap from the garage, he's not involved. What was he doing there then?"

"His sister had told him to look in on Flynn, get the boy a bottle, and when he got to the castle, he was already gone. We'd already found him that morning. He said he just felt he needed to go back and take another look – curiosity, I suppose. A bit like us."

Chrissy blew her cheeks out at the news of yet another person entering the picture. The mystery was growing in size with every day that passed by.

CHAPTER 45

Maureen did the calculations in her head before responding to the vague group text. She hadn't got any plans for the evening and wasn't due to be back on the road again until the following night shift anyway, so she had oodles of time to oblige and then get some rest before work. Not waiting to see if anybody else responded, she quickly tapped a message saying she would do the pickup. A moment later a regular location popped onto her screen. It was in Liverpool, one she was quite familiar with, one just on the outskirts of the city. She checked her watch; it was already getting late. The message informed her the destination was Dublin which meant she needed to have the package on the 2.30 am ferry out of Holyhead. It was too late for anything any earlier. Three hours on the ferry, then someone else would meet her to offload it, allowing her to drive straight back. The message said no paperwork. Maureen hated that aspect; it was far riskier if she got caught, but still, this was her way of giving a little back. She quickly tapped a reply that she had received instructions, and all was good at her end, before going upstairs to grab the few things she needed for an overnight bag.

Maureen had worked out on the road for many years, enjoyed

the quality time alone with her own thoughts and music, and when she was feeling a little more sociable, she picked up the odd hitch-hiker along the way. A masculine-looking woman with close-cropped grey hair, she had tattoos of various domestic animals around her arms and, by her own description, sported a duvet-covered body shape. She was a regular up and down the motorway networks, stopping at service café's, and lately on the ferry crossing across to Dublin and back. Call it a hobby. With no one sitting at home waiting for her to return, her time was her own. She took a can of Coke from the fridge and a couple of energy bars and stuffed them into her bag before grabbing a jacket and leaving. It would be almost lunchtime the following day before she'd get back home for a proper rest but that didn't worry her. She headed out to her car, drove to the lock-up nearby, swapped to the van, and made her way across to Liverpool and the pickup. No paperwork was far riskier but once they'd made their decision to leave and a rendezvous was set, there was precious little time to do anything about it. They left with no possessions, no bag, no ID, no nothing. Another member of the team will have organised to get them to the address she was now heading to, before they were passed over to Maureen and her network, and beyond.

Immigration could be tricky, but after so many successful cross-ings, they had their system down pat and she'd never been stopped yet. It was always in the back of her mind though, there was always a first time. It was worth the risk though. People have been smug-gled across borders since time began almost and it was Maureen's job to make sure they got across safely without any interest from the authorities. Their current set-up was working a treat.

An hour later she pulled up at an old warehouse in Liverpool. She knew the collection point well and pulled in through the old metal gates which were open, waiting for her. She spotted the light on in one of the old outbuildings and headed towards it, reversing up to the door ready for collection. She wound her window down, popped her head out and nodded to a silhouette as the man loaded the cargo in the back. No one said a word. No one needed to. A thump on the rear door told her she was ready to go. Maureen waited while a passenger jumped up into the seat beside her and nodded his greeting. She pulled out of the dark warehouse grounds and headed out to the motorway and on towards Holyhead. It would be a couple of hours' drive, but at least there was little traffic and they would be in plenty of time to catch the early ferry. Finally, when they'd been travelling for about an hour, her passenger said, "I hope you didn't have plans for this evening?"

"Hardly ever have plans," answered Maureen. Her deep, gravelly voice sounded almost male and she coughed a little as if for emphasis. While she'd never smoked a cigarette in her life, the many years of second-hand smoke in the bars she'd worked in had played havoc with her lungs.

It was coming up to 1 am when they finally hit the port at Holyhead and parked the van in the loading queue. This was the bit she hated the most. While she and her passenger had their own documents, her cargo didn't. Over the years though, she'd perfected her poker face and the contents of her van had never received more than a cursory glance. Wicker storage bins weren't of much interest to anyone and that was why it had been designed that way. Tonight was no different and at 2.30 am on the dot, the ferry pulled away from Holyhead harbour and headed out on the Irish Sea towards Dublin. By 6 am, they would be rolling off and on to their next organised destination where her cargo would be handed over and she would be free to return back home.

CHAPTER 46

Maureen drove to the assembly point, one of three they used not far outside Dublin Harbour itself. It was yet another remote and disused warehouse, so there would be no prying eyes to witness what went on. It was early, most people still in their warm beds, as she prepared for the swap. She had hardly slept on these journeys, there was no time for it, but there would be an opportunity for a nap on the return ferry. A long yawn told her she needed it.

As she pulled into the yard, she spotted the van easily and pulled up alongside it. It was identical to the one she was driving. A man she had seen on many occasions got out of the driver's seat and she got out of her own. The two exchanged brief pleasantries, nothing more. She watched as he swapped over the vehicle registration plates before climbing into the other van. When her old plates were attached to the new van, she was ready to go, but she paused for a moment to make sure that the first vehicle drove away with its cargo before her. They would be heading in a very different direction. She was back on her own now, her passenger with the new driver as they moved on through Ireland and ultimately to their destination. It made her smile; she hoped her earlier cargo made a go of it without having to watch over their shoulder for the months to come. Things always settled down for them, but the start, she knew, could be rough.

Maureen made her way back towards the port to wait for the 8 am ferry. There was plenty of time to get something to eat and drink, so she pulled in at a nearby service station that she often used. It was her treat, her celebration of another swap-over successfully completed. She high-fived the steering wheel before getting out.

When the van was about half an hour out from the port of Dublin, it pulled over in its designated lay-by, a quiet one again, where no one would be overlooking. The passenger slipped out, opened the rear door and entered the back of the van. He spoke quietly, knowing the stranger would be able to hear him as he removed the lid from one of the wicker coffins. Inside lay a man of about forty years old.

"You can get out now. I hope the journey wasn't too arduous?" He offered the man a hand to pull him up and generally gather his bearings before the passenger suggested he sit up front with himself and the driver.

"Bet you need to pee," he asked, smiling.

"I do," he said, and made his way over to the hedgerow where he relieved himself. The other two watched as the man stretched out his shoulders and shook his legs out individually. Being confined to a coffin for several hours wouldn't be fun or comfortable but their system worked, that was the important thing. Once he was seated, the passenger handed him a sandwich and a bottle of water. He'd be hungry and thirsty after his journey, having been told not to drink anything for several hours prior to his pickup. They couldn't risk a mess in the van, it was too dangerous for all concerned.

"How are you feeling?" the passenger asked.

"Glad the worst is over." He spoke with a certain finality in his voice that said he didn't want to talk about it, but there was no mistaking the relief that he was on his way to a new life. The worst indeed was now behind him, the rest he could cope with. "How far have we got to go?

"A couple of hours," said the passenger. "Everything will be ready for you. A lot of work goes into this."

"And I appreciate it," he said. "I really do." He sounded weary, though it wasn't from the lack of sleep. Every one of their 'packages' sounded the same at first, worn out from the stress of it all and anxious to get on with the next stage. They rarely felt like talking. The rest of the journey passed by in silence apart from local radio chatting away in the background, nobody really listening to it. It filled the usual void. The job almost over, the destination almost in sight, the 'package' almost delivered.

At mid-morning, they pulled up at a small bungalow in a town somewhere in southern Ireland. The man had no idea where he was, and he didn't much care. It was only temporary until he could move on again. The driver pulled the van down the side of the of the property where it would be tucked away out of sight of the main road. Not that there was much traffic, but again it was better to be cautious and away from prying eyes that they didn't need. The passenger turned to the man and said, "Everything you need is inside. The key is under the mat. Someone will contact you shortly and be around at lunchtime to see if you need anything else and give you your new contact details. The best thing you can do now is sleep for a while and wait for the call. There will be a phone inside."

Behind the front door lay his new life and he approached it feeling lighter than he had done in many months. Things could only get better from now on and he couldn't help the smile that pulled at his lips. It was the first one in a long time.

CHAPTER 47

Elliott Wilson looked at the sparse surroundings of his new home. It had all happened so quickly, but he'd got out and what stood in front of him was now his, for a while at least. Everything he needed was here, as he'd been told it would be, and he couldn't have been more grateful. There were clothes in the cupboard, second-hand, but that didn't matter. There was food in the fridge. Magazines and books would keep him entertained and an older TV sat in the corner. He walked through to the master bedroom, where he'd be sleeping, though it wasn't much of a master. A large single bed filled the room along with basic furniture that had seen better days. It was functional, that's all he needed. It was the same set-up in the other bedroom. He wondered what she'd be like when she arrived.

A phone that sat on the kitchen counter would presumably ring at some point during the day and he'd find out the next steps of his life. The house felt chilly. Likely nobody had lived in it for a while and it reminded him of his grandma's place when he'd visited not long after she'd passed. It had felt like its soul had died along with her. He glanced around the rest of the small property, reaching out to touch various items as he went. Everything was used. The curtains, the towels, everything he touched had had a previous owner, a previous life, much like himself.

"I think we'll get along just fine," he said to the empty room and made his way back to the master bedroom. Elliott found some sleepwear and then headed to the bathroom to freshen up. It had been a long journey and it had played with his mind somewhat, being smuggled across the border in a wicker coffin. But the team had assured him they'd never been caught, never once been questioned and Elliott wondered about that. Perhaps they had a contact at the ferry terminal, someone that turned a blind eye when needed. It wasn't his concern though and he shook the question from his head. He turned the shower on and was grateful it had decent pressure.

Soon enough the small room filled with warming steam and he stepped under the water, letting it cascade over his head and shoulders, washing grime, tears, and a previous life away. His nostrils filled with pine from the supermarket shampoo and he scrubbed himself clean with a new vigour. By the time he stepped out to dry himself, he felt a whole lot better. He knew he'd made the right decision, no matter how painful it had been at the time, and everything was going to be just fine. Slipping into fresh pyjamas, he retrieved the new mobile phone from the kitchen then slipped in between the sheets. Deep sleep engulfed him almost immediately.

It was about four hours later when he was disturbed by the sound of a phone ringing and he struggled to sit up in bed and orientate himself. It took him a moment to remember. "Hello, Elliott" he answered. It was a woman on the other end. She had a soothing Irish accent and sounded pleasant enough as she said, "Don't you mean Ronan?" There was a slight ripple of laughter at the end of the question. "No bother," she added, "I'm teasing."

He felt groggy and Elliott rubbed his eyes in an effort to try and grasp what she was saying. He switched the phone to the other ear, as if that was going to make any difference in understanding what was going on.

"Sorry," he said.

"I hope you managed some rest," she said with more Irish lilt. "I'll be there in an hour. Does that suit?"

What else was he going to do? Since he had nothing else planned, he may as well get moving with things. "An hour is fine," he said. "I'm guessing you know where to come?"

The same light laugh filled his ears and made him smile for the second time in one day. He was beginning to get the hang of it.

"Of course. Can I bring you anything? Maybe something you're missing?" He'd gone straight to bed almost and hadn't looked through his new belongings in any detail, nor the kitchen cupboards. He suddenly fancied a fresh coffee.

"Maybe a cup of strong coffee if you pass somewhere?"

"I can do that. In the meantime, don't answer the door to anyone. When I arrive, I'll knock four times, okay?"

"Got it."

"See you shortly." The line went dead.

Almost an hour to the minute later, there were four taps on the door and Elliott approached it feeling a good deal more awake than he had earlier. Dressed in faded jeans and a sweatshirt, he looked more like an advert for the Salvation Army than *GQ Magazine* but at least he was clean and felt human again. He could see a female silhouette on the other side of the glass panel and so pulled open the door. The woman had a bright smile, a perfect match for the voice he'd heard on the phone earlier. Wavy brown hair stopped just below her jawline, and trendy plastic glasses perched on her tiny nose. She looked about the same age as he was.

"Hello, please come in," he said, stumbling a little on his words as he opened the door wider for her. He'd get used to it all in time he was sure. She held out the coffee cup and Elliott took it, taking a long drink, cherishing the strong flavour within.

"You look like you needed that," she said, making her way through to the living room.

"Please, take a seat," he offered.

Elliott sat opposite her, waiting for whatever came next. He felt as if he were in a game of some sort, and one that he didn't know the rules of, the steps, the way things worked. He waited for his instructions.

"My things are in the car outside, I'll bring them in shortly, but I wanted to sit and chat to you for a while first, if that's all right?"

"I have no expectations, no knowledge on what happens from here, so you're the leader in that respect," he said. "You tell me what happens next."

"You start your new life is what happens next. Though you can't go calling yourself Elliott any longer. From this moment on you're Ronan. Elliott has gone."

He nodded his understanding. She pulled out an envelope and slipped the contents into her hand and passed him his new identity. It was so small. "You've got a driver's licence in the name of Ronan Walsh, but no passport, there wasn't time and you shouldn't need one yet anyway. Photo ID is enough for local and I don't suppose you'll be holidaying in Spain quite yet." He shook his head, 'no'. He sipped the rest of his coffee.

"There will be someone coming with a few more boxes, and he'll be here around 6 pm. I'll give him a hand. You need to stay indoors for the time being."

"Right."

"I'll be with you most of the time, as part of your new set up, and we'll work on you during that time. I must warn you though, you may find it quite intense, but experience tells us it's worth it. We'll have plenty of breaks to begin with. As time progresses, you'll be allowed outside. How does that sound?"

"Fine by me. I'm happy to get going. I just hope I can keep up."

"You'll be fine, I'm sure." There was that bright smile again, and it put him at ease. He was beginning to like the woman already.

When it was clear they'd finished talking for the time being, 'Ronan' stood and suggested she bring her things in. As they headed towards the door, he asked, "So, you know I'm Ronan, what's your name?"

"It's Ciara," she said.

CHAPTER 48

Adam had chosen to drive over to Father Ted's house and Chrissy hadn't tried to dissuade him. Not that it was called Father Ted's since it was a private residence. Glanquin Farmhouse was its local name and it sat proudly in the small town of Lackareagh, about forty minutes' drive from where they were staying. Since Adam was driving, he'd decided to take the more scenic route rather than the direct, choosing instead to have a look around some of the smaller villages as they passed through. It had added about ten minutes more to the journey and by the time they'd finished their detour Julie's head was well and truly buzzing, the painkillers from earlier not making a dent. Chrissy glanced across at her sister, they were on the back seat together, and could see that she was still in pain. Knowing the full story that she'd been whacked on the back of the head, she wondered if her sister perhaps had a concussion and whether she should take her to hospital to get checked out. Not that they'd be able to do anything but instruct her to rest. And how was she going to do that without raising suspicions with both Adam and Richard? Maybe she could say she'd had a fall, hit her head. Julie glanced across and gave her a weak smile as Chrissy reached out for her hand and stroked the back of it gently for a moment.

"Not long now," said Adam, catching Chrissy's eye in the rear-view mirror. Maybe he'd seen the exchange between the two sisters.

The scenery was sparse and they hit the last small village before turning up a road that was almost single-lane width and looked like many others out in the country. The colour of the stone walls gave the place a look and feel of Derbyshire perhaps, with its mainly limestone walls, though any stone was used in these parts. The colours matched the sky with darker variations of grey on one side of the stone to the other, just like the ever-thickening clouds above. Overgrown brambles and mixed shrubbery lined the narrow lane, muddy gateways gave farmers a place to pull in, and a handful of almost derelict dwellings looked like they'd been there forever. As they neared their destination, the once white wrought-iron entranceway held a sign that informed them it was a private residence and visits were by appointment only. Adam turned up the unsealed driveway and headed for the huge two-storey house in the distance. Chrissy counted three chimney stacks though suspected the place was stone cold inside. She shivered. There didn't appear to be anything else around and indeed it stood looking out as if it was on Craggy Island. The whole place looked bleak. Kind of Emily Brontë-ish. Heathcliff wouldn't have looked out of place stood by the door.

"It looks quite foreboding," said Julie from the back seat as they approached. Adam pulled into the small car park and waited for everyone to get out. There wasn't much to see from the front entrance. The building stood on its own, surrounded by deep green fields where a handful of woolly sheep grazed the grass to a neat carpet length. They headed inside the huge, old Georgian-style property and immediately it wasn't hard to see the place didn't look any different than on the TV show. Dark wooden floors, white sash windows with oak-coloured wooden panels to either side, sofas with throws over them. It didn't look like anything had changed from the set but that was the point. Chrissy glanced around at the other visitors that were enjoying their afternoon tea, some taking selfies of themselves by the fireplace Father Ted himself had stood next to on many occasions. Adam slipped his arm around her shoulder and they made it known to the receptionist that they had a booking. As soon as they were seated, Chrissy offered Julie more painkillers and she waited for a glass of water before taking them. Since it had been her idea to take afternoon tea, it was a shame she couldn't enjoy the experience properly. The likelihood of them returning to this particular part of Ireland in the future was almost non-existent.

It turned out to be a fairly arduous event for Julie, who all but picked at her food, before throwing up what little she had consumed in the ladies. She returned sweaty and shaking, and the four decided it best to beat a hasty retreat back home. Julie wouldn't be going out later, whether there were white linen table-cloths or not.

She rested her head in Chrissy's lap as they took the main route back home. Adam offered to cook and suggested they drop Julie back at the house before going off in search of supplies, and Chrissy volunteered to go with him. Everyone seemed happy with the plan of a quiet night in and another casual dinner. Julie blamed it on a migraine and would likely go straight to bed with her eye mask. Sleep and a dark room was all she needed.

After dropping Richard and Julie at home, Chrissy and Adam headed back out, for the town of Ennistymon. For Chrissy, it was the second time in one day, with her earlier visit to the Guards, and she directed Adam to a grocery store she'd noticed earlier, hoping they would get everything they needed in the one place since it was touch and go anywhere else would be open. It was hardly Englefield Green with its late-night Tesco and the like.

They were in luck as they pulled up out the front and the two headed inside to see what they could find to create a casual meal from. Or that Adam could create a meal from. Fifteen minutes later they were back in the car, two bags of supplies loaded and heading back, Chrissy munching through a packet of salt and vinegar crisps, passing occasional ones to Adam which he clamped with his lips then crunched as he drove along. They were almost at Doolin when a van caught Chrissy's eye as it turned into a property just ahead of them. Could it be...?

"Pull over!" she instructed urgently as she turned back to look over her shoulder.

"What's up?" Adam asked as he slowed to a standstill. Chrissy stayed silent as she watched the van drive down the side of the house. A tall man got out and headed to the side entrance door.

He had blond curly hair. The barman. Again.

"Chrissy?"

"Can you pull back around, drive back the other way? Just for a minute."

Knowing he wouldn't get an answer as to why he should if he asked, he did a U-turn and headed past the house she appeared to be interested in. He saw the van, but nothing else.

"Are you going to tell me what this is about?"

She could hear an ounce of frustration in his voice. She watched the barman undo the back of the van and retrieve a large box. He took it inside.

"I thought I recognised someone, that's all," she said, smiling and dismissing his question. "Sorry, let's get back."

Adam didn't need to be asked twice and headed off in the direction they should have been going in while Chrissy rummaged in her bag for her phone. Maybe he lived there, it being his van; nothing wrong with that. Or the van might belong to someone else. She tapped the registration plate details down for later. Either way, she knew it was the same one as she'd seen at the castle during the night; it couldn't be a coincidence. The large box looked the same style too. Maybe he was moving in? As Adam pulled past, she was just in time to see a woman appear on the doorstep for the briefest of moments before vanishing back inside.

Something about her seemed familiar.

CHAPTER 49

Who the hell did the van belong to? Was it the barman's? Not that she even knew his name, but that wouldn't be too hard to find out, she could simply ask at the pub, but if it belonged to someone else? Where did he fit in? She grabbed a carry bag and helped Adam with the groceries they'd bought and headed inside. She dumped her own bag on the worktop and went straight through to have a chat with Richard to see how Julie was.

"She's gone to bed. She'll be fine in the morning, just a migraine, she thinks," he said, dismissing it and Chrissy hoped it was just that. Even if it was a concussion, and she doubted it was, not from being whacked with a lamp base, there was nothing to be done but keep a close eye on her. Anyway, Julie suffered with migraines, so since she'd vomited earlier and had had some rest, she'd likely be back to her normal self tomorrow. Satisfied that all was well with her sister, she grabbed her phone and headed to her room to make a call.

Maybe Bridget would be feeling amenable. A woman answered quickly, and Chrissy smiled as she imagined her sitting at her desk beavering away on something through the proverbial 'back doors', or surfing the dark web as she was prone to do.

Bridget Knox was a talented though tiny woman who liked to think of herself as a bit of a Lara Croft. While she didn't carry a gun on her hip, she did kill people with her tongue and her strong attitude was polarising to many. Plus, Bridget either liked you and you her, or you didn't, and she didn't lose any sleep over it. But talented she was, particularly when it came to digging into things where she shouldn't be digging. She had a knack for finding answers that usually involved borderline illegal means, and borderline illegal tools. Her day job was as part of a Kent-based detective team, working just outside of Ashford, while technology was her side interest. Often the go-to girl when the official tech team were too busy, with her prowess and knowhow she'd kept cases moving that otherwise would still be sitting in a queue waiting. Getting the name and address of the van owner would take her all of two seconds. As long as Bridget liked you. Chrissy had worked with her on a case that had taken them to France and the woman had been a godsend and instrumental in getting everyone back safely. All power to her. They'd kept in touch.

"How's it?" Bridget asked by way of greeting. Chrissy smiled. She'd not heard the woman's dry tone for a while, and not those words either. There were only so many times she could tap into Bridget.

"It's good," said Chrissy.

"What the favour?" Bridget, straight down to business. There was no small talk. There was no need.

"Need a plate run." Chrissy gave the details.

"Is that all? Hang on." Chrissy could hear keys tapping in the background and waited the few seconds for the information to come back.

"It belongs to Ethan Duffy. Quite an attractive looking man actually," said Bridget. "Lovely blond hair."

"Blond curly hair by chance?"

"A girl's dream actually. I'd almost die for natural curls like that." Bridget was also blonde, though out-of-the-box. "He's stunning. Rather jealous."

Chrissy smiled at the amount of information Bridget was offering, most unusual for her to pass an opinion. Maybe she was in between boyfriends and liked the look of the guy herself. "Do you have an address?"

"Of course I do. What's your interest?"

"Not sure yet, but he keeps popping up in unexpected places. I'm just trying to put things together."

Keys tapped in the background. "You want to know more about him?"

"Of course," said Chrissy. She hadn't wanted to push her luck, the reg details would have sufficed, but if Bridget was offering...

"He's got a sheet but has never done time," she said. Chrissy waited for more to come and could imagine Bridget's own blonde head scanning the screen in front of her. "He's had a couple of run-ins but, funnily enough, all the charges have always been dropped. There's four or five of them here – assault, looks like. I wonder why."

"How can you even get into the Guards' system? No, in fact, don't bother answering that, I don't want to know." Chrissy heard Bridget almost grunt down the phone though it wasn't really a grunt. It was more a loud grin, if a grin had a sound.

"Who mentioned the Guards?"

"You mean offences in England then?"

"Indeed, though this cutie pie seems to have the luck of the Irish." Chrissy's phone pinged with incoming text as an address was relayed to her phone. Bridget worked at the speed of light in everything she did, which is why she accomplished so much during her waking hours. The address was in Dublin, not local.

"I wasn't expecting a Dublin address. I was expecting something a bit more local, to say County Clare, Doolin maybe."

"Hang on," she said. Chrissy waited, wondering where Bridget was breaking into. She could imagine her screen looking more like a spider's web with various lines running off in all directions, connecting with others. She was reminded of her bubble chart from when she'd gone out for a walk trying to link things together.

"It's not his only vehicle. I've just done a cross reference. He's got the van and has got a regular Honda Civic as well, I guess his run-about. I'll send you the reg details, you might spot it locally."

"Perfect, thanks." Chrissy's phone pinged again with the new information.

"Best get on."

Bridget was gone, leaving Chrissy wondering about the barman with blond curls Bridget would almost die for. That was her power-house token gone for another few months. Shame, she'd have liked to have asked a few more questions after all.

CHAPTER 50

After Brocc had bumped into Julie at the castle he'd headed straight over to Bronagh's shop before returning to the garage. He'd been conscious of time, having left Jake on his own for most of the day already. No apprentice should be put in that position, particularly with customers collecting their vehicles at various times. While he had a business to run, that didn't stop his inquisitive mind running overtime. His visit to his sister's shop hadn't unearthed any further clues, though he hadn't really expected anything to shine out for him. What exactly could he have found? A big neon sign with an arrow pointing to what he needed to know? No, but whatever Bronagh was involved in, he intended to squeeze more out of her later. He checked his watch; time was marching on. As he pulled the garage roller doors closed, his last customer gone, Jake well on his way home, he figured he'd have to make himself a sandwich when he got home later because by the time he'd taken a quick shower and driven across to the hospital, visiting time would be almost over as it was. Again. He looked at his shiny new phone and wondered about calling her to let her know that he was on his way. She had been adamant earlier on that he mustn't go back, she'd be home tomorrow anyway. He could ill afford more time away from the business, but someone had to pick her up, assuming of course the doctor said she was able to go home.

"Get on with it, Brocc" he said sternly to himself, grabbing his keys and heading out to his car.

He entered the ward for the second time that day and was pleased to see her sitting up in bed, looking a whole lot brighter with colour back in her cheeks. A chemical disinfectant fragrance mixed with the odour of long since delivered hot food, and his stomach rolled at the lingering stench. Or was that at his own hunger? An empty dinner tray sat in front of her, she'd obviously eaten a meal. Bronagh looked surprised when she saw him ambling over but then changed into a full smile. Everyone liked a visitor in hospital, if only to break the boredom.

"I wasn't expecting to see you again today," she said as he bent to give her a peck on the cheek, brother and sister love.

"I wasn't sure I'd make it, what with the garage." He pulled over the single chair, the same one where he'd spent the night only recently.

"You look tired," she said. "You should pull up a bed."

"I am tired," he said, "but I'm not planning on stopping here overnight."

"Visiting time is nearly over anyway," she said, glancing at the clock on the wall.

"I know, but there's something I wanted to tell you. I didn't want to say on the phone, so I thought I'd pop over in person."

"Oh?"

"The child, the baby. He's safely in care. I thought you'd want to know."

"How do you know?"

"Let's just say I met a woman earlier on today. She knew all about it."

Brocc watched as the colour drained from Bronagh's face, she'd be wondering what woman.

"You all right, Bron?" he asked

"Yes. Yes, of course I am. Why wouldn't I be?" she said, gathering herself and forcing a smile across her face.

"Because you just lost all your colour. I'm guessing you're wondering who the woman is?"

Bronagh didn't say anything for a moment before finally adding, "I don't know what you're talking about."

"That's bull and you know it," said Brocc. "But just to put your mind at ease, the woman has nothing to do with whatever it is you're doing. She's just an innocent bystander. Like me really."

"Where did you see this woman?"

"I'm not telling you anything else until you start telling me what's going on. I just came to tell you that the boy was safe."

"Well that's good news the boy is safe, but I'm concerned now there's somebody else involved. And that is risky."

"Involved in what Bron?"

"I've told you Brocc, you wouldn't understand. I'm not telling so stop at me. There's too much at stake, so please don't push me any more." Her eyes held a warning he should leave it alone but that was against his nature.

"Is anyone likely to get hurt, or another child abandoned, perhaps?"

"On the contrary. Nobody is going to be abandoned. Nobody is going to get hurt, but if more people find out that could all change pretty quick. So, whatever you know, whatever you've seen, Brocc Bowen, you've got to promise me you won't tell a living soul."

"Oh, Bronagh, this doesn't sit right with me."

"I don't care where it sits. You've got to promise me you keep this to yourself, and whoever this woman is, you don't tell her anything that you think you know. Leave it to me."

"Well, answer this," he said. "Is what you're doing illegal?"

Bronagh readjusted herself in the bed and thought for a moment before answering. Technically, it was all pretty much illegal, but the outcome really wasn't.

The look on her face as she thought the answer through told

Brocc what he needed. "I guess you're not going to tell me, so is there anything I can do to help?"

"I appreciate the offer, Brocc, but no, you've done enough, thank you. Whoever this woman is, she can't get involved. There's too much at stake."

"So you keep saying. That's all you say."

"And that's all I can say."

Brocc glanced at the clock. Visiting time was over. All around him, people kissed their loved ones goodbye and wished them well. Brocc stood to go. "Is there anything I can do for you, for the shop, maybe?" he said, bending to peck her on the cheek once more.

"I don't think so. I'm hoping to be out tomorrow. I'll give you a ring and let you know when I know, though I could just get in a taxi. I'm sure you've got things to be going on with." A taxi would cost a small fortune.

"I'll come and get you. You just let me know." He waved lightly, grey fingers stained with years of grease moving through the air in an affectionate manner. Bronagh lay back and watched him leave, the smile falling from her face. While it was good that the child was safe, she wasn't pleased at how things were turning out. The woman, whoever she was, had inserted herself into something that didn't concern her and Bronagh could only hope she wasn't going to be a problem. She picked up her phone. All she could do was let the others know that there was someone local, on the periphery, on the outside.

And they were looking in.

CHAPTER 51

Chrissy was sitting on the edge of her bed wondering about what she'd heard. It sounded like the barman had been in trouble in the past for assault, though no charges were ever laid against him. Whomever he'd hit had had a change of heart, frightened of repercussions, perhaps. Just who was this barman, Ethan Duffy? He didn't look the violent type.

"Damn! I should have asked her about the ANPR cameras on the van. Can I even I ring back?"

"Should you ring her back?" said Adam, surprising her. She hadn't realised he was standing in the bedroom doorway behind her.

"A missed opportunity is all. I could kick myself," she said.

He walked into the room, serious written all over his handsome face.

"Why don't you tell me what you're really up to. And I mean all of it." She'd been rumbled. Adam knew her too well, which was only a good thing. "I'm guessing that call," he said, pointing to her phone, "has got to do with Flynn and his missing parents?"

"Yes. I've just been talking to Bridget. Remember, the blonde that got us out of France?"

Adam smiled at the memory of meeting the woman. Unique didn't cover it. Neither did interesting. "How could anyone forget Bridget?" said Adam with a slight smirk. She'd be close to many men's dreams, though in reality they'd find a very different person underneath compared to what their own dreams contained. "So, what does Bridget have to say?" Chrissy took a long, lung-emptying breath and said, "Here goes, long story short: when I just asked you to pull in at that house earlier? I saw the barman from the pub in a van that I've seen knocking about, and at the castle, and I'm suspicious of it, that's all."

"And I assume you think he or the van is somehow connected?"

"I think there's something going on, yes. I've not got to the bottom of it yet, but Bridget's done a quick search and the guy's got a sheet, several assault charges. And they've all been dropped. That in itself is odd, though I'm not sure how that links to the missing pair. There must be more behind it, I can feel it."

Adam sat down next to her. "I thought you were going to have a break, have a holiday, some time out," he said, showing the start of frustration again. It wasn't the first time he'd raised it.

"I am. But this is important. A young child's been abandoned. His parents have run off amidst some strange goings-on and I intend to find out what's happening. I'm not entirely sure quite how much effort the Guards are putting into the case since Flynn is now 'safely' in the system."

"So, in true Chrissy form, you take it on yourself." He sounded defeated. Maybe he knew he was. It wasn't a battle worth fighting, he'd never win this one, he knew Chrissy all too well. Tell her to stop and she dug her heels in. Plus, her day job was as a private investigator, so he knew she'd be sensible about her own involvement and safety.

"Yes, in a nutshell."

He stood. "Well, call her back and ask your question. Then will you come and help me in the kitchen? You can keep me topped up with wine."

"I can do that," she said, dialling Bridget's number again. It went straight to voicemail, so she left a brief message, hoping she had a little virtual credit left to afford Bridget's headspace. Chrissy headed back to the kitchen and slipped her phone into the back pocket of her jeans.

Julie had gone to bed. Richard was buried in his book and the house was quiet as the two sipped wine in the kitchen, waiting for the beef hash to cook. Adam hadn't asked any more awkward questions and Chrissy was grateful for an understanding husband, though she was painfully aware she should focus on the rest of their holiday instead of working a case, paid or not. Adam would only stay cool about it for so long and she'd noticed his frustration peeking through.

"So, tomorrow we might have two patients in tow," said Adam. "Richard's still not up to moving very far and if Julie is no better, she'll want to stay in bed. If that's the case, what you fancy doing tomorrow?"

Thinking quickly, she asked, "Are you up for horse riding?" Adam's head shot up. He looked horrified and Chrissy couldn't help but laugh. The last time they had been horse riding, he hadn't quite mastered the rise and fall of the saddle hitting his undercarriage when it came to trotting, and he'd hardly walked for a week.

"How about mountain bikes instead?" he suggested. "I feel safer on a bike than a horse."

It was a good compromise. "You're on." It was the least she could do. "But if Julie is feeling better tomorrow, I'm not sure she's ever been on a mountain bike. In fact, I'm not sure she's been on a bike since she was a child."

"You never forget how to ride. Plus the fresh air will do her good. We don't need to go far or too fast so let's see how she is when she wakes up." At that moment Chrissy's phone vibrated in her back pocket and she glanced at Adam. It was Bridget.

"I'll take this on the deck," she said, nodding towards the living room, indicating that Richard could easily overhear.

CHAPTER 52

Chrissy slipped outside the back door into the cold, wishing she'd grabbed her jacket from the peg first off. It was dark now, hardly any light visible as waves crashed away in the distance. A stiff breeze whipped by, and she hoped that Bridget would be her usual brief self. Once she'd got the information she so desperately needed.

"I hope you've got a good memory because I'm not sending this through. No trace from me, not on this, you understand." All business.

"I get it. What is it?"

"It seems your man changed his name some time ago, quite legitimately I might add, to Ethan Duffy from Nathan Jones. So, Ethan, Nathan, not much difference there. Jones, Duffy, obviously nothing alike, but he did that all legal and above board. Plenty of people change their names every day."

"Right."

"Okay. While he might look cute, he's not my favourite kind of man, but then anyone that is involved in domestic violence disgusts me. I'd like to kick the shit out of him with my heavy boots on."

"Ah. Not good, not cool."

"Apparently there were numerous call-outs to the property, usually by the neighbours. Things often got heated and items could be heard crashing about, but charges were always dropped."

"So where was all this? Dublin or Doolin?"

"In Manchester actually. Your boy is not a local to where you are. I'm assuming you are still in Doolin?"

Chrissy had no idea how Bridget knew where she was right there and then and at a guess would have said it was something to do with her own mobile phone. But Manchester? That's the second person from Manchester she'd come across this week.

"So he's not really Irish."

"No," she said. "If he sounds Irish, he's likely got a fake accent along with his change of name."

"Right. Do have an address for me?"

"I do and it's easy to remember: 1, Rooska," and she spelt it, "Lisdoonvarna. Small cottage, tiny village; perfect for hiding, I'd say."

"Hiding from what though. He works in the local pub, it's hardly hiding."

"The guy's got to earn money, he's got to keep himself somehow. Maybe he changed his name after those assault charges. Maybe he doesn't want anybody knowing his background."

"Makes sense I suppose. And the ANPR, any joy there?" The van's reg plate picked up on the night Lorcan and Ciara disappeared would be more valuable than gold at this point.

"Before I tell you, tell me more. The part you're keeping from me."

It seemed Adam wasn't the only one interested. She had no choice but to fill her in if she wanted the information. She brought Bridget up to speed.

"And you think Duffy is somehow connected. Well, this guy doesn't deserve my adoration of his curls now I know more about him. After I've kicked his head in, I'd like to finish him off with my boxing gloves." There was a certain chill in the woman's voice that Chrissy wondered about. She didn't doubt her intentions.

"Steady on Bridget. I thought you didn't like violence?"

"Anyone that beats his wife deserves far more than I could give them." Then, like flicking a switch, Bridget changed tack. "Anyway, I can tell you the cameras pinged that plate at various locations on the way south that night, but ultimately the pings stopped at Cork since there's nothing much else at the end of the M8 but ocean. Having said that, the same plate has been on the move back up to Dublin and across to Holyhead, Liverpool included. It's been getting around quite a bit in the last few days."

"That's a puzzle then. I wonder what's at Cork?"

"Besides water? A day or two's rest from my tracking. Just watch yourself, Chrissy. Anyone that can beat their wife needs a serious talking to."

"I couldn't agree more," said Chrissy. "I don't know anything about where Lorcan and Ciara have gone but this Duffy guy seems to keep popping up. It's too much of a coincidence to ignore.

"Just look after yourself and you didn't get any of this from me."

"No problem there, and thanks again, you've been really helpful."

Bridget had already gone.

Chrissy went back inside and, sitting at the kitchen table, watched Adam make a salad. It seemed too cold for lettuce. She reached for one of the throws that was lying about and draped it around her shoulders while she warmed back up. A long drink of red wine helped to warm her insides as she watched Adam chop tomatoes.

"I'm guessing that was Bridget? Anything useful?"

"Everything Bridget tells you is useful in some way," she said. "It's just sometimes you don't know quite where the pieces all fit in and I can't take advantage of her generosity as much as I'd like. I have to kind of earn my rewards from her or hope she's feeling benevolent. But it's starting to take shape in my mind now. I need to do a bit more digging."

"Will your digging wait till after dinner?"

Chrissy looked up at her husband and put the disappearance of two people and an abandoned baby to the back of her mind for a moment. "It can wait until after dinner," she said, noticing the warning note. But she needed to nip out, follow up on what Bridget had told her. The address wasn't far away.

"How would you feel if I popped out for an hour later, though?" She was tempted to wince at his response before he'd even given it.

"Well, if you're going to do that, you'd better hold fire on that red wine you've been knocking back," he said. "And jot the address down, just in case."

CHAPTER 53

Chrissy drank water over dinner and said very little while she mulled over what she'd learnt in the last hour or so, leaving Richard and Adam to talk men's stuff. Julie stayed in bed fast asleep and Chrissy hoped she'd sleep through and not be wide awake at 3 am. Since she'd not long ago eaten afternoon tea, her own appetite was almost nil and she picked at her food, which didn't go unnoticed by Adam. A sandwich would have done her. Eventually she made her apologies and waited for them both to finish. Then she gathered cutlery and crockery and loaded the dishwasher, clearing away. It was only fair since Adam had cooked. She glanced at the clock. It was coming up to 8 pm and she was anxious to make her trip out. She had two destinations in mind.

"Can I get you boys a coffee?" she enquired, hoping to settle them in the living room like you might two young children.

"Please," said Adam.

"I'll bring it through," she said. "Richard?"

"Not for me, thanks. I'm going to have a brandy. Join me, Adam?"

"Just a small one," he said. "It would be rude not to since you offered," he added cheerily, and the two men headed off into the living room like old pals. Mission accomplished. It was good to see them getting on so well. Richard, like Julie, seemed to be mellowing a little around the edges. Neither were as stiff and uptight as they were at home in their big house. Chrissy knew a lot of it was for show, keeping up appearances. She knew her sister was as down to earth as she was inside, though needed to relax and be the real Julie, the one that was starting to shine through again. With Richard's continued support, the shoe shops were having a positive effect on both of them and with plans to expand online, she could see Richard taking that aspect over in a career change.

She busied herself making a coffee for Adam and took it through, and when the kitchen was all cleared away, she went to their room to collect the car keys. As she breezed back through, she kept away from Richard, hoping he didn't ask any questions. He appeared to be back engrossed in his book, a brandy by his side. Whatever it was he was reading he was certainly enjoying it. Adam nodded at her furtively, a warning in his eyes to stay safe at all times, and she nodded back. Grabbing her jacket from by the back door, she quietly left the house and headed out into the dark. As the car unlocked itself the interior glow was the only light showing her the way. It was pitch black otherwise.

Judging by Google Maps, Lisdoonvarna was local, so not far away, which fitted with the fact that Ethan was a barman in Doolin. Being local was ideal when finishing a late shift, he wouldn't want a long drive home at midnight.

It didn't take her long to find the address and park up outside No. 1, Rooska. There was a bed-and-breakfast place opposite and she pulled into the driveway and turned her lights off while she surveyed the street. It was nothing more than a row of small cottages that looked like any other row in a small picturesque Irish village. All was quiet, curtains drawn in each window. No Honda Civic. He was likely at work, but she wanted to see where he lived, see if there was a van parked nearby maybe, something she could have a look inside, something to pick over, like the remaining carcass from a Christmas turkey. But after fifteen minutes sitting in the freezing cold with nothing happening and nothing to see, she pulled away and headed back towards Doolin, and on to the second place of interest on her list. It would be the third time in one day she'd headed off to Ennistymon.

Since she'd seen the van outside the house earlier, she was doubly keen to take another look. Perhaps peer through the windows and look inside. She doubted whether the van would still be there now since Bridget had mentioned an address in Dublin. Maybe his Honda Civic would be parked outside instead, though that could easily be with him if he was working and there was no point going there. What was she going to ask him? What are you mixed up in and by the way I know your real name? No, that wouldn't work.

She pulled up outside the bungalow, which resembled any other in the street. Curtains were drawn tightly, though slices of light were visible down the outer edges. All looked warm and cosy on the inside, the flickering of TV light told her someone was likely home and watching it. She parked up the street a little way along so she could watch any comings and goings, but all was quiet, just like it had been at the cottage. With the engine turned off, it wasn't long before the cold evening seeped into her vehicle as she watched and waited. How could she find out who was inside? She could knock on the door potentially, pretend to whoever opened it she had got the wrong house. That would give her a face-to-face with the occupier, but if it turned out to be the barman, that could be tricky since he was bound to recognise her. Then what?

She pulled her hood up on her jacket against the cold, slipped her phone into her pocket and locked the car before walking the few steps towards the house. The street was deserted, only herself out in the damp air, and she wished she'd put another layer on before heading out. She stood outside the bungalow listening for noises but couldn't hear anything, not even the TV. Carefully, she undid the front gate and walked up the path quietly, glancing at the darkened downstairs windows that she passed. It seemed whoever was in was only in the one front room. She quickly made her way to the rear of the property and all the way back around to the front to confirm that no other rooms were occupied. From the side of the property she made her way across to the bay window and hoped that nobody was looking out from across the road through their own curtains and watching her. She looked like a prowler and didn't relish another meeting with the Guards. There was a small crack in the curtains where they hadn't quite met. She could see the TV was on but couldn't see anything else, any inhabitants likely in a chair well out of her sight.

"May as well knock," she murmured to herself quietly and headed back to the front door. She hoped it wasn't the barman she'd come face-to-face with. With a traditional knock on the door, tap tap tap tap tap, tap tap, she waited. Whoever had invented the common door rap had taught generations to pass it down to the next since everyone knew the tune when knocking. She waited. Nobody came after a moment or two. She tried again. Tap tap tap tap tap, tap tap. But the door stayed firmly closed. Whoever it was inside, and she felt sure there was somebody inside, was not going to answer the door. Giving up, she wandered back to her car up the road and turned to look over her shoulder for a second or two. That was when she saw the curtains twitch. Somebody for some reason hadn't wanted to open the door to find out who was there. Another 'why?'

CHAPTER 54

There was little point Chrissy watching the house any longer. It was quite clear they weren't going to answer the door. But Chrissy knew that didn't mean anything sinister was going on. It could have been an elderly relative of the barman who simply felt unsafe opening up to a stranger on a cold autumn night. She wasn't buying her own logic.

She may as well go home now, Adam would be wondering where she'd got to, and if Richard hadn't got his nose still stuck in his book, he might ask questions too. She started the engine and pulled slowly past the house, giving it one last look, but there was really nothing to see. She chewed over once more what she knew as she drove, wondered what thread she could pick at and unravel a bit further. The only one that sprang to mind was that Julie had mentioned a man from the garage who she'd seen at the castle after being whacked on the head. Since it hadn't been him and the only person in the picture at the moment was the barman, Chrissy assumed he'd been the one to assault her sister. Had he been at the castle that morning? Why, she'd no idea. Tomorrow, she'd go and chat to the man from Brocc's garage. Julie had mentioned his sister's possible involvement, so he wasn't going to go to the police and drop her in any trouble. Not yet anyway. Maybe between them they could come up with a plan because at the moment Chrissy had got nothing.

She wondered where baby Flynn was and if he was being well cared for. She hated to think of him in the system, at someone's house that perhaps wouldn't be looking out for him quite like his own parents, but then again, perhaps he was better off without them if they'd abandoned him in the first place. Perhaps being with a brand-new family was the best for the little boy in the long run. As she pulled up in the driveway of the holiday home, she was relieved to see the living room lights were still on. Someone was still up. She hung her jacket up and went through. Adam was reading the newspaper; Richard still had his nose in his book and barely looked up as she plopped herself down on the sofa. Adam glanced across and she smiled and nodded that everything was okay. He went back to his newspaper, content she was back and safe. An unexpected yawn told her it was time for bed, but she knew when she slipped under the covers she'd lie there tossing and turning while her brain attempted to untangle the threads.

"I'm off for a shower," she announced and went through to the bedroom to grab her pyjamas and robe. Changing her mind, she turned the bath on, feeling the need for a soak instead, and added blue Radox to the flow and stood watching the bubbles growing in the bottom of the bath as the water filled up. It reminded her for a moment of bathing baby Flynn only a couple of days ago, the poor boy sweaty from his tears, hungry, and in dire need of a change of nappy. She'd wrapped him in a soft blanket to comfort him as he'd taken a warm bottle. Chrissy tested the water temperature then climbed in and slithered down under the bubbles herself to keep her shoulders warm, her feet poking out the end. The warm water soothed her, joints relaxing as the magnesium entered through her skin's surface and did its thing. She focused on her breathing, taking deep breathes in and letting each one out slowly, willing her heart rate to decrease slightly. She wanted to make the most of her relaxation time, head off to bed ready for sleep and a peaceful night, but her mind had other ideas.

She needed to know where Lorcan had gone. Duffy's van was in Cork, was Lorcan with it? The van had pinged cameras down there and then stayed quiet for a day or two, but then had travelled north again. She couldn't just drive down there without a destination in mind, it was too big a place. He could be in any of the surrounding smaller towns or villages, where a camera hadn't been located. A simple Google search had not shown the locations of the cameras in Ireland itself, the Guards keeping their locations secret for obvious reasons. She thought of Bridget, her only resource when it came to the techy stuff, her old contacts in the field long gone on to other roles in life. She had already asked for two pieces of information; she couldn't push another. Plus, Bridget had all but said she wasn't getting anything else this time around, she didn't want anything traced back to her. Her loyalty was with Kent police and nothing to do with Chrissy's investigations at all. She was lucky she'd found out so much so far, but Bridget couldn't be pushed any further, not without ruining their relationship. Chrissy knew she was too valuable to do that.

Steam covered the mirror, misting it up totally, and little clouds of moisture hung around the lamp in the ceiling as they wafted up from the warm bath and circulated around the room before clinging to cold surfaces. There was a gentle knock at the door and Adam put his head around.

"Can I come in?"

"Of course you can. There's room in the other end if you want to get in?" She raised an eyebrow, teasing.

"You look like you're enjoying yourself wallowing there. I'm not going to squash you up."

It was true that if he'd joined her at the other end, at over six-foot tall, there wouldn't be much room left for the water, never mind Chrissy. Still, it was a nice thought.

"Wash your back?"

"Please," she said and slithered up from under the water like a mermaid, her pink skin glowing as she leaned forward, water running off her, steaming. Adam grabbed the bar of soap and the nearby loofah.

"Did you find anything out?" he asked conversationally.

"Nothing at all," she said. "Although there was definitely somebody in, but they wouldn't answer the door." He grunted his acknowledgment then changed the subject to the following day.

"Are you going to come cycling tomorrow?" he asked.

"I hope so. I'm going to go for a run first, but I'll back in time for when Julie wakes up. Let's see how she feels tomorrow. Hopefully it's just a migraine and she'll wake up refreshed and ready to go."

"Do you think she'll want to come with us?"

"I don't know, but we've got to at least ask."

When he'd finished washing her back, she slithered back down to rinse the suds off. All that was visible was her head among the white bubbles.

"Then we need to come up with another plan for tomorrow's entertainment. Something that includes everyone really, not forgetting Richard," said Adam. "We can't leave them both again, they must be getting bored by now."

Chrissy pushed up through the water and stood dripping, white foam sliding down her legs. Adam passed her a fluffy towel and she wrapped herself in it before getting out and standing on the bath mat. Adam stripped, then slithered down under the bubbles himself. His feet stuck out and rested on the back of the bath. "Do you want me to come with you for a run in the morning then?"

She screwed her face up a little and felt mean when she said, "Would you mind if I went alone?"

"It's no problem to me," he said. "I'll see you back here when you've done what you need to do." That knowing look again filled his eyes.

Chrissy bent down and gave him a lingering peck on the lips.

"Thank you."

THURSDAY

The following morning Chrissy was up around 6 am and standing in the kitchen with her first cup of coffee of the day. The rain tumbled down outside, a constant deluge from the sky as if whoever was up there had their hosepipe on full pelt, finger over the nozzle, creating a wide arc of spray. But she'd learned during her stay that the weather in Ireland at this time of year changed almost hourly. It could well be a sunny, clear day by mid-morning. She watched as the wind belted the rain sideways across the window, so it sounded almost like hail on the glass. A grey sky reached down to meet the equally grey sea below and large droplets of water ran down from underneath the gutters looking more like snow in their dense form. Bushes around the edge of the garden bent as the wind whipped at their tops, green leaves splintering off and flying away in all directions. It was a foul day to be outdoors just yet.

There was nobody else up. Chrissy had done her best to sleep and had managed a few hours, a soak in the bath had helped, but in the end she'd lain there listening to Adam's gentle snoring, trying to use his rhythm to drop off back to sleep herself. The last time she'd looked at the clock it had been almost midnight, the next 5.30 am. Looking out to the bleakness beyond, she concluded it wasn't the weather to go mountain biking and she doubted very much Julie would entertain going even locally in this weather. That left the problem of what to do in Ireland on a rainy day for four people on holiday, one of whom couldn't walk very far. She sipped her coffee and cogitated a plan. She'd still go for a run and get wet, the weather never bothered her, it was only water that fell from the sky after all, nothing nasty. Those that questioned her judgement and asked, 'you're not going out in this weather, are you?' she'd say the very same thing to. When she returned, she was only going to get in the shower, though granted it would be much warmer than nature's own version. So, rain, what did it matter really? She got wet in the end either way.

There was little point heading out just yet for the simple reason the garage wouldn't be open for another couple of hours anyway, so she enjoyed the tranquillity of the quiet house and watched the rain carry on its drenching. She was halfway down her mug when she heard the door open behind her and turned to see Julie standing in her pink robe and slippers. Her first impressions were that Julie looked a good deal better, her own personal storm had passed.

"Good morning early bird," Chrissy said brightly. "You're up early. I don't think I've ever known you be up before 7 am," she quipped, smiling.

"I'm fine, thank you," Julie replied somewhat sarcastically.

"Sorry, I meant to ask you that first. How are you feeling this morning, Julie?" she said, making a big thing of the 'how are you feeling', exaggerating the sentence with outstretched arms. "It's good to see you up so early." She knew she was ladling it on.

"There's no need to be sarcastic, but I feel much better, thank you for asking. The sleep did me the world of good."

"Well, you did go to bed early. Plus, you missed dinner, so you probably had a good ten hours' sleep. Lucky thing."

Julie walked over to where Chrissy was standing and peered out. A misty spot formed on the window from her warm breath against the cold glass. "What dreadful weather," she said. "What we going to do then, because it doesn't look like an outdoors kind of day, does it?"

"I was just thinking the same. I'm going for a run in about an hour but after that I don't know."

"You're not going for a run in this, are you?" she said. Chrissy rolled her eyes a little. One down, two more to go.

"Got to keep my fitness up," she said in a sing-song voice, avoiding the question. "We thought we might go mountain biking, but unless this rain stops, I don't expect you'd want to." Julie turned back to her sister quickly.

"Mountain biking?" she queried. "Do I look like I mountain bike?"

Chrissy smiled at her sister's horrified face. "Well, riding on a mountain bike. I don't think we were planning on going *into* the mountains per say. More a gentle ride across some of the flat tracks that go around the villages. We don't have to go up onto the cliffs. Plus, I thought you'd like to blow yesterday's cobwebs off. How's the lump on your head today?"

Julie rubbed the spot that had been whacked. "Sore."

"Well, what about Richard? It seems unfair to leave him on his own, again," said Chrissy. "He can't go for a walk and he can't very well pedal I don't suppose."

"I'm happy to stay with him. There's probably not a lot else to do around here when it's raining anyway; I'll keep him company. Plus, he seems to be enjoying his book, whatever it's about, it's appealed to him. I don't think I've seen him read so much since... Well, let's just say since forever."

Chrissy smiled at her sister who had taken on a kind of dreamy state as she pushed her mind back someplace trying to recall Richard's last book interest.

"Why don't you and Adam go out and I'll stay here with Richard?" Chrissy suggested.

Julie looked incredulous, as if she'd proposed a walk to the moon and back in flip-flops.

"I don't mind," said Chrissy. "You've not been out really,

yesterday was a bit of a write-off for you, and I'm sure we'll be fine. In fact, I've enjoyed his company, he's been quite relaxed actually," she added.

Julie looked at her sister sideways, not sure if she was taking the mickey or not. "Let's see how the weather goes," she said matter-of-factly before heading over to the coffee pot and pouring herself a mug. Chrissy watched and downed the remainder of her own. She may as well go and get changed. A longer run would do her good and by the time she'd circled back around, the garage could well be open. There was no point sitting around waiting for something to happen and drinking more coffee.

"I'm off to get into my gear," said Chrissy, putting her mug in the sink. "I might as well get off now and get back, I suppose. You decide while I'm gone what we are doing today in case it does stay wet."

By the time she'd returned to the kitchen to grab her trainers, Richard was pouring himself a coffee. "You're not going out in this, are you?" he said.

One to go.

Smiling, she said, "I'll be back later." She slipped buds into her ears and jogged off down the path towards the village and beyond, glad to get out of the house for a while, even in the rain.

It was an hour and half later before she circled back down into the village and she felt a lot better for expending some energy. She slowed her pace to an easy jog and rounded the corner, heading directly towards the garage. She could see someone at the front of the property; they were likely opening up for the day.

"How convenient," she said as she neared a younger man in a dark hoody and jeans.

CHAPTER 56

Chrissy could hear the rumble of the old roller door as the man helped it on its way before finally letting go as it took on a life of its own. It crashed to the top with a loud smack. She smiled at the fact that the door probably did that to him every single day. There would likely be some sort of pole with a hook to pull it back down at the end of the day and she imagined it standing proudly just inside the doorway, waiting for its one job. The man disappeared inside.

She slowed her pace down to a walk and wiped the mixture of sweat and rain off her forehead with the long sleeve of her running shirt in an attempt to make herself look a little more presentable before she headed over. She was drenched, her hair plastered to her head, but that didn't matter. She always felt good after going for a run, it eased the tension in her shoulders and dragged her thoughts kicking and screaming into order. The young man returned holding a pavement sign advertising the fact they were open for business then vanished back inside. Chrissy watched for a moment and wondered about the other man, the one she'd come to see, the one that Julie had almost whacked. What time did he start work, would he be along shortly or not? If she hung around too long, she'd get cold, and she'd have to dream up another excuse to come back later. While it was all right to tell Adam and Julie what she was really doing, she didn't want Richard to know what she was up to, not wanting to have to explain herself. She put her head around the open doorway and spotted the young man at the back of the unit by a small office.

"Good morning," she said brightly. He swung around, startled, probably not expecting anyone so early in the day. "I'm looking for the owner," she added.

"He's not here yet, he'll be along shortly though." While he seemed pleasant enough, there wasn't a hint of a smile on his face. This morning's shave hadn't happened, and stubble sprouted from his chin in an uneven manner.

"Okay if I wait?"

He shrugged. "If you like," he said. "Want a coffee? It's only instant," he offered, pointing to a nearby jar with a teaspoon.

"Thanks."

He nodded to a chair in the corner by the office door, offering for her to sit while she waited. Since it was an old wooden one, she took the weight off her feet while he made her a hot drink.

"Any idea how long he's likely to be?"

"Usually here by now," he said. "But with his sister in hospital, he's been a bit more erratic with his hours." He spooned two sugars into his own mug and turned to face her. Brown fingernails stained from his oily job held her drink and she wondered about the cleanliness of what she was about to sip from. Just then a car pulled up outside.

"He's here now," he said and nodded into the distance towards the front pavement. Chrissy turned to see a weather-beaten older figure get out of an equally old car and head towards them. It must be the man the Julie met yesterday at the castle, judging by the description of him. He walked as if he was exhausted.

"Morning," she said, approaching him as he entered the building.

"Morning," he replied. She was dripping water to the floor. He looked her up and down, her drenched state of interest but not in a leery way. He didn't pass comment.

"You must be Brocc. I believe you met my sister yesterday?" she said, getting straight to the point. She watched as his face clouded over, likely wondering where the conversation might go and where she fitted in.

"I did, yes," he said slowly. "Scared me half to death, so she did."

"I'm Chrissy," she said and smiled in the hope that it would put him at ease and that he would return one, but he never did. "She can be scary can Julie," she added, trying to lighten the moment, but still no smile. Figuring he wasn't the talkative or smiling type, she ushered him gently towards the entranceway, away from the possibly prying ears of the young man. She didn't fancy going outside back into the rain just yet.

"I believe your sister may be involved in something," she said in a low voice.

He flicked his head up quickly and said, "What's your business?"

"Trying to find out what's going on. Probably like you I'd imagine. You were at the castle, remember?"

Brocc grunted. He must have figured if the dripping woman was the sister of the one he'd spoken to yesterday, she was okay to talk to. He let a moment or two pass before responding. "She'll not telling me anything."

"You think she's involved then?"

"I know so. I just don't know what it is or how deep she's in. But I do know I don't want her in any danger, she's too old for all that."

"Then if she's not letting on to you what it is, we need to figure out a way of finding out without her."

"Why do you want to know? You don't look local to me."

"Let's just say I'm a holidaymaker with a nosey interest. The young child that was left at the castle? It was me that found him."

"Yes, your sister did say. Well, he's safe now, that's the main thing."

"I intend to find out more though. I can't leave it there."

"I don't think I can be much help. I don't know anything to tell you."

The young man, now working under a car at the far end of the garage cursed then wriggled out on his creeper from underneath an Audi. "Bulb's gone," he said, pointing to the handheld lamp. Brocc, remembering he'd got a torch on his phone that he hadn't had a chance to use yet, looked across and said, "Use this for a minute," he said, walking towards Jake, who glanced at the phone and disappeared back under the car. Brocc went back to stand with Chrissy when his phone began to ring. The lad once again wheeled himself out from under the car and handed the phone back to Brocc who looked at the caller ID. Chrissy caught the glance, she could tell he wasn't entirely sure what to do with it, so she helped him out by saying, "Green button, tap it."

She stood for a moment while he had a brief conversation, though it was mainly one-sided, before he hung up and looked at the phone.

"New phone. I haven't figured it out yet," he said by way of explanation.

"Flash," said Chrissy. "A smart new iPhone."

"Got it yesterday. Got two yesterday actually."

"What do you need two for?"

"One for me, one for Bronagh. Hers got smashed in the accident. I'm still getting to grips with it. The last one didn't have so many fancy bits, just made phone calls. I reckon this could fly a spaceship." At last, a morsel of a smile at his own analogy. "Anyway, that was Bronagh. She's being released from hospital this morning, I'm to pick her up at 11 am."

"Well that is good news." Better still it gave Chrissy the seed of an idea. "So, you've got identical phones then?"

"Yes."

Chrissy told him her quickly forming plan.

"I don't know..."

"Do you want to find out and help or not?"

CHAPTER 57

Brocc wasn't convinced at the strange woman's plan, but if he wanted to find out anything, it was clear Bronagh wasn't going to tell him and he'd have to figure it out for himself. The two women he'd now since met seemed intent on getting to the bottom of it so he may as well lend a hand where he could, for her sake and for perhaps the young child's. She was all the family he had left, and if she was putting herself in harm's way, he had to do something about it. All he had to do was make sure that he came away with Bronagh's phone, leaving his own one behind, and hope she didn't notice. Chrissy had taken it from him and cleaned it so it was devoid of grease and grime and hoped Brocc could make the swap when his sister wasn't looking. It would work, but finding the right moment to make the switch would be the tricky part.

Once again he parked up and headed inside the hospital and straight to the ward where his sister was sitting on the edge of her bed with her belongings alongside her, such as they were. He bent to give her a kiss on the cheek and asked how she was feeling.

"Pretty good, actually," she said. "I'm ready for home."

"What did the doctor say this morning after his rounds?"

"Take it easy. I told him I'd got someone at home to help look after me. That seemed to satisfy him, otherwise I think he'd have made me stay longer."

"What did you do that for when you quite clearly haven't got anybody?"

"Because I'm sure you'll pop in and I can manage. I'm young enough to hobble around and sort myself out. I don't need much more."

"Well, I hope so," he said, almost scolding her. She'd always been fiercely independent for as long as he could remember so there was no point in trying to convince her otherwise. He could keep a close eye on her.

"Then we should have a quick run through," he said. "Walk to the end of the ward and back and I won't grass you up."

"Really?" she exclaimed.

"Yes, really. Now, you heard me, get on with it."

"Well, you cantankerous old man," she said, "I don't believe you'd do that."

"Try me."

Bronagh locked eyes, tutted as loudly as she could to show her dissatisfaction, then got up on her crutches and set off towards the end of the ward. It was now or never to make the phone switch. While she wasn't looking, he quickly unzipped her bag, slipped his hand in and felt for her phone, all the time watching to make sure she didn't turn around. When he'd got it in his grasp, he pulled his own out of his pocket and did the switch before quickly zipping the bag up again. By the time she'd reached the end of the ward and turned, he was stood with a grin on his face, feeling more pleased with the fact that he'd managed to do something covert than with his sister managing to hobble along on crutches for few metres. He felt a thrill travel up his spine at what he'd just done. He pulled hers out of his pocket and flipped it on to silent as Chrissy had shown him to do earlier, having already done his own. The last thing he wanted was either phone ringing while Bronagh was still in the car and her to realise it was the wrong ring tone. He doubted she changed hers from the standard one as yet, but he couldn't be sure. By the time she'd reached him back at the bed, she wore a pink glow from the exhaustion.

"That's enough for you today," he said. "You're as red as a beetroot."

"Will you stop fussing?" she said, annoyed that she was breathing hard. It had taken more out of her than she'd realised.

"Do you want a wheelchair to get to the car?"

"No, I'm fine," she said. At that moment a nurse passed by and Brocc thought better of it.

"Stay here," he said, and wandered off to catch the nurse's attention for a chair. A moment later he was back. "She said she's already offered you one, which you'd refused, but you're getting one now anyway. Don't be a fool, Bronagh."

"I don't need the fuss, I can manage."

"Clearly, you can't." The nurse arrived and held the chair while Bronagh seated herself. Brocc put her bags on her lap and thanked the nurse as the two left, working their way slowly towards his car parked outside. Part one of the plan was now complete. The second part would take someone else's skill set, not his. And the woman, Chrissy, had volunteered to do the rest. All he had to do was take Bronagh back home and meet Chrissy at the garage. He was ahead of schedule and it felt good, so he allowed himself a slight smile behind his sister's back. He could get used to being devious.

He pulled up close to the kerb outside Bronagh's house and helped her from the passenger seat and up the path where he unlocked the door with his own set of keys. The house felt cold and damp with the rainy weather and without an occupant, and he hadn't thought to make sure the heating was switched on for her arrival home. She shivered as she stepped inside.

"You go through to the sitting room and I'll wet some tea and put the heating on," he said helpfully. He made sure he grabbed both her bags, taking them into the kitchen out of reach. Five minutes later he took her a mug of tea and a half-eaten packet of biscuits he'd found and asked if there was anything else she needed.

"I've got to get back to the garage for an hour, but I'll call in again just after lunch, okay? Make sure you're fine."

"I'll probably still be sitting here," she said. "But I'll see you later." He gave a nod and left the house feeling pleased with himself that he'd managed to accomplish the important part of the plan. Without Bronagh's phone there was no other way of finding out the contact details of others involved.

And that's where Chrissy would come in handy.

CHAPTER 58

It was gone midday by the time Brocc got the phone back to Chrissy at the garage, where they'd arranged to meet earlier on. He felt pleased with himself, like Oliver Twist handing over to the Artful Dodger after a successful morning pickpocketing.

"Excellent work," said Chrissy. "I need it long enough to go through and figure out what these texts mean and who they belong to, who the contacts are. The end of the day preferably."

"Can you do it quicker? Only I'm going back for a late lunch. I told her I'd go and check on her so it would be best if I could slip it back then. Will it give you enough time, do you think?"

It wasn't ideal. She needed longer than an hour or so, but her brain gave her another solution. It would work. "Should be all right," she said. "Let me use your office."

"It's over there," he said, pointing to a grimy space nearby. A tyre company calendar hung on the open doorway and she could only imagine what the pictures were of. The space was as dirty as she'd assumed, but there was somebody's jacket hung on the back of the door, so she turned it inside out before sitting on it. Grease was a pig to get out of any clothing and she didn't want to spoil her own. She got to work quickly; it was a bonus that the shop assistant hadn't put a passcode on already. Brocc had given her the password to Bronagh's account, which she'd written on a piece of paper in case they needed to do a whole new download, but Chrissy was confident they'd manage with what they'd got. She got to work first on the texts, figuring that that would be the preferred form of communication, as it was with many people, and she scrolled through the list looking at the names, not that they meant anything to her at this stage. There were some strange ones other than the normal Graham or Jeremy or Julian or whoever else, as if they'd been given code names. They made no sense. Carrying on scrolling through she came across 'Ed Sheeran' and 'wine bottle top'. She doubted Bronagh really had a direct line through to Ed so it had to be code for something. There were several others in the same vein. Just what were 'Autumn Climb' or 'Old Line'? Chrissy figured the woman had a sense of humour or liked cryptic crosswords and made a mental note to ask if she did. She took photographs of the details contained within each contact with her own phone, but didn't pay any attention to what the information said or could possibly refer to at this stage. She could do that later when she'd got more time. With all the texts gone through and copious photographs taken of each conversation, she carried on through the contacts list and clicked on recent, but again most of the names made no sense. Anyone else that picked up the phone would be equally stumped but that was likely the point. It was Bronagh's own form of security. A quick look through the apps told her she did indeed like puzzles, but there was little else of interest, and no social media channels. She clicked on the photos icon and quickly scrolled through the last few, though the majority appeared to be views of the sea from various places around the country. There was no location obvious for any of them.

There was one other place that Chrissy needed to check so she tapped into location services, scrolled all the way down to the bottom, tapped system services and clicked on *significant locations*. It was a little-known detail, unless you were techy minded, an area that automatically recorded places visited regularly and how much time was spent there. If Bronagh spent every Sunday morning at church for an hour, it would show the location and length of time the phone was there. It was a goldmine of information if someone wanted to spy on your whereabouts. Chrissy was pleased Bronagh hadn't turned it off and scanned the list quickly. It made interesting reading and she photographed the entries to look at in better detail later. She now had everything she needed from the phone, which was perfect because she was conscious of time. Brocc had to get back to his sister and she to their holiday home. She gave Brocc the phone and said, "I'll need some time to sift through this lot. It makes interesting reading if you know what you're looking at and since it's clear she's being cryptic, it might take me a while. I'm assuming she's a crossword girl?"

"Does one every day. She's probably doing today's right now. Mad for the puzzles, she is."

"Let's see what I can come up with and I'll get back to you. Now all you've got to do is make the switch back again."

"No problem." He was confident.

CHAPTER 59

Chrissy left Brocc to his work and called in at the bread shop, the one thing she'd escaped from the house for in the first place, before racing back home. The rain had since stopped, though the day was not at all warming to the soul and after her earlier drenching she could feel herself getting cold. The last thing she wanted was a chill. She made her way back, mulling over everything she'd seen in Bronagh's phone. There were plenty of photos to sift through and try and understand. The location reading settings on the phone were the most interesting and something that she could figure out almost straight away. The names and contacts meant nothing at this stage, but the places the woman had visited on a regular basis were all nicely listed for her to figure out. She was surprised at how varied the locations were across the southern part of Ireland and in particular a couple of locations further south near Cork – Kinsale, to be precise. Doolin was mentioned but she lived in Doolin so that was a given. Other areas included Castlebar and Templemore, as well as Kilkenny and Ennistymon, just down the road. She wondered if it was the same address as the one she'd been watching only last night. What were the chances? Now all she needed to do was figure out what happened at these locations, which would be easier said than done. From the messages it looked like Bronagh received packages of some description, but Chrissy wasn't fooled that they would be for the shop either. What were these packages and where did they come from and why were they so important? Did she then distribute the contents, perhaps? Bronagh didn't look like the average drugs mule to her. Ciara's earlier quip about being a drug baron pricked at her mind. Still, it didn't seem plausible for the older woman. By the time she'd reached the house, she'd got more questions than answers. But a crazy thought had surfaced – could she and Brocc put a fake order through the system perhaps? Or send a package? She'd need Bronagh's phone again to do so, the message would have to use the same mobile number. Brocc's phone wouldn't work in that respect. She tossed the idea around some more. If they did send a text and requested a package it could be dangerous since they'd no possible clue what the woman was involved in. It might also be nothing, an embarrassing something that Bronagh wanted to keep hidden and nothing to do with anything else. Maybe she had a fancy man, maybe she was a part-time mature hostess, though Chrissy doubted both of the scenarios. Being a babysitter, or a cleaner, she wasn't likely to be driving such distances to do so, it was too far-fetched.

Flynn popped into the mix – where did he fit in? Surely he wasn't a 'package' to be picked up or dropped off? Trafficking in Doolin? She doubted that too. She started her brain on the cryptic contacts list. Richard enjoyed a crossword, perhaps he could inadvertently help? If the code names were for a person, they might take some time to decipher, but they could also be for a location, so it was worth investigating. Perhaps she could pretend it was a game later on and ask them to break the code? Four heads were better than one. Maybe after supper they could have a go, she'd write the names out on scraps of paper and everyone could pick one and try and work it out, like Pictionary or literary charades. It could be fun, and no one need know what they were actually doing. If they deciphered a few, it should then be easy enough to decipher them all. Impressed at her simple plan, she upped her pace to a jog to get back to the house for a later than scheduled lunch. They'd wonder where she'd got to, yet again.

CHAPTER 60

It hadn't been ideal nor part of the plan that he'd had to flee the castle at Doolin. And just when things were starting to feel comfortable and he was beginning to enjoy life again. It had all been so rushed, so little time to gather their things and then it had almost broken his heart in two to find out that young Flynn had been left all on his own. But as he gazed down into the buggy out in front of him, he was thankful for small mercies that they'd been reunited so quickly, and the boy was fine. Things could have all gone so very, very wrong.

The town looked very much like Doolin, only on a grander scale with much more history and places of interest to look at. Quaint streets and shops sat amongst buildings as old as the hills themselves. A seventeenth-century fortress overlooked the River Bandon, the courthouse dated back to the sixteenth century and now held the Kinsale Museum. He'd looked at it many times, for something to do really. Flynn gurgled in his buggy and he stopped for a moment to watch the boy smile. How he could repay them, he had no idea; he'd be eternally grateful for their help and in their debt for the rest of his life.

His new life.

A chill wind whipped around his head and reminded him he needed to settle all over again, though it would be just him and Flynn. The sun glinted on the boy's hair. He noticed for the first time the regrowth, the blond shining through at the base of his skull. He needed to attend to it before it got much longer and someone spotted it. He hated dyeing it. Something so young and delicate didn't deserve such harsh chemicals, but needs must if they were to keep their identities until it was safe to change back, if they ever did. He'd become accustomed to being called Lorcan now, and calling the little one Flynn. He thought back to his previous life as he walked, not much else to fill his mind with, and for a fleeting moment wondered about Tess, his wife. She'd think he'd vanished off the face of the earth. That had been the plan and he felt sure she'd never find him on the south coast of Ireland. Why would she think to look there, and look for who? He was Lorcan now. She'd give up searching one day, let it be and he'd grow old with Flynn by his side, just the two of them, and she'd eventually meet someone new. Somewhere inside him, there was the tiniest spot that wished her well.

He needed to start looking for a job now, his extended holiday well and truly over, and he was almost bored except for the time he got to spend with Flynn. He'd get a job in a bar perhaps, something seasonal maybe, though since it was moving on to winter, it was not the ideal time for it. The cold wind caressed his ears; it wouldn't be long before the tourists were all but gone until the warmer months returned. He'd look at other employment opportunities in a week or two, though childcare might be an issue. Could he trust to let the boy out of his sight for several hours at a time? He turned into the small park and headed for the centre where the water fountain stood and people gathered on the various benches that surrounded it. A little boy perched on his father's shoulders, giggled as he hovered near the water, waiting for the fountain to disappear down and return again with a giant splash in front of them. A skateboarder entered from the other side, flipped around the perimeter of the fountain then carried on his merry way. Lorcan spotted an almost vacant park bench: an elderly woman sitting at one end, he could take the other. He sat for a moment, the buggy alongside, enjoying the delights of the weak sunshine and those around him. He was conscious of the older lady looking his way and he turned, meeting her cloudy eyes. White hair escaped from under a pink hand-knitted hat that sported a black pom-pom on the top. Lorcan absent-mindedly wondered about the colour match. Maybe she'd run out of pink and only had black to finish the look. She smiled a toothy grin and nodded down to the buggy where Flynn was half asleep, half awake.

"Bonny," she said with a surprisingly deep Scottish accent.

"Thank you. He's my pride and joy." They sat in silence and observed the pantomime in front of them as other small children watched the water, all wrapped up well in their own hats and coats, some with gloves on, some in Wellington boots. The leaves on the nearby trees had all but gone, winter was well on its way. They sat for a few more minutes before deciding it was time to go. He'd stop for a coffee or maybe put his head in at the bookshop as they passed, or even get fish and chips for a late lunch. He hoped for Flynn's sake there was to be no more hassle and the two of them moved on because they wanted to and not because they had to. Being settled and in a routine was important for both their souls.

CHAPTER 61

By the time Chrissy got back with the bread, three hungry adults were waiting for her at the kitchen door.

"I thought you'd got lost," said Adam sarcastically.

"Patience has never been your strong point," she said pointedly, "but I assure you, this loaf will be worth the wait."

"What sort is it?" Julie asked.

"It a fresh Irish soda loaf, and anyway I'm back now," she said, passing the loaf to Adam, who had his hands outstretched ready. Salad, sliced cheese, and ham all sat nearby on a chopping board waiting to go into the bread. She felt almost guilty for holding up their lunch, her own stomach rumbling, reminding her she hadn't eaten anything since breakfast.

"Have you decided what we're doing this afternoon?"

"Well, I had a quick look at the map," offered Richard, "and I think we should drive down to Limerick. It's only an hour or so away, quite direct, and we can have a look around the shops. I can hobble on behind. Julie wants to look at the shoe shops, as per usual," he said, casting a glance sideways. "Purely research of course," he added.

"I'm up for that," said Adam. "No point in sitting here all day long. How about you, Chrissy?"

She had hoped to go through the photographs she'd taken and make some sense of them. Maybe she could use the time on the way down to sift through. It could work.

"Sounds good," she exclaimed. "Let's all get out for the afternoon, good idea." She couldn't have sounded any more thrilled if she'd tried. "Has anyone organised where we're eating tonight? Only I just saw the menu for the bistro up in the village and it looked quite nice. I thought perhaps you'd like to eat there?"

"Has it got white linen tablecloths?" enquired Julie.

"I don't think so, sis. Is that what you require? Are you getting withdrawal symptoms from the lack of formality?" she asked jokingly.

"No need to be snide," she said. "I just thought it would be nice to wear the only dress I brought with me before we go back home. And since yesterday's afternoon tea..." She let the words linger. Julie had missed her fix of being dainty for an hour or two.

She spoke as if she were Marilyn Monroe, desperate for a night out with a Martini between her fingers.

"Then you should choose the venue," said Chrissy, "white tablecloth eating we can do. Why don't you book something, and I'll help to make the sandwiches?"

That would keep Julie happy for a few minutes, and be something to look forward to later. It wouldn't hurt her and Adam to get glammed up a bit tonight. She had brought something smart to wear herself; it could be pleasant. "Is there much at Limerick?" Chrissy asked Richard.

"It's a medieval town, like many in Ireland, so there'll be some old buildings to view and some walks to be had, or hobbles in my case," he said, smiling. "A change of scenery, learn something new; it'll be fun. Life is what you make it," he said emphatically. Richard seemed to be gaining energy as the days went by, though an energy for life and not being his usual drab self. He'd been as such for all the years Chrissy had known him, and she wondered what was making him re-energised. Was he having a midlife crisis? Surely he wasn't seeing someone else? He didn't look the type to be interested, never mind actually do it. But then Julie had a spring in her step again too. Maybe the shoe shops were good for both of them, given them both a goal, something to do together, something to look forward to for their future.

She watched as Richard hobbled into the living room, probably to retrieve his book – he had to be near the end of it by now. When the coast was clear, Adam turned to her and said, "How has your morning been then, what have you really been up to?"

"If I don't tell you, you can deny all knowledge when later questioned," she said, grinning.

"Sounds ominous."

"You love the mystery I provide, Adam Livingstone, and you can't tell me you don't."

"You're a mystery in itself," he said, adding cheese and lettuce to a sandwich. She took the plate to the table, while Adam carried on making sandwiches for the others, putting them on various plates before calling everyone through. Lunch was finally ready. When everyone was seated and tucking in, a peaceful silence settled on the room. It was like feeding time in a nursery when babies suckled quietly, a certain air of tranquillity as their own stomachs were filled. The human body needed the same few things all through its life from infancy to old age: warmth, shelter, and sustenance. Everything else was immaterial.

"Limerick," said Julie suddenly. "What's the difference between a limerick and a poem?"

"Google it," said Chrissy through a mouthful of bread and cheese.

"Why don't you just tell me?"

"Because you won't learn if you don't find the answer for yourself."

"Can I borrow your phone then since you've got yours there?"

Chrissy couldn't very well say no, so she closed the photos and slid it across to her and watched as pretty pink fingernails tapped out the search words. Everyone seemed to wait for the answer. "There we go," said Julie. "Limerick is a humorous poem, usually five lines, like what you'd hear at school, often rude." She closed the browser down and slid the phone back towards Chrissy.

"So now you know. If I'd simply told you, you wouldn't have known the full explanation."

"You would have told me the same things as what was on the search," she said satisfied. The two men glanced at each other over the stupid conversation that was going on between the sisters; they sounded like fifteen-year-olds again. Neither husband dared say anything. Something buzzed in Chrissy's head. Could it be that simple? Another name for something the same?

CHAPTER 62

Chrissy was anxious to get everybody in the car and get going so she could bury her head in her notebook while travelling on the back seat. Julie, it appeared, was taking an age getting ready for an afternoon out in town, obviously excited about wearing something other than jeans and walking boots. She was like a kid in a sweet shop. What would she be like later on at dinner?

In a perfect world, Chrissy would have Bronagh's phone for herself so she could look back and cross-reference points of interest, but she hadn't. There was no way of Brocc getting it back unnoticed unless he gave her a sleeping pill and knocked her out and that wasn't going to happen, so she hadn't even suggested it. As they travelled south along the N85, she jotted down the strange list of contacts and where the texts had come and gone to, and then the locations that she'd found that the woman had visited over recent months. The list sounded like gobbledygook. *Autumn climb, old line, citadel pub* didn't make any sense to her from the list of contacts. On the list of locations, there had been plenty going on in Doolin, Castlebar, Kilkenny, Templemore, and Kinsale, along with a whole list of others. The locations unfortunately didn't give a firm address when she studied the map, but from the image of where all the location beacons were, she could see roughly whereabouts in the town each was situated. It was figuring out the cryptic contact side of things that needed her full attention, and maybe of the others too. She thought back to earlier with Julie and the limerick question. It was a type of poem, usually short and funny. The two things were similar. She contemplated Bronagh's love for the daily crosswords and the list of regularly visited locations she had. She pulled up a web page on her phone and found the Thesaurus website and clicked on synonyms. She looked at the first noted down, *Autumn Climb*. She typed and pressed enter: *fall, harvest, autumnal, equinox*, but nothing meant much to her. So she removed autumn and put climb in on its own then hit enter: *clamber, go up, mount, rise, scale, soar, top*. The words glared back at her, nothing shaking itself, shouting 'It's me!' More's the pity. The Irish countryside flashed past the window as Adam chauffeured them out for the afternoon and she tried to lose herself, hypnotise herself even, in the grey tarmac that sped by below the wheels. If she watched it long enough without blinking, it eventually fused into a dark grey blur and she willed the filing cabinets of her mind to open drawers and show her the answer. Mount niggled away for some reason, but maybe that was because they'd only recently been talking about horse riding. Or was it something else?

Mount, climb, rise, top... Something fell into place, like a locking mechanism enables a safe door to open, and she flitted her eyes across to the list and looked back at the map where location dots sat teasing her.

"Got you," she exclaimed, a little too excitedly, causing all eyes to turn to her brief outburst. "Cracked a puzzle, that's all," she said by way of explanation and smiled at as if she'd won a prize. In a way, she had. When you knew the answer, all questions were easy. Autumn Climb had suddenly turned into Spring Mount. Bingo! It really was that easy; basic but clever. Spurred on, she moved on to the next one, *Old Line*, so she put old into the thesaurus and received *aged, ancient, decrepit, elderly*, none of which made any sense to her list. She tried line and watched as it returned *boundary*, *channel, edge, border, bar*. Maybe Bronagh hadn't used the thesaurus for this one but her own brain. She checked the map to find another alternative to line. Row beamed at her. It would have smiled if it could have, so Chrissy did instead. Old Line suddenly became New Row. Chapel Less became Templemore. She had the most part of the addresses. Now she had got the hang of it, Citadel Pub became Castlebar and Slay Rogers became Kilkenny. After twenty minutes, she'd solved the majority of the addresses and where they were.

Could they be safe houses of some type? Or addresses for drug dens, maybe, or where paedophiles lived? Was Bronagh on some sort of crusade? She doubted the older woman was dealing opioids or worse, and the cryptic address could be for any number of activities. They were obviously meant to stay private, but why? The list of possible goings-on at each address was endless. She closed her notebook and rested her head back on the seat and closed her eyes for a moment to think through how what she'd learned might fit in with the missing couple and why they'd abandoned their baby at the castle. The place was much more than a holiday home for someone, and Chrissy wondered if the owners even realised it was being used for something she couldn't yet explain. She thought back to the cellar, the wicker bins, the coffins, but her mind was blank. There was still so little; was it now time to bring in the Guards? But tell them what? A few code names and cryptic addresses? That was it. Would they even be interested since the couple had fled and Flynn was now in care? They'd likely have bigger crimes to solve since no one was in danger. She thought about the woman that had taken Flynn. She seemed caring enough. Family services often got a bad rap, sometimes warranted and sometimes not. She'd wondered herself, not at all happy young Flynn was now a part of the system.

Bridget sprang to mind, and the locations the van had driven through on the night Lorcan and Ciara had fled. The ANPR cameras had picked up the vehicle heading to Cork, in the south. Which of the deciphered addresses had they gone to? She pressed the Google Maps app on her phone and studied the area. Kinsale, or Clan Bargain as Bronagh had referred to it, was not too far away, on the south-east coastline. She flipped back to the photos she'd been studying and deduced the contact 16 Autumn Climb was the address of 16 Springmount, Kinsale. It was easy when you knew what you were looking for. With her newfound knowledge, she cross-referenced the two lists to see if anything fitted the castle back at Doolin. Was the address significant enough to have a code?

"Stone me," she said, louder than she'd wanted, and felt the attention once more of the three others in the car, if only via the rear-view mirror from Adam. She ignored her own outburst and hoped the others would too. Glaring out from the page in front of her: Ed Sheeran. While it wasn't quite the same code as the others it made sense now. 'Castle on the hill'... Whatever went on in the tiny holiday home was what went on at the other addresses too.

She now had to figure out just what that was.

CHAPTER 63

Looking inside Bronagh's phone had been invaluable and the fact she'd put everything in a code that was reasonably easy to decipher had been a blessing. The only thing Chrissy could think of doing now was to set something up and see what happened, and for that she'd definitely need Bronagh's phone again. If she was going to send a text to those involved about a package, it had to be Bronagh's she used. There was only one way to get the phone back and that was via her brother. She pushed her new knowledge to the back of her head to percolate for a while.

For the rest of the afternoon, Chrissy, Adam, Julie, and Richard sauntered slowly around the streets of Limerick and she tried her best to appear interested. When they pulled into a small bookshop that had a café at the back, she was glad of the space it created, as everyone browsed and she could lose herself in her thoughts for a few more moments undisturbed. They arranged to meet inside the café in twenty minutes' time.

Richard was still browsing the shelves, injured leg cocked like that of a horse standing in a paddock. Adam was ordering at the counter and Julie flicked through her phone. Had Chrissy been visiting on her own, she'd have been tempted to carry on the rest of the journey down towards Cork to Kinsale and check out the address. It wasn't that far from her current location, and from Google Earth, it looked like any other small village urban development. Regular houses for everyday people. But who lived there, who was staying in the one she was particularly interested in? She had a feeling she might find Lorcan and Ciara behind the door. But what of Flynn? Had he since been placed in a proper foster home somewhere? There was little point calling the guard she'd met that day; he couldn't tell her anything.

"Come on, Chrissy,'" she said to herself under her breath. "You need to go directly to the horse's mouth. That's the only way you'll find out." Adam arrived back with a tray of silver teapots, jugs of milk, and a plate of tiny cakes. He set them down and played mother by dishing everything out. Richard was too engrossed by a shelf to notice, and rather than call him, Adam strode over. Chrissy watched him go. Could she make up a feasible enough story for family services, if she pretended she was from another agency? Perhaps back in England? Watching the two men walk back to the table, she made her mind up to at least try. She dug inside her bag for her phone and, as the two men sat down, made a big show of looking at the screen then pressed it close to her chest.

"Sorry, I need to take this one," she said, pulling a face and left the table to walk outside onto the street, quickly putting her phone on silent. Once outside, she slipped out of view from the front window and googled family services, Tulsa, and waited to be connected. In her best authoritative telephone voice, she asked to be put through to the caseworker for a little boy, Flynn, that entered the system on Tuesday. She waited while she was transferred, and a woman answered. From the tone of her voice she was either annoyed at the interruption or just generally stressed and bordering on downright rude. Chrissy explained that she was from a UK family service agency and was checking up on a little boy that had come to her attention on Tuesday evening. There was a long pause before the woman finally said something.

"I can't give you any information, I'm afraid. You need to go through the proper channels, and with a case number."

"I understand that," Chrissy tried again, "but I'm simply enquiring as to how the boy is, not any particular information about his case. Are you at least able to tell me that much? He was such a cutie and I'm almost embarrassed to say he's stuck in my mind somewhat. I just hope he's settled in somewhere nice. You know how it can be."

Was it enough?

The line stayed silent for another long moment and Chrissy hoped the woman was checking her computer screen, or at least finding something useful and not ignoring her. "I still can't tell you anything," she said finally with an exasperated sigh.

"May I ask why not?"

"For the simple reason that I have no record of a little boy being entered into the system on that day or the following."

That was something Chrissy hadn't expected. She'd personally handed Flynn over to Tilly Murphy, back at the house.

"That can't be right. My information is that Tilly Murphy took charge of the little boy. Can you check again for me, please?"

"I don't need to," she said. "Since there's nobody at this agency called Tilly Murphy."

CHAPTER 64

Chrissy couldn't believe what she just been told, and a chill settled down the base of her spine. There was no record, no notification of Flynn ever entering the system and no woman by the name of Tilly Murphy worked at the agency. Who the hell had she handed the child over to then? She stood on the pavement outside with the phone pressed to her ear, pretending she was talking on a call, while she tried to make some sense of it. The Guards had been present – surely they had checked the woman's credentials, perhaps even knew of her from previous dealings? No, there had to be some mistake somewhere. She fought to remember the scene back in the living room that day. The sergeant had moved to the far side of the room to make the call, and Chrissy had thought no more of it, she'd assumed he was calling family services, there was no reason to doubt that. Was he somehow involved in this mess, turning a blind eye even, or was he unaware and it a pure coincidence? Sure, he made the call, had spoken to someone, but was that someone Tilly Murphy? Or maybe he'd spoken to someone else who had then in turn called Tilly Murphy and maybe Sergeant Staines was simply an officer stuck in the middle without realising it. Perhaps she should call him, but that came with its own set of problems because if he did know, what did that mean for her? The whole thing was like a ball of wool coming unravelled and Chrissy was trying to undo the knots it was creating. The wool was winning. She turned back to the bookshop café and all that it contained. Three of her holiday companions had likely finished their tea and cakes and were ready to go. She'd better get back to them before stiff questions were asked and she was *persona non grata*. The tinkle of the bell above tried its best to lighten her mood as she entered. She spotted Richard hobbling his way back to the table and Julie and Adam deep in conversation. By the smile on Julie's mouth, it seemed Adam was telling her sister something amusing. If she didn't know better, she would have said they looked almost conspiratorial. Chrissy sat down with a heavy thump and tried to look like she hadn't a care in the world. Adam glanced her way and, knowing her well, knew there was something on her mind. The way her features contorted gave it away and he caught her eye questioningly. Knowing she'd just taken a phone call, he could afford to be more obvious and so asked, "Everything all right?"

"Not really," she said honestly. "One of my cases has just taken a strange turn."

Julie looked up at that. "Oh, how?"

"I'll tell you later if you're still interested," she said, dismissing it. "Let's enjoy tea and the rest of what Limerick has to offer," she added finally and hoped she didn't sound rude. She could run the news past Julie when the opportunity arose. Perhaps her wisdom would help in what to do next.

When everyone had finished, Chrissy suggested they split up so the men could go one way and look at whatever, and the girls could peruse the shops without having to think of them being bored, trailing behind them. It was agreed they'd meet back in an hour's time. As the girls turned left, and the boys right, Julie wasted no time in asking for an update. "What's happened? Come on, tell me."

"You're not going to believe it but here goes." She paused before blurting her concerning news out. "Remember when the Guards came to take Flynn away?"

"Of course, it was only a couple of days ago. What's happened?"

"I just rang family services. Only it appears that Flynn has not been entered into the system and not only that, but Tilly Murphy doesn't work for the agency. She doesn't exist on their records."

"What?" Julie exclaimed, incredulous. "Who the hell has Flynn then?"

"I don't know. And that's the worry. What I need to know now is what do I do about it?"

"Go to the Guards of course."

"I'm not so sure. Remember who made the call from the living room? I'm wondering about his involvement in this whole thing."

"You can't be serious," said Julie. "A Guard officer wouldn't be involved in something like this, surely?"

"I don't know," she shrugged. "But I do know that little boy is now missing, and I do know Bronagh knows more than she's telling us all. Maybe she knows where the child is and how this all fits together."

"You need to put some pressure on her, threaten her with the Guards and see what she comes up with. If you don't get anything from her, you'll have no choice but to go to report your concerns. Maybe speak to Sergeant Staines's boss. Doesn't have to be him remember, there's more than one officer in the place. If Staines mentioned it to a colleague, it could be the colleague that's bent, or whatever."

"That's what I'm coming around to thinking too," she said. "He may have thought he was doing the right thing and the culprit is at the agency. I don't know what else we can do."

"So, what were you beavering away at in the back of the car on the way down? It was obvious something has come to light."

Chrissy had almost forgotten what she'd been doing, that she'd cracked the code. "I've been trying to figure out the contacts and the locations out of Bronagh's phone because she had them written in some sort of crazy code. And now I've figured it out, I've got locations and addresses but they still make no sense in terms of what they are for."

"So now you're thinking Flynn is at one of these locations."

"It's possible," she said as they walked on thinking about everything they'd just talked about, not really interested in window shopping or anything else.

"I hope he's not in trouble or harm's way," said Julie. "You hear of such wicked things…"

"I know, it doesn't bear thinking about. We thought he was safe, now we've no clue about his whereabouts or his situation."

"Well, I vote when we get back and meet up with the boys, we should head off home and you need to go and talk to Bronagh, and see what she says, find a way of digging deeper. You've got these addresses now, haven't you?"

"Yes and I've got one for near Cork too, where the van was seen, and I'm wondering about Lorcan and Ciara, if that's where they are. Could Flynn be with them perhaps, though why would he be?"

"You've got to find out, Chrissy."

CHAPTER 65

Before the two women met up with their respective husbands, Chrissy had another call to make. While she wasn't going to get very far with Bronagh herself, she could tell Brocc what was going on. After all, he seemed just as interested as she was, and now they had new information to work with. Unfortunately, it didn't sound like Bronagh would cough up any time soon, though if she knew Flynn was missing... She dialled the garage and waited for him to come on the line before saying, "I need to speak to Bronagh and urgently, and I think it's probably best if you're there too."

"What's happened?"

"I'd rather not say on the phone, but let's just say it's urgent, and if I don't get any answers from her, I'm going straight to the Guards myself."

Silence filled the airwaves as Brocc registered what would happen next. He didn't want to see his sister in trouble with the law, but at the same time if she was up to something criminal, then what was he supposed to do? "Okay," he said. "Meet me here at seven and we'll go around together."

Chrissy checked her watch. It was doable but there would be no white linen tablecloth for her this evening. While it wasn't ideal for a family dinner, with Flynn missing and possibly in harm's way, this was far more important. She hoped Adam would understand, and since Julie knew the whole story that would have to suffice. "See you at seven then," she said before hanging up.

"I hope this works, Chrissy. She'd be a fool if she doesn't tell you."

"Let's just hope she does. There's nothing else I can do apart from go straight to the Guards right now. I've got my doubts there still. I suspect at least one of their officers are involved so I need to tread carefully."

"So, if she doesn't say anything, what then?"

"Then I'm going to drive down to Cork and on to Kinsale and take a look at the address myself. We know the van was seen down there from the ANPR cameras. I wonder if the Guards know about that?"

"I don't see how they'd know to be looking for the van. You only got the reg plate details by chance, your eagle eyes. And our joint snooping in the dark at the castle that night."

"True. But I suspect the Guards were monitoring the ports for Ciara and Lorcan. Maybe they found out their real names, or at least their surname?"

"Not heard anything or seen anything in the local paper, but that doesn't mean they haven't found them yet."

"Perhaps I should try the Guards after all, they may tell me," said Chrissy. "It also makes me think the pair are still in the country, have not gone back to England. My bet's on the south, and now I know the address, that's what I'm going to do tomorrow. It's too late to go now, it's a three-hour drive."

"I'll come with you," said Julie. "Richard won't mind, I think he's quite enjoyed himself relaxing and reading on his own for a time." Chrissy thought about Adam, who liked to go out and do stuff and not hang about, he could be bored stiff by now, though he hadn't said anything. Yet. It was his break away too. "I'm going to have to make this up to Adam somehow because I'm going to miss dinner tonight."

"You'll be in the doghouse," said Julie.

Chrissy grimaced.

"If you're meeting Brocc at seven, you're not going to be round at Bronagh's house too long anyway. You can still meet us at the restaurant later."

"We'll see. All I can think about now is getting Bronagh to talk to us without turning the screws on her. I'm hoping when she realises we know Flynn is not safely with family services, her conscience will encourage her to spill the beans."

"That's the best outcome." Changing the subject slightly, Julie added, "I'll keep the menfolk happy. If we book the table for 8 pm, that should give you the time to slip out, do what you need to do and hopefully be there for the most part. There must be a local taxi so the three of us can get there and you take the car. You do what you need to do and meet us later."

"Right." Chrissy could see Adam and Richard walking towards the arranged meeting place ahead and she waved lightly as if they'd had the time of their lives. In actual fact they'd barely looked in a shop, preferring to mull over the current predicament and saunter along at the same time. As they got closer, Richard wore a surprised look, his eyebrows almost up in his receding hairline as he enquired, "No bags, Julie?"

"No, there was nothing I needed," she said sweetly and gave him a quick peck on the cheek. His brows resumed their normal position at the news, not something he was used to hearing. It didn't matter whether she needed it usually. If Julie wanted it, Julie bought it, their credit card bill testament to that.

"I'm ready for home," she said, slipping her arm around his waist affectionately. "I'm sure your leg must be aching by now, isn't it?"

"It is somewhat, it's the furthest I've moved all week," said Richard, sounding exhausted.

Chrissy grabbed the chance. "Then let's get back and you can rest up a bit before a later dinner. Relax a little, have a whiskey or something beforehand." The four moved along together, back towards the car park, leaving Chrissy and Julie smiling inwardly at their manipulation.

Chrissy decided it was her turn to drive them back and not risk detours with Adam the explorer behind the wheel. By the time they reached the house, Richard was almost asleep in the back, his head resting on Julie's shoulder, showing his tiredness. Julie in turn was resting back on the headrest, her eyes closed behind giant sunglasses. Neither of them looked like they were up for an exciting evening's entertainment at a posh restaurant, but more ready for pyjamas, cocoa, and a good book. As the car came to a standstill, Richard and Julie both stirred in unison and pretended that neither of them had been asleep. Adam glanced at Chrissy and smiled as they watched the pair head straight for their room.

"I need to ask a favour of you," said Chrissy.

"I wondered when it would come."

"I need to slip out before dinner. Something's come to light, so I'll organise a taxi for everyone and I'll meet you there a bit later. I should be there in time as you sit down to order."

"It's fine," said Adam. "Not ideal, but it's fine. Where're you going?"

"I'm just meeting up with Brocc from the garage, we're going to go and have chat with his sister, so only local, but I'll need the car. I'm meeting him at seven but just in case the timings don't work, that's the taxi part. I could be back here in time anyway."

"Okay."

"I just hope she finally sees sense, and I get some answers."

CHAPTER 66

As Brocc and Chrissy walked up the path towards his sister's place, Chrissy noticed the curtain twitch. She must've heard the car door slam. When they reached the door, it opened and a woman looking almost identical to Brocc stood waiting. If she remembered Chrissy from her recent purchase in the sweater shop, her face never gave anything away. She wore a cast on her leg and another on her wrist. Chrissy figured it must be difficult to get around and certainly tiring for the older women who looked much older than she had when she'd first seen her only a few days before. Pain registered on Bronagh's forehead as deep wrinkles – or was that confusion?

"I didn't know I was having visitors, Brocc. You should have told me, I would have baked a cake." The two women smiled at one another and Chrissy went inside.

"Not sure how you'd manage to bake a cake with one arm and one leg out of use," said Brocc. "I hope you've been resting today?"

"Stop fussing," she said, but it was light-hearted banter. "Put the kettle on, will you?" Bronagh obviously had no idea why Chrissy was tagging along. Brocc disappeared for a moment then returned. The pair waited until Bronagh made herself comfortable in the small living room. A roaring open fire made it feel stuffy, and with three bodies in the room, Chrissy soon felt like she was overheating.

"Please, take a seat," said Bronagh. "What can I do for you? I'm assuming this isn't a purely social visit?" she asked, looking at Brocc for confirmation.

"I'll check the kettle," said Brocc, as if it would help him avoid all involvement. Perhaps he'd thought his sister would talk to Chrissy a bit more openly without him being present. After all, she had said he wouldn't understand. Maybe it was a woman's thing? "I'll go and wet some tea," he said and left the two women to it.

"How do you know Brocc?" said Bronagh, opening the conversation.

"I don't really if I'm honest. I only met him yesterday, but we do have something very much in common. And that's what I want to talk to you about, if I may."

"Oh?" She adjusted herself in her seat while she waited for Chrissy to go on.

"It is complicated, I'm not entirely sure where to start," she said – or was she buying time?

"I find the best place is usually the beginning," Bronagh said with a kind smile. "What's on your mind? I can see something is."

"I know you're involved in something and I also know you won't tell Brocc for reasons of your own. Now, I don't know if that's because it'll put others in danger or you in danger or quite what might happen." Chrissy paused to allow the older woman to cotton on to what she was talking about. The older woman faded back into her chair. Chrissy could almost see the shutters closing in her eyes.

"I see."

"Look, I don't care about your reasons, but I do care that the little abandoned boy who should be in the system, being looked after, is not, and I know that you've got something to do with that. I don't how you fit in, but I'm going to get to the bottom of it. I'm just hoping with all my heart he's safe."

"You don't know what you're meddling in," said Bronagh.

"Then try me," said Chrissy. "I'm guessing it's illegal?"

"Kind of. But let me assure you the little boy is being safely taken care of. If you're thinking I'm involved in one of those filthy rings that do unspeakable things to young children, you're wrong. It's nothing like that. I'm no angel, but I'm no monster either." Flames from the fire danced in the woman's eyes as she leaned forward to deliver her speech. Chrissy believed her.

"Then why don't you tell me exactly what's going on. Has he been kidnapped? It's not right he's not with his parents, wherever they are."

"You'll just have to take my word for it that all is well, and the boy is safe. It's your meddling that could put him and others in danger, so please, just leave it well alone if you want to help."

The discussion wasn't exactly going how she'd planned it, but seeing as how the conversation was taking a more direct approach, Chrissy boxed on.

"Where is he?"

"I'm not telling you where he is. Like I said, he's quite safe but you need to leave it alone. Don't get involved."

"So who took him then? It wasn't family services. Tilly Murphy doesn't work there."

"You have been digging, haven't you? And no, she doesn't."

"Tell me where Sergeant Staines fits in then?" Chrissy waited for recognition to that piece of information and got it.

"I'm not saying any more, so if that's what you've come to talk about, you've had a wasted visit." She crossed her good arm with her bad and they rested awkwardly on her stomach. At that moment Brocc walked into the room carrying a tray, three mugs of tea.

"I just made some, I don't know what everyone wants," he said, placing it down along with the bowl of sugar. Chrissy glanced at him and shook her head gently. It would have been difficult not to pick up the vibe that had settled on the room in his absence.

"Now come on, Bron," he said. "This is getting silly, because I tell you, she'll go to the Guards."

"I wouldn't do that," said Bronagh. "Not if you really want to help."

"Why not?" he asked.

"Like I just told your friend, there's too much at stake, too many lives could get hurt, so please just leave it be. The boy's safe. That's all I will tell you."

Chrissy, figuring the woman wasn't going to budge on her decision to talk any time soon, changed the subject unexpectedly.

"May I just use your bathroom, please?"

Bronagh looked confused for a moment but said, "Of course, upstairs on the left."

Chrissy left the room and took the opportunity to climb the stairs, looking as she went, trying to peer inside the rooms that had doors open. It was obvious and easy to spot Bronagh's own bedroom. The pink eiderdown folded back on the bed, her dressing gown hanging on the wardrobe door, a pot of moisture cream on the bedside cabinet. It was a room that was used regularly. As she got to the top of the stairs, she could see the bathroom, but it wasn't the room she was interested in, just an excuse. She strode on to another door and turned the handle, hoping it wouldn't creak. She stepped inside and took a quick look around. It was set up with a small single bed, a set of drawers, and in the opposite corner sat a baby's cot. A freestanding wardrobe was the only other item in the room that was visible. The decor was generic but childish. It certainly wasn't a spare room for an adult to sleep in. She pulled open the wardrobe door and peered inside. An array of clothes and children's belongings hung there and she quickly rifled through. Sat at the bottom was a box of toys, everything from a small soft duck to a pickup truck that would be pushed around the living room floor by a toddler perhaps. There were nappies, shoes, blankets, everything a child might use from newborn to around the age of about ten. Why? But she'd been upstairs a while and seen enough so she left the room silently and went to the bathroom where she flushed the toilet before heading back downstairs. As she entered the living room, it wasn't hard to feel the atmosphere, tense words had obviously been exchanged, though she hadn't heard any.

Chrissy took a seat and looked Bronagh straight in the eye before asking, "So, how many children come to stay here Bronagh?"

The woman was instantly angry. "You've no right to be snooping. You didn't really need the bathroom, did you?"

"Tell me where he is," said Chrissy. "Or you'll leave me with no choice but to talk to the Guards and believe me, I will." Nobody spoke, each waiting for another to fill the void. Sparks flickered from the fireplace, a crackle as a piece of wood fell down into the fire, tiny explosions contained in the grate.

"I don't know exactly where he is. But I know he's with safe people." Bronagh clearly wasn't going to be deterred, her bond to whomever she was protecting was as strong as glue.

"Has he gone somewhere near Cork by chance?" Once again Bronagh's anger flashed in her eyes as she turned to Chrissy and stared her down. There was the answer she needed. Chrissy rose, there was little point asking anything else.

"I'll show myself out," she said, leaving Brocc open-mouthed. While he likely wanted to remain loyal to his sister, the child's situation supposedly concerned him too. Just whose side was he on?

Chrissy hadn't the energy to convince him either way.

She was on her own.

CHAPTER 67

Chrissy was absolutely seething as she reached the road and her car by the kerb. Brocc hadn't left with her; he'd have to make his own way back to the garage to get his vehicle and she was sorry about that, but she couldn't hang around and wait for him to decide which side he was actually on. When she'd last felt so mad and worked up at another human being she couldn't quite remember. The woman had been so calm the whole time except when she'd realised Chrissy knew so much more than that Flynn was missing. Cork, that's where she needed to go and first thing in the morning. Bronagh had assured her that the child was safe, but with whatever she was mixed up in, could she be sure? She certainly didn't want the Guards to be involved, that much was obvious.

Brocc's voice called down from the front step. "Hang on," he shouted and made his way towards her awkwardly, he wasn't built for hurrying. She glanced up at his face to see if she could figure out what he was thinking, but he slipped inside the passenger seat uninvited, making it impossible. Chrissy joined him, the pair of them sitting there in silence, staring straight ahead through the windscreen. Orange lights from nearby street lamps gave them both an eerie glow. Chrissy didn't feel much like speaking, she felt more like shouting but that wouldn't get them anywhere. After what seemed like a couple of minutes, Brocc finally spoke in a low voice, by which time Chrissy was beginning to feel a little calmer.

"Looks like we've no choice but to involve the guards," he said. "We can't go harassing others she knows from her phone, and we can't prove she is involved in a crime, but if it's the only way to get the boy home safe then we have to take that chance. If she really wants to look out for him, she has to cooperate."

Chrissy turned to him in the semi-darkness, "You sure about this?"

"I've made plenty of mistakes in my time. I don't want to add to them and always be wondering about a little boy that vanished, what happened to him."

Chrissy started the engine and drove back to his garage. Little was said along the way and when they pulled up outside, he got out then bent down and stuck his head in to say goodbye. "Let me know what you decide to do next," he said. "You've got my number."

"I can tell you that right now. I'm going to drive down tomorrow first thing and see what I can find out at the address. Then I'll take it from there."

"If that's what you think's best."

"I've no idea of what's best actually, Brocc, but I've got to follow the only real lead I have."

"That you have. Then have a good night," he said and slammed the door shut and headed over to his own vehicle parked on his forecourt. It was not far off eight o'clock. She'd just got time to quickly nip back to the house, slip into something more suitable and still be at the restaurant around about on time. She dropped Adam a text to tell him to cancel a taxi, she'd take them after all. He texted a response.

Great, see you soon, not cancelling the taxi. You'll probably want to have a drink too.

Damn right she would. And more than one. She texted back: *See you shortly.*

As soon as she got back to the house, she went straight to their room, having almost bolted through the living room where the three had gathered for a pre-dinner drink. Nobody said a word. Nobody asked a question and five minutes later she appeared wearing a pale blue dress that hugged every inch of her figure, hair tied up loosely with blonde tendrils cascading to her jawline. A light application of make-up and a pair of diamond studs in her ears and she was ready. Adam whistled his approval as she walked back into the room. "You look stunning, Mrs Livingstone," he said, openly looking her up and down. It wasn't often she dressed up, but when she did heads turned just as much as they did for Julie.

"I concur," said Richard rather formally and Chrissy couldn't help but laugh and she gave an exaggerated curtsy.

"Are we all ready now?" asked Julie.

Just at that moment a car horn pipped outside and the four headed out to the taxi together.

Chrissy did her best to enjoy the evening and be present in mind as well as body. Nobody asked any questions about where she'd been earlier which she was thankful for. Maybe Adam had made something up about where she'd gone, mainly for Richard's benefit, since he was the only person out of the loop. While he knew of her day job, Chrissy often felt his disapproval, that she was 'playing at it', and it irked her. Best to leave him out of it.

While liqueurs and chocolates were served, she gazed around the table at her family. It wasn't often they went to such formal dining places together, occasionally was enough since she found it all a little pompous in truth, but looking round at Julie and the two smartly dressed men, it was nice to be able to do so for a change. Life wasn't all about her choices, it was about compromise with those she loved and lived with. And there were often plenty of them. The trivial as well as the larger things, the things that perhaps she'd do differently if she lived on her own. The downside of being by herself would have been never having anyone to share a laugh with, to smile with, share a joke with, or even to share the dishwashing with. While it was nice having a bit of time on her own, loneliness was a different matter and she was glad she'd found her soulmate in Adam. No, she didn't do too badly at all, she was happy with her lot. Adam was a good man and the rest of the family, too, for most of the time. It'd been a great holiday despite the saddening discovery early on, and it would be a shame when it was over and it was time to head back. It would be good to see her own boys again though, she'd missed them. Maybe tomorrow she'd find out just what had happened to young Flynn.

CHAPTER 68

Chrissy lay in bed, looking up at the ceiling, thinking back to the really quite enchanting and relaxing evening she'd had in the restaurant. It had been right up Julie and Richard's street, though Adam and Chrissy had found themselves enjoying it just as much as they had. With wonderful food and even better company, it had been a roaring success and Chrissy smiled to herself in the darkness at Adam's reaction when she'd walked through all dressed up. She knew he appreciated it, and it was a great confidence boost to know she still scrubbed up well. Having had two children, it was easy to wear their casual influence on her sleeve and live in jogging bottoms for the rest of her life. No, she should do it more often. Her mind wandered to the journey the following morning and hogging the car all day, which wasn't fair. She needed an alternative, but there were no car hire companies in the village. It was too small, plus it was too last minute now to figure out getting one. Brocc and his garage sprang to mind – maybe he had a spare he could lend her? Or, indeed, could she borrow his car, perhaps giving him some petrol money to cover it? She reached over gently so as not to disturb Adam and picked her phone up off the bedside cabinet and sent a text to Brocc. Even if he was sound asleep, he'd get it first thing.

There was nothing to be done before then anyway. A moment later and the reply came through.

What time do you need it?

Hope to leave about seven, will that work?

I'll drop it yours at seven. Address? Will you drop me to the garage?

She gave him the details. *The least I can do. Thank you!*

With the vehicle sorted, she felt better about leaving everybody again since she'd be gone for most of the day. It was a good three hours down there and depending on what she found, she didn't know how long she'd stay. Perhaps she'd take an overnight bag? No, Brocc would need his car back. One day would have to do. She slipped the phone back onto the cabinet, then turned on her side. In no time at all she'd drifted off into a deep sleep filled with green fields and a woolly looking dog. That was something else she'd still to take care of, they couldn't possibly take him back home with them.

FRIDAY

CHAPTER 69

It was never hard for Chrissy to get up in the morning. She was always the early bird and usually the first in the kitchen making coffee. Today was no different. As the rest of the house slept after a relatively late night at the restaurant, Chrissy busied herself buttering toast then took her breakfast to sit in the window and watch the weather outside. It was going to be another wet, grey day, but that didn't much matter since she'd be in the car for a chunk of it. Plus, it could be doing anything on the south-east coast of Ireland.

When she was ready to go, she grabbed her bag and began walking up the lane to meet Brocc. She'd written a quick note to Adam that he'd find on waking, knowing again that he'd understand, but she knew she was pushing his patience now. It wasn't like she was working a paid case. He hadn't said as much, he never would. She'd given the address of where she was going and said she'd see him later on and to have fun whatever they chose to do without her. She'd agreed to tell all later, hopefully she'd have some news.

She spotted Brocc's old vehicle coming towards her down the narrow lane; it had seen better days. It suited the older man really

and she couldn't grumble at his offer for her to use it. As long as it
had a radio to keep her company on the journey, that's all she could
hope for. The car pulled over a little and when it came to a standstill, she walked round to the driver's side and Brocc shifted over.
For an older car, it was surprisingly clean.

"What time do you think you'll be back?" he asked as she
fastened herself in and turned the car back towards the garage.

"I don't know in truth, I'll have to play it by ear. Can I text
you?"

"If you're not back when we close, Jake will run me home, I'm
sure." She pulled up outside and left the engine idling. He turned to
her once more before adding, "Watch yourself. You've no idea what
this is yet."

"Always," she said and gave him a light wave before watching
him head to the garage and open up for the day. She paused a
moment, hoping she hadn't disturbed his routine too much, then
pulled away, driving south towards Cork and beyond.

It was almost 10 am by the time she arrived at Kinsale on the
south-east coast of Ireland. The weather had changed since she'd
first left and a weak, watery sun hung low in the sky, still trying its
best to climb and warm the town below. She drove down the 607
towards the town centre, the River Bandon out in front of her. It
would had been tempting to have a quick look around since, she'd
likely never return again, but there wasn't time for sightseeing.
Google Maps directed her across to Spring Mount, the address
she'd deciphered from Bronagh's cryptic code; it was only a couple
more miles away. All the time she'd been driving, Chrissy had
wondered what she might find, how she'd approach things, and
decided that first off she'd just sit and monitor and see what, if
anything, was visible. That was about as far ahead as she could plan
under the circumstances.

Spring Mount turned out to be small, town-style houses in an equally small estate. A car park for residents split the two rows of houses in half, a grassy area in front. It would be too obvious to park in the residents' area so Chrissy carried on a little further up the road before pulling in. A couple of cars were parked on the narrow road itself. All was quiet, nothing to see or hear so far, but then it was mid-morning, folks would be at work. She turned the car around so that it was pointed in the direction of the house and waited, gathering her surroundings. She observed the other vehicles that were nearby, and any movement, but there was nothing of interest to note except for one. A car parked further on down caught her attention as a bright flash of light glinted off something inside. Maybe it was someone's watch, maybe it was a woman's compact mirror. Perhaps a woman doing a make-up or someone with a laptop even. She reached inside her bag, pulled out Richard's small binoculars and focused closely on the vehicle, but all she could see was the top of a man's head. He was obviously looking down at something in his lap. Possibly a local resident on his way out of his house, or coming home perhaps after an evening shift, a salesperson even. There was no reason he would be anything else and Chrissy labelled him as uneventful. Her stomach rumbled and she ached for a fresh coffee, not to mention the loo. She should have stopped somewhere along the way. While she needed to take a look around the back of the property or knock on the door, the man in the car prevented her from doing so. He may not be anything to be concerned about, but she most certainly would stand out snooping through windows and couldn't risk taking a look while he was sitting there. Was he going to be long? She saw his head lift and glance across at the small row of houses again, the same as she was interested in. Perhaps he had an appointment.

"I can't sit here all day," she mumbled to herself. "Move on, would you? Then I can go and knock on the door." As if he'd heard her, the man started his engine, reversed into the residents' parking area and slowly pulled out of the road. He'd finished what he'd come for.

"Thank you," she said to the empty space. Chrissy was about to get out and head towards the front door when it opened. She pulled her own door closed as she watched a man push a buggy towards a small car parked outside the house opposite. She gasped at the realisation of who she was looking at.

It was Lorcan.

He was on the move. Could it be Flynn in the buggy? It looked like the same as the one she'd pushed the child in earlier in the week before handing him over to Tilly Murphy. It was obvious he was in a hurry as he loaded the child into a booster seat, put the buggy in the boot and then quickly got into the driver's side and started the engine. It took only seconds – practised, Chrissy wondered – and she watched as the two of them pulled away.

She was ready to follow.

CHAPTER 70

Chrissy stayed well back as she followed the car out of Spring Mount and it turned left at the junction. There was no chance of him recognising the car she was driving since it was Brocc's and as old as the hills, but still she didn't want him to know that he was being followed. He took a series of lefts and rights, weaving his way through the back streets, seemingly heading towards the town centre. It was along one of these that Chrissy noticed a car pull in behind her. Glancing in her rear-view mirror, she immediately recognised the vehicle. It was the same one that had been parked outside the house only moments earlier. Had he known that Lorcan was going to be on the move or was it purely a coincidence? She was tempted to pull in herself and let the car pass so she could follow him at the same time, though didn't want to be too obvious about. She needed to find out where Lorcan was going, that was the important item on her agenda right now. On the other hand, he was definitely being followed, so was he in danger? He may need her help yet.

It wasn't long before they arrived in the town centre and whether Lorcan had noticed the two cars behind him or not, he pulled over at a telephone box anyway. Chrissy drove on past, and turned to see the other car drive on up a side street where it pulled in. Watching through her rear-view mirror once more, she waited to see what the other driver would do before pulling over herself. A car behind her blasted its horn at her lack of attention as she dawdled along, focused on the activities of the two people in her sights. She watched as Lorcan headed inside the phone box to make a call. Maybe he hadn't got a mobile phone any longer. Or maybe he didn't want any record of the call he was about to make. She waited.

The town was busy. It was a weekday morning with holiday-makers and local businesspeople mixing as they walked, some grabbing coffee, others lunches for later, and it was hard to keep her eye on the phone box for the traffic driving up and down the road. She wasn't sitting in the perfect place, but she didn't want to let on that she'd seen him just yet, content to monitor and see what he would do next. Would he go back to the house or go on somewhere else? And what about the other vehicle? Would they continue to follow?

Finally, Lorcan finished his call and got back in his car and pulled away. She let him pass so he was in front of her and waited to see what the other car did and wasn't surprised to see him pull in behind Lorcan's. All she could do now was join in the tag team and follow. It seemed somebody else was interested in Lorcan too. Chrissy soon realised, as the road wrapped back around, that he was driving the long way to get back to the house. Maybe he was aware he'd got a tail or he was simply being cautious, just in case. Or just maybe he was trying to get Flynn off to sleep. Many parents drove around aimlessly at night in particular, the soothing motion of the car allowing the child to be rocked to slumber. She'd done it herself. As Lorcan turned right towards home, the other driver turned left over the bridge and away from the town. She suspected he'd be pulling over shortly, figuring where his target was travelling back to, and not wanting his tail to be spotted. He would be back in the vicinity of the house in a few minutes. The road was quiet for a time, which was a shame, she could have done with pulling in herself and letting a car or two drive in between her and Lorcan to take her out of his rear-view mirror. She hoped he hadn't spotted her. There was no other choice but to tail him from a distance and it wasn't long before Lorcan turned back into Spring Mount. He was, in fact, heading home. She turned off down a side road just before his address and figured out what to do next. Would the other man reappear shortly? Would he drive past the end of the road where she was sitting or maybe come back later? Her bladder let her know it was getting time to do something urgently before she created a puddle in Brocc's car. That would never do. It was unfortunate timing and she cursed herself for not stopping sooner. She had to confirm he had indeed arrived home, so she pulled out and entered Spring Mount once again, driving straight through, glancing exactly at the place where she knew Lorcan had parked his car earlier. It was sitting in the space opposite again. Her bladder pressed a little more, she had to take care of it and soon. Now she knew Lorcan was safely back, she pulled out of the road once again and headed down to the town to find a public toilet. She'd grab provisions before returning, she could be sitting there a while to come.

Having picked up a sandwich and a bottle of water, and with the all-important bladder relieved, she headed back up to Lorcan's place and prepared to wait it out. It wasn't long before a familiar car once again turned into the road and cruised slowly along before finally pulling in a little way down from its previous position. Balding man was back. She slithered down in her seat, not wanting him to see her, though it was obvious now he was looking at the house. How long was he going to hang around? She had no idea, but he was becoming a pain. An idea came to her and she smiled to herself, wondering if it would work. It was worth a try.

CHAPTER 71

If she drove past him, he'd likely twig that he'd seen her car recently and know she was up to something too. So all Chrissy could do was pretend she was a local resident out for a walk, heading down to the shops. She slung her bag over her shoulder and had her phone ready, finger on the button to take a photograph. All she needed was the registration plate of his car and hopefully, as she walked by, he'd be busy doing whatever he was doing in his lap and not pay her any attention. She now knew he too was waiting for activity at the house, maybe for Lorcan to go out in his car again, and that's why he was tucked in at the end of the road. What was his interest? Was he an investigator too? As she approached it was easy enough to accomplish her goal and she snapped a few frames before stopping a little further on to check she'd got what she needed. To any other observer, she was just like any other woman on her phone before carrying on her way. While the picture was a bit blurry, she was able to make out the registration from the shots she'd taken. She looked up the number for the local Garda station, there was no need to make an emergency call. Walking along, she dialled, amused at what she was doing. She told the officer what she knew, that she'd seen a car loitering for most the morning, having left and come back and that it was currently sat just off Spring Mount. She gave the registration plate and was assured that someone would be up to have a look shortly. Once she'd completed her call, Chrissy headed straight back to her car to sit and wait for the pantomime to begin. It was about twenty minutes later when the first Guards vehicle turned into the road and stopped by the offending vehicle. What would he say, she wondered. Would they simply move him on? That would be the best outcome. A nosey neighbour reporting him to the Guards – he'd be annoyed, frustrated, and may not be back again today. That said, depending on what he was up to and how urgent it was, he might chance it. It was another ten minutes or so before the Guards left and she spotted both vehicles leaving the vicinity and could only imagine the fumes that would be seeping from the man's ears at being moved on.

With the coast now clear, she took the opportunity to walk up to Lorcan's house and rap on the door. She wasn't expecting anyone to answer. If he was in hiding, and she had every reason to think he was, he'd likely be watching from an upstairs window. The door stayed firmly closed. She pulled out her notebook and wrote *Lorcan, we need to talk. Chrissy*. She added her telephone number then slipped it through the letterbox in the hope that he'd read it and give her a call. She could only hope. Even though he'd just been out and used the telephone box, there wouldn't be many people without a mobile, burner or otherwise. Or maybe the property had a landline. She walked back to her car and waited. There was little more she could do if he wasn't going to answer the door or call. After another hour, she decided on another message and wrote *He's gone now. The Guards have escorted him away. I reported him for loitering. I'm outside, just give me a sign and I'll come over. I'm on your side. Chrissy.*

She folded it in half and slipped it through the letterbox again and hoped for the best as she walked back to her car. Chrissy wondered where Ciara was, she hadn't seen her at all, yet she'd seen Lorcan and, presumably, young Flynn. Maybe she was at work? Maybe he was left looking after the child. She sat hopeful in her vehicle, waiting and hoping he'd make contact.

It was nearly half an hour later when the front door finally opened and Chrissy let a long breath out. She approached him with her hands in surrender, though she'd already said she was on his side. He opened the door fully for her without saying a single word. As soon as she was in the hallway, he closed it behind them and put the chain back on. A bolt top and bottom didn't go unnoticed.

"Hello Lorcan," she said gently.

"Hello again," he said curtly. He didn't look too happy to see her. "I suppose you want to talk?"

"I most certainly do."

CHAPTER 72

Chrissy took in the sparse surroundings; the furniture had seen better days. The room was warm from an electric fire in the hearth. They stayed standing, Lorcan's eyes filled with anger.

"You must be out of your mind coming here," he said as they entered the small living room. "And thanks for dragging him along too." He pointed with his thumb over his shoulder for effect.

"I didn't drag anybody along, I've no idea who he is. He was parked up when I arrived."

"Well it's funny how you both show up on the same day. It's been nice and quiet until this morning, and now two of you."

"Why don't you tell me what's going on?"

"Not likely," he scoffed.

"Then why did you let me in?"

"Because at least you managed to get rid of him. So thanks for that." Chrissy ignored the comment.

"Are you in danger, Lorcan, is Flynn in danger?"

"Well, we could be again, thanks to you." He sounded deflated as he sat down in a nearby sofa chair. While it had seen better days, it looked comfortable enough and Chrissy sat down opposite. Flynn crawled around on the floor, unaware of the tension in the room.

Neither of them spoke for what felt like minutes, but Chrissy needed to start somewhere and put him at ease. She knelt down on the floor next to the child and said hello, giving him a small tickle under his chin. Flynn looked back with a glazed look on his face. He didn't seem to remember her.

She made a start on the conversation ahead. "I was concerned about Flynn and when I realised I'd handed him over to someone that wasn't part of family services, I couldn't just let it be. I'd no idea what had happened to him or where he fitted into any of this. Nor you and Ciara for that matter."

"So many questions," he said, deadpan. He wasn't joking. He looked deadly serious, looked worn out. Dark circles sat heavily under his eyes, the product of so many sleepless nights. "Who knows you're here?" he asked.

"Just Adam, my husband. Nobody actually knows the exact address, although I daresay Bronagh's been here before, has she?" He lifted his head up at the mention of her name.

"How is she? I saw the accident on the news."

"She's doing well. A broken leg, broken wrist, but she's managing." He nodded his understanding, fell silent again, obviously mulling over what or how much he could possibly say. He knew nothing of Chrissy. A decent night out in the pub back in Doolin was about it and it all seemed like a lifetime ago, though it had only been earlier in the week.

"Why don't you start by telling me who that man was outside and what he's got to do with any of this, because I suspect he's more foe than friend, am I right?"

"I can't tell you anything about him, because I've no idea who he is actually. I suspect he's a private detective, would you believe." Chrissy hadn't been expecting that piece of news, not from Lorcan's mouth.

"What makes you say that?" She didn't want to add that she was too, not yet.

"Because my wife will not have accepted me just walking out, she would have sent someone to find me, drag me back. She's that type of woman. Everything has to be on her terms."

"Ciara?"

"No," he said, smiling. "Ciara is not my wife. Tess is my wife for all of a whole twelve months. That's how long we lasted before I couldn't stand living with her any longer." He seemed to go off in a dream state, staring up at the corner of the room that bore nothing of any activity or interest. It was just a place to focus his eyes while he thought back to whatever it was that was clearly upsetting him. Whoever Tess was, twelve months of marriage didn't sound like it had been a good relationship.

"So, you left Tess, and took Flynn, then came to Ireland. I'm also guessing Lorcan isn't your real name then, since you come from Manchester."

"You're quite smart, aren't you?" he said. "Not only to find me in the first place but to put all this together after just two short meetings. Why did you pick it up, by the way, why didn't you just leave us be?"

"Because when I found Flynn all alone that morning, I couldn't just leave it," she said, raising her voice. "I had to find out what had happened, why two adults would leave their child alone while they ran off someplace. And it's a good job I was there, after Bronagh ended up in hospital. Heaven only knows how long the poor child would have been there, uncared for and upset. He was in a bad enough state when I found him as it was." Chrissy spat her words at him, her patience waning. She gave herself a moment to calm down a little – an argument wasn't going to do anyone any good. She changed tack: "I wonder what your private detective outside has been told to do, how far to take it? He may just be taking some photos, or he may have a grander plan to follow."

"Well, Tess will certainly know where I am by now, he'll have informed her of the address, so she'll be well on her way."

"It'll take her some time to get here from Manchester, I'm sure."

"I doubt she's been in Manchester for a while. When they'd realised that I was down here in the bottom of Ireland, she probably came over here, could be standing outside now even." The way Lorcan spoke sounded like he'd given up, almost like someone had pulled the plug out of him and he was winding down like a doll that had lost all power from the mains. Flynn was sitting on the floor, looking up at the two adults occasionally, peaceful and content with building blocks and a cardboard box to put them in. He hadn't a care in the world, unlike his father. Lorcan was clearly worried, anxious, and upset about how events had taken a turn. Tess turning up was adding to it. What had Chrissy stirred up? Bronagh's words of warning filled her ears.

"What will you do if she is on her way?" asked Chrissy.

"I can't go back, but I don't know if I can go forward either, because even if I take a restraining order out, that doesn't mean anything, she'll not abide by it. They're not likely to throw her in prison when she ignores it, as she almost certainly will."

"Why would you need a restraining order?"

Lorcan turned and stared straight into Chrissy's eyes. She couldn't help but see the sadness mixed with fear that lay there like watery pools. Whatever had gone on in the past, the man sitting in front of her had nowhere near recovered from it. Not even close. She didn't expect the words he uttered next.

"To stop the violence. To stop her hatred of me. To stop her taking over my life. And to stop the pain she's caused over the last few months." It took Chrissy a moment for it to sink in what he was saying. Domestic abuse was relatively common, but you seldom heard the cases where the roles were reversed. Tess had been hurting Lorcan both physically and mentally.

"Did you try conventional methods when you were at home, go to the police?"

"Male victims don't get taken quite as seriously as a female one, I'm afraid," he said. "Particularly when it comes to sex. If I was a female and I'd been raped, they'd be all over it like white on rice, but turn the tables and you're almost laughed at. How can a man possibly be forced to have sex with someone he doesn't want to?"

Chrissy felt herself pale. It was much more than just abusive conversation that Tess had enjoyed. She was beginning to understand why Lorcan had run away. "And to answer your question, yes, I did report it. And do you know what the officer said to me that first time?"

Chrissy waited, shook her head.

"He said, 'Every man's dream, isn't it? To have a woman force herself on him?' He'd laughed for a moment, but when he realised I was deadly serious, he tried to cover his mistake up. I remember wanting to vomit, but I held it together until I'd left the station and threw my guts up outside. I doubt much was ever done with my paperwork after that. I know I never heard anything back from them, it likely went in the bin. The whole experience was a total joke."

Chrissy sat quietly, taking in Lorcan's ordeal, wondering where to start to help him. She thought again of Bronagh's words, that she wouldn't understand, lives could be in danger.

Chrissy was finally beginning to see what she was now involved in.

CHAPTER 73

It registered with Chrissy that a car had pulled up outside. She'd heard a door slam and wondered where the occupant might be heading. There had been so little activity around the street as she'd been sitting watching a peaceful neighbourhood. Now, after what she'd only just learned from Lorcan, her antennae went into overdrive. No sooner had the thought entered her head than a fist banged angrily on the front door. If someone was trying to be make a quiet arrival, they'd failed miserably. Lorcan flicked his eyes up quickly and connected with Chrissy's. There was no mistaking the fear that glowed there. Tess's angry shouts broke through the quiet.

"I know you're in there, you coward, let me in!"

"What have you done?" he said quietly.

She had no answer, not at this point, but assessed the situation quickly before saying, "Take Flynn upstairs right now. Pack a bag to go. I'll look after this."

"You can't," he said. "You can't let her in, you don't know what she's capable of."

"I'm not going to let her in. But please get Flynn and take him upstairs," she urged.

Lorcan seemed frozen to the spot, his eyes looking past her at nothing.

"Now, Lorcan!" she urged. Even through their brief conversation, Chrissy had heard the sound of yet another car door slamming. Somebody else was with her. Could it be the man that she'd spotted earlier, the private investigator? Tess banged again, her words ricocheting around the small estate and Chrissy could only imagine the angry woman's face. Judging by her chosen vocabulary, she wouldn't be a pretty sight. She glanced out the window briefly, in time to see a familiar figure walking towards the front door. It was Sergeant Staines. "What the—" she started and then it registered. Bronagh must've had called him, had a conversation and explained Chrissy's plan. She knew full well that she was coming down here and would undoubtedly find Lorcan. The officer was a welcome sight under the circumstances as the angry fist thumped once more.

"Matthew, open up right now, or god help me!" she yelled as her foot made contact with the bottom of the door itself. Maybe the vision of a guard in uniform would ease the situation and stop things getting out of hand. Even though he was well out of his local jurisdiction, that didn't matter, the woman outside so intent on getting in wouldn't know that at this point.

"Go!" Chrissy said urgently to Lorcan. "Take Flynn, get your stuff, be ready to leave when I shout you."

Bang, bang, bang, as Tess hammered again. A woman's voice screaming, followed by a male one in the distance. Chrissy was grateful of his presence and wondered if the local force were on their way too. She opened the curtains properly to look outside and locked eyes with Staines. He was not surprised to see her, though likely unimpressed at the hornet's nest she'd stirred up. Now was not the time to tell her she should have kept her nose out since he'd got his hands full with a ferocious angry female.

"I'll ask you again, madam, to come away from the door," she heard him say, but Tess ignored his directive and carried on banging and yelling for Matthew to come out. So that was Lorcan's real name, Matthew. Matthew what? she wondered. Chrissy could see people starting to gather on the small grassy area out front, wondering what was going on in their normally so quiet neighbourhood. The sight of an angry woman banging on a man's door, a guard trying to rein her back. It was an odd sight. The vitriol that Tess spewed would have made a sailor's hair curl. Chrissy was aghast at her word choices, the names she conjured up and was calling her still husband. She must have been an animal to live with and Chrissy wondered at what point it all started to go wrong for them, what the trigger had been.

Bang! Bang! Bang! Accompanied by more obscenities, more shouting, more screaming. Chrissy could hear Staines warning her with what would happen if she didn't calm down, but the woman was on a mission, she was having none of it. When he finally said, "You leave me with no choice," Chrissy watched as he arrested her, grabbing her hands behind her back and putting them in handcuffs. She heard a siren in the distance, and registered the look of confusion for a moment on Staines's face before she realised that someone else, an onlooker perhaps, had made the call. That might need some explaining, thought Chrissy to herself, knowing full well that two different Garda forces on the doorstep was going to be confusing to explain. She only hoped Sergeant Staines wouldn't get in trouble; she doubted he'd informed the locals of his arrival on their patch, never mind his intentions. The extra siren did the trick and the woman moved away from the doorstep, back towards Staines's car, without too much trouble, though she continued to spew ferocity from her mouth at the increasing gathering of people. A moment later and a liveried Garda vehicle pulled up alongside Staines's own and two officers got out. Chrissy wasn't sure whether to help sort it out or not and opted to stay where she was for the time being. She'd caused enough trouble for one day and could only hope it would have a happy ending. Right at the moment she couldn't see how that would be possible.

In her experience, restraining orders didn't work as a deterrent when someone was adamant to get their hands on their prey, and depending on what the Guards charged Tess with, breach of the peace, threatening behaviour, the likelihood of her going to prison was remote. Unless, of course, Lorcan had evidence of the assaults. Maybe he'd finally be taken seriously if he tried to report her actions again and she could be charged successfully. Chrissy watched as Sergeant Staines handed Tess over to the two officers then waited for them to leave. She wondered what he'd told them, likely that he'd drop into the station and give his side of the story before he returned back north. At least Tess had gone.

CHAPTER 74

It all happened so fast. Chrissy watched as the two local officers drove the hysterical woman away. Tess was clearly not happy with the outcome. She'd come for a fight and had almost got one, though not with the man she'd wanted. He was still upstairs along with Flynn. Chrissy opened the door and locked eyes with Sergeant Staines. He didn't look best pleased as he stood on the step.

"I told you to leave matters to the Guards," he growled in a low rumble. "You've no idea what you've disturbed with your meddling."

Chrissy's patience was running out. "Then rather than tell the whole street, why don't you come on inside and fill me in!" Guards or not, she was angry at his blaming her. "Since I'm not the only one to have figured it out." She closed the door behind him and, like Lorcan had, bolted it top and bottom.

"There's no need for that."

"It's for Lorcan and Flynn, not you or I," she said, ignoring his instruction.

Footsteps padded down the stairs and Lorcan reappeared, Flynn in his arms. His face was devoid of all colour, and tiredness filled his eyes. He joined them in the living room and Chrissy took charge, instructing everyone to sit. Flynn stayed in his arms, upset now at sensing the disruption. He had a dummy to suck on, but tears stained his pink blotchy face. There was a certain calmness among the adults, everyone taking a moment to simmer down, before Lorcan finally spoke.

"Our bags are packed. She'll be back when they've done with her."

Sergeant Staines was ready. "I have somewhere arranged for you, though it's not properly set up yet. We weren't expecting a move quite so soon," he said pointedly and turned his full gaze towards Chrissy. If she was meant to sizzle under his stare, it wasn't going to work.

She had a better idea. "There's a spare room back at mine, if it helps. She'd not think you'd return to Doolin, I'm sure. Maybe for tonight, at least."

"I'm not so sure that's a good idea," Lorcan said, looking at Staines for confirmation. He gave a sideways nod, that it wasn't a bad suggestion.

"It's actually likely the best idea," Chrissy carried on. "Until your new place is sorted. You've a little one to think of." She looked over at young Flynn and reached out a hand, giving him an exaggerated smile, one adults only gave to young children. A light giggle escaped his lips and helped put everyone at ease. Staines sat back a little in his chair and everyone followed suit, the pressure easing on all of them slightly.

"It's not a bad idea," Staines added again. "She'll not think you'll go back there." Chrissy was still wondering about Ciara – where was she and where did she fit in all of this?

"Will Ciara be joining us?" she asked, searching their eyes for an answer.

"No, she's at another location," Staines offered. That didn't make any sense, but he wasn't going to expand on it. She'd find out herself how Ciara fitted in, and soon. "We can't move her on from there, it's too early," Staines added. She nodded, as if she understood.

"Bronagh will be able to help with Flynn, though, if you need anything straightaway," Chrissy offered. She was slowly dropping in the bits she did know, all the time trying her best to figure out the missing pieces. Let them think she was further along in her deductions than she really was. They might just make a slip up and reveal more.

"Will the local Guards sort things or have you got to go and make the peace? Only I'm thinking we should take off soon."

"I'll drop in. Make it work," said Staines.

"And the investigator that was hanging around? How did he find the address, do you think?"

"Same way as you, I expect," Staines said curtly. Chrissy wondered about the phone details. How could he possibly have got a copy of what she herself had?

"Somehow, I doubt that very much. Not unless he had access to Bronagh's phone."

Staines thought for a moment. "It was smashed, at the crash site. Come to think about it, it looked like someone had put their heel through the screen."

So he'd already looked and discarded it without anyone the wiser. Was the investigator the cause of the crash, to get at Bronagh's phone? That raised another question if so, how did they know Bronagh was involved?

"I guess we'll find out how soon enough, when we talk to him."

"There is no 'we'. I think you've had enough involvement for now." It was his way of telling her once again to leave things alone. She checked the wall clock.

"Whatever," she added, waving him away. "But can I suggest we start the journey back? Perhaps you'll come around to mine when you arrive home?"

Staines nodded. "Where is this investigator now?"

"I don't know. The local Guards moved him on earlier. They have his number plate so you can check your cameras. Perhaps he's scarpered back to where he came from."

"Let's hope." Staines stood. "Safe trip then. Watch your rear-view mirror, eh?"

"I'll grab your bags, shall I?" she offered to Lorcan, and headed off upstairs, thinking they needed to swap the car seat over before they set out. Staines must have had the same idea because by the time she'd arrived back downstairs, the pair were making the switch, Flynn flopped lazily over his father's shoulder. He gently lowered the child into the seat, strapped him in and laid a pale blue blanket across his body. It reminded her of the one she'd wrapped him the morning she'd found him. She loaded the bags into the boot and remembered the buggy, which Lorcan grabbed from his own car. He then tossed the keys to Staines. Once all three were safely in Brocc's old vehicle, he gave a quick nod as they pulled away. Through the rear-view mirror, she watched Staines get into his own vehicle and drive back towards the town centre and the local station. He'd got some explaining to do but that wasn't her concern.

Lorcan was silent, not wishing to talk nor relive recent events, and Chrissy let him be, even though she still had so many questions that needed answers. The weak sunshine filled the car, casting a warmth over the three individuals inside. By the time they'd reached the main road home, both Flynn and Lorcan had dozed off and were fast asleep. The stress he must have been under had taken its toll and Chrissy watched over them both as she made the three-hour journey back in silence. A few minutes out from the house, she made the call.

It was almost dark when Julie, Adam, and Richard met the three of them at the door and helped take their few belongings inside.

It felt good, being in someone else's care for a while. Like a small child might snuggle into the ample bosom of its grandma for comfort, Lorcan, or Matthew, as he had been known previously, felt like he was being wrapped up in the comfort of the very same. Even a grown man needed to feel safe, and when that safety had disintegrated, he'd run, and it had frightened him nonetheless. It wasn't just children that needed a hug once in a while, or a loving and caring relationship, it was everyone. As Chrissy pulled up at the holiday home, he pretended to stir from his deep slumber, though in reality he'd been awake, lying there thinking, for the best part of the last hour. He was avoiding talking, he knew, but he did owe her an explanation at the very least. Should he tell her the whole story though? Or just the pieces that would satisfy her? Was it his place to put the good work of the group, maybe other lives, in jeopardy? Bronagh would know, but she wasn't there to advise. She was the bosom that had saved them all.

He stretched as he pretended to come around, glancing at Flynn still fast asleep in the child seat behind him, his perfect little cherub face resting to his right. He hoped the little boy didn't have a stiff neck from the journey back, he was obviously tired out too. Children picked up on fear, on anger, on worry, and Flynn had been no different. He could have played up more, been a good deal worse than he had been, and Lorcan was thankful for the child's goodwill in that respect. Perhaps he'd sensed adding any more to Lorcan's plate would have toppled him. Chrissy's voice sounded in his ears.

"We're here," she said gently. The left side of his own face bore a line where he'd been resting on the seat-belt strap, and it had manifested itself as a deep crease. He sat up awkwardly, a real case of bedhead without having had a full night's sleep. He forced a smile, rubbing his eyes to awaken himself more. At the sound of voices and the car coming to a halt, Flynn stirred in his own seat, bleary baby eyes greeting them both.

In a low voice, Chrissy said, "Hello little man." He stared back at her; he was still in his own state of half awake. Should he cry or not? Lorcan stepped in to help him understand. Flynn wriggled in his seat and screwed his face up, threatening tears, and Lorcan soothed him with a hand to his head, stroking gently.

"Let's get you both inside." Chrissy stepped from the car as he opened his own door and released Flynn from the booster seat and into his arms. It was then he noticed the small group gathered by the front door as he headed towards the house. Rupert bounded towards him and he quickly ruffled the dog's head before refocusing on the group of adults. How much did they know? he wondered. Would he be welcome? How much had Chrissy told them? He hadn't heard her call anyone, but then he had drifted off when they'd finally hit the road. Adam stepped forward and reached out a hand, and Lorcan shook it heartily, searching the other man's eyes for confirmation he was welcome. The last thing they'd want would be a wild woman turning up on their own doorstep, making a scene. He shuddered at the memory of only a few hours ago and hoped Tess was miles away someplace. Where? He didn't much care.

"Hello again. Come on inside," Adam suggested with a sympathetic smile, leading the way into the living room. "Make yourself comfortable, I'll go and get your gear."

Lorcan placed Flynn down on the sofa for a moment and let him settle himself, which he did by lying out flat and closing his eyes again. It wouldn't be long before he'd be back asleep. He sat himself, closed his own eyes, head back, just for a sweet moment, and let his shoulders fall back down to their normal resting place. He hadn't realised how far up by his ears they had been, a sure sign of the stress he'd been under. Someone entered the room. Julie. He remembered dancing with her on their first night in the village, and he managed a smile.

"Adam has put your things in the spare room, you'll be quite comfortable in there. There's even a travel cot so Flynn will be safe too." Did she sound a little businesslike, or was that his imagination? Perhaps she didn't approve of his impromptu overnight stay.

"I'll be gone first thing, but thanks."

Julie sat down in a chair opposite and studied the man who had caused so much intrigue of recent.

"You're mad, aren't you? At me," he said.

Julie studied him for a moment before speaking. "Mad isn't a word I'd choose. Confused, yes." Her tone was cool, untrusting, and Lorcan knew he'd have to appease her if he wanted her on his side.

"Is this where I say I can explain?"

Rupert sauntered over and flopped down by his feet.

"Why don't you try me. I've never sat opposite a human being that deserted his little boy and ran off before. I'm interested in hearing what could possibly be so important." The words stung, but he would have thought the same had the roles been reversed. Lorcan fixed his mouth firmly, chewing his lower lip while he contemplated what to say next.

"Leave the man alone, Julie!" Chrissy said as she entered the room with Adam and Richard right behind her. "Lorcan will speak when he's good and ready, I'm sure. Won't you, Lorcan?" she asked, eyeing him almost like a matron on a hospital ward in an old movie. He held her gaze for a long moment as everyone sat down.

"I know I owe you all an explanation."

Julie harrumphed and tucked her legs underneath herself as she did so, turning the other cheek. He carried on: "I can only tell you so much. Not because I don't want to explain, but if I go into too much detail, there'll be others at risk, in danger."

"Others?" Richard asked. Chrissy had kept him out of the loop.

Lorcan took a deep breath in and released it noisily. It was time to start filling in some of the pieces. "Yes. Men mainly, like me. Men that have been victims of domestic abuse, many far worse than my own experience." Richard raised his eyebrows in surprise, it was not what he'd been expecting to hear.

"So I'm guessing you ran away, escaped?" he asked.

"Flynn and I, yes. I couldn't leave him with Tess, my wife, I couldn't trust her not to harm him too."

Another harrumph from the corner as Julie again looked the other way, unimpressed so far. Richard sent her his best glare, but she'd turned to stare at the opposite side of the room.

"So, who is Ciara then? If Tess is your wife, where does she fit into all this?"

"I don't think I can say where she fits in, not yet, for her own sake. But I can tell you she's a therapist, a psychologist. Maybe that will be enough for you."

"Tell us about what happened that night," Adam said.

Lorcan again took a deep breath and bowed his head a little, thinking back. After a few beats, he spoke. "I had a phone call, when I was last here. Somehow, she'd got my number. Scared the hell out of me, I can tell you. She said she was on her way, knew about the castle, that I couldn't escape her. I was terrified, so I called Bronagh, told her we had to move on, and quickly. There was no time to do anything more than grab our clothes and flee. Tess could have been parked up the lane for all I knew." He gathered his emotions that were threatening to spill over as his voice caught on leaving his child alone, even for a short time.

"Where does Bronagh fit in then?" asked Chrissy.

Lorcan paused while he contemplated his answer without saying too much. "She's a marvel. She takes care of any children as the need arises; we refer to her as 'the sitter'. She's looked after Flynn on many occasions – like when Ciara and I first met you in the pub that night, he was with her."

That fitted. Chrissy nodded for him to carry on.

"We'd had to travel separately, Flynn and I, to get here. To keep away from the authorities. They'd have been on the lookout for a man and his child so separating us made more sense. Safer. When we had to leave on Monday, Bronagh was to babysit, take him back to hers and we'd sort it from there. I couldn't risk Tess finding him if she was on my tail, so it was best if we split again, for a while. She was on her way over when..." Lorcan's voice trailed off as the group filled in the blanks. "But she never reached him that night."

Julie turned to him, all negative thoughts about his actions visibly gone, tears in her eyes at the revelations so far. She'd obviously no idea how much he'd been through and had jumped to her own conclusions about why he'd abandoned his son. She could never have thought it would be something so frightening and heart-wrenching. He'd never meant for any of it to happen, events had taken hold and he'd had no way of knowing what was going on behind him. Thank goodness Chrissy had found Flynn when she did.

"I had the pleasure of meeting Tess earlier," Chrissy added sarcastically.

"Tess hated Flynn with a passion. More than she hated me. There was no way either of us could stay." Shock waves filled the room – how could that be?

"She sounds like a piece of work does Tess. How can a mother hate her son so much?" Julie asked.

Lorcan glanced at Julie as he said, quietly, "Flynn isn't hers." All eyes were on him. He could see Chrissy doing the rough maths in her head as she pondered a possible but obvious explanation. Flynn must have been from a previous relationship of Lorcan's, but still, even that equation has an overlap time. Flynn's age didn't stack up right.

"Flynn is— was my sister's child," he said. "She passed away six months ago, and I took his care on at her request. I'd have taken him anyway, he's family, and a lovely boy into the bargain, and I could never have handed him over to the state to look after, never."

"That explains the hair colour," said Chrissy. The room sat silently as they each digested what they'd been told. It sounded horrific because it was. There was so much more to understand, but it was getting late. The day had been tough on both Lorcan and young Flynn, who was now sound asleep again.

"I've been calling him Flynn for so long, I wonder if I'll remember to call him by his real name ever again," he said, watching the child sleep beside him. Could he love him any more than he already did?

The room seemed to wait for him to reveal what it had once been, what he'd been christened. As he glanced at Chrissy, it was obvious she was dying to know.

"Blue. He's called Blue. His mother was a bit of a stargazer at times. She'd wanted to call him Cloud, but settled on Blue, thank goodness," he said, smiling at the memory. While it had been her decision, Lorcan— Matthew had thought she'd gone mad. Blue it had been.

"It suits him," Julie offered, her olive branch. "Little boy Blue."

Adam took charge. "Well I suggest we all go and get a good night's rest. You'll be safe here, I'm sure. We can talk more in the morning, figure out what happens next," he said, stifling a yawn himself. Lorcan nodded, relieved at having said enough to explain the worst of it but not all of it.

Chrissy stood. "I agree. Let's see how you feel in the morning. I'm sure Sergeant Staines will be here first thing."

Lorcan just hoped the Guards weren't going to be too hard on him.

"Come on, I'll show you to your room."

Lorcan picked Flynn up, who uttered a tiny whimper as he stirred, and followed Adam to the spare room at the back of the house. There was little point disturbing the sleeping child and so he placed him straight in the travel cot and covered him over with a blanket. He turned back to Adam.

"Thank you."

"It's Chrissy that deserves the thanks, not me," he said warmly and headed to his own room, leaving Lorcan and the child to get some rest.

CHAPTER 76

Tess had finally calmed down after spending the afternoon being interviewed by the local Guards. She'd been released with a warning to steer clear of her husband, and the English police had been notified of her recent actions. While she was in Ireland, there wasn't much else they could do. Banging on someone's door and causing a scene wasn't worth getting too excited over. No doubt when she returned home, there'd be a knock on her door and a visit from her local police force. She'd deal with that then, with her lawyer present. Until then, she had work to do and that involved tracking Matthew down and making him pay. She doubted he'd have headed back to England, so that meant he was still in Ireland. She just had to figure out where. Nobody walked out on her, not ever. She'd keep control of things, the child and all – he was her bargaining chip. And what was with the name change? Where had Lorcan come from? He was about as Irish as her little finger. She sniggered as she sat in her hotel room and tossed her third vodka back and gazed at the map of Ireland displayed on her iPad in front of her. His car tracker, the one the investigator had planted, showed his vehicle was stationary at the address she'd visited earlier, and hadn't moved. But she knew he wasn't anywhere close by; he was smarter than that. The tiny icon pulsed its location, but she'd been back to the property, even though she'd been warned against it by the Guards. It had been in darkness. The curtains all open, she'd peered in and looked at the meagre furnishings with disdain. A rental, with crappy second-hand-shop bits and pieces like you'd find in a halfway house for a criminal out on parole. It had been pitiful, certainly not what he'd been used to in their home together.

She'd provided well for him, and him for her, both with excellent, steady career jobs, but then the boy had come along and spoiled everything. He'd robbed her. She hadn't asked for him, had had no choice in the matter, and resentment had taken hold early on. No sooner had he entered their lives than she had felt Matthew pull away a little. As the child received more and more of his attention, it seemed there was less available for her and so she'd shown him quite how she'd felt about being second place in his affections. Small at first, almost jokingly, little nips and pinches to get his attention, to make him aware she was still in his life, and that there was more than the little one that needed him. They'd laughed it off early on, neither realising what was happening, how things would then progress.

He'd spilled a mug of tea all over the kitchen floor one evening, right in front of her. He'd said it was an accident, caught the mug handle all wrong and down the whole thing had gone, smashing to the floor. Pieces of ceramic had shot off in all directions, the beige liquid running under the fridge. As he'd bent down to start the clean-up, she'd lashed out with her foot and kicked him in the side of his ribs. He'd yelled out in shock, staggered to his feet and got straight into her face, demanding to know why she'd done it. At last, a reaction, some attention, he'd noticed she was there. But it had only lasted a second or two as he'd yelled at her and she in return had slapped his face, and hard. It had stunned him. The pathetic excuse that was her husband hadn't the balls to strike her back as she'd egged him on that night. She'd goaded him, begged him to, but he'd simply walked away. And that had been that. The thrill, the adrenaline, the anger even, whatever it had been had lingered a while and she'd enjoyed it immensely, had celebrated it. She'd slept beside him wordlessly, relived it over and over in her mind for the rest of the night.

He never mentioned again.

What a weak man.

The following day he'd gone to work as normal, but she'd noticed the shift in his attitude towards her. The distance he put between them hurt and she despised that even the tiniest spark of attention to herself had all but died. So she'd upped her attempts to make him see her, want her, desire her again, make him understand he couldn't ignore her. That was where the child had come in handy. Pinching his flabby upper arms had got the reaction she so craved. He'd looked at her and though she knew it wasn't affection in his eyes, it would do nonetheless. From there it had been easy to keep the attention up and it became almost a daily event to look forward to. But then a nosey neighbour had called the police over the screaming and shouting going on one evening and they'd had to deal with that. No charges were ever brought, because no one figured it was a woman administering the violence. When asked if she wanted to make it official, she'd played the attention game once again and pleaded no, she was just fine. The sympathy she saw in various officers' eyes was almost better than the attention Matthew afforded her. At least theirs was genuine, the emotion lingering just a little while longer than anything she received from her loving husband.

But like a rogue sheepdog after attacking a lamb, she had a taste for it. Now she wanted more.

She made a call to her private investigator. Matthew had to be found. And soon.

CHAPTER 77

His instructions had been clear: find him in the next twenty-four hours and there would be an extra ten thousand in it for him. That wasn't to be sniffed at. It would take the immediate pressure off his own life's problems, though it wouldn't stop the avalanche once it started to roll. He'd deal with that when it happened. Sitting at a scuffed desk in a dreary hotel that smelled of cheap pine air freshener, he'd wondered about being moved on by the Guards and had assumed at the time it'd been a concerned neighbour. But since the turn of recent events, it looked more likely he'd been spotted and reported during surveillance, possibly by his target himself and that had been that. It had been embarrassing to say the least though, and Tess had torn into him when he'd called her with the bad news. Since she had already been on her way to the address, driving down from Dublin, she'd told him to leave things to her, that she'd take over and had it in hand. He wondered what had then gone wrong since she'd not long ago called and offered him the extra incentive to get back on the case and be quick about it. While she was a tough bitch to deal with, she paid well and on time, though it was one job he couldn't wait to see the back of. If she ever called him for help in the future, he'd steer clear. Unless he was desperate again.

He knew the man's car hadn't shifted, the tracker he'd deposited still pulsing slowly at the house location, and she'd told him her husband had already fled, the place in darkness, deserted. That left him to wonder how the man had travelled and where he might have gone. Having a child along with him would undoubtedly slow him down, but that could also be a saving grace, a bonus for finding him.

He looked at his watch, time was marching on. With no fresh leads to go on, it was like starting again.

Or was it?

He grabbed his notes and scanned each of the cars he'd noted coming and going, along with the odd delivery service. There hadn't been many arrivals to the sleepy estate, but with the advantage of hindsight, maybe one of them could have been the husband's guardian angel, or his co-conspirator? It was worth taking another, closer look. Several cars had left while he'd watched, all likely heading out to work, he figured, and since none had returned during the morning, he'd discounted them all. He'd made a note of the details nonetheless. It was surprising how often something so innocuous could turn into being nocuous later on in a case. He made a call and gave the man at the other end of the line the three vehicle registration plate details he'd recorded. It was a costly service to use, but the case now warranted it with the bonus on offer.

It didn't take long to run a simple background check and get the results. A local florist, a woman in her twenties and the owner-driver, gave him no reason to investigate further than finding out she lived locally and had been in business for all of two years. He doubted she'd be a likely candidate for smuggling the man and his child off somewhere, though the van aspect interested him. He'd go back to her later. The second was an elderly man, probably too old to still be behind a steering wheel he thought, and likely visiting family. The house he'd stopped at had been a good way further up than his target's and the old man had stayed for about an hour before leaving. Coffee with a daughter perhaps? That left one more vehicle, an older car with a woman at the wheel. It was registered to a garage, the woman driver not listed as the owner. The address flashed at him like a lighthouse beacon.

"Bingo!" he shouted, springing up from his chair in the run-down room. Now why would a car registered to a garage in Doolin, some three hours north, be parked up near his target? There could only be one reason. She'd arrived mid-morning, but had she gone before the Guards had moved him on? He couldn't be sure. He hadn't made a note of it.

It must have been her. He grinned at her ploy as he realised she'd been the one to spot him and have him moved out of the way. And he'd been so careful, blended in, or so he'd thought.

"Sneaky cow," he said. But where was she now? More importantly, was Tess's husband and child with her? If not, she'd likely know where he was, where she'd taken him. Surely he hadn't gone back to the castle, had he? There was only one way to find out. It made sense. Who would think he'd go back to where he'd fled from? It was genius in its simplicity, hiding in plain sight almost. He quickly threw his few belongings back into his overnight bag and left the room. It would be a long drive up in the dark, but since he could feel the bonus money getting that bit closer, he brushed it off. There'd be a coffee stop at Mallow, hopefully, in an all-night service station. If there was one.

Should he call Tess now, or wait? She might want to set off north herself if she hadn't done so already, but if he was wrong, he didn't fancy her wrath a second time in one day. Or ever again.

"No wonder the husband left," he mumbled to himself as he started his engine. A light drizzle fell making his windscreen smeary as his wipers did their best to clear his vision. There was hardly a soul on the deserted streets of Kinsale as he pulled away and headed north, back up the N20, towards Doolin, and the castle on the hill.

Even though she was exhausted, Chrissy was restless as she turned over for the umpteenth time, trying to find a spot where sleep would come. Neither numbers nor alphabet, nor sheep, nor breathing exercises appeared to help as her mind rolled with events of the day like the ocean outside. Two exhausted individuals were likely sound asleep at the back of the house and she was grateful she'd found them. While they seemed well, Lorcan, she couldn't think of him as Matthew yet, was a nervous wreck and, recalling Bronagh's words, she hoped she hadn't put them both in more danger by investigating their disappearance. Tess had acted like something demented back in Kinsale and Chrissy had been glad of Staines's involvement. Sure, she could have called the local Guards herself, but with him on their side, it had most likely worked out better. He'd arrived at just the right time.

Where was Tess now? Was she still in the country or had she flown back to Manchester? She doubted it. Having come all this way and involved a private investigator, she was intent on seeing her husband again, of that Chrissy was sure. No, the woman would be licking her wounds some place – and waiting.

Sergeant Staines would be around in the morning. She was keen to hear of his involvement, where he fitted in. Had he knowingly handed the little one over to someone impersonating family services? Or had he acted correctly, had he contacted them and someone else had intervened? She doubted he'd admit to any wrongdoing, he could lose his job over it. His presence and the sight of his uniform had saved the morning back in Kinsale and she was grateful for that part at least.

It was just after midnight that sleep eventually came for Chrissy and the rest of the house slept peacefully and undisturbed. Tomorrow there would be more questions, and hopefully more answers.

He could see the castle was in total darkness as he approached from the narrow lane, but he expected it to be at midnight. He turned his headlamps off and drove the last few metres carefully before pulling up just outside the boundary. He'd make the rest of the way quietly and on foot. He grabbed his torch, tugged his jacket closer and pulled the hood up, then set out across the grass to take a closer look. Clouds covered the moon, making visibility almost impossible, so he had to be quick while using his torch. The last thing he needed was a nosey neighbour reporting his torchlight, or worse, if the husband was inside, that he be seen snooping through the window. As he approached the first downstairs window, he pressed his nose to the glass for a closer look, but it was useless, he needed the torch. A quick burst of light inside told him the ground floor was empty. There was no way of looking in the rooms further on up, so he risked turning the torch on again for a closer look at what he could see from where he was standing. The kitchen looked unused, everything in its place, and he wondered if there were any signs of life at all in the old building. He slipped around the other side of the castle and shone his torch through from the other side. There didn't appear to be anything of note, no bags left in the door-way, no meal remains on the table, no nothing. Perhaps the husband wasn't inside after all. Moving back towards the front door, he tried the handle. The door was locked. Damn, he couldn't even creep inside, not that he particularly wanted to. He did, however, want the extra ten grand.

With nothing else to look at or do, he consoled himself for having got it wrong. Though it was possible the man was hiding out in Doolin somewhere else, just not at the castle. Walking back in the darkness towards his car, he had one last destination on his mind. While he wasn't expecting to see the old car parked outside the garage, he did suspect the owner was involved and would know the husband's whereabouts. Should he call Tess now?

Sitting in the darkness, he made the call.

"Doolin, eh?" Tess said. He could hear the smile in her voice, even though he'd obviously just woken her.

"I'll go and see him first thing in the morning."

"After today's debacle? No, you won't. Leave this to me." There was no mistaking her intention, but it raised a concern for him.

"What about my money, the ten grand?"

"That all depends on what the man from the garage has to say."

He was about to protest but Tess had already hung up on him.

SATURDAY

CHAPTER 79

Julie had taken to strolling up to the village for fresh bread and a newspaper. It reminded her of being in France on leisurely holidays gone by, though always watching her weight, she'd rarely eaten the croissants she'd returned with, let alone the soft cheese and ham. While she still monitored her intake with precision, she'd found that the longer walks she now took a couple of times a week, not to mention working at the boutique, had done wonders for removing the extra calories, and so had found herself relaxing her intake a little more often. After all, life was too short to be so strict with her food, there were other more pressing things to concern herself with. Chrissy had opted to stay behind and play with Blue while Loran, or Matthew, as they now knew him to be, hung out with Richard and Adam, mainly drinking coffee and dissecting football matches while they sat in the living room or on the deck. He was looking a good deal more relaxed than when he'd arrived the previous night, though knew he wasn't out of the woods quite yet.

As she passed the garage, the lad she assumed was the apprentice Chrissy had mentioned working there, was just leaving, likely on his way to either the pub for lunch, or home. Everyone in Doolin seemed to live where they worked, and it wouldn't be far if he was indeed heading there. She could see Brocc just inside, talking to a woman. Maybe she was a tourist having trouble with her vehicle; something about the way she was dressed told Julie she wasn't a local. Even Julie had found herself dressing for the weather and far more casually than she did back in Surrey. A Mercedes SUV parked by the kerb looked as if it perhaps belonged to her. It had a sticker in the back window that informed anyone following it was on hire from the same company as they'd used for their own hire car. What would she need a garage for with a hire car? Julie wondered. She thought no more about it as she headed on to the bread shop.

She'd miss the place, she was sure, miss the routine they'd found themselves in, each of them enjoying the restfulness of it all, though she doubted Chrissy had found it quite so. She was never one to sit still for very long, she'd proven that by getting involved with young Flynn, Blue, in the first place. She smiled to herself at the vision of them both crawling along the living room floor together, the toddler's giggle as she tickled him, let him ride on her back like a cowboy on his horse, and her own memories of her own two girls when they were small came flooding back. Did they really enjoy their boarding school or was it time to consider bringing them home, schooling them more locally? It wasn't the first time she'd wondered about it in recent months. Perhaps she was getting soft, mellowing as she aged, and she wondered what Richard might think of the idea. After all, he'd been the one that had pushed for their places away right from the get-go. Maybe she'd ask him. She reached the shop and stepped inside to the lingering aroma of freshly baked bread. It was warm and cosy on another bright, crisp day. A woman wearing a white apron greeted her, wiping her hands as she did so, causing flour to billow in the air. Her smile filled her flushed, round face as she asked, "What can I get you?"

"Two soda breads, please."

The woman wrapped each of them in tissue. "They're still a bit warm, is that okay?"

"Even better," she replied as she studied the cakes. Unsure

which to take back, she asked for a selection for six people and watched as the woman filled a box. When she had everything she needed, she paid and left the shop, heading back towards the house. As she approached the garage, she couldn't help but notice the front roller door was now down, the place looked closed up. In the few days they'd been staying in Doolin, she'd never once seen the place closed during the day. The Mercedes was still parked by the kerb, though the vehicle itself was empty. Since she'd only seen Brocc's apprentice leave a few minutes ago, he'd likely still be away on his lunch break.

Something felt wrong. She glanced about her; there wasn't another soul nearby, but that wasn't unusual in the small village. With everything that had been going on of recent, an internal unease filled her chest and she stood still for a moment to let it pass. It was taking its time and after a couple of long beats, she was still standing fixed to the spot. And then a pull, an imaginary magnet from the building, urged her to detour and she let it take over. Walking slowly as she approached the garage door, she placed her head against the metal to see if she could hear anything. A faint murmur of conversation, though she couldn't decipher any words, nor hear who was speaking. That made it even more intriguing, that there was someone inside, yet the door closed. She knew there had to be a rear entrance – should she take a look? Balancing bread and a box of cakes in her hands, she berated herself for not getting a plastic bag, but it was too late to concern herself with that now. She placed them on the floor, the bread on top. Hopefully the loaves wouldn't squash the contents below. She pulled out her phone and wondered about sending a text to Chrissy, she'd know what to do, but what would she say? The roller door is down at the garage, seems odd? She'd laugh out loud.

"Come on, Julie, you're a big girl," she said under her breath as she headed behind the building in search of another way in. Surely it would be unlocked during the day, unless Brocc *had* actually closed up for some reason. He'd have taken the 'open' sign in though, wouldn't he? It was still standing proudly out front.

The sound of voices was much clearer as she slowly opened the old wooden door and she hoped the hinges were well oiled as she pulled it wider. Not a sound from the old thing and she let her breath out, which she'd been holding in her lungs as if that too might make a sound. It took a moment for her eyes to adjust to the darker interior, though a small dirty window allowed a modicum of outside light to enter the room. It appeared to be some kind of storeroom, there was an old sink in the corner for getting water for the kettle. She paused to try and understand what might be happening on the other side of the wall. A woman's voice sounded frustrated, angry even, her tone an octave higher than it would be in normal conversation. A male voice, Brocc's, she assumed, was the total opposite, dull, flat, and steady. Whatever was going on, the woman was seething about something, and for something like a repair to her car gone wrong, such a clandestine discussion seemed a little over the top. Julie decided to text Chrissy, something was definitely amiss.

At the garage, something not right. I'm inside the back door. Drive up.

She waited for a reply, hoping her sister had her phone nearby and didn't miss the message. It didn't take long.

On my way. Don't do anything dumb.

Like what? Julie thought, tutting at her sister's orders.

A hollow yell, the sound of someone in pain, came from the other side of the wall and had her re-evaluating her next move in an instant.

CHAPTER 80

There was no way she was going to wait for Chrissy now. If Brocc was in some kind of trouble, she might be able to help him. Slowly, she moved from her side of the internal door and dared a quick look at what was going on around the other side. She whipped her head back in an instant and hoped she hadn't been seen. After a couple of heavy heartbeats had passed, she took stock of what she'd managed to see. The back of a woman's body, according to the hairstyle, but it was what she held in her right hand that caused Julie to inwardly gasp in horror. It was the blue flame of a blowtorch. Her father had had one in his shed, for welding and repairing things she or Chrissy had broken over their childhood years. The flame was on full blue, giving it the ability to burn anything it touched in seconds. She must have been using it on Brocc, judging by his cry of pain only moments ago.

Could it be Tess?

She needed to alert the Guards, and she needed to warn Chrissy, but right at that moment, she needed to help Brocc before the woman did some serious damage. She was in a garage, so there were tools lying about, and she searched for something she could use to deflect the woman's attention, preferably a crowbar she could wrap around Tess's head. As Brocc experienced obvious pain and yelled out again, Julie could wait no longer. She quietly grabbed the cordless kettle from its spot on the sink drainer and was pleased to feel the weight of water inside. It had been recently boiled judging by the heat, and she could only pray Brocc didn't end up getting scalded in the bargain. She stepped into the room soundlessly and, in a split second, ran forward a couple of paces before stretching her right arm out. Then, with all the force she could muster, she swung the hot kettle at the woman's skull. It struck with a sickening thump but it did the trick. Down she went as her brain gave up for a moment and forced her body to crumple onto the floor in a heap. Julie stood for a second and looked down at her handiwork. There was no obvious blood coming from the woman's head, but then the darkness inside the garage could have covered it up. Never in her life had she attacked someone with such ferocity, never had she needed to, and she stood momentarily in a state of shock. Julie finally turned her attention to Brocc who was sitting slumped forward in an old chair. His hands and feet were tied to it with what looked like thin rope. A hole in his overalls on his thigh showed where the woman had pointed the naked blue flame to burn his skin.

"Brocc!" she said urgently. "Are you okay?"

He was out cold too. Julie's nose picked up an acrid smell to one side of her and she spun around to see where it was coming from. A pile of rags was already engulfed by flames that were spreading rapidly as the oil and chemicals they contained acted as an accelerant.

Flames climbed the wall. The garage was on fire.

"The blowtorch!" she yelled, running towards the flames, but it was too late. It must have been thrown from the woman's hand as she'd fallen and had already made a start on creating a blaze that was well on its way to destruction. Julie was momentarily transfixed and motionless.

"Oh hell!" shouted Chrissy. After a quick glance at Brocc tied to the chair and a woman on the ground out cold, she spotted Julie statue-still, watching the flames climb up towards the roof.

"Julie!" she yelled at the top of her voice. It did the trick and her sister was instantly dragged back to the here and now, the sound of someone else in the building releasing her from the paralysis. Her eyes shone in the glow from the flames as she joined Chrissy.

"We need to move Brocc first," Chrissy yelled, and the two women took a side of the old chair each and shuffled him outside through the back door and planted him firmly in the yard. Chrissy started to run back inside.

"There could be all sorts in there that could blow," Julie yelled.

"I'll be quick. We can't leave her," she shouted as she disappeared around the corner again. Thick black smoke belched from the door and Julie could hear a siren in the background. Someone had called the fire brigade, help was on its way, but would they be in time? A side window blew glass outwards, it splintering on the uneven concrete a few metres away. Julie glanced down at Brocc who was now coming too, but Chrissy still hadn't appeared. She dashed towards the door again and went inside to lend a hand, but dense black smoke choked her back and filled her eyes. There was no way she could go in after her.

"Chrissy!" she screamed above the roar of flames, but it was no use. Remembering the kettle had been on the sink, she closed her eyes and fumbled her way over to feel for a hand towel she could soak and put over her mouth to help her breathe. There was no way she was going to leave her sister inside on her own.

There was one! She turned the tap on and soaked the cloth before wringing it out and using it to protect her lungs. She set off in what she hoped was the right direction but a firm hand on her shoulder suddenly pulled her back. Confused, she turned to see the mask and breathing apparatus of a firefighter before he bent to pick her up and carry her back outside.

"My sister!" she yelled in his face, but he didn't respond, concentrating on getting her away to safety. Julie thumped his chest for him to let her go but he was twice the size and strength of her.

Smokey tears sprang from her eyes as she sobbed for him to help Chrissy then bright daylight forced them to close against the sun. He placed her on her own two feet as a paramedic rushed to her aid.

"My sister!" she howled again, hysteria settling in, her sobs bursting through her chest in torrents.

"They'll find her," a friendly voice said, though Julie wasn't listening as they put an oxygen mask on her and attempted to wipe the worst off her sooty face. The mask made it impossible to shout, and her throat burned at the effort, but it didn't stop her trying to make them understand. A firefighter approached her and asked if she knew how many were inside.

"Chrissy, my sister! You've got to find her!"

"Anyone else?"

"A woman, on the floor, that's all. Please, find Chrissy!" Julie watched as the fire officer conferred with two colleagues and they went back to search once again. What had happened to Chrissy? Brocc was wheeled by on a stretcher, and she gazed at his ashen face as he passed. She wanted to wish him well, tell him everything was going to be all right, but her strength to speak had evaporated. She turned her concentration to the building in front of her that was now fully engulfed in flames. Chrissy was the only thing that mattered now, getting her out, getting her to safety. She thought of Adam and the boys; did he even know where Chrissy was? Had she told him anything when she'd driven up only a few moments ago? But then, a fireman emerged carrying a woman in his arms, her filthy blonde hair resting by the man's shoulder.

It was Chrissy.

Two paramedics rushed over to help as the fire officer laid her on the ground in the recovery position. They both worked frantically as the fireman returned back to the fire for the remaining woman. Julie sat transfixed at what she was witnessing and so it didn't particularly register when they quickly turned Chrissy onto her back, and a paramedic commenced CPR compressions to Chrissy's chest. It was only when Adam filled the picture that she jolted back. Suddenly Richard was by her side, holding her head and shoulders awkwardly in his arms, crying with relief. She gazed up at him, hoping he could read the worry that had settled in her own eyes before they both turned to the scene nearby. Adam was down on the cold concrete, stroking Chrissy's hair, words moving from his mouth, though neither of them could hear what he was saying. They could only guess. It felt as if the world had stopped as each of them willed Chrissy to take another breath, for her heart to restart, for her lungs to once again fill with clean air.

SUNDAY

CHAPTER 81

It was Bronagh's turn to play visitor to a patient in hospital. Brocc lay propped up in bed looking a whole lot brighter than he had done the previous day when they'd brought him in. Having suffered from smoke inhalation and a badly burned thigh from a mad woman wielding a blowtorch, he was now feeling a good deal better than of recent.

"The article says she didn't survive the fire," Bronagh relayed sadly. "Still, she knew what she was doing," she said, showing no sympathy and shaking the paper out before folding it in half, her almost complete crossword ready for another attempt when she had time.

"Don't be so hard on her."

Bronagh could only sniff, her disdain evident.

"Shouldn't have been meddling where her nose wasn't wanted." She folded her arms across her chest triumphantly, as if she herself had won a battle. Her cast rested oddly with her good arm. "She could have done untold damage that woman, mark my words."

"But she didn't, did she?" Brocc added, trying to appease his sister. "No real harm done. In fact, for the lad, you could say it worked out well in the end." He tried his best to shuffle up the bed a little and relieve his left buttock of being numb. Pain shot through his thigh; it would be a reminder of recent events for a few more days yet to come.

"Anyway, you've some more visitors," she said, changing the subject and smiling broadly as a group and a toddler in a buggy headed towards his bed. Chrissy sat in a wheelchair, her head bandaged from a nasty cut on her forehead. Other than that, she was fine. She'd only been released herself an hour or so ago, having passed the doctor's tests easily and promised to take things easy and stay put on the sofa. He'd agreed to her release on the proviso that she travel to the car park in a wheelchair and stay in Doolin for at least one more night. They should have left for home this morning, but events had prevented them from doing so. Adam stationed her beside Brocc so she could reach forward and take hold of his hand.

"How are you doing?"

"Good. Though I believe the garage isn't." There was no malice in his words.

"Ah, about that."

Brocc smiled. "Not your fault. I dare say she'd have torched *me* had it not been for blondie here," he added, holding a beckoning arm out to Julie. She stepped forward, all traces of smoke gone and smelling of fresh roses. "I broke a fingernail in the process," she quipped. "I just hoped I wasn't going to scald you when your kettle made contact with her spiteful head. That's all you needed." Richard watched on proudly. A gurgling laugh from a small mouth caught everyone by surprise – young Blue. Matthew pushed the buggy next to Chrissy's wheelchair so the older man could see what his efforts had been for. Matthew held out his hand to shake and Brocc took it.

"Thank you for your help. I can't apologise enough for dragging you into my mess."

"Ah, happy it's sorted now. I guess you'll be going back to Manchester soon. Back home?"

"I'm not so sure actually. Now I've nothing to run from, I might investigate Ireland on a better footing, we'll see. Plus I've still got to see where the Guards and I end up. The DPP may still charge me with neglect, even though Bronagh was on her way when we took off. You all know the rest," he said, glancing round, "it was no one's fault, just bad luck."

"And a couple of youths out joyriding with no lights on," added Bronagh grimly, remembering back to the accident. It could have been a very different outcome that day. The Guards had since received a report from another driver about an unlit vehicle out on the back road two nights since. It seemed the youngsters thought it would be fun to intimidate solo drivers, fancied themselves as junior James Bonds. They were being dealt with. While it didn't fully explain how Bronagh's phone had found its way out of her bag, the theory was perhaps they'd stopped at the scene and rummaged through her belongings, looking for something of value. They would never know for sure.

"Well, thanks to a barking dog and a private investigator on holiday, there was no real harm done. Blue was found safe and sound," Bronagh added, smiling warmly at Chrissy, who was wearing the scarf she'd bought from the woman's shop on their first day on holiday, a souvenir of another case with a happy ending.

"I still have one unanswered question, Bronagh, if I may," said Chrissy.

"I'll see if I can answer it."

"The barman. Where does he fit in? He has a record, for violence."

Bronagh dropped her chin, while she thought how best to respond most likely. "He's a victim, now a volunteer. He helps make up the accommodation when needed, hence the boxes you saw."

"But his record?"

"Same story as Matthew here, I'm afraid. It was all *her* doing, no violence from himself. That's why the charges were always dropped, because *she* never laid any since she was the perpetrator in effect." It made perfect sense. The man wasn't violent at all. Chrissy wondered about his current situation, if his personal storm had calmed yet.

Adam slipped his arm around her shoulder and squeezed it gently. It was time to go.

"Well, I guess we should say goodbye then. We head back home tomorrow, though Matthew and Blue are staying on for another couple of nights, since there's no urgency for them to go off anywhere now," she said, smiling his way. "And Rupert, of course, for the time being anyway."

"Ciara will be happy to be reunited with him," Matthew added. "And I guess I'll figure out what to do next from there, though all our IDs say Lorcan and Flynn so that might prove tricky."

"But since things have come to a permanent close for you, you can probably revert back now anyway. I've still got your wallet and phone from when you first arrived," Bronagh said.

"I wondered what had happened to them."

"All safe at the house," she said.

"It's been a most memorable holiday," Richard chirped in. "One I certainly will never forget."

"I agree," said Julie. "And when I see that barman again, I'll ask him about a certain lamp base," she said, showing her disdain and rubbing her head for effect.

"What about a lamp base?" Richard asked.

Forgetting he'd no clue of events that particular day, Julie quickly covered it up by suggesting it was time to leave Brocc in peace. But not before she'd locked eyes with Chrissy.

"Come on, let's leave Brocc to his rest," Chrissy encouraged.

"It was nice to meet you all," he said, waving a little as they each said their goodbyes and he watched them leave the ward as a group.

CHAPTER 82

Bronagh and Brocc both looked like they'd been in a recent war between them, what with bandages and plaster casts. They had of sorts. "I don't think I will ever forget this week of my life. It really has turned out to be something pretty special in an odd kind of a way," Brocc said as they watched them go. "But now I know the whole story about what you and your network of volunteers do, why did you think I wouldn't understand?"

"That's simple. Men of our generation invariably don't. 'Harden up' and all that. 'Give her a slap back' mentality. And that's no one's fault, more deep-ingrained culture and history. I remember the leather belt dad used on our backsides occasionally. That was how things were back then, how we were brought up, but times have changed. Now, we talk about all sorts of things that we once swept under the carpet, even only ten years ago."

Brocc had to concede the point, it was true. "Well, I've had my eyes opened now, I can tell you. But I do have a question of my own."

"What's that?"

"How does it all get funded, who pays for it all?"

"Benefactors. Those that have sought refuge with us and are

safely out the other side. You'd be surprised how generous people can be when they've been touched by an abusive relationship in some way. Some do so with the loan of their property."

Brocc nodded his understanding. It made perfect sense.

"She was a piece of work though, not only to Matthew and Blue, but the way she hurt you too," she went on. Brocc brushed the comment off with a flick of his hand.

"See what I mean? Anyway, should I move into yours or you move into mine?" she asked suddenly.

"What are you talking about?"

"When you get out of here. Since we're both banged up, maybe it would be a good thing for a week or two, keep an eye on the other for a while."

Brocc had no intentions on going anywhere, he was too independent. Plus it was only a burn, he hadn't lost a limb.

"Will you stop that, woman. But I can tell you I will be heading to the pub as soon as I get out of here. So why don't I buy us both dinner, and you can tell me where I might be able to help you, in the group?" It wasn't often Brocc smiled, but the occasion warranted his biggest in a long while. Bronagh was aghast at his surprise suggestion.

"Really? Are you sure? And I don't mean about buying dinner."

He nodded, his smile broadening across his face. "No one deserves to live scared in their own home, so yes. I'm doubly sure. If there are other 'Tess's out there, then people need to be protected from them. And I'm sure I can be of use somewhere, if only with my old car."

She bent down and hugged him, her broken wrist awkwardly dangling to one side, but the sentiment was there. She blinked back the tears that had started to well, but it was too late, he'd seen them.

"Easy now," he said. "Don't go getting all soft on me."

Bronagh spluttered a laugh of sorts. She knew she could find a role for her brother somewhere.

Tomorrow, somebody else may be in need of their help.

CHAPTER 83

EPILOGUE

Two months later, December

Doolin seemed the obvious place for them both to settle. With a nearby babysitter that doted on Blue, it was easy for Matthew to pick up a driving job once more, and return to his previous occupation, though this time without the long-haul distances. It also gave him the opportunity to give back to the network that had saved him, as a volunteer, as so many past victims went on to do. Pay it forward.

Blue pointed at something in the distance, an undecipherable attempt at putting his own words together half lost on the chilly breeze that whipped off the sea as they walked. The little boy turned towards him from his buggy, and Matthew marvelled at his rosy-pink cheeks and ever-present smile. The tension now gone from his home environment, he'd settled into his new routine and surroundings with ease. He steered them into the small supermarket and placed Blue in the child seat of a trolley. Mitten-covered hands waved at anyone that looked their way. His cute cherub face topped with a blue woollen hat had heads turning as he gurgled, travelling down the various aisles with his dad. They stopped at the deli counter and waited their turn. A few days out from Christmas and the shop was busy, but that didn't matter much, they had all the time in the world. A woman's voice caught Matthews attention, and he turned at the familiarity of it. He'd not seen her for some weeks.

"Hello little one," she said, first bending to give Blue a kiss on the cheek, before pulling Matthew into a tight bear hug and planting another one on his. It was Ciara, her long, deep auburn hair visible from underneath her knitted hat. Long gone was the wig she'd been using from her last case, her work there finished. Matthew returned the squeeze; it was good to see her again. Since his own treatment with her had stopped with the turmoil of moving south, he hadn't had much of an excuse to stay in touch. He'd certainly missed her.

"It's good to see you," he said, beaming. It really was.

"And you too, both of you!" she exclaimed with some theatre, mainly for Blue's sake. "Have you time for coffee, perhaps?" she asked excitedly. "When you've finished in here, I mean. It would be grand to catch up."

Blue shot an arm in the air and yelled his approval as if he was the one making the decision for both of them. It was a habit he'd started only recently. Laughing, Matthew said, "We'd love to. Give us twenty minutes?"

"Great. Let's say Oh La La? They're doggy friendly in there. Rupert is waiting outside for me."

"Perfect, it will be lovely to catch up, and see the mutt again," he said, smiling just as much as the toddler sitting in his trolley was,. He'd missed her company more than he'd realised, but then he had been through the emotional wringer of recent. Now things were a little more settled, he too had begun to relax. Finally, life felt good again.

Twenty minutes later, he parked the buggy alongside a table in the back of the café and waited for Ciara to arrive. She was only a moment behind them, and Matthew watched as she breezed in with Rupert close by her side. He waved as she made her way over. Matthew stood to greet her, and Rupert waited patiently for his pat.

"Hello, boy!" he said as he made a fuss before the dog settled on the floor beside them. Blue pointed and yelled his approval. Again.

"Still drinking hot chocolate?" he asked. "I'll go and order." They'd spent the best part of three months living and working together, he wasn't about to forget her usual drink.

"Please," she said, taking a seat as he made his way back towards the counter where he ordered two hot chocolates and a mini for Blue. He added two slices of apple cake to their order – Blue could share his. Having paid, he returned to the small gathering at the rear of the café. So close to Christmas, it was warm and cosy inside, and a tinsel-covered tree in the corner with fake presents underneath it added to the festive feel. He unzipped Blue's coat and removed his hat and mittens. Ten tiny fingers reached out to touch whatever they could, which happened to be Ciara's leg. Grinning, she bent down and unbuckled him from the buggy and he sat happily on her lap, the action of her doing so uninvited feeling natural to all three of them. Matthew took a deep cleansing breath as he realised how much he'd missed the woman's company. He caught her eyes for a second and smiled.

"It really *is* good to see you again," he started. "Where are you working now, in Ennistymon?"

"I've just finished actually, so I'm, shall we say, 'in between homes' at the moment?" Matthew smiled at the thought of her actually staying at her own small cottage for a change. He'd only been there only once, a tiny place on the edge of Doolin. She rented it out for the majority of the summer months, the extra income welcome cover for when she worked on an intense case. There weren't the funds in the network to pay her a full salary, but the work she did was invaluable. He imagined her sitting curled up on the sofa alone, reading one of the many books she had displayed on floor-to-ceiling shelves in the living room. She was a real bookworm. "I guess that's a good thing," she added. No one entering their system was generally a positive thing, though there were plenty of people in need that simply weren't aware of their existence or help on offer. It was hardly something the network could advertise.

Matthew cleared his throat and prepared to speak. He felt like a teenager as he took the plunge.

"Well, maybe you'd like to join the two of us at Gus O'Connor's pub, perhaps for lunch tomorrow? I know Blue would like to share his meal with you," he said, grinning. "He told me so only this morning," he added, more to fall back on humour as he nervously awaited her reply. Since they were no longer working together as patient and therapist, there was no issue there – unless of course Ciara simply didn't want to. He fixed his grin and waited, watching her face for a sign, a tiny twitch even, as to which way her decision might go. Her eyes held his when, finally, they started to dance.

"I'd love to," she said gently.

"Sorry?" he asked, a little surprised. Had he heard her correctly?

Louder, she replied, "I said, I'd love to!"

It was Blue that broke into the awkward moment with his own way of doing things. Right on cue, he threw both arms up into the air and yelled 'yeah' at the top of his voice. It was all the two adults needed to help the nerves between them and finally relax with each other, as they had been before.

This time around though, things would be different between them, and Matthew could look forward to the start of something new.

～

Missed the beginning of the series? There's more from Chrissy starting with Tin Men.

ACKNOWLEDGMENTS

This book is most definitely a work of fiction, though some of the physical places featured are indeed real. If those places are not portrayed entirely accurately, that's my doing to make it fit the story – it is a work of fiction after all. Doonagore Castle isn't within earshot of the nearest holiday home, not by a long way. It is owned by a family that keep it for themselves as a holiday home and is a kilometre from the village. The characters, however, are all figments of my imagination, though I'd love to meet Chrissy, Julie, and the rest of the cast in person someday. Are you reading this, Netflix?

It was my audiobook narrator, Aoife McMahon, that first gave me to seed of an idea for the setting, since she has such a wonderful Irish voice herself. It made the decision to set the book in southern Ireland an easy one. Her suggestion of Doolin is perfect for the story, the castle a bonus, so I simply had to send Chrissy off on holiday and let her stumble on a case.

My special thanks to Ciaran Keogan from the Kilrush Garda Station in Co. Clare for his valuable input on keeping the policing stuff straight. That part of a fictional story should still be accurate where the story allows.

Not forgetting my editors, Jenny and Jon, whom I thank for their sterling advice and accuracy. It's a pleasure to work with you both as usual.

I always enjoy hearing from readers, so do drop me a line about anything to do with my books at linda@lindacoles.com.

Finally, thanks to you, the reader, because if you didn't buy my books, there would be little point in me writing any more.

ALSO BY LINDA COLES

The Chrissy Livingstone Series:

Tin Men

Walk Like You

The Silent Ones

Jack Rutherford and Amanda Lacey Series:

Hot to Kill

The Hunted

Dark Service

One Last Hit

Hey You, Pretty Face

Scream Blue Murder

Butcher Baker Banker

Book set 1

Book set 2

Book set 3

Book set 4

Book set 5

If you enjoyed reading my story, here are the others:

The Chrissy Livingstone series:

Tin Men

She thought she knew her father. But what she doesn't know could fill a mortuary...

Chrissy Livingstone grieves over her dad's sudden death. While she cleans out his old things, she discovers something she can't explain: seven photos of schoolboys with the year 1987 stamped on the back. Unable to turn off her desire for the truth, she hunts down the boys in the photos only to find out that three of the seven have committed suicide...

Tracing the clues from Surrey to Santa Monica, Chrissy unearths disturbing ties between her father's work as a financier and the victims. As each new connection raises more sinister questions about her family, she fears she should've left the secrets buried with the dead.

Will Chrissy put the past to rest, or will the sins of the father destroy her?

Walk Like You

When a major railway accident turns into a bizarre case of a missing body, will this PI's hunt for the truth take her way off track?

London. Private investigator Chrissy Livingstone's dirty work has taken her down a different path to her family. But when her upper-class sister begs her to locate a friend missing after a horrific train crash, she feels duty-bound to assist. Though when the two dig deeper, all the evidence seems to lead to one mysterious conclusion: the woman doesn't want to be found.

Still with no idea why the woman was on the train, and an unidentified body uncannily resembling the missing person lying unclaimed in the mortuary, the sisters follow a trail of cryptic clues through France. The mystery deepens when they learn someone else is searching, and their motive could be murder...

Can Chrissy find the woman before she meets a terrible fate?

The Silent Ones

An abandoned child. A missing couple. A village full of secrets.

When a couple holidaying in the small Irish village of Doolan disappear one night, leaving their child behind, Chrissy Livingstone has no choice but to involve herself in the mystery surrounding their disappearance.

As the toddler is taken into care, it soon becomes apparent that in the close-knit village the couple are not the only ones with secrets to keep.

With the help of her sister, Julie, Chrissy races to uncover what is really happening. Could discovering the truth put more lives at risk?

A suspenseful story that will keep you guessing until the end.

The DC Jack Rutherford and DS Amanda Lacey Series:

Hot to Kill

When a local landscaper vanishes, Madeline Simpson knows she was the last person to see him alive – because she killed him.

With a serial sex offender on the loose, Detectives DC Jack Rutherford and DS Amanda Lacey already have their hands full. It's only when another death occurs that a link between the two cases comes to light, and Madeline finds herself the focus of their investigation.

While attempting to keep her deadly secret, Madeline stumbles upon clues that point to the true identity of the sex offender. She's closing in when tragedy strikes, and the death toll increases.

But DS Amanda Lacey has no idea how close she is to the killer as her work and personal lives collide.

How long will she have to wait to find out the full truth?

If you like interesting characters, imaginative story lines, and British crime drama, then you'll love this captivating story.

The Hunted

The hunt is on...

They kill wild animals for sport. She's about to return the favour.

A spate of distressing big-game hunter posts are clogging up her newsfeed. As hunters brag about the exotic animals they've murdered and the followers they've gained along the way, a passionate veterinarian can no longer sit back and do nothing.

To stop the killings, she creates her own endangered list of hunters. By stalking their online profiles and infiltrating their inner circles, she vows to take them out one-by-one.

How far will she go to add the guilty to her own trophy collection?

Dark Service

The dark web can satisfy any perversion, but two detectives might just pull the plug...

Taylor wakes frightened and alone in an unfamiliar hotel room with no idea how she got there. On the desk nearby is a note of warning: "Tell no one".

During a chance conversation, DS Amanda Lacey learns of the incident and discovers the traumatised woman is only the latest victim in a long string of disturbing and highly unusual thefts.

Amanda and partner DC Jack Rutherford venture deep into the underbelly of the dark web in search of answers. It soon becomes apparent one of them will have to go undercover – alone.

When an unexpected event sends their sting operation spiralling out of control, their only chance at catching the culprits lies with a local reporter...and a scandal that could ruin them all.

One Last Hit

The greatest danger may come from inside his own home.

Detective Duncan Riley has always worked hard to maintain order on the streets of Manchester. But when a series of incidents at home cause him to worry about his wife's behaviour, he finds himself pulled in too many directions at once.

After a colleague Amanda Lacey asks for his help with a local drug epidemic, he never expected the case would infiltrate his own family...And a situation that spirals out of control...

Hey You, Pretty Face

An abandoned infant. Three girls stolen in the night. Can one overworked detective find the connection to save them all?

London, 1999. Short-staffed during a holiday week, Detective Jack Rutherford can't afford to spend time on the couch with his beloved wife. With a skeleton staff, he's forced to handle a deserted infant and a trio of missing girls almost single-handedly. Despite the overload, Jack has a sneaking suspicion that the baby and the abductions are somehow connected...

As he fights to reunite the girls with their families, the clues point to a dark secret that sends chills down his spine. With evidence revealing a detestable crime ring, can Jack catch the criminals before the girls go missing forever?

Scream Blue Murder

Two cold cases are about to turn red hot...

Detective Jack Rutherford's instincts have only sharpened with age. So when a violent road fatality reminds him of a near-identical crime from 15 years earlier, he digs up the past to investigate both. But with one case already closed, he fears the wrong man still festers behind bars while the real killer roams free...

For Detective Amanda Lacey, family always comes first. But when she unearths a skeleton in her father-in-law's garden, she has to balance her heart with her desire for justice. And with darkness lurking just beneath the surface, DS Lacey must push her feelings to one side to discover the chilling truth.

As the sins of the past haunt both detectives, will solving the crimes have consequences that echo for the rest of their lives?

Butcher Baker Banker

A cold Croydon winter's night and pensioner Nelly Raven lies dead and naked on the floor of her living room. The scene bears all the hallmarks of a burglary gone wrong.

It's just the beginning.

Ron Butcher rose to the top of London's gangland by "fixing things". But are his extensive crooked connections of use when death knocks at his own family's door?

Baker Kit Morris will do anything to keep his family business alive. Desperate for cash, he hatches a risky plan that lands him in trouble. As he struggles to stay out of prison, he forges an unlikely friendship with an aging local thug.

And then there's the Banker, Lee Meady, a man with personal problems of his own.

Just how does it all fit together?

As DC Jack Rutherford and DS Amanda Lacey uncover the facts surrounding the case, the harrowing truth of the killer's identity leaves Jack wondering where the human race went so badly wrong.

ABOUT THE AUTHOR

Hi, I'm Linda Coles. Thanks for choosing this book, I really hope you enjoyed it and collect the following ones in the series. Great characters make a great read and I hope I've managed to create that for you.

Originally from the UK, I now live and work in beautiful New Zealand along with my hubby, cat and 6 goats. My office sits by the edge of my vegetable garden, and apart from reading and writing, I get to run by the beach for pleasure.

If you find a moment, please do write an honest online review of my work, they really do make such a difference to those choosing what book to buy next.

If you'd like to keep in touch via my newsletter, use this link to leave your details:

http://eepurl.com/gwfVqL

Enjoy! And tell your friends.

Thanks, Linda

Keep in touch:

www.lindacoles.com

linda@lindacoles.com

Follow me on BookBub